THE LONG FIRE

A NOVEL

MEGHAN TIFFT

The Unnamed Press
Los Angeles, CA

The Unnamed Press
1551 Colorado Blvd., Suite #201
Los Angeles, CA 90041
www.unnamedpress.com

Published in North America by The Unnamed Press.

1 3 5 7 9 10 8 6 4 2

ISBN: 978-1-939419-44-6

Library of Congress Control Number: 201594171

This book is distributed by Publishers Group West

Printed in the United States of America by McNaughton & Gunn

Designed & Typeset by Scott Arany
Illustration & Cover Design by Jaya Nicely

This book is a work of fiction. Names, characters, places and incidents are wholly fictional or are used fictitiously. Any resemblance to actual events or persons, living or dead, is entirely coincidental.

For Tony

Contents

THE LONG FIRE

THE LONG FIRE

A NOVEL

PART ONE
SPIT OR SWALLOW

1

RIGHT NOW THERE'S ONE CHOICE I MAKE THAT DECIDES WHO I AM. It divides me up, connects me back, turns me in, takes me out. One choice I live by: Spit or swallow?

Not so long ago I swallowed everything. I was numb, cheerfully depraved, a hang-jaw dummy flapping away on the lap of an anonymous master. I was that nose-picking child hunkered down in primitive dread, barbaric and vague, deeply insistent, my body cramped and churning with secret shame. I was that dim, lumpish primate skulking through the Stone Age, neither dead nor alive, my sustenance only yet a vague, urgent experiment. I was there in every form, my mind blank and unfurling, a warm wet seed in a dark fallow field. I was anything and everything and nothing. I was what I ate.

And what did I eat?

Old grimy sponges from the kitchen and dusty wax candles and rubber bands blackened and bitter with newspaper ink. Latex gloves, powdered and silky, from under the sink, those rough and crackling balls of twine at the bottom of drawers, and paper, paper everywhere—so much paper. Junk mail of every grain and weight. Envelopes, coupons, circulars, all those promotions on slick, heavy card stock. Books too—whole meals eaten one chapter at a time, their pages yielding into gobs of fibrous pulp, my saliva pooling in a bitter juice of ink—the final tacky product flattening densely between my teeth. The same thing went for the more brittle aromatic delicacy of wood, pencils shaved to delicate curls in sharpeners, spicy and dry, and the blunt metallic taste of a stick of lead rolled across my tongue, snapped like the frailest bone. What else? There are so many ready torments in the world of non-food, so much to make a monster of me. Greasy lipsticks? Chewy foams? Pliable plastics? All of the above. So set up a lab. Build an experiment. Pay me. Or call me crazy. It has a name—it's pica.

But it's not pica if you don't swallow. If you pinch the valve and say no. Then it's something else. It's sampling, tasting, testing. It's a connoisseur's careful inspection. And that is what I am now: a specialist, a sampler, a taste tester—an investigator of sorts. I put things in and I take them out. In this way I've managed to slither partway out of my darkness, but it's when I'm out in the world that it hurts the worst. I'm twitching and unsure at every turn, instantly discharging each communal offering that enters my mouth, every partial submission a rejection too. And rejection is what I feel out there.

When people catch me, their noticing glance becomes a long gaze, worried and disbelieving, a warning signal that tells me I have to cancel this latest display, smother down whatever unseemly urge I'm trying to satisfy. When it happens it's hard to hide, and sometimes I can only make a show of it, a public experiment. Look what I'm doing. Look what I'm trying. Isn't it interesting? Now it's your turn. This is a vital performance, a survival tool and a necessary dishonesty. It's important to make it look less like an affliction and more like a choice. Choice makes all the difference. I learned that from my mother. Choice is sometimes all we have to believe ourselves human.

And now the next choice I have is harder—the choice to close my mouth, refuse altogether the tactile sensations that urge me through life. That will be many times more difficult, maybe even impossible. But I can try. At this very moment—I can clamp my mouth and resist.

"Do it," I can say.

Or maybe what I should have said was *Don't do it.*

Now the pink curler was in my mouth, the old-fashioned kind with the plastic snap that swung down over the age-stiffened foam to clamp into place. I gave the mirror a nasty look.

"Thupid."

With brute ferocity I crushed the whole morsel between my teeth. It yielded with a surprising flexibility, the bent plastic providing a rigid spring action that was viscerally pleasing while my tongue explored the wet crispy tension of the sponge. It had the stale mineral taste of dried water.

In the mirror I looked ridiculous. Three curlers at the top of my head, chewing like a dog at a bone, the pink stuff in my mouth. I was about to give up, dismiss the curler project altogether, go to bed. I could hear the slow heavy footsteps of some weary person coming up the stairs outside my apartment door, their deep lethargy signaling how late it was. I looked at my unhappy victim in the mirror, her face contorted, beseeching me to stop as I clenched my jaw in tormented gratification. The footsteps stopped on my landing. For a second I felt like two people, one coming and one going. Then a fist thudded on my door.

My heart gave a heave. What time was it? Who could that be? But I had hardly asked myself that question before I knew. Only one person would come over at this time of night. Maybe he would go away, I thought foolishly. I stood still in the bathroom doorway and waited while he continued to chop away at my door. But I knew it was hopeless. I crossed the apartment and gogged an eye into the peephole at a raspy-looking smudge of brown.

"Jah?" I huffed out around the curler. I noticed I wasn't opening the door.

There was a grunt of recognition. "Natalie. Let me in now."

"Uh, Gnatalie—thee ithn'd—" I swallowed back a geyser of drool and listened to these spluttered foreign tones, wondering what accent I was doing. "Thee's gnot here." Not convincing, whatever it was.

"I have to sit down. I saw a movie tonight."

I had seen a movie tonight too, and just now I was feeling like those hostages in the storage closet, gagged and bound, pleading with their captor on the other side of the door. "Pleathe," I said. "Thpare me."

"I need some water."

"You can shange your mind. I won dell."

"I know it's you!"

"Yesh. I'll do anythig. Jushet me fee."

"I can hear your voice! Whatever it is you're doing." There was a disgruntled murmur and then he began stabbing something at the lock on my door. I realized he was trying to use the spare key I had given him.

"Courth you can hear my voith," I said, giving up. I opened the door.

My father heaved past me with a grunt of agitation.

"Hewo," I said.

"I have to sit down." He walked into the kitchen and collapsed heavily on the chair at the table.

For a moment I stood there, swallowed down in the wake of his rolling bulk, and then I let it carry me into the kitchen after him. Without bothering to be discreet, I turned to the counter and bent over and spit out the foam curler.

"What do you want on this fine evening?" I asked, straightening up.

My father gave me a heavy squint, as if doubting what he had just seen. For some reason this pleased me, and I gave him a face-splitting grin.

He shook his head. "I need some water."

I smothered down the ghastly smile, feeling guilty. "Right," I said. "Of course." I went to the sink, reminding myself to be friendly. What was so hard about getting my father a little water? I knew why he was here, so I should be able to forgive him. As I filled up his glass I concentrated on working up a reserve of compassion that would see me through the rest of this visit. When I had gathered enough of it I turned and looked at him.

He was sitting in the chair like a whale on a training potty. It was a small white plastic chair because I had gotten it at a junk sale down the block at a private elementary school, and I liked to sit there with a snack whenever I wanted to have the special feeling of being a kid again. The brown, greasy ends of his coat flapped out wanly at the sides of his body like crippled fins. I could smell the stale fishy reek it gave off and the cigar stench of his hat as he shook drops of icy rain onto my floor. The coat and hat had come from the thrift store he was living over now and they were replacements for the ones he had lost. He didn't seem to notice that he was smothered in an unseemly concoction of odors, and I wondered if he was getting used to the emissions of his clothing. I put his water on the table in front of him and folded my arms and looked down.

"What would you like to talk about, sweetie?"

He snarled at me, then folded sadly around the cup of water and took a little sip. "That's an ugly robe."

"Thank you," I said. "I poop on it."

He looked at me in grave astonishment. Then his face sagged. "It's green."

"It's not green. It's *chartreuse*." I fondled the word on my tongue, replacing the urge to be rude again with the pleasure of sensation that the syllables stirred along the floors and crannies of that great, heroic mucus membrane we call the mouth. "Charrrtrreuusse," I said again.

My father gave me a feeble look of disapproval and then he shivered—probably because he was still inside the wet coat.

"Wet out there?"

He nodded.

"So, how was the movie?"

He swiped the air irritably.

I leaned my tailbone back into the counter and propped my hands behind me. "What was it about?"

"I don't want to talk about it. There's nothing good in the movies anymore. It's all this killing and sex everywhere." His face bloated. "And these gays and homosexuals. They have to be in everything now. Even monkeys in the damn picture."

"Oh—I think I know what you're talking about. What did you go to see a horror movie for? You don't like horror movies."

I could tell by the look on his face that he had not expected it to be a horror movie. He was still shaking his head in disbelief. "Trash," he said, covering his eyes. "All such trash."

I was embarrassed now that he had seen the movie, which was based on a book I had literally devoured back in my impetuous youth. I had long since given up the dangerous pleasures of reading books like that—too many digestive reprimands. My father took a last violent swig of his water and scowled at me across the table as if I had made the movie myself. The clock on the microwave behind him said 12:37. I went to the refrigerator and pulled out my midnight snack bowl. "So why are you here, Boris? I was sleeping."

He gave me a beady look, as if to tell me not to use his first name, and said defiantly, "I want to talk about your mother." We both knew he wanted to talk about my mother, but he was not usually so direct as this.

"Okay," I said. "Let's talk about her." I took a lick of cold batter and waited, my eyes widened in a *go ahead* manner.

"I think she called me on the telephone tonight."

I paused, pretending to consider this. "Shipsy lady cawl you?" I said, the glop in my mouth urging me back into my earlier performance with the curler. But seeing his expression I got serious. "How can she do that?" I asked. "She's *deceased*."

My father gave me a hard, petulant stare, as if he had been expecting me to point out this flaw in his logic. "She left me a telephone message."

As I thought this over I opened a drawer and pulled out my favorite gnawed-up wooden spoon and dipped it. I was trying hard for his sake to look thoughtful. "So, okay," I said cautiously. "What'd she say?"

"Nothing. It was only a murmur. It was *her* murmur."

"Okay. A murmur." What could I say? "Interesting."

"This is what I don't like," my father said suddenly, batting his hand at the air. "You don't listen to anybody. You don't want to hear what anybody says to you."

"What do you think I'm doing?" I asked.

He puffed out an agitated breath of air. "What are you eating?"

"Pancake batter," I said, lifting my spoon for him to see. "Want some?"

I couldn't quite hear the words he grumbled out next.

"Excuse me?" I cocked an ear. "You're speaking into your mustache again."

"Listen." Now he got up and palmed the bowl in one hand and ripped it from me. "This is how you'll get fat. I will not let you get fat. No man will have you."

"Boris," I said, putting on an offended look. "I just broke up with a man one month ago. I'm not interested in letting another one *have* me just yet."

"Yes you are. You're almost thirty."

I was twenty-seven. For a moment I wondered if my father was rounding up or if he didn't actually know my age. "Well, I'm trying to get my childbearing hips first," I told him. "I need to start looking like good mom material."

"No. You're good enough already." He put the bowl in the fridge without the tinfoil. "Cook those tomorrow"—he pointed inside at the shelf—"and stop fooling around. This is serious." He was close enough now that I could see the deep gaze of love sunk down inside the inert mud of his eyes, all the way to that molten core where he kept his most hidden feelings.

"Okay Daddy," I said, hugging him around the roll of his waist. I squeezed and sent air out of his nose.

"Okay, fine. Good." He ended the embrace with a blunt karate chop down the middle of us, then looked seriously down at me and held my gaze for a brief, halting moment. I had the feeling he wanted to say something more, and I raised my eyebrows for him to go ahead. I waited, watching the muscle in his jaw poke out as he clamped the words down, and for another few seconds we stood there, trapped inside the rising pressure of his silence. Finally I decided to help him out.

"Yes, darling?"

The look on his face broke. "Listen now," he said. "Be serious. I want you to be serious."

"Okay. I'm being serious."

My father held his finger up in the air. "I have to tell you something. You need to listen to me now." His mouth opened and stuck that way, as if he was embarrassed or afraid to say more.

"Okay, what?" I was beginning to feel too serious. "I'm listening," I said.

"Your mother—" The words cut off, strangled down in his throat.

So we were back to my mother again. "Yes?" I said. "What about her?"

"I don't think it was—" For a moment his eyes touched mine, stricken, then he let out a heavy breath and turned away scowling.

"You don't think it was what?"

He shook his head, cleared his throat, and picked up his little dead hat and went to the door. He opened it and pointed at me. For a blank moment he stood there, his finger vigorously aimed, and then he seemed to realize it was there and dropped it. "Go to sleep," he said.

What could I do? "Okay." Before he turned I reached up and blew him a kiss goodbye. He whacked it away in the air in front of him, still holding militant eye contact across the room.

"I'm not crazy. I saved the message."

I said nothing and turned the kissed hand into a dramatic wave, as if I were a lover on a shore that my father was leaving behind forever. "Farewell. Until the next time we meet," I said in a departing voice to my father's ship. "Which will be *tomorrow*," I added reassuringly. "For church."

But my father had already turned and was staring pensively out, thinking past me into the foggy darkened sea where he was headed, and without looking back he drifted into the hall and closed the door behind him.

Under cloudy skies I went out for my run still in curlers, my head bagged in an elastic-lined shower cap, having pep-talked myself into a little early-morning perspiration as a final volume enhancer. The air was gusty and metallic, my breath prickled in my throat, the light a frozen sludge on the windows. I passed the Laundromat and saw two people inside, the warming tingle of my limbs waking me from my misery just as I was introduced to theirs—dull, indolent looks, already doing thankless chores before the break of day.

It made me think of a book I ate once, in which a housewife in Africa who gets tired of doing her housework begins to talk incoherently and falls down on the floor, and *extravagantly demeans herself.* When her husband sees this, he bows down to her like a servant to a god and she doesn't have to do housework anymore.

I huffed past brick warehouse conversions and Victorians housing various social services offices, my plastic bonnet riffling, and thought about what happened to my mother and father—how striking the similarities to the book: one day my mother unintentionally promoted herself out of her household duties into another realm, and now she is out there somewhere, her divine presence rearranging the elements, massaging the air, tickling molecules into sound, channeling frail currents of electricity—out in the distant swell, making phone calls.

My mother the deity.

It was shortly after her abrupt ascendance that I began to suffer my father's new conversion. Every Sunday morning he began plugging up my hallway, looking pained and bloated in his tightly pinched shirt collar, quietly assuming the chastened attitude one needs for church. If I didn't answer the door he came in anyway with his spare key, waking me up and standing impatiently in the entry space while I put on clothes and brushed my teeth, checking his watch and blasting air from his nose to tell me I was running us late.

Lately I had been making the best of this weekly trial by dressing myself in costume, starting with my favorite characters from centuries past, present, and future. Now every Sunday my father would come in and scowl when he found me ready and waiting for him.

"What are you doing?" he asked me last week. "Why do you look like that?"

I was dressed as a Pilgrim—in a heavy lackluster dress of faded dark blue material and a white bib front. My hair was in a braid, and I had found a pair of secondhand shoes with overlarge buckles, like the ones I had once worn for a second grade presentation. I had skipped the bonnet.

"Thank you," I told him. "Are you ready?"

He looked at his watch and made a sour face and went briskly to the door. In the hallway he got his wallet out and thrust a twenty-dollar bill at me. "Here. Get yourself something nice to wear to church. None of this," he gestured darkly. "You need something else."

I had taken his donation and spent it diligently at the thrift store in preparation for today's costume, opting for something a little lighter in color and more palatable in style for my father. I was going to be a retro-futuristic nurse from a 1950s sci-fi movie, and Boris was going to be my nearly recovered patient, a brave-hearted man still enfeebled by the wounds of galactic war, whose elbow would need to be clutched for support as we walked up the center aisle. It was the sort of dress-up fantasy Mitch would have mocked as juvenile—until he'd had one or more drinks, and then he would have been all in. I had a stiff white vinyl dress that encased me like a shiny cone, creamy tights, and white leather ankle boots that were a little yellowed with age but close enough. The curler project had made it through my jog and my shower, and now my hair was a huge and gentle dome of curls that had come out nicely. This was the finishing touch I had hoped for, the soft angel's halo, a cloud of burnished amber light.

I smeared on a layer of chalky pink lipstick and immediately began scraping the oily chemical paste with my teeth and rolling it into a tiny ball on my tongue. I went to the hall mirror and reapplied it. The clock said 9:16, which was usually the time my father was huffing at my door, jingling his keys as if I were a dog he could stir into action. Where was he? I stood for a few more minutes at the mirror, patting my hair and feeling uneasy. Just as I wondered if we were going to be late, I heard his heavy footsteps coming once again up the stairwell. I picked up the last of my accessories—a white vinyl purse that dangled at my side like a deflated lung—and emptied the contents of my other purse into it. I hung the strap from my shoulder and stepped out into the hall.

On the second-floor landing I intercepted him. He was coming up the stairs with a weariness that looked sleepless and strung out, and he glanced up at me with sullen surprise, looking unsure as to who or what I was. I flapped my hands at him to get him to turn around.

"We're going to be late. We only have ten minutes to get there." This got him turned around and walking back down the stairs. By the time we got to the car he was muttering under his breath.

I got in on the passenger side, feeling guilty. Maybe I had taken the costume too far this time. "Is everything okay?" I asked.

My father picked up a road atlas on the bench seat between us and studied it for a moment, then reached across me and opened the glove compartment and threw it inside.

"Dad?" I said.

He stretched his mouth into a wide, smiling grimace and turned to me. I watched his eyes drift blankly up to my hair.

"What's wrong?"

For a second longer he stared at my face, his mouth twisted into that distracted rictus of pain and agitation, as if he weren't really seeing me. Then he seemed to process what I had said. "No," he barked. "Nothing. I think I have a stomach flu."

"Well why are we going to church then? You could have called and stayed home."

He said nothing and bucked tensely behind the wheel.

"Hello?" I said. "Why are we going to church if you're sick?"

His head swiveled around to face me, like a monster in a horror movie. He stared through me for a moment and then unclenched his jaw and said, "What? We're not going to church."

"We're not? Where are we going?" I was disturbed by this news. It occurred to me that wherever we were going, I probably wasn't dressed for it. Angelic space girls might be appropriate for church, but not much else.

He didn't answer me. He turned on the car, teeth still gritted in that fierce ghoulish smile.

We drove for a few minutes in silence, me wondering when I should try again to prompt him for information. We passed the church and stopped at a red light, and he took off his coat and balled it up and put it on the seat between us, then rocked back forcefully like he was testing to see if the seat would recline. He leaned suddenly forward and swiped his hand across the dashboard in front of him, sending a cloud of dust into the confined air of the car. I sneezed.

He swiped a second time, this time whisking the dust in my direction. I sneezed again.

"Would you stop that?"

He looked up with fretful, distracted eyes that didn't see me. The light changed, and he stamped the gas pedal down and zoomed under the bridge and merged onto the highway.

"We're leaving town?" I said. "What is going on? Where are we going? *Boris,*" I said, my voice sharp enough this time to have an effect. His eyes met mine and snapped into focus. "*Where are we going?*"

He cleared his throat loudly at me. "I'm going to see about your mother," he said, his voice husky and grim. Then he turned his gaze straight ahead and tilted his chin down in silent defiance and refused to say another word.

2

ON MY FATHER'S DASHBOARD WAS A PLASTIC HULA GIRL WHOSE HIPS gyrated with the movements of the car. Boris had stuck her up there in obligation to my mother, who had put her in his Christmas stocking two years ago. Now as I sat in the parked car alone I peeled up the suction cup and brought the woman in for a closer inspection. She reminded me a little of my mother herself in her younger years, with ballooning hips and deep copper skin. I blew some dust off her face.

"Sorry," I told her, and put her head in my mouth. This was something I had been desperate to do for a long time, and with guilty relish I crushed the morsel between my teeth and chewed fiercely for several seconds. Beneath the surface malleability I could feel the solid resistance of the plastic core, and I squeezed my jaw tight against it for pure pleasure. In the side mirror I looked like a barbaric dimwit—the lady's head in my mouth, her body clamped in my fist. Even so I went on gnawing, reminding myself that I was alone on an unknown street in a nearly abandoned town an hour from where I lived. There was nobody walking on the sidewalks. Nobody even had a reason to look out their windows on a street like this. Just me and hula girl.

The shack-like dwellings that surrounded me seemed to be sinking back into the earth—the street and everything on it sloping gently down in front of me toward a small, muddy basin into which a concrete drainage pipe leaked brown water. A murk of graffiti coated the pipe, and a few stray tags sprawled up nearby porch columns and dribbled over the lumpy concrete pads propping up rusting clothesline poles. A more legible script on the stop sign read *STOP—your stink*. Behind the sign was a small eroding brick building that I wouldn't have recognized as a church if not for the name painted on a wooden placard that hung over its door: *Mount of Olives Church*. Ten minutes ago my father had left me in the car and passed under that sign and disappeared.

I'm going to see about your mother.

I chewed on this awhile, considering the possibilities. One thing was obvious. This was the town my mother had grown up in. She had left when she was seventeen and never come back. I remembered the exit; she would point it out sometimes. We had taken it once and driven through without stopping.

She still had relatives here, gypsy relatives, relatives I had never met because she had been cast out in disgrace for getting pregnant by a *gajo*, a non-gypsy, before she could be married off properly. I had not thought people in America lived like that, and I remembered being appalled when my mother had told me about it. There were a lot of things she had told me about her family, some of them with a fondness I couldn't fathom. Now that I was here looking at a sample of the life she had lived all those years ago I was glad she had been banished from it.

It was obvious that this was a gypsy neighborhood—everything claustrophobic and unkempt. I was parked fifteen feet away from a busy street, but still I had the sense that I had passed an invisible barrier into a different world, someplace far away from the cars swishing by just behind me, someplace sucked in on itself by a certain sickness and decay. The detail that had me convinced was the sign in the window of the house my father had parked me in front of, directly across from the church. The house was pitching forward into its splintered wood porch and puffy clots of yellow fungus were growing out of its many gaping crevices. One stray shoelace of spray paint bent around from the street-side wall, almost touching the large front window, which had a gauze of fuchsia and turquoise draping the perimeter as if it had been tacked all the way around. Centered in the middle was a hand-painted sign that said *Madame Zadie, Fortune Telling, Palm Reading, Services*. Maybe it was a smudge, or a simple case of syntax confusion, but my mind kept snagging on that last, most cryptic word on the sign, *Services*, pushed out by the comma to become its own mysterious item in the list, suggesting things of an ambiguous and illicit nature. Something else my mother had told me more than once—gypsies have no qualms about pursuing their own economic gain and will buy and sell anything, in brazen and audacious contempt of the law. I was still considering all the appalling, potentially criminal implications of the word "services" when the door opened and a woman stepped out.

Madame Zadie herself, I presumed, tall and molten, with long heavy hair and a neck that flexed like a horse's as she tilted her head back and briskly smelled the air. In my mind I immediately invested her with all the qualities I had given to my mother's estranged family—principled cruelty and aloofness and pride. She was draped in satiny fabrics of green and blue that spilled across her like bright heavy water—her professional costume, the effect showy and artificial. She stood on the porch exuding her magnificence as if it isolated her from every tangible thing here, and this too felt like a performance. Since I was the only one out here, it occurred to me that she might be performing for me.

Discreetly, I took hula girl from my mouth. Her head was crushed in at the sides, her face narrow and elongated and pitted with what looked like terrible acne scars. "Sorry," I murmured with genuine regret. I suctioned her back onto the dashboard, hoping the damage wouldn't be noticeable.

I knew the woman was watching me from her porch, but I didn't want to look up and accidentally catch her eye. I opened the glove compartment instead and stared inside. There was the road atlas Boris had been studying. I took it out. It was folded back to a close-up of a street map and there was a wobbly penciled line tracing our route from the highway. To my surprise there was another line too, smudged by the opening and closing of the book, and it led from the highway to a different street nearby. I was beginning to feel alarmed. Had he been to this neighborhood before?

I stole a nervous glance at the woman. All I caught was a movement of her arm that suggested she was smoking, and rather hurriedly. I looked back down, realizing I was waiting for her to do something. With growing consternation I found myself staring at another object in the glove compartment, sitting on top of the car manual. It was a small, blackened silver rectangle, slender with rounded edges. I didn't recognize it, but it felt disconcertingly familiar in my hand. Something leftover from the February fire.

In his apartment my father had dozens of objects like this one sitting around—whatever he had been able to pluck from the rubble of our lives in the week before it had all been carted away in two enormous city dumpsters. All of it was laid out on various pieces of furniture like mysterious artifacts of some ancient, impractical culture, a series of tortured instruments maimed into inexplicable shapes and blackened beyond recognition. Every time I went over I could imagine him going back to the house, searching in bushes and gutters, leaning over fences and into flower beds and plucking out any last thing that had been tossed up in the smoldering rush of collapse. I had thought he had finished cleaning up our great family barbecue weeks ago—all the bags unpacked and each savage little relic meticulously cleaned and placed. Maybe this one had been forgotten.

I flipped the object over and studied the other side. Suddenly I knew what I was looking at. It was a cigarette case I had once given my mother for a gift, a silver one that was engraved on one side and studded at the clasp with two topaz stones—her birthstones. The fire had scorched them cloudy and lifeless, but I remembered how they had looked years ago when I gave the case to her. I remembered when she opened the gift. She had looked at me like I was crazy.

"What do you want me to do with this?"

"It's a cigarette case," I told her.

My mother snorted. "What am I, the queen of Newports?"

I shrugged. I had bought it knowing she would never use it, but I hoped it would be the thought that counted.

My mother leveled a stare at me. "Don't think that someday I'm going to give this back to you so you can start smoking and feel like some fancy-pants."

"I'm not a fancy-pants," I said, my feelings hurt. "I don't want to start smoking."

"If you say so," said my mother.

After that I never saw the case again. I had assumed she had gotten rid of it, but apparently she hadn't. She had kept it somewhere out of sight—perhaps so I wouldn't be tempted. But she had kept it. Maybe she had liked it after all.

The sudden flicker of a voice broke through the damp morning silence, and I looked back at the porch, startled. Madame Zadie had one hand up to her ear and was speaking into a cell phone. I watched her take it away and hang up, then flick her hair back and bring her cigarette up to her mouth again. It all looked wrong to me, all these unmatched gestures—the cell phone and the cigarette that had nothing to do with the costume. There was something about her manner too—a distracted energy—as if she hadn't really needed to make that phone call, or didn't even want that cigarette, and had only used these things for an excuse to come outside. I put the atlas away and closed the glove compartment and turned to look at the church across the street, hoping that the back of my head would discourage her.

The church was a little building, further dwarfed by a line of tall cypress trees planted down both sides of the walk all the way out to the street. The winter-brown grass around them looked badly kept, thinning into patches of dirt and dead weeds that mingled with wind-blown wrappers at the edge of the asphalt. There were no curbs. In the cloudy midmorning light the whole scene felt contrived, as if I had just joined hula girl inside a depressed child's ugly diorama. I listened to the breeze rustle its way through the stiff brown grass and brittle winter limbs. It would be easy to set this place on fire, I thought. The dry swish of un-mowed blades became a broken, hissing crunch that grew louder and more rhythmic behind me. I realized that I was hearing footsteps, and then a knock on my window.

I turned and the woman's face hung down sideways in front of me like the smiling head of a ragged, worn-out doll.

"You come?" she said in a sweet, simpering voice through the glass. "You get fortune?"

"No. No thank you," I said, cracking the window to be polite. Up close she was older than she had looked on the porch, or else the details of her face made her look older than she was. She had the deeply neglected look that my mother had had at the age of forty-five—puckered brown skin, cheeks flushed red with a scattering of broken blood vessels, the yellow hooves of her teeth still clamped around what was left of her cigarette.

She pointed up to her decrepit house. "You never get fortune before? You want?"

"Oh, I'm just waiting for somebody."

"Not take long," she told me, and I could sense now a steely insistence behind her sweetness. "Not expensive."

I told her that I didn't have any money.

She took the lie in stride. "No? Just a little? Ten dollars I give you a reading," she said, motioning to the house.

"No, really," I said. I shook my head at her, my smile apologetic.

"You park here you come in," she told me, as if I had no choice.

I was still shaking my head. "No thank you," I said. "Sorry," I added, and I rolled up my window.

She stood back from the car, her smile gone. Had my mother ever warned me about rolling up your window on a gypsy? Then her foot came out and kicked the door, the thud like a shockwave in my chest.

"Get out of here!" she shrieked.

I threw up my hands. "I'm sorry"—I mimicked turning the ignition on Boris's car—"I don't have keys."

Helplessly I watched her kick the door several more times before stooping again to pound the butt of her fist against the window at my face.

"This is my parking! Don't sit in front of my business!" The wheedling foreigner act had fallen from her like a blank veil and now I was looking right into her real, furious eyes. My mouth had gone dry with fear. Behind her I glimpsed a face peeking out of the darkness of her front window. It was a kid, maybe five or six years old, watching placidly with big eyes, as if this sort of thing happened every day.

I turned to the church, hoping to be rescued, and almost instantly my prayer was answered. My father came plunging down the stairs. "Stop!" he roared. "Get away!"

Without a moment's hesitation the woman strode around the car and into the street to meet him.

"What do you think? You think you just park your shitty car out in front of my business?"

Boris was gliding swiftly at her with loose weaving strides, as if the very sight of her had stricken him. "I can park where I want to! You people! What's wrong with you goddamn people!"

As if she were snatching something out of the air, the woman reached out her hand and dragged it down my father's face.

He staggered back and howled in agony. I felt my stomach drop away.

"Gajo!" she said, spitting on him as he covered his eyes. "Trash! Don't come here!"

I could hear my father's subvocalizations of rage as he stumbled toward me blindly, the woman following and kicking his legs. He staggered under her assault, unable to see what was happening to him.

The woman walked around the car up to her yard and stood on the porch yelling at us. I slid across the bench seat and unlocked the door and pushed it open.

"Get in!"

He took the keys out of his pocket and sank into the driver's seat, then sat there bellowing like a bear while he tried to find the ignition.

"Let me drive," I cried. "You can't see." Red lines had puffed up on his face where the woman had scratched him, and a few drops of blood beaded up on his fluttering eyelids.

"You need a tissue," I told him, searching furiously through the trash in the backseat.

He started the car.

The woman was still yelling at us from her porch when he pulled us into the street and yanked the wheel into a U-turn and then kept going into the dead yard of the church. There was no curb to stop us. My father turned the wheel sharply and accelerated hard and aimed us straight for a cypress tree.

"Look out!" I told him, bracing myself.

He turned the wheel again, and we passed the tree and careened over bumpy ground as my father battled for control. I felt the car surge as if he had accidentally pumped the gas instead of the brake. For one disoriented moment I felt like we were going backward instead of forward. Then we passed into the busy street. There was an instant of silence, long enough for me to suck in my breath, before my ears filled with the hideous crunch of metal and I felt the dizzying swerve as we spun around. My head hit the window at the same time I registered that we'd just struck another car—a moving one—and I got a blurry view of the churchyard as we jostled breakneck over the grass toward the same cypress tree again, from the opposite direction. We hit with a sickening thud and I felt my seat belt snap hard against my chest. My face came close to the dash, where I caught a glimpse of the violently shuddering hula girl, and in my periphery I saw my father's head hit the steering wheel and ricochet back. The car made a squeal of protest and sat ticking like a bomb.

I stared at the splintered tree bisecting our car's front bumper for a blank moment. Beside me, my father let out an eerie whimpered exhalation, and then his head dipped forward, like a Buddha in deep meditation.

"Dad?" I said hoarsely.

An engine revved loudly outside. In the busy street, the car that had hit us was backing up and righting itself in the lane. There was a squeal of tires as it sped away. I had no idea what to make of that. I turned back to my father.

"Dad," I said, more loudly this time. No response. I put two fingers beneath his nose and felt the breath going in and out. His window was broken and the side mirror dangled outside of it. My father's face seemed to be turning a boiled gray beneath the festering scratch marks. I opened my door. The woman had vanished. I stood unsteadily and looked around at the church, and in the silence that reverberated through the street, I heard my voice call out, "Help!"

A feeble and hollow attempt—I tried it again. A few moments later the door at the top of the church stairs opened, and a man leaned out and peered at me, his expression as blank and stunned as I felt.

"He's hurt," I yelled. I pointed inside the car to my father. "Do you have a phone?"

The man's black eyes moved from me to my father to the tree and he said nothing. I saw how young he was, maybe late teens, and painfully thin and tall, with a wild nest of black curly hair on top of his head. His dress shirt was a bright cherry red, and he had matched it with a sea-green tie.

"Can you understand me?" I yelled at him, realizing I didn't have time to waste. I started to stumble around the front of the car on shaky legs. "Is there a hospital around here?"

He took a step off the porch. "Who are you?" he said suspiciously, in perfect English.

This unexpected fluency surprised me for some reason, and then I was angry. "He's hurt!" I yelled. I floundered to blame somebody for the situation, quickly growing absurd in my mind. "That woman attacked him!" I pointed at the woman's house, where nobody was on the porch. "Will you just tell me where the hospital is?"

He stared another moment and then walked down the stairs toward me. I stiffened, irrationally preparing to strike the man, then thought better of it. Instead, I ran around to my father's side of the car and opened the door. This was a mistake, because he promptly poured out onto me like a heavy ooze.

"Huuhrr," he moaned.

"Dad," I gasped into his ear, trying desperately to catch his weight and tilt his body back the other way. "Sit up."

I heard the passenger door open, and the next moment I felt the load of flesh lighten and lift off of me. I looked across and saw the gypsy clutching my father by the shoulder. I almost thanked him, then stopped myself. Boris was taking deep, rasping breaths now, his eyes blinking furiously. "Move over," I told him, shoving on his leg, trying to get him to respond. "I have to drive." As I pushed, the gypsy leaned in cooperatively and tugged my father by his belt, and together we got him to the middle of the bench seat. The blood had smeared across my father's face and the front of his shirt. The gypsy wiped his hands on his pants and stood back.

"Uh, yeah," he said, too calmly, leaning into the open door. "If you go up and take a right at the next street over. Then go down to Parkview and take another right on Harbor. The hospital's on the left."

I was already in the car and waiting for him to shut the door.

He continued to peer in at me. "What's your name?"

"What?" I started the ignition.

He pointed at my father. "Are you related to him?"

"Who are you?" I said. "Was he talking to you inside?"

For a moment we looked at each other, neither of us willing to answer. Then he shrugged. "You look like him," he said, and shut the door. I glanced at my father. He was sinking like a blob of biscuit dough into the seat. The man stepped back to let me drive away, and carefully I started backing the car through the bumpy yard and into the street while he made guiding gestures with his hands. As I pulled forward into the road he lifted his hand in a wave.

3

WE DROVE FAST DOWN A FOUR-LANE STREET, THE CLOUDS DISAPpearing in a blaze of cold blue sky. The sun spread a thin blinding light on everything metal, parked cars and windows searing my eyes.

As I drove I held my arm uselessly across Boris. He had slumped over sideways and wasn't belted in, and now I was afraid my driving would slide him right onto the floor in one big puddle.

"Do you want to sit up?" I asked.

He responded with a gurgle. "Where did he go? I don't understand where we're going."

"We're going for a little drive," I said. "Enjoy the scenery."

"He'll bother you," he said. "Don't let him bother you."

"Who—that gypsy kid?" The drastically skewed rearview was giving me a disorienting view of most of my father's face, slack jowls melting into neck, puffy gobs of closed eyelid. "Hey, can you hear me?" I had an uncertain feeling that I had to keep him awake. Because that's what they did in the movies, right? They talked to keep the other person awake. "Are you there?"

"Where?" he said. "You stay away from him. That boy's a criminal."

"Which boy? The one who came out of the church?"

For a while he didn't respond, and I figured he was going to ignore the question. Then his voice darkened and he growled, "It's all the sex. They're all having sex these days."

"They only have sex in the movies," I said.

His eyes fluttered and snagged on mine in the rearview for an instant—or at least I thought they did. I couldn't tell what the look was, but it was meaningful. Was it fear? Was it anguish? Was it just nausea?

"He took the money."

I was getting annoyed. What money? His speech sounded infuriatingly scripted, like he was reciting movie lines to me.

"Where are we?" said Boris, looking up in distress. "Are we going there? I told him not to come."

We were passing a graveyard, a blank, treeless corner of it where the new plots were being dug. On the other side of the street we passed several buildings of residential apartments set back on a deep manicured lawn, and then we came up to the block that the hospital was on, its proximity to the graveyard like a bad joke. Across from it, quiet residential streets stretched away, full of large, swaying shade trees, their branches empty, huge in comparison to the tiny turn-of-the-century bungalows that squatted beneath them.

"That poor girl," said Boris in a heartbroken voice.

"Don't think about it if it bothers you," I said bracingly, utterly lost in the spaces between his thoughts, those dark synapses firing their delirious connections. "Just look outside at the nice morning."

For a moment I took my own advice, looking out at all the bungalows painted in their artsy purples and yellows—it looked like some kind of bohemian enclave. I thought about all the carefree Sunday activities that were going on across the street from this hospital. On the other side of the street, I found the sign that said EMERGENCY and turned where the arrow pointed. It took me down a single-lane road and deposited me into a parking lot in front of a long beige building that looked more like a high school than a hospital. As I pulled into the parking lot I could hear Boris still chewing down words of agitation beside me. I swerved into a parking spot near the entrance.

"We're here!" I said, and got out. I waited for something to happen on my father's side. Nothing did, so I ran around and opened his door for him, but I couldn't get him out—he was too heavy and uncooperative, pawing me back like I was an unwelcome dog who was trying to join him on the seat.

"Okay. Just a minute." I closed his door and locked him in. "I'll be right back," I called through the window, stepping away. Before I turned I saw his eyes snag on me through the glass.

"Alepa?" he said, his voice a vague murmur behind the window. I didn't have time. I waved and turned around and rushed to the entrance.

The doors opened for me and I passed through, stumbling as my ankles buckled sharply in my boots. My eyes locked immediately with a hefty clerk who was standing behind a desk.

"Help!" I said, tripping up to the counter.

She pulled her chin back into her neck as if I had just insulted her. "Please don't yell, ma'am."

I blew air in her face. "He's—I can't get him out of the car."

She looked doubtful but she lifted a phone and spoke into the receiver. After a few seconds she hung up and turned away.

I felt like I had missed something. "What?" I said. "What do I do?"

Before she could answer, a double door split open beside her, and two beefy men in blue scrubs appeared with a gurney. "Somebody need help?" said the taller one, and looked at me. "Is it you?"

We all looked over at the clerk, and she widened her eyes as if it were unbearably obvious. Outside I pointed them to my father's powder-blue Oldsmobile Cutlass, its paint gently faded like a pair of denim pants, the front bumper crushed and dangling.

"What happened?" said one of the men as we ran toward it.

I stumbled and caught my breath. "We hit a tree."

He glanced at me, his round pink face full of tiny glistening blond stubble, his eyes wary. "Is he unconscious?"

I told him no. But when we pulled up with the gurney and opened the door, we found Boris inside snoring. I called to him and he remained perfectly still, his face sinking down into his neck, his eyes twitching beneath a heavy batter of swollen eyelid. If not for the blood streaked across his brow, he would have looked like an old man taking an afternoon nap. I patted him hard on the cheek. He kept snoring.

"He was awake when I went in!"

I watched as they climbed through the front seat of Boris's car and began to lug my father out like a roll of carpet. As they were loading him onto the gurney his wallet fell out of his pocket and I bent down to pick it up. It was still warm, like some last glowing ember of my father himself, and instinctively I pressed it between my hands.

It seemed like only seconds passed before they had arranged him on the gurney and were rolling away from me, the mound of my father's body gliding over the asphalt and into the hospital and then through the same double door beside the desk. I stood watching the door flap closed, my heart still hammering in my chest.

"Ma'am?"

The desk clerk was holding her arm up in the air, her mouth opening and closing in a dull, gum-chewing expression. For a moment I stared, unable to interpret this signal, waiting for her to say something more. Then it occurred to me that the clipboard in her hand was for me, and she wanted me to take it. I moved on rubbery legs in her direction. As I approached I watched her eyes roll down my body like beads of slow black ink. I stared back insolently before I remembered what I was wearing. I felt a warm glow of embarrassment. The accident hadn't changed certain details. Like the church outfit I was wearing. I stood before this clerk as a fellow health worker—a visiting space nurse from the 1950s.

I could see from the clerk's expression that she had no idea what this outfit and hairstyle signified and suspected that I was crazy—a deranged bum in a tawdry suit of clothes from the thrift. I carried the clipboard into the waiting area. It was small and shabby—patterns of mud were stamped into a floor that had not been mopped since last night's storm and a dingy fluorescent glow filtered through plastic panels in the ceiling. I sat down on a brown vinyl chair facing a little woman who was looking around in a startled way, holding her enormous purse in her lap like a baby that had just learned to sit up. Beside her a man was reading a book. He glanced up and accidentally caught my eye. He smiled.

He had a mouth full of small, perfect teeth. I noticed the way they lined up inside his soft, well-tanned cheeks. His book was a big thick paperback, battered and well worn, the kind that had led many lives since it had been in the bookstore. It was the kind of book I hated to read because I knew I would have to eat its germ-packed pages anyway, and I would even be a little excited to do it.

I watched his smile linger. It's something I've known since high school. The crazier I feel, the more I can always count on men to be interested in me.

He held up his book. "You should try one of these. It helps."

I nodded, and then I found myself completely unable to respond to that. I opened my mouth and closed it again.

The man gave me a quizzical look, and I thought I saw his eyes pass quickly over my outfit. They were small, vivid blue eyes.

"Uh—I can't read books," I said, my voice breaking halfway through the sentence.

His face puckered in confusion and then concern, and I realized of course that this was the wrong thing to say. What did that even mean for a normal person? That I was illiterate?

"I mean I *can* read books," I corrected. I tried to think of something that would make what I had said seem reasonable and not crazy. "I used to love reading horror novels." I pointed at his, which had given itself away by the savage red script on the cover. "But all the gore. It just made me too queasy."

"Oh." He smoothed his face out into a polite smile, nodding to show he understood. The woman raised her eyebrows and looked away.

"Well." He lifted his book to show me it was still there and went back to reading.

My heart was slowing down and I was beginning to come to my senses now. My father was going to be okay, I told myself. He was in the hospital now. They were helping him. I opened his wallet to look for his insurance card. He had had this wallet for years, and the worn leather smell was so attached to him that I brought it up to my nose and sniffed it. Then, of course, I fought the urge to bite it. I found the insurance card in a front leather pocket and started to fill out the first of the forms. When I was done with them I brought the clipboard back to the desk. The clerk took it silently, staring past me into the waiting area, as if she couldn't risk the consequences of accidentally looking at me.

I went back to my seat. The horror fan showed me his small, striking teeth again and went back to reading. I found myself wanting to talk to him. There was something physically comforting about all that unassuming bulk so close to me, as if this man could console away the thoughts in my head. I kept thinking about who my father had been talking to in that church. What did it have to do with my mother? And who was that gypsy kid who came outside? Why did he want to know my name? I found it perplexing that he had said I looked like my father. I looked nothing like my father. Boris was white as whale blubber. All I had gotten was a small measure of that whiteness, enough to blanch my skin to yellow clay and dull my hair and eyes to an uncertain dishwater brown—I certainly didn't look like him. I had always thought of myself as a diluted version of my mother—her tall, willowy proportions, her thick, wavy sheath of hair, which I had recently made the mistake of cutting too short, so that it sat propped on my head like a short, broad wedge of congealed pudding.

But not today. My hand came up impulsively to check on the stiff, fluffy hood around my face, and I felt vaguely incredulous. I locked my eyes on the vending machines across the room, trying to sweep my mind clean. For several minutes I studied the machines distractedly, a whole brightly lit assembly bulked up against the wall—chips and candy and soft drinks and even hot cocoa. Then I realized I was hungry. Right on cue, a slow guzzling wave of hunger rolled through me.

Nervously I looked around. Had anybody heard that? The reader hadn't twitched a muscle, his little mouth tucked down in concentration, utterly oblivious. I felt the swell of another wave, promising to break with an even louder crash. I stood up and got out of the aisle just as it rolled out in foaming gurgles. It carried me all the way to the vending machines, where for a minute I stood there looking in at the chips and pretzels, everything dry and unappealing. I went to the hot chocolate machine, and before I could help myself I thought of the Styrofoam cup it came in. I reached into my purse for change. As I dug to the bottom something smooth and metal slid into my hand. Startled, I pulled it out. The cigarette case. I had forgotten it was there.

I rubbed my finger over the rough black surface. Strange. After all these years that my mother had kept it, now it was back in my possession. I clicked apart the clasp and opened the case as if she might be inside, like a genie in a lamp. But there was something else in there, a folded piece of paper pressed into the shiny interior. I watched it fall out and flap down to the floor.

It was a small paper, folded once in half and twice in quarters. The creases were soft, as if it had been folded and unfolded many times. A brief handwritten note was scratched onto it.

Emilian is dying. He wants to see you. Be at the lot at 10 A.M. on the 16th. Park on the street and stay in your car.

I stared at it for several minutes, unable to make any sense of it. I didn't recognize the handwriting. But the name, I knew the name.

I put the note back and dropped the case into my purse, troubled. Did my father know about it? Probably. He would have opened the case. I pulled out some change and fed the coins into the slot and waited through the loud mechanical hum while the machine produced my drink. Emilian. As I stood there I could feel the name rising to the surface of my mind and stopping just before I could grasp it. The cup came out. I lifted it and took a careful sip. The chocolate was warm, sweet, and thin. I went back to my seat and sat there sipping, each time uncomfortably aware of the Styrofoam rim against my lips. Why couldn't I think of how I knew that name? It gnawed on my thoughts, like something I needed to remember now so that I could forget it and move on.

I brought the cup to my mouth and bit down.

The foam was light and crispy and had good compaction. I took another bite. Already I knew I was going to chew up the whole cup—and so what, the people sitting across from me could watch. But I would need to find a place to spit it out. With my hand in front of my mouth I looked around for the bathroom.

I located the sign behind the head of the horror fan, and I was about to stand when suddenly he clapped his book shut and let out a short bark of triumph. He gave me a satisfied look. "Here," he said, leaning out across the aisle and holding out the book. "I just finished. It's a good one. You should try it."

I fluttered my hand in front of my mouth.

"Excuse me," I tried to say, pushing the chomped-up bits aside with my tongue. I stood up with my hand over my mouth. He must have thought I was going to vomit. With a look of apprehension he tucked his knees to the side and I stepped past them in the aisle. And despite all this I knew that if I came back out and sat next to him, he would keep on smiling, and eventually ask for my phone number, suggest we chat about gory books we love over coffee. A voice stopped me in my tracks.

"Natalie Krupin?"

There was a doctor at the desk, short and Indian, and when she saw me she gave a guarded, closemouthed smile. My heartbeat scattered in my chest like buckshot. With a delicate lift of her hand she gestured me back into an alcove on the other side of the desk, and mechanically I turned and walked toward her. As I went I realized that the clutter of foam was no longer in my mouth but stuffed somewhere up high in my esophagus, not moving. I had swallowed it. When I got to the alcove I stood facing her beside a small metal bench. Her eyes passed over me once with a slow look of surprise, then her face took on the pinched, careful expression of somebody who was trying politely to ignore my appearance.

She cleared her throat. "Okay, Miss Krupin?"

I took a ragged breath and nodded. I could feel the intensity with which I was staring at her but I couldn't stop myself. The pain in my esophagus was long and deep as the unchewed foam drifted like an iceberg slowly down toward my digestive organs.

The doctor said, "We've done a scan and it looks like your father has a small fracture in his skull where he hit his head."

I fell into a frantic fit of coughing. "What?" I said, though I had heard her perfectly.

The doctor waited for me to finish, then she repeated herself. I pressed my hand over the pain in my chest and she went on in a composed voice. "He has an epidural hematoma forming at the point of fracture," she said, speaking more slowly. "He needs to have a surgery to remove it."

Oh my God, I thought. I drew in an unsteady breath of air and didn't let it out.

"We're transferring him down to the general hospital in Worcester where they have a neurosurgeon to perform an emergency surgery," she said calmly.

Emergency surgery? What was she talking about? Why did she look so unbothered by this? Was my father going to be okay?

The doctor was studying me as if she were squinting into heavy sunlight. "I know this is a lot to take in," she said.

I was aware suddenly that I needed to let my breath out. With a short burst I exhaled, and the question spilled out of me. "Is he going to be okay?"

She gave me a hesitant look. "We really won't know until after the surgery. You should know that there's a chance there will be some damage to the area."

I kept breathing in and out, my chest clogged and heavy. She seemed to want a response now, some verification that I was hearing her, but I couldn't make myself understand what she was saying.

Damage? What damage?

"Of course, with the surgery itself there is some risk too."

I could feel my mind chugging along somewhere three sentences behind her, still trying to catch up to what she was saying. "Wait. You mean brain damage?"

"Well, let's wait until he gets through the surgery. We won't know the extent of the damage until afterward. But you should understand the risk of surgery," the doctor said patiently. "There is a small risk of fatality." She squinted hard again and I squinted back, unable to speak, my throat pinched all the way closed. What chance?

Suddenly I had to sit down or risk pitching over. I sat on the bench in the alcove. The doctor hovered over me and looked down with grave sympathy, and I dropped my head and concentrated on the floor. I listened to her voice telling me the name of the hospital in Worcester where they were taking him, and assuring me of the advanced surgical procedures and highly experienced specialists they had there. The name of the hospital was familiar to me. Mitch's hospital. Conveniently located just four blocks from my apartment. Then she named the doctor who would be performing the surgery and what was going to happen in there. There was a roaring in my head as she talked about putting bolts in the skull and draining fluids. I didn't think I could stand to hear any more. For several minutes I nodded at her words, which sounded like utterances in a foreign language. Then she said, "Are there any family members you need to call? Anybody to inform? Or anybody who could be with you right now?"

At these words an unexpected gust of grief swept through me. Before I could help it all the anguish of the past few months was sucking up into me like a choking black cloud. *My family,* I thought. *What had happened to my family?* First my brother, then my mother, now my father. I didn't know what to say. There was nobody left but me.

I closed my eyes. I took in several slow, deep breaths and let them out, feeling waves of heat escape my body. A steady dread was burning up through me. What happened next seemed like a part of it, as if a hot black ash had suddenly come loose from the burning of my own heart. Somewhere in that smoldering darkness the memory clicked and I felt stupid for not recognizing it right away. The name.

Emilian is dying.

My mother had used that name before. Except now that I remembered it, it didn't do me any good. According to my mother, he was already dead—and had been for a long, long time.

Eventually I put one foot in front of the other and walked back through the waiting room toward the glass doors. I passed down the aisle of seats where I had been sitting, and on my way I saw an empty seat with a book in it. The horror fan was gone. Instead the book was there, like a leftover scrap of his large, soothing presence.

I picked it up. It felt rumpled and thick and all too familiar. This had been my bread and butter over the years, the endlessly replenished supply of mysteries and horror stories in serialized dozens, churned out as fast as I could consume them. The tattered front cover was curled back from the title page and the title on it was *Sleep, My Lovely.* Then I did something I knew I shouldn't. I put it in my purse.

PART TWO
NO ESCAPE

TOO OFTEN I FEEL WHAT A FREAK I AM, WHAT A PARIAH, WHAT A NATURAL disaster. There is no escaping it, my mother told me at a young and impressionable age. It runs in the blood. My mother's daughter: that's what I am. I've heard the stories. I know what I come from. I've heard all about what spreads behind me: a long line of crazies and quacks, people with circuits loose and chips on their shoulders, people living in the moral and mental gray, twisted but functional, not committable, delinquent and duplicitous, shameless and shifty—my other family. I've tried to be proud of it, like a deranged superhero with an alter ego. All my life, certain girls, and then young women, have been attracted to my attitude, intrigued by my air of quirky mystery. Our friendships never last long.

I never told them—though it would have helped—all the stories. My mother once told me that her own mother gave herself seven home abortions after she gave birth to her first child, a son, and then later had three more children—all girls. She also told me that her father, a scheming businessman, sold everything from hot plates to hot cars to TVs to handguns—back and forth across the black market and everywhere in between without discrimination. Their names were Yana and Mircea Czacky. They were second-generation American gypsies. My mother's father had learned all his business tricks from his own father, who had used them to establish his immigrant family against all odds in Depression America. It was 1938 when the first Czacky stepped on American soil. And his name, my mother told me, was Emilian.

That was in June of 1938. That summer, something had happened to my great-grandfather that had driven him to leave his family and his homeland, something that ended up becoming a fortuitous event in the end, because it had led to his marriage and sown the seeds of his life in America. That something, that fortuitous event, which my mother told me about, was a fire.

And here my mother would say that fire is part of our heritage. Wherever gypsies go, fire follows. It's a way of life. Houses and businesses are always burning down. The future and the past are always going up in smoke. Nothing is forever. And whether foretelling fortune or disaster, fire is always there, reminding us of this fact, coaxing us along toward our inevitable destiny. It was fire that brought her family from Europe to America, fire that introduced my great-grandfather to my great-grandmother on the boat ride over, fire that bought them land in a dying town, and it was on these fires they had built their lives and livelihoods. Fire had brought my mother into this world, and I couldn't help noticing that forty-seven years later fire had taken her out of it. Just like that. She may have escaped her family, but she had failed to escape her family's legacy.

I always knew that smoking would kill my mother, but I pictured her taking a long time with it, wasting away in a hospital bed, choking up green sludge until she was an empty husk of cancer or emphysema. I never imagined she would be caught by something so drastic, incinerating completely in a hot bitter wind of smoke and ash one day, leaving at the center of the conflagration only a charred scattering of remains barely recognizable as human.

When the shock had worn off, I was left with a horror that was almost satisfying, as if her death were the final consummation of a life that was leading her always toward this one certainty, where she would become in death the one thing that she had been a willing slave to in life, the one thing she had lived with in total devotion—that stick of fire from which she had drawn breath all the years I had known her.

I picture my mother on those nights she sat telling me stories about her family, her mouth zippered shut around her bobbing cigarette, her eyes squinting against the acrid curl of smoke that left her nose. According to her, we were descended from a long-lost gang of adventuring nomads, shifty and roving, dusty characters in a story far removed from my life in the here and now. It occurred to me later that all this seemingly backwards itinerant living had been going on throughout the last seventy years, not so long ago, and that even after my mother's family had moved to America and become citizens they had carefully, suspiciously, preserved most of that lifestyle, out of value for their separateness. Separateness—another gypsy legacy that my mother bore until she died.

She never got used to thinking of herself as an American, as one of the *gaje*. Even after her banishment, she had identified herself first and foremost as a Rom, a gypsy, a Kalderash. That part of her was too deeply ingrained to be swept away by bad feelings. The same had been true of her grandfather, who had claimed until his death that he was a Lovara, even though he had lost those ties to his *natsia* when he came to America. But his departure had been different from my mother's, because he had simply picked up one day and left of his own free will. He had been acting out of one of the most basic practices of gypsy existence, that necessary nomadic wandering that was becoming easier and easier in the twentieth century, but paradoxically less lucrative and more unwelcome as the old trades lost their value. Groups and individuals were striking out for weeks or months before they returned, treating the *kumpania*, the community, as a sort of base camp for their excursions. The kumpania itself would move and halt, move and halt, settling briefly outside of towns and villages to trade horses or do copper work until it was time to pick up and move on again, only deciding it was time to go when there was no more business to wring out of a nearby town, or else overstaying their welcome until they were run out or burned out by incensed townspeople—their rhythms with the gaje following that same constant flux of acceptance and rejection, separateness and isolation, escape and banishment, that they had practiced among themselves. My great-grandfather had lived through many of these cycles, and they must have been as regular to him as the seasons by the time he left. So when he abandoned his kumpania in Romania, it would have been an act that was unprincipled, but not unprecedented.

One day, after he had sold some radios in a nearby town—the last sale of two years' worth of miscellaneous trading and buying from which he had been saving his profits, growing rich by gypsy standards—he headed back to the tough scrap of land on which they currently lived and saw the dirty smoke belching up into the pale midsummer sky. Coming down the road, he watched his house along with all the others burn down. All he had was his money, every small bill he had gathered and exchanged in town for fewer, bigger ones and then stitched into the hollowed heel of his shoe. He knew that his parents and brothers and their wives and children would pick up and move to some other discreet fringe of land, hang their lives up on another temporary settlement and steal and sell and barter until they were driven or burned out again. He knew that they would continue making their way to the mountains, chased by rumors and bad omens, refugees from an approaching war. But not him. No—he wasn't going that way. He made a choice. One of those first choices that changed lives for generations afterward. He took his money and spent it on a long boat ride to New Jersey.

There were other gypsies on the boat with him, other people fleeing Europe, fleeing the concentration camps, fleeing war. Among them was a group of Kalderash, who were eager to invite into their company this lone Lovara who stood a class above them, who wore fine clothes and exuded wealth and status, who was all alone without his family, his *vitsa*. There was a young woman among them. She was sixteen, long and lithe and sharp featured, with eyes that were large and brooding like a long night of soft rain. Her name, she told him in a voice that was low and steady, was Alepa.

The conversations on the boat began with questions about family and lineage, then delighted outbursts when vitsas were recognized and common acquaintances named, and soon nudges and winks were being exchanged, optimistic speculations filtering through the bated exchanges about war, about capture, about death. My great-grandfather could hardly believe his good fortune. When the proposal was made, spoken by her father in some dark airless corner of the cargo hold, the Atlantic spread flat as glass around them, Emilian agreed. He took Alepa as his wife, and shortly thereafter they stepped onto the shores of America.

This was Depression America, and Emilian and his new family knew how to be resourceful. They lived hard and never noticed, staying in pitched camps and slums where other immigrants, some of them gypsies, were doing the same thing—all of them using the universal language of buying and trading, picking up English little by little—and making their way slowly up through the region into Massachusetts. In the cities they got coppersmith work in shipyards that paid good money until it was discovered they were gypsies, and then they were fired and told to move along. They travelled in from the coast, spread out to the rural areas. Here they found seasonal work as farmhands and added a stable income to the stealing and bartering and selling they had been doing, until two years later Emilian found himself with another wad of cash in his shoe in a dying industrialized farm town outside Boston, looking at a FOR SALE sign in the window of a shabby singed-looking shed next to a corner lot of charred-up, smoking metal that was being hosed over by county workers. What had been there was a little family-operated amusement park, a long-failing venture that everybody in town whispered had been finally set on fire for the insurance money.

It was the fire that told him. Emilian could see the whole wheel turn—one fire had led him to another, disaster had led him to fortune. This was his destiny. He purchased the park. The fire damage had not been as bad as it looked, and only a small portion of the park was irrecoverable. Emilian had that debris dismantled and hauled off, and then he and his family pitched a tent right there on the spot.

The timing was almost perfect. It was 1941. The war had come to America, industry began to boom, and ever so slowly money began to flow, and it flowed little by little into Emilian's neighborhood amusement park. Eventually he emerged as the leader of his vitsa, and was known by the gaje of the town by his *nav gajikano*, his non-gypsy name—an assimilated citizen. He was happily married with three children. And life went on for a time like this, every year that passed giving the next generation stronger roots to grow on.

But over the years enmities grew up in the town—social misunderstandings at first, rifts in lifestyle and custom, grievances scumming the waters of a people that had never been sedentary. It began with the job disparities after the war. Dark strangers wandered in from out of town to work the park and then disappeared, while the town's own unemployed factory workers languished—the flux and flow of unfamiliar faces was unseemly, the lack of community spirit unconscionable. Fewer and fewer people came to the park and the patrons were mostly from out of town—family caravans passing through on vacation. The locals gave the park a wide berth, and while teenagers partied in it and vandals plagued it, the town police barely patrolled it.

By the time Emilian fell ill and his firstborn son, Mircea, married and took over the amusement park, his inheritance was outdated, rusty, a danger and a liability. His father had kept it barely in repair, had done the minimum to keep it running. Laws were stricter now. A new inspector came and handed over a long list of mandated repairs and upgrades. Mircea saw that what he had was a money pit, and because his father had never instilled in him any bit of sentimentality or nostalgia for anything he had lived with, and because he needed a fresh start as much as he needed this burdensome property, he pooled all the vitsa's remaining money and promptly had the whole park razed and turned into a used-car dealership. His childhood experiences of carnival music and rusting metal were absolutely erased, replaced by a hot flashy sea of asphalt and chrome. This was the world he introduced his children into, the world where my mother grew up.

And this was where my mother's people were still living. For seventeen years she had grown up among them, a gypsy, one in an extended family of outsiders, and then the outsiders had cast her out. Yet less than ten years later, in the disgraced depths of her exile, she was telling me the stories that she had been told, passing down her family's heritage as if it were still important.

More than once I had heard her use the name Emilian when she spoke of my great-grandfather. Now I supposed it was a family name, a name that had been passed along through the generations, just as she had been named Alepa after her grandmother. There could be any number of Emilians in that gypsy kumpania now.

But which of them had been the subject of that note? Which one, on his deathbed, had asked to see my mother? And why? It was hard to imagine.

5

"YOU SHOULD BOTH KNOW SOMETHING ABOUT THEM," MY MOTHER said one night, looking from me to my brother. She was drinking, and her usual flush was deeper and ruddier, her face already burned red from a day in the sun. "They're your family too."

We had been to the beach that day, and after hours of exertion my brother and I were strewn out on the carpet, our bodies limp and radiating warmth, limbs stiff with sun and exercise and salt water.

"But you hate them," Eliot told her, his voice light and drowsy. "You'll never see them again."

My mother fixed him with a gaze that was both scornful and tender, and shook the ice in her glass. "I see them every time I look at you." She often seemed to me like a recently tamed barbarian after such a day outside, her hair crisp and wild with salt air, her pink eyes blinking and wet. She tipped her glass and finished her drink. "And you're the reason I'll never see them again."

She was drunk. Always after a day at the beach, my mother would get too drunk to send us to bed. The hour would come and go, and Eliot and I would lie there sapped of strength, giddy with our secret success, waiting for somebody to notice and push us into our rooms. "What do you think about that?" my mother asked.

My brother tried not to look hurt, but I had seen that flinching look cross his face and disappear. He shrugged. "It's not my fault."

"No it's not," said my mother. She pointed at my father. "I met him."

We all looked over. My father had gone to sleep in his chair watching the ten o'clock news, and his gentle snoring, which a moment before had left me triumphant to know that I wouldn't be going to bed any time soon, now made me feel uneasy, as if in his moment of weakness he had left us all at her mercy.

If my brother and I could have lifted ourselves up and gone to our bedrooms, we would have. But our only defense was to sink down silent and languid, pretending not to listen. That night my mother told the story of her exile, how she had once been promised away by her family like a sack of goods, and had meanwhile met my father on her own and gotten pregnant. When she was done, she kicked us with her feet and said into our faces with unnatural cheer, "And now here I am. With you."

Mesmerized by our own exhaustion, minds soft, we watched her.

"See—I wanted to be here. It was my choice to be with your father even before they turned me out. That's what I wanted to tell you."

But somehow I knew, and my brother knew, that was not what she had wanted to tell us. Because by telling us this story she had somehow taken herself from the place she was sitting and moved out of our reach. She had left us for a different world, a past world that stood between us and her like a dark, reflective glass, one that threw us strangely back onto ourselves and kept her in the shadows of her former life. It was the same world she had gone to, and always went to, when she was out on the beach. Out there, my mother seemed to stand at the edge of her own life in order to meet some unfathomable punishment. And we were there, my brother and I, to see it.

It was in this way, I later realized, cast into my mother's darkest moment with her, that she had made her punishment ours too.

We were born into punishment, my brother and I, our mere existence implicating us. My mother had given it a kind of religious ceremony in our lives, lifted it to a creative and mystifying act that passed through her from somewhere else—never in scale with the original misdeed and never predictable, but always swift and decisive and nonnegotiable. As punishment my mother would leave my brother and me stranded in drugstores and Laundromats for two or three hours at a time, children of nine and six, just young enough to feel the agony of her abandonment. When we were older she would tiptoe into our rooms to read our most private confessions in our journals, and then write sneering notes back to us in the margins. *Don't be a moron,* she wrote once after I had made an outraged complaint about a boy in my class. *You're obviously in love with him.* I was terrified when I saw this, afraid that my mother would say something to the other mothers, or tease me in front of my brother. But she preferred silent acts of torture—fixing us a meal full of our most despised foods and making us eat it, leaving all our laundry unwashed so we had to fish dirty underwear and socks from the hamper to get dressed for school. By high school we had taught ourselves to be watchful of these tricks; we learned to use the washing machine and plucked up the courage to refuse her dinner, so she simply humiliated us by walking up onto the school bus in the afternoon, draped in the same ragged seafoam-green robe she had been wearing that morning, and pulling us off in front of all of our classmates—never explaining what we had done but leaving that to us to figure out, in our bedrooms later, where we sat nursing our wounds and humiliations, vowing to get her back someday.

What all of my mother's punishments had in common was the element of surprise, that sharp stab of clarity, that moment of realization diminishing us, prostrating us before the great mystery of her knowledge. What had we done this time? How did she know? Over the years, her tactics had made us churlish, independent, full of defensive mockery and distrust. But while we thought we were tough, grown to be survivors in her cruel world, I later looked back and realized that at the bottom of all that bluster we had submitted ourselves to my mother's earliest vision of us—and in that vision she was perhaps subscribing to her family's—that we were weak and culpable, her unhappy rejects, dirty little gaje, deserving of what we got.

It was her earliest punishment that had first annihilated us before we could even save ourselves. When we were young, too young to be embarrassed or threatened out of our utter devotion to her—when her anger only made us cling harder in love and fear—my mother had a special way of punishing us. She took us to the beach.

At the beach, while we played in the waves, she looked down on us from a rusting deck chair and wept. We always knew if she took us there that we had done something bad, and since we didn't know what it was, the day often unfolded around the mystery of what deviant act we had committed to make her willing to sacrifice us to the worst peril she could imagine. My mother couldn't swim, and we vaguely understood that we were here because of her fear of drowning, because she could not imagine us going into that water and coming out alive.

At the age of six, I was terrified of the beach: the loose grit in the bottom of the car from the last day trip we had taken, the wet billowing air on my bare shoulders, the brackish gray sand dented and churned by thousands of feet, the malicious little bits of shell that stabbed me when we walked to our spot, the rubbery clumps of cloudy green seaweed strewn everywhere, and worst of all, the appearance of that great glittering ocean surging up in heavy powerful waves, which was there, I knew, to search out the shame and guilt I couldn't find inside myself and then swallow me under it forever.

Still smoking the cigarette she had lit in the car, my mother would lead us to a spot just behind the soggy line of the tide and set down the cooler and straw shoulder bag she was carrying, and then she would command us to arrange our towels. She stood above us dropping ash into the sand while we followed her instructions with the grim solemnity of those preparing their executions. As she was setting up her chair she would give the word for us to go, and still we would linger, half afraid to do what she said, feeling our will and substance dissolving already, until she turned around and gave us a look that made us run.

And surprisingly, once we got to the water's edge we felt better, and with our courage plucked up we played fiercely and bravely, making ourselves forget about her, digging up sand crabs with our buckets and knocking our chests into the crashing surf to see who could stay up. Sometimes it went on for hours and hours, us playing resolutely in her view while she sat smoking and weeping above us.

I remember that feeling of vital relief sweeping through me like a gale when finally I looked up the beach and saw that my mother was done with her weeping, that she had pulled one of those thickly furled books out of her bag, the ones with roses and windswept men and women on the covers, and leaned back with it propped against her chest. That was the sign. When her eyes left our bodies, held us no longer to the shoreline, we knew she was now too tired to push us back from our towels. Exhausted from hours of play, our bodies shivering and buffeted and raw, we would drag back up to where she sat, eerily quiet in her chair, and she would shift her gaze to us and point to the cooler to tell us we could have a soda. I remembered the taste of that soda—always grape because she knew it was our favorite—the first sip of it taken as I sat wrapped in my towel and slowly warming in the sun. The cold bright sparkle would hit my throat with a dazzling burst, and it was like awakening back into the sweet world of the living. And that feeling came with the understanding that we were all sorry and it felt good to be sorry, because now we could all be absolved of our bad deeds.

My brother and I would sit in the bliss of our restored grace, drinking and chatting, drowsy and sated, our mouths deepening to purple stains, and my mother would sit back and watch us—a fresh, curious affection blending with the lingering contempt in her gaze, contempt for our sticky purple mouths, for Eliot's shrill uneven speech, and for my compulsive fingers pulling my bathing suit straps up into my mouth to be sucked and chewed incessantly. And we watched her watching us, both of us dimly aware that these helpless acts were somehow connected to our transgressions that day, lingering evidence of our depravity, linked to her certain disapproval: her strange children, strangely alive.

It was that gaze of my mother's that over the years could turn me back into myself and show me what I couldn't see otherwise: those deeper tremulous corners of my being, dark unreached places where my soul like a spider dwelled, in cringing strangeness and fear. As we grew up, my mother continued to watch us as if we were bizarre creatures who had stolen her flesh and blood right out from under her nose. Who were these creatures in her house? And her love for us despite our monstrosity was a rare thing she periodically held out in our sight, like something of grotesque beauty she had found and wanted us to glimpse. *Look, don't touch,* she seemed to tell us. *Or you might get nothing.*

This was how it looked to us over the years, my mother's love like a thing of fragile design, something that could hardly withstand all our prodding needs and demands. We hovered as near as we could, searching it out with a complicated sense of wonder and fear, shrinking even in our advances, shy and eager for any little portion we could get. But we lived in dread of her vacillations, those small refusals of love that accumulated over the years, each one making us more aware of our own uncertain worth, warning us of inevitable rejection, and so finally to avoid being pushed away, we fled. We sought our own escape.

My brother sought escape first in the most prosaic fashion—showing interest first in my mother's booze, taking bottles out of the house to sit behind the church parking lot with neighborhood boys who would otherwise be jumping him for his money or for fun. In buying his own safety he set himself up in their group as the goon, desperately bartering for the lowest place among superiors, shamelessly bearing the gifts and offerings of his own survival—the weakest sort of gypsy in him. My mother, immune to all this, perhaps even ashamed, smacked him around herself, and then bought a padlock for her liquor cabinet. My brother started taking her cigarettes instead. When she got around to noticing this, the bulk cartons went behind the padlock too. He was fifteen then and a sophomore in high school, coming home every week under the banner of some fresh attack, one day arriving without his shoes and another with hair slimed with loogies and another with his face and neck branded in black and red marker scrawl, the barely legible letters spelling out slurs like *FAG* and *QUEER*—always too battered to speak. For it was speaking that had done this to him. Even years of therapy, which had finally smoothed and perfected his pronunciation, could do nothing for the manic pitch of his voice, still singling him out and exposing him to the violent fears and aversions of those boys at his school and in the neighborhoods who felt the imperative to make him sorry—sorry for the way he sounded, sorry for the way he was.

So my brother found some other people to hang out with, tough angry fags who carried knives and needles to school, who took their shelter in drugs and gathered together for the communal benefits of cutting parties. Leaving the house at all hours, locking his door so Boris wouldn't talk to him. By the end he was using only my father's first name to address him, reveling in all the distance and condescension it implied. At first Boris had given him long, smoldering looks, but Eliot had seemed to enjoy those too, and eventually my father had given up. By then I had heard my father's name so much that I began to think of him as Boris too. It wasn't long before Eliot was lost in cravings and lined with mutilations, all his fraternal bloodletting making him sallow and listless around the house, until finally he slipped bodily away too, like a snake leaving behind a damaged husk of skin, slinking out one night and never coming home.

I was fourteen when he left. I had spent most of that time lost in a book, trying to hide. My habits of escape had always been more subtle, more physically sedentary, but even in her greatest distress over my brother my mother would periodically startle me to alertness, reminding me that she hadn't forgotten me. She made it clear that my habits were equally troublesome to her—neurotic and shrinking, queer and dullish. And there *was* something unhealthy about the kind of reading I did. My eyes and mind would glaze. My whole conscious being would soften to putty, only the most involuntary functions still working. One time I found myself standing up with a book in the kitchen, a string of drool stretching slowly down to touch the page I was reading, and I snapped out of it long enough to feel a writhing disgust and swipe my slobber away. My mother might have been there to see it, and I didn't even bother to turn my head to find out.

Whenever I did notice her, it was usually after she had tried to get my attention and had succeeded only in bringing me dimly to the surface, because she was often walking away from me with a stormy look, her face brimming with contempt and disbelief. Surprisingly, whenever I saw her like this, I felt a surge of cool satisfaction. Alone again, bobbing in the ripples left by my mother's gusts of agitation, I knew that, for the time being, I had found something she couldn't touch—I had gone somewhere my mother could not follow.

6

UNDER THE INFLUENCE OF THE WRITTEN WORD MY MIND LOOSENS, wanders, sinks deep into unknown places, places I can't control or even fathom, leaving so little of me at the surface that I don't even notice what I'm doing there. Page after page comes out, and each one goes into my mouth, but with only enough of me present to observe it passively, to bear witness in sweet surrender. I've consumed whole histories and populations without ever knowing it, I've eaten up entire cultures and devoured distant galaxies, I've sampled philosophies and religions and tasted the bitter strife of politics and the minor pains of pet ownership and digested the handbooks of hobbies I will never have and the fantasies of fiction I will never live—all of this with a hunger I could not satisfy. It took a long time for me to learn that the only way to stop eating was to stop reading. And the only way to stop reading was to stop handling books, to never bring one into my house—to seal the valve, pinch it right at the door. It was the strictest and most necessary rule of this regimen, the only way to maintain sanity, to keep from getting lost in the deep oblivion of my physical urges, and to stay on the right side of the rule—the right side of my mind. But, like any addiction, there are moments of relapse and submission, stress-induced backslides, painful regressions into the drooling, chomping moron I worked so hard to shed.

This one started at the hospital, waiting for my father to come through surgery.

My mind was a distant squall. How had I gotten here? It seemed the drive from that other waiting room had taken only minutes, and I only vaguely recalled the car's ominous knocking and the low steady squeal that had accompanied me all the way back into town. I brought the book into the hospital hoping I wouldn't run into Mitch. I let my eyes drift over the page, and slowly, dazedly, I felt myself submitting to it like a sleep tonic I couldn't possibly resist. I read myself into oblivion, pulling pages as I went, looking at no one, wanting only to lose myself. When I came to, I was sixty-eight pages into the story and every page had been neatly layered onto the supple wad that was tucked against the roof of my mouth. The nurse was speaking to me.

My father was alive. All his vital signs were good. He had made it through the surgery. And so had most of the book.

I went home and ate and showered and called in sick to work and had a fitful night of sleep. The next morning I got up early and called to report the car accident, then went back to the hospital, where I had the presence of mind to stop and look at the directory, to see that the psych unit was up on the fifth floor in this wing. That was where Mitch would be, strolling around with a clipboard, giving everybody that serious look out of the tops of his eyes. It wouldn't be hard to avoid him. I took the elevator up to the second floor to my father's room and sat down at his bedside with my purse jammed uncomfortably into my hip. With a slight quiver of shame, I fished out the offending article.

For a moment I held it, then put it down on the table, trying to resist. I was sitting in the chair by the window, and I twirled open the blinds, looked studiously at the monitors and machines around my father's bedside—the bag of clear fluid going into his forearm, the yellow pouch at the end of the catheter tube hanging half full from the bedrail, the heart monitor, the tube of pink fluid spurting from his head—then I stole a wincing glance at the ripe purple bloom on his shaved scalp and the circles around his closed eyes and pulled the book off the table. I folded back the blood-spattered cover that was drooping all alone in front of the gap of bare binding that I had left, and stared at the page until the words began to make sense.

By the light of the window, I read the horror fan's gift to me. I read with a reckless abandon, without regard for the nurses coming and going around me. Every half hour I would sense the presence of a quiet body come to administer medication or adjust fluids, and once I was kicked out into the hallway so that two nurses could change the sheets, and even then I kept reading, standing against the wall, oblivious to passing traffic. In this way the time passed, and it seemed like only minutes had gone by before I was sitting by the bed in that deep blue light that made me feel only half there. I had the pages in my mouth, a dumpling of disintegrating fibers that was hard to keep together. I took out the sodden gob and tore it into two soggy halves. What would my mother say? As always when I read I could feel her sitting on her high perch somewhere gazing down at me, that barbed angry look in her eyes. I knew what she would say.

For years in her house I had eaten up the terrors of things done in darkness, the blood and guts of murders found by flashlight and moonlight and lamplight, my appetite insatiable, my urges themselves a horror story. I finished one book and started another. I couldn't stop myself. My earliest method of escape had become, over the years of my adolescence, something I could not escape. And the person who had seen the danger before I did, even before I had begun to rip pages out and pack them in my mouth, was my mother, stalking me in various rooms of the house, her gaze agitated, just waiting for me to step over the line so she could interfere at last. I could imagine it now, there in her eyes all along—the terrible certainty of foresight.

But I didn't see it. I flinched away over and over and departed to another room where I could read my book in privacy, moody and withdrawn, all jellied limbs and blanched skin and plastered hair shaped to the back of a chair. I was addicted by then to mysteries and thrillers and horror novels, anything that would scare me, and it was in the trance of these books that I began to tear out dog-eared corners of the pages while I read and anxiously ball them up into little pellets and put them into my mouth. I chewed each pellet experimentally at first, and then with a rush of visceral gratification, discovering a new activity that urged instant exploration—and that brought, somehow, a material comfort, a deep, soothing consolation even as I went on in my rush of apprehension toward the end of the story. When the corners were gone, I moved on to other available blank spaces, and soon I was gnawing on the bottom margins and nibbling up that hefty blank expanse at the end of chapters.

Perhaps my mother had been spying on me, coming into my room while I was at school and going through my stacks of partially digested books with a growing concern, and then had decided how best to act—or maybe one day she simply found the evidence and reacted. But she began periodically to come into my room and wipe every surface clean of reading material and then would refuse to answer my questions. Where were my books? What had she done with them? They were gone, she said. And that was all she said.

In my room I started hiding my books and then eating them whole before she could steal them. After I read a page I tore it out of the binding and stuffed it in my mouth, nothing left of me now but a machine, physically grinding the raw material that was regularly fed through it. I finished every book with the disturbed conviction that I was bad and dirty, my own perversion blending now with the perversions of my characters—the inhumane, incomprehensible slayings like a shameful hunger that was feeding my shame and hunger.

At some point my mother found my hiding spot in the closet. And while she thought she could fight down my behavior, that it would be easier to win with me than my brother, she underestimated the need I had, and just how deep it went, failing to understand that I was living now on these physical reassurances, on calm, inert substances that secretly soothed my cringing soul. Yes—I knew what my mother would say. She would say what she always said.

"What I want to know," she always said. "Is how I got these two children. My two little sickos," she said, shaking her head at us, incredulous and mocking. "All mine. How lucky I am."

I put the book on the table and sat back.

In his sleep Boris's mouth puckered up like a mummy. I checked my watch. In four minutes he would be ready for another dose of pain medication. I stood up and went to the doorway, and just as I stepped through it, the nurse arrived. She was not much older than me, but the thin, beakish face, heavy midwestern accent and big rubber shoes all made me feel relaxed and nurtured. Her name tag said Jenna.

"He's doing it again," I said.

"Alrighty." She wagged a little vial at me. "Are you leaving then?" She cocked her head and gave me a kind, sympathetic frown. "Oh, you look tired."

Seeing myself in her eyes, I felt suddenly exhausted, as if I were a child who had been waiting all this time for somebody to gather me up lovingly and put me to bed.

I nodded.

"Well you go home and get some sleep." She reached out and rubbed my shoulder. "I'll see you tomorrow." With a final little pat, she passed me through the doorway.

When she had gone inside the room I stood there for a moment, quite still, absorbing all her casual affection as if it were a rare and exquisite cure to a lifelong deficiency.

PART THREE
FORTUNE SAYS

7

I WOKE UP THE NEXT MORNING IN A CHILL, BIRDLESS PREDAWN, WITH a bright moon still shining in through my window, three-quarters full. I brewed coffee and stood at the window with my mug, mentally preparing myself to return to work. The three days I'd been gone felt like much longer. One car passed, its yellow headlights softened by a light fog. I opened the window and listened to it fading out to a distant hush, then heard only the cold quiet throb of the air in my ears. It seemed to me that at the age of twenty-seven I had accepted a fate of unhappy solitude and was now making a plummeting descent into the life of an old maid, just as my father had feared. For a long time I had argued that "old maid" was not even something that existed anymore, but I was beginning to fear that perhaps this was wrong. Perhaps it did.

I heard a thin clatter of footsteps in the street below me and looked down. A figure was coming out of my building onto the sidewalk. It was a man, walking quickly, curling his shoulders down into his chest like he was cold. I watched the figure cross the street and walk down the block, his steps echoing. It was rare to see somebody out this early. I must have been in a strange mood. The more I stared at him, the more I thought he looked like Mitch.

Why was I brooding like this? What was it—my job bothering me? Was that my problem? It had been Mitch who'd warned me about it. For the nearly four years we lived together I had been rising at four a.m. so that I could be at the TV station by five to contribute my meager portion to the preparations required for the six a.m. newscast. I ate dinner at five p.m. and was in bed by nine at the latest. This routine had always been a problem for Mitch, who had been the first to suggest that I was an old woman trapped in a much younger, sexier body that was not getting its proper treatment. Then he tried to treat it properly and I said I was too tired.

"But tomorrow's your day off," he said, talking into my neck where he usually started.

"But I got up at four o'clock *today*," I said. "I'm sorry. You know my schedule. Try me before nine next time."

"Okay, fine." The edge in his voice implied that he didn't believe my excuse. He seemed to think my problems were more than schedule related, and that I was using the schedule as a justification he couldn't argue with because it was my job that was making the money for us while he went to med school. Now he had finished school, and was one year into his residency, and could consider himself in the last stretch of his long path to becoming a psychiatrist. And I was still here, right where I had started.

Thirty minutes later I was walking that same direction as the Mitch-ish figure had gone, hunched down in my hooded rust-red corduroy trench with the quilted satin lining, my favorite coat in all the world, a lucky purchase from the thrift store under Boris's apartment. I headed toward Boris's apartment so I could rummage through his car before going to work. The insurance company had determined the car totaled. I had been advised to take everything out of it that I wanted before the tow truck came to haul it away.

After a short search of the car I determined there was nothing to salvage apart from the hula girl, which I plucked from the dash. Then I opened my father's glove compartment, pulled out a door opener that went to a garage that no longer existed, and took out the road atlas. I walked up to my father's apartment with these items and let myself in. It was narrow and dark, painted an underwater blue, the living room sandwiched between a small kitchen on the street side and a bedroom and bathroom on the parking lot side. Two little windows in the kitchen burned dim shafts of early-morning light through the apartment, like portholes on a submarine. The brown plaid couch was sitting in one of these pools of blue light. It had been left by the previous tenant and it smelled like dog hair and smoke. The rest of the furniture I had purchased in the thrift store below the apartment, and it wasn't much better.

I still regretted the evening two months ago that I had stopped outside that thrift store and looked in the window. That day, it wasn't the clothes that had caught my attention, but a sign propped in the corner of the glass: *Apartment Upstairs For Rent*. At the time, two weeks after my mother's death, still stunned and raw, stumbling through the investigation and insurance claims between work and sleep, trying to find a place to put my grieving father, it had looked like the best thing I had ever seen. Now I was painfully aware that I had put my father in a dump.

In the kitchen, I set my father's car pickings down on the counter. A red light on his answering machine blinked that he had messages. I hesitated, then pressed it. There was a message from the insurance company, a recorded advertisement for carpet cleaning, and then a garbled muttering in a raspy female voice. All I caught was the end of her last sentence: *"if you don't come soon I'll be"*—something, all the words barely distinguishable, the last word spoken as she was taking the phone away from her ear to hang it up with a sloppy clatter. The voice was ornery and impatient. It sounded like an old woman who had called a wrong number. I stared at the machine. Then I realized what this message was. It was the one Boris had been talking about the night he came to my apartment—the one he had thought was left by my mother.

I listened to it again. What frenzied train of thought had led him from finding that note in the cigarette case to hearing this message and then on to pursuing my mother's family? Beyond the superficial qualities of pitch and tone the voice was too creaky, too full of quivering need, too *old* to resemble my mother's. I pulled the atlas off the counter, where the two lines led away from the freeway and into that dismal neighborhood. And what sort of contact had my father been attempting? How many days had I walked by here on my way to work thinking he was upstairs in this hovel when he was actually a town away, pursuing some mysterious madness? My eyes felt hot and singed. Clearly my father had brought me to the street in that town because he wanted to alert me to something, to bring me in on some part of it, but he had not been able to tell me what it was. He had given me access to the road atlas and the cigarette case. He had wanted me to know about this phone message and had tried to tell me something else. What had he said that night? What about my mother? *I don't think it was*—was what? An accident? The words fit themselves into the unspoken words of his sentence like a puzzle piece snapped into place.

I sat down in the living room, my thoughts rushing back over my mother's death. The investigation had been pat. She had pulled the oven out from the wall. The scorched vacuum canister was still there beside it. I had seen her do this cleaning task before, whenever she did a thorough cleanup of the kitchen. She always started with the dirtiest appliance, the oven, and moved out from there. The brittle gas tube at the back was cracked at the point of strain. The slim gold lighter was there in the debris, as if, after cleaning the oven and the rest of the kitchen, my mother had paused in front of the oven before pushing it back into place, and lit the cigarette that killed her. Years of chain-smoking had all but banished my mother's sense of smell, and it was entirely feasible that she had gone about her business and not noticed the telltale odor piling up around her. It was even possible that she had been doing a three-phase cleaning of kitchen, laundry, and family room, all in that back corner of the house, and had not gotten back to reposition the oven for several hours. It was all so natural, so true to my mother's habits. Did he think somebody *else* had pulled the oven out from the wall to crack the gas tube behind it, and then struck that lighter?

I lifted my eyes to the digital clock and saw that I had only six minutes to get to work. Maybe I was making all this up. Maybe those words I had filled in for my father were not the ones he had wanted to say. I picked up the road atlas from my lap. One more time my eyes followed the other smudged line across the page, the one that led somewhere unknown. Dread flooded my heart like black water, the way it used to that summer before my brother disappeared. Even if it was pointless, I told myself, tucking the book under my arm—even if it told me nothing—I could find out where that line led.

8

MY JOB AT THE NEWS STATION HAD STARTED FIVE YEARS AGO WITH script feeding and edits and filing and copying, all the usual assignments given to a college intern. Then when I quit school I was hired as the assistant to the weatherman, and I was doing all the same things for him alone, with the addition of scheduling and correspondence. Now over the years my job had gradually morphed and I was something less easy to name, way beyond assistant and bordering on personal attendant to the world's oldest weatherman, Salt Pfeiffer.

In recent years my efforts on behalf of Salt had helped to preserve his image as the beloved, recognizable figure of our community—erased the lurid details of age, the crust of premature senility, the greasy archaic soils of decay that had begun to gather in the creases of his forty-one-year career. These efforts, I was fully certain, were helping to delay his long-overdue retirement from this distinguished and locally revered news group.

Though his coworkers were beginning to be startled and offended by his behavior, the city loved him as they would a grandfather standing at the head of a long-established family, and the station manager was hesitant to let him go—disregarding complaints, citing Salt's spit-spot forecasts in defense. Most recently, he had been stringently ignoring Salt's habit of driving to work in the sweats and t-shirt he had slept in the night before and wandering the station in a bleary, bedheaded fog with his coffee and newspaper until I arrived to dress him. This morning Salt outdid himself. I was sipping coffee from the distinctly unchewable aluminum thermos I kept at my desk, when he appeared in the studio wearing only a pair of overlong boxer shorts and a stiff collared shirt left open over his undershirt.

"Good morning, Salt," I chirped.

I stood in the back under the bright lights where a little station had been assembled for the news team to refresh their makeup and retouch their hairstyles. This professional-looking vanity had been procured for Randall Birnoff, the morning anchor, who, because of the ratings he had brought in over the past three years, had some clout with the general manager, clout which had also allowed him to recruit one of the interns to play makeup girl for him, of which he had selected the prettiest and dullest one. Though this exceptional setup was supposed to be for everybody who wanted a little sprucing before a live broadcast, Birnoff had accidentally intimidated the other members of the news team away from it in the mornings, leaving only Salt, who was attracted to the bright vanity bulbs like a moth to flame, and who showed up every morning to sit beside Birnoff in the empty chair and wait for something to happen. When I saw this I began arriving ahead of him at the idle chair. Birnoff was satisfied with this arrangement as long as I made Salt look presentable. Today I clamped my mouth and rolled the cut-metal flavor of coffee across my tongue and said nothing when I saw the underwear. If one didn't look closely enough to see the buttoned flap at the fly, one might assume these were plaid cotton shorts—inappropriate, but not obscene. I tapped the chair I had reserved for Salt and he sat down in it.

"Good morning, Salt," I chirped again.

He slammed the heel of his hand into the armrest. "Mr. Pfeiffer. Mr. Pfeiffer," he enunciated tiredly. Not in a good mood today. In a good mood, he let me call him by his first name. I got out my pancake putty and caught a distressed glance from Raina, Birnoff's makeup floozy—a short, adorable blonde of no more than twenty-two who liked to dress like an oversexed version of the anchorwomen. Behind her and facing into the mirror was the smooth, easy mass of Randall Birnoff, reading a newspaper and sipping his coffee in a dark suit. He hadn't yet looked up to see the vision that was Salt Pfeiffer.

"I deserve my dignity. I have been a weatherman for forty years."

I batted his roving hand away from his temple, where I was applying a layer of paste. "Is it cold up there?"

"Yes it's cold, and it's sticky. What are you doing to me?"

"You are fussy today." I stopped daubing him and hoisted his bristly chin to tilt his face under the lights.

Under his breath, he said, "I am a *weather*man."

"I thought you had to wear pants to be a weatherman."

His eyes hooked savagely on me for a long moment. I could see I had confused him.

So far no response from Birnoff one seat over. He was too busy reading to hear our conversation.

"I asked Meredith to iron your pants for you," I reminded Salt. "She's going to put them in your office when she's done."

"I know that," he snapped.

"Well, did you know that you were expected to keep on your *other* pants while she was doing that?"

He gave me a cloudy look of irritation. Instructions were not something he took well. "Why don't you do your job, Nan? I mean…" His bluster sagged for a moment. "I'm in a hurry."

Everyone at the station called me Nat, except for Salt. When he called me anything, he called me Nan, after his sister. It wasn't affectionately used.

I shrugged. "If you say so."

Salt's skin demanded an oil-based coat of makeup, due to his loosely creased jawline and a badly shaved neck waddle where a smooth, flawless transition was required. Compared to Ms. Sexy Skirts beside me, my job was the tougher one by far. I made old age look natural and dignified. Raina only made a young man look like a peanut butter cookie. Just now her brush was fluttering wildly over Birnoff's cheeks and leaving behind a rusty orange flush of color, over which his white eyeballs rotated ominously as he shifted his gaze up to me in the mirror. I tried not to notice.

"Mr. Pfeiffer, do you have your report all prepared for today?" said his deep, bell-heavy voice.

"Mmph."

Birnoff sighed heavily, his face half obscured by Raina, who was needlessly defining his eyebrows with a pencil—after which he had two charred logs on his face that he raised in disapproval. His eyes moved to look Salt over.

"Oh Christ. Shit almighty. Really?" he said, looking up at me.

"Excuse me," said Salt, turning a withering look on him. "I don't like that language."

"Just—finish him quickly, Nat—he only has twenty minutes."

"He'll be ready," I said, and winked. "Trust me."

Birnoff shifted in his seat and looked profoundly uncomfortable. It was a miracle to him that Salt got on every morning and performed, and I allowed him to think that I was the one holding him together by a thread. What he didn't know was that Salt was in his office at four A.M. with a stiff cup of coffee every morning, looking over all the scans and feeds and compiling his weather data and doing his analysis and putting everything together while he was still half asleep and half naked. His weather research and reporting was as deeply ingrained in him as moving his bowels. All I did was prepare and move his papers from one place to another and then prepare and move him from one place to another.

I had finished the base coat and now I picked up my round brush and rolled it firmly in the blush compact, getting that embalmed face ready for a rosy flush. Salt closed his eyes in anticipation and I blew on the brush and swept it briskly over his whole face, talking quickly as I worked.

"So, guess what? I'm going on a hunt after work."

"A hunt? Do you have a gun?"

"No—I do not have a gun."

"Well you can't hunt without a gun," he said, as if only a stupid girl would forget that.

I paused to take another sip of coffee. "Actually," I said, "it's not a traditional hunt. It's more like a scavenger hunt. I have a map telling me where to go. Only I don't know what I'll be looking for when I get there."

"Natalie," said Birnoff in warning. He stood up and brushed himself and gave me a look that was more severe than his voice. "He can't be distracted by all that now—he has to give the weather."

I gave him a dismissive wave and turned back to Salt. "Almost done. We have to do lip gloss." I snatched the compact from my counter with a flourish and waited for Birnoff to walk away. "Make your face for me," I said to Salt. He flattened his lips against his teeth like the pro I taught him to be, and I dragged the brush through the color. "That's it—thank you baby."

"Excuse me!" he burst out, almost thrusting his nose into the lipstick brush. "This girl," he said to Raina, "keeps calling me names. Can I get someone else? Why can't *you* do my face dressing?"

She gave me one of her brief looks of terror, like she wanted me to come to her rescue but disliked me anyway, and then said, "Mr. Pfeiffer, I have to take care of Mr. Birnoff." As she spoke she glanced nervously into his lap, where his hands were restlessly flicking elastic.

"Underwear," I said. They both turned to me with the same look of infant astonishment. "That's what it's all about, Salt. You need my services because I provide you with underwear."

"No you do *not*."

"Yes I do," I said. "It's like this—if you don't wear the right underwear it shows through the old britches—or skirt suit, as it may be—right Raina?" I glanced at her backside in suggestion. "Lines and wrinkles and such show through. My makeup is like good underwear—it adds to the beauty and respectability of the subject without even showing. You are wearing *fine* underwear. I'm done." I spun his chair to face into the studio.

Salt got up sputtering and I waved him bye-bye, all the while feeling Raina's impotent stare on my right temple. "Toodle-oo. Raina says don't forget to put some pants on before doing the weather."

I heard a little noise of irritated disgust from her, a sound that had to be forced, as if it had taken significant resolve to communicate this one small indignation, and then she whisked past me in her red skirt suit, as if running from possible retaliation. I felt a little sorry as I watched her go. She was a nice girl, and I didn't know why I tortured her. I supposed she reminded me too much of one of those girls in high school, the girls who hadn't liked me, who couldn't understand why their boyfriends tended to talk to me in the lunch line, their mocking questions inevitably misting over with awkward flirtation. As I stood there in the wake of her jasmine perfume, I realized something. I was biting the bristles off the lip brush.

9

NEW CLOUDS HAD GATHERED IN THE SKY, AND THE AIR WAS COLD and heavy and suffused with a thick white glare. I consulted the road atlas once more. The line stopped on its smudged path somewhere in the middle of two large intersections on Harbor Street, and I had already driven back and forth three times under a bridge and past a handful of nondescript buildings. There was a Rhonda's Burgers and an indoor flea market on one side, and a bank and a bowling alley on the other. On the second pass I saw a dry cleaner and an auto body shop, and then a paint store with a picture of a tipping can of paint on its overhead sign. This time I kept going several blocks beyond the end of the pencil-drawn line, just in case Boris had stopped it ahead of his destination. Several barren storefronts later, I pulled into the driveway of a convenience store and parked at the far side of the lot to look one more time at the map.

I was on the right street, between the correct major intersections, so it had to be one of the places I had passed. I looked out my windshield, thinking back on what I had seen, staring out over a dirt lot beside the convenience store until my eyes rested on a brick building with a large metal sign that said CHINESE GROCERY. The sign was a dented, once-white rectangle with red block letters, streaked brown from the rusting bolts that had been used to mount it onto the building. I took a sip of my coffee. It tasted like rust. I looked at the sign again.

My first boyfriend in college liked to go to a Chinese grocery down the street from his apartment and buy egg noodles and bulk-sized bags of fortune cookies. He thought it was funny at the time, how I would compulsively eat the cookies one after another, message and all. I took another sip of coffee, my stomach churning, and wondered if this grocery sold bags of fortune cookies. I thought of the delicate glaze on the shell and the brittle crunch of the cookie around the resiliency of the paper. It was no use resisting at this point—I could feel the familiar pluck of desire, that tight chord vibrating with sudden need. I got out of the car and crossed the dirt lot to the front of the grocery, where a neon OPEN sign was mounted on the inside of the cloudy yellow glass.

The door was heavy, and barely swung open for me before it closed swiftly on my heels.

The store was deep and narrow, and the air had a nauseous smell of refrigeration and raw fish. From somewhere at the back I heard an impatient voice rapping out instructions to somebody. I walked across the front of the store, and when I passed the refrigerator aisle I saw a man with a bottle of cleanser on his knees wiping down the glass door. He looked up, his eyes small and narrow above wide, bulging cheekbones. I smiled and kept walking. When I came to the dry foods aisle I saw a middle-aged woman in a quilted purple coat looking up at a shelf. In the back, behind the counter that went across the back wall, a Chinese woman held up a latex glove shellacked in something slimy and orange. "Too far, too far," she yelled.

She flapped her bloody glove. "Back other way."

"Oh," said the lady apologetically.

"Up. Top shelf." Her eyes settled on me. "You need help?"

"Oh no," I said to everybody.

"What you need?"

I felt silly. "Fortune cookies?"

The clerk nodded and gave her hand a vigorous flick. "Right there. Bottom shelf."

I looked down. There was a package the size of a bag that would normally hold noodles. I was a little disappointed. My boyfriend had brought home bags three times this big.

"You find?" she said, watching me.

I pulled the bag from the shelf and held it up.

"Okay. One moment I finish and be at register."

I turned back up the aisle, listening to the smack of her gloves as she pulled them off and rinsed her hands in a sink. At the front of the store I found the other customer already standing at the register.

The shopkeeper came up to the counter and began picking up the woman's items and speedily punching prices into an old, bulky register. "Oh," she said, bending. "You look at something." She brought up a little piece of stiff paper and pushed it at her.

The woman took it and looked down at it. "I don't. Hmm." She turned halfway around to me, an uncertain smile on her face. "She's, uh—Lin is asking me if I know what this means. She heard it somewhere—is that right? You wrote it down from something you heard?"

The shopkeeper was bent over the woman's driver's license, copying the number onto the top of a credit card slip. "Something I saw on TV. Advertisement."

I took the card. It was one of those "Have You Seen Me?" flyers that came in the mail, with two pictures, a missing child and a woman, her photo filled up with a wild mane of sun-streaked hair, and in the top left corner was the shopkeeper's quivering handwriting. *I pity dafoo.* The woman pointed at it. "Do you have any ideas?"

I sounded it out in my mind. *Dafoo.* Oh. The fool. "It's a saying that Mr. T is famous for."

"Who Mr. T?"

The other woman had signed her credit card slip and was moving to the door. "Bye Lin."

"Okay. Bye." Lin turned back to me.

I tried to think of how best to explain Mr. T. "Was there a big black man with a mohawk on the TV?"

She gazed up at my hands as they shaped a wedge of hair on top of my head. "Yes, yes," she said, nodding me on.

"He used to be on a television show for kids. He fought crime and drove a van." I put the flyer on the counter, imagining my explanation to be sufficient.

This woman, Lin, was not satisfied. "Why? How that related to cell phone advertisement?"

"Hmm… I don't know," I said, beginning to feel a little flummoxed. "I guess that anyone who doesn't buy that telephone is a fool? In other words, he really meant to say, 'I pity the fool who doesn't buy this terrific cell phone.'"

For a moment she continued to peer at me, then she snatched my bag of cookies and rang it up. I handed her some cash and she put the cookies in a grocery bag, all without a word. Before she handed the bag over, she stuck her hand into the box by the register and plucked two candies out of it and threw them inside.

"For you," she said. "For help."

"Oh, thank you," I said.

"You welcome." She held out the bag. "I work on my English."

I nodded. I wanted to say *good for you,* but I didn't want to sound patronizing. I was suddenly speechless, as if my proper phrasing was now going to embarrass us both.

I waited until I walked out of the store, and then on the way to the car I cracked a cookie in half and read the message. *You will be successful.* I put it in my mouth with half of the brittle shell and munched them together while I got into the car. I cracked open the second one. *You will find luck when you least expect it.* Slightly better. I needed some luck. I didn't like to eat the fortunes that I hoped would come true, so I took out my wallet and put it behind my license window for safekeeping. Then I ate the remaining cookie shell while I started the car and pulled out of the parking lot.

Passing the dry cleaner, the body shop and its fading sign—BIG M'S—I still didn't see anything that explained why my father had come to this neighborhood. I cracked another shell open. *Don't ask, don't say—everything lies in silence.* That one was nice—rather poetic. I ate it, and then another. The fortune cookies were only making me hungrier. I wondered if this was going to be my dinner. It was already four o'clock and I wouldn't be getting back to town until after five. And I still had to go to the hospital to visit Boris. *The name does not make the person; the person makes the name.* I considered that to be true, though it was rather obvious. *Someone you know will make you proud.* These cookies were like drugs—the more I ate, the more disappointing they were, and the more I needed to eat them. *The hunger for knowledge is never satisfied.*

By the time I got to the hospital there were only a few cookies left. I took one more out and crumpled the bag down to keep the last two fresh, then threw it on the floor in the backseat. I cracked the cookie open. *You will meet an old friend.* Not likely, I thought, putting it in my mouth. I didn't have any old friends.

In my father's room, Jenna was adjusting his pillow under his head to help him sit up. A sharp pain plucked at my heart when I saw his wakened face, still looking just as slack and gaunt as it had been in sleep. Jenna saw me and smiled.

"Oh, look, your daughter's here to visit you."

I felt a smile stretch my face tight. My father's murky eyes rested on me. Was there recognition in them? I couldn't tell.

"Your dad here woke up this afternoon and he's been sleeping on and off, getting ready for you, right Mr. Krupin?" Jenna leaned down and hung her face where he could see it. "Are you alright now? Comfortable?"

He made a sound, feeble and dismissive, and looked down at his hand as if he wondered how it came to be resting on top of the remote control for the bed.

"Those are your buttons for moving the bed. Remember I just showed you those." She patted his hand and an expression crossed over his face, vaguely irritated, or else perplexed.

"Okay," Jenna said. "You're okay then? You don't need anything else?"

He looked at her for several heavy moments, his face stuck in a dumb expression, and then suddenly his mouth opened and he said, "Nho." Before I could help it my eyes brimmed with tears.

"Okay," said Jenna, as if nothing miraculous had happened. "Well I'm going to leave you to talk to your daughter. Just push this button if you need me."

She smiled her way across the room, gave me another rub on the shoulder. When she was gone I walked in and sat down in the chair.

"Hi Dad. Are you feeling okay?"

His mouth opened and closed a few times as if he were reminding himself how to do it, and then stayed hanging open. "Eh," he said, signaling me to do something.

"What?"

I watched his eyes turn inward in a concentrating expression. Then a word came out, so crisp and loud that I wanted to clap for him. "Dry!" He looked at me, waiting.

"Dry?" I repeated.

He opened and closed his mouth again.

"Oh, your mouth is dry? You want some water?" I stood and went to the tiny bathroom and filled a paper cup with water at the sink, then came back and held it to his mouth. With one look of chagrin he let me tilt the water into it until the cup was empty. I settled back into my seat.

"It's getting warm outside," I told him, as though it had been weeks, and not days, since he had been conscious. "Spring is finally here."

He gazed at me, his eyes heavy in the sunken dough of his face.

"You should see the crabapples." I mentioned this because the crabapples were the only thing about spring that my father noticed. There was one week every April when he would go to our front window at least once a day and whistle at our tree in appreciation, as if it were some hot girl passing by. "Remember that crabapple tree we used to have?"

He put his head back on the pillow and let out a tired breath. For a moment he lay still, and I wondered if he was falling asleep. Then his mouth opened and another word came out. It sounded like my mother's name.

I wasn't sure what to do with that. For a long pause he was silent, his face puckered in that look of pain that had bloomed periodically in his sleep. I began to think it was too much effort to talk, and I was going to ask him if he'd like to rest again when his mouth opened and out came an exhalation of words.

"Hur tree," he said.

"What? Oh, her tree?" I repeated. "Because she planted it."

He nodded. I waited as my father clacked his mouth a few times to work up moisture for the next words.

"Do you need more to drink?"

He shook his head. "On his birthday," he said.

"Oh, okay." It must have been my brother's birthday he was talking about. He had been born in April. "I didn't know that," I said. My father let out a breath and closed his eyes. At first I felt a warm glow to think that my mother had done something so sentimental, then I wondered why she hadn't done anything like that for me. Or maybe she had.

"Did she plant anything for my birthday?"

Boris was silent. I thought I saw his head twitch. Either he was thinking about what I said or falling into a doze. After a while he opened his eyes and looked at me, an expression of bitter searching on his face, like he was trying to come to some secret conclusion about me. Under his gaze I felt my face turn quietly to stone.

I opened my mouth to speak and then closed it. My father let out a tired sigh and turned his head up to the ceiling. For several minutes we sat together silently and I watched him, wondering what was going through his mind. *Don't ask, don't say—everything lies in silence.* I told myself I had to be patient. This wasn't the time. Tomorrow there would probably be a battery of tests, and explanations and medications to keep track of, and plans for therapy and rehabilitation, and all of this would need to come first. Then we would talk about what had happened that day. For now I would let him rest.

"Dad?" I said quietly. He didn't answer me. Either he was sleeping or pretending to be sleeping. I told him in a low voice that I would come back again tomorrow and then I left him there, unresponsive, his eyes closed, his breathing calm and even.

I walked out to my car and drove home, eating the last of the fortune cookies on the way, thinking about the events of the day, wondering which of the buildings I had passed on that street had once been my father's destination. It wasn't until I got home, when I was throwing the crumpled fortune cookie bag away in the parking lot dumpster and looking through the papers I had saved, that I realized how obvious it had been. *The name does not make the person; the person makes the name.* I ran upstairs and rummaged through a drawer until I found it—the sweatshirt. Still there, as thin and droopy as I remembered, one of those rare relics that would have thrilled me in the aisles of a thrift store. I had once found it unworn in the back of the linen closet after a basement flood had depleted our regular towel supply. When my mother saw me wearing it, her eyes blistered.

"Take that off."

"What?" I shrank back in the doorway.

She was already flinging down her oven mitt, hand out.

"Mom," said Eliot. The sound of his voice from the table snapped her neck back. My knees went soft.

"Who cares?" he said, as she stopped to regard him.

She turned to me, the fumes of her silence withering. "I don't care," she said, and went back to her cooking. I glanced at Eliot, slumped over a plate of food he didn't seem to have the stomach to eat, and retreated to my room. I took off the sweatshirt and looked at it. Just a kitschy ad for a place called Big M's.

Later that night I went to his room. "Don't you remember?" he said. He'd been out with my mother that day and his eyes wouldn't settle. "It's that place her father owned. The car dealership."

A sketch of the building was right there on the sweatshirt, accented in sherbet colors to enhance the retro 50s architecture: rounded corners, big plate-glass window under an awning, sign like a speech bubble in a comic strip.

It had been right there in front of me every time I passed by. *The person makes the name.*

Big M's Auto Body. Big M was for the name Mick Thomas, and Emilian Czacky had made it. It was his nav gajikano—the name he used with the gaje.

10

THE NEXT DAY I WENT BACK, AND WHEN I SAW THE SIGN FOR THE AUTO body shop I turned the car into a parking lot on the opposite side of the street and sat looking at it. The smooth walls had been given a dirty off-white stucco job, and a profusion of cracks spidered in all directions. The garage door was open and inside three dark figures moved about, backlit by a window on the far wall that was letting in gray afternoon light. Two junky cars were parked by the garage, waiting their turn to be worked on, and several more cars were parked out at the edge of the lot with fluorescent dollar signs on their windshields, marking their sale prices.

The sign for the shop was on a pole beside the window of the business office—turquoise letters affixed to a milky fiberglass marquee. There was no doubt in my mind now that this was the same used-car dealership that had belonged to my mother's father. BIG M'S, named for the head of the vitsa, Mircea's father. Probably the auto body shop had been added on at some point. If Mircea was alive, then he would be about seventy now. Maybe he was still running it. Or maybe his son was running it. Maybe all those people in there were my uncles and cousins. I lifted my thermos and took a bitter sip of coffee, feeling vaguely queasy, and watched a man in slacks and a dress shirt step out of the business office and walk rapidly with long, arm-swinging strides to the garage. He entered the open darkness and approached a figure at a car. For a minute I watched their dim outlines together, and then I began to feel ridiculous. Now that I had come here, there was nothing left to do. I didn't have the courage to cross the street and talk to anybody. Even if I did, what would I say? The tall, narrow figure was walking back toward the business office. He was the one I would be talking to if I went over there. At the door he paused and put his hand up to smooth out his tie. It was a metallic sea green, and it streaked like a jet of cold water down the bright cherry red of his shirt.

It was the young man from the church. I watched him go inside, my mind racing. For another minute I sat there, wondering if I had the courage to go and talk to him about what my father had been doing at the church that day. Then the door to the business office opened again and he appeared holding a briefcase. He turned and locked the door behind him, holding the briefcase nonchalantly, as if he didn't realize that leaving his little greasy office with such a prop made him look absurd. Instantly this very absurdity made him seem sinister. He stepped from the parking lot into a dirt alley at the side of the building and disappeared.

Where was he going? Why take a briefcase into an alley? I felt my heart knocking inside my chest, certain that I had seen something incriminating. It seemed like I had been given an opportunity of some kind. Paralyzed by the mere idea of it, I realized I was not going to do anything but sit and stare at the vacant alleyway. Then a perky white sedan with a mismatched purple door appeared and stopped at the edge of the alley, waiting to turn into the street.

He was driving. I could see the bright red shirt through the windshield. He made a broad left turn across the street and pulled into the right lane. I had a flinching impulse to duck my head as he passed the parking lot where I was stationed. Then I realized he was getting away. I started the car and followed at a distance for a block, then a car changed into the right lane and got between us. I could see the convenience store and the Chinese grocery up ahead on the right, two shabby buildings standing on either side of a dirt lot. The driver in front of me rolled down his window and tossed out a cigarette butt that hit the ground with a shower of sparks, and pumped his brakes at the same time. In front of him, the white sedan was turning into a parking lot. It was going into the grocery. I cruised by slowly, then lurched into the convenience store parking lot. I sat in the car, watching out my side window while the gypsy got out and went to his trunk. He opened it, pulled out the briefcase, closed it and walked into the grocery.

Right in front of me the door to the convenience store swung open and two men came out, their mouths moving in conversation. One was wearing big black sunglasses and holding a large beverage cup, and he lifted it into the air and smiled—a flat, humorless smile that was either for me or a response to something his friend had said. I turned my face back to the grocery. The only other car besides the gypsy's was a maroon sedan. Why had he gone into a

Chinese grocery with a briefcase? I thought of the clerk, Lin, and wondered what business she had with a gypsy who carried a briefcase. I could still hear the two men, leaning against the building somewhere in my periphery, their voices getting louder. One of them let out a husky bark of laughter that made me turn my head. It was the one with the cup and the sunglasses, standing alone now by the payphone and watching his friend walk across the dirt lot, past a dumpster overflowing with rubble, and over to a porta-potty.

"You're nasty," he said.

At the porta-potty his friend turned with a grin and went inside and closed the door. Three minutes went by. I wondered what he was doing in there. There were the normal things, of course, you do in a porta-potty, but I suspected he was not doing something normal. Another several minutes went by and then he came out at a jumping trot, hooting as if he were congratulating himself.

"No way," his friend said.

"Oh you don't believe me? Go in there and see."

"Hell no, I'm not going in there."

I was watching them out of the corner of my eye when the door of the grocery opened, and I turned my attention from their phlegmy laughter to look at a short woman stepping outside with two grocery bags.

The door closed behind her and then immediately flung back open, and the gypsy came out right on her heels. He stepped sharply to her side with a sudden flash of teeth and passed her, nodding as he went, walking with a jaunty stride. I could see the ankles of his white socks between his black pants and black shoes. The pants were noticeably too short, and baggy. He looked like somebody dressed in the hand-me-down clothes of a person much shorter and wider than him. He was at his car now, putting the briefcase in his trunk and closing it. A flash of movement passed across the edge of my vision, arcing swiftly over the dirt lot like a bird flying too low, and the gypsy jumped back as something hit the ground beside him with a gushing clatter. Two figures came rushing in from the edge of the lot, the profiles of their white faces tensed—the men who had been leaning on the wall of the convenience store.

As I watched them run I realized what they had thrown. It was the drink cup.

I gaped as the gypsy flailed back like a spring-loaded toy and hurried to get inside his car, but the two men caught up to him and grabbed him from behind. The one in black sunglasses was tall and heavy, built like a wrestler, and he lifted the gypsy off his feet and twisted him around, his white hand over the gypsy's mouth. The other one took a smiling dive at his face and said something in a loud taunting voice. The wrestler pushed the gypsy through the parking lot. He said something to his friend, his voice a low rumble I couldn't make out, then the friend ran into the dirt lot and opened the door to the porta-potty. I heard his cracked giddy voice over the low rush of the traffic. He was asking the gypsy if he wanted to eat shit.

"Come over here," he said. "You know you like it."

I felt a rising sense of doom as I watched the gypsy twist and thrash, trying to get out of the clutch of the wrestler. Just in front of the porta-potty, his flailing arm smacked the sunglasses off the ruddy white face behind him. The wrestler cursed and thrust his hand up against the back of the gypsy's head and shoved him forward into the porta-potty, pressing down hard until the thin narrow figure was curling toward the bench with the outfitted hole in it. The gypsy collapsed onto his knees. I cringed, a familiar recoil twisting inside me. I realized I had seen this before. This very thing had happened to my brother a dozen times. The same feeling of flinching empathy washed over me every time the neighborhood boys got that glint in their eyes and I couldn't stop them, every time he came home scuffed and wincing from a school beating. For a moment, all the sympathy and helpless compassion I had felt for my brother was directed at the gypsy. But then I had to tell myself that I didn't know this gypsy. I didn't know what this was about.

Still pushing him down, the wrestler looked backward over his shoulder and made a gesture at his friend, who scurried around to the back of the porta-potty. As it began to rock forward the wrestler stepped back and pushed the door shut, then reached up and gripped the roof and pulled. The booth tilted and I had a moment to imagine the gypsy tumbling backward as the whole thing heaved forward onto the dirt with a dull heavy thud.

The wrestler took several hopping steps away, and his friend jumped on top of the upended booth and pounded it with his feet, took a flying leap, and landed at a trot. I had the impulse to duck my head as he came toward me through the lot, but then the wrestler stepped back up to the booth and crouched down and began pushing it through the dirt, wedging it back into the tight space between the wall and the dumpster. Now they were both coming my way, and I slumped sideways into the passenger seat. A moment later I heard the sounds of their breath-heavy voices and the scuffing of shoes on pavement as they passed behind my car. I lifted my head and watched them running away on the sidewalk until they reached the end of the block and turned the corner.

I looked back at the porta-potty. As the moments passed I could hear the traffic flowing by me in the street, like the rushing of my own blood. Nobody had stopped. It had all happened so fast. I was the only one who had seen it. I looked at the front of the grocery, at the cloudy yellow window covered in peeling posters. What was I supposed to do? Timidly, I got out of the car and walked to the edge of the lot. With the break in traffic there was silence, and I could hear the muffled sounds of a body shifting around inside the plastic booth.

"Hello?" I called, walking forward into the dirt, plugging my nose as the odor of chemical waste thickened in the cold air. The booth lay suddenly quiet, like an animal that goes still when it senses it's not alone.

"Are you okay?" I said loudly through my pinched nose. "I saw what happened."

After a moment of silence there was a fretful scramble inside the booth and it gave one mighty tilt upward, hit the dumpster, and fell back down. Then a muffled thump suggested that he had sunk down inside of it. I could hear him taking thin, rapid breaths.

"No," came the unhappy voice.

No? I had forgotten the question. "Uh—should I call someone? I could call the police," I offered, taking out my phone. "I saw the guys who did it."

"No," he said quickly. "Don't call the police." Then his breathing broke into heaves and there was a telltale splatter of vomit hitting plastic.

My own stomach recoiled and I stepped backward in the dirt. I felt a crunch of metal under my foot. I lifted it and looked down. It was a set of keys.

The gypsy groaned and said something inside the booth that sounded like a curse, but it was in a different language. "Go into the market," he said, not very nicely.

"What?" I was still looking down at the keys. They were his keys, to be sure. They must have fallen out of his pocket during the struggle.

"Next door. Get the guy in back to come out here. He knows me."

I realized he was probably asking me to go get the man he had just been to see with the briefcase. At this thought my heart skidded in my chest.

"Okay," I said. "I'll be right back." I paused to see if he would say any more, but all I heard was a thick, queasy silence. Before I turned away I bent down, and with a guilty rush of adrenaline I picked up the keys. Then I headed through the dirt toward the parking lot of the Chinese grocery.

There were five keys attached to a red rubber tab with the name and address of the auto shop on it. Threaded between two of the keys was a gold ring with a bright amber stone in it, the metal soft and greasy looking. As I walked I found the key that went to the car. I could open it right now and search it and he would never know. I felt my skin prickle hot and then cold.

At the gypsy's car I bent and peered in the driver's window. The cloth interior was a dirty beige, and the console between the seats was filled with trash. I looked in the backseat and saw a pair of dumbbells crushing the cushion down on the far side, ones I couldn't imagine the gypsy having the strength to lift, and a pile of rolled newspapers in orange bags. And then I remembered the trunk. The briefcase was in there.

As I walked around to the trunk, I took one look back at the porta-potty, which sat like a big blue piece of abandoned play equipment in the dirt, and then glanced at the door to the Chinese grocery. Nobody was here to see me, except the traffic going by at my back. And all those people would see in the momentary glimpse they caught on their way past was a person opening the trunk of her car.

I told myself to pretend what I was doing was completely ordinary, and then I stuck the key in the lock. This was the way to do something without being noticed—right out in the open, with complete transparency. I had learned that from my mother. The lock clicked open and the trunk lid rose a few inches. I pushed it up, half afraid of what I would find, but there was nothing there but the maroon briefcase, lying in the middle of the cloth interior. I reached inside and pulled the handle toward me and tilted the case up on its end.

It was a cheap Naugahyde piece with shiny gold-plated hardware. A tiny key slot was centered under the handle. I looked on the key chain for a small key and found one dangling beside the ring. I put it in the lock and the briefcase unlocked with a dull click. Inside was a camera sitting on top of a manila folder, and I lifted them both out and set them in the trunk. A stack of loose papers filled the folder—typed and neat. They were invoices from a chiropractor. Jane Stevens was the name of the first bill recipient, and the tests and services she received were itemized: cervical subluxation and two forty-five-minute sessions each for neck realignment and spinal adjustment. I picked up another one. This bill recipient was Peter John, and the services were the same. The next one was written for Mike Adams, and it listed something called surface EMG. All the bills said PAID at the bottom and the payment type was cash. They were paid receipts, not bills. The chiropractor's name was Mary James. *Jane Stevens, Peter John, Mary James*—all first names. I closed the folder. The only thing left was the camera, and I picked it up. It was a cheap digital with a brand name I didn't recognize. The instant I had it in my hand, I knew what I was going to do. I told myself to do it fast and get it over with as the black display screen lit up with a photo.

It was a picture of a man and woman smiling up from a couch, wearing paper birthday hats. The woman was broad with a profusion of yellow hair, and I was pretty sure the man was the same one I had seen working in the Chinese grocery, the bowls of his cheekbones pushing up against narrow eyes. In the next photo they were standing in a little kitchen beside two other women, both of them white, and a man who looked either Indian or gypsy was bending over a cake at the counter lighting candles. All I could see of his face were his chin and white teeth. In the next photo, the Chinese man was holding the hefty blonde by the waist while she cut the cake through the message

Happy Birthday Michelle. I scrolled through the photos quickly, trying to get past the party to something else, but after several more pictures of cake in the kitchen I came back again to the first one. And that was it. A birthday party in somebody's apartment. I put the camera back and closed the briefcase, then lowered the trunk and latched it lightly, trying not to appear suspicious. Glancing up, I thought I saw a silhouette looming in the register window, a dark liquid movement behind the glass. I didn't want to stare and I didn't want to stay where I was. I could feel my heart jumping in my chest. How could I go back into the Chinese grocery now? I didn't want the man in there to know what I looked like. What if he had watched me? What if he described me to the gypsy? Would the gypsy recognize me? With a glance at the porta-potty, I walked away from the car and stepped onto the sidewalk.

My pace seemed to quicken almost to a scurry, and I found myself hurrying back up the parking lot of the convenience store, looking behind me and finding nobody on my heels. I was at my car door. My eyes rested on the dinged-up pay phone a few feet away, and I made a decision. I stepped up and dialed in an anonymous phone call to the police. In a trembling voice I told the operator that I had just seen a gypsy attacked and trapped inside a porta-potty. As I gave her the name of the street, I felt guilty. I had done nothing to help him. All I'd done was sit idly by while he got pushed into a public toilet and then I broke into his car and quietly raided it. And now I was doing the one thing he asked me not to do: calling the police.

PART FOUR

GET WELL

11

I WAS IN THE HOSPITAL CAFETERIA EATING MY DINNER, HAVING WANdered through several food stations at random, my mind buzzing with distracted anxiety, filling my plate until I had something resembling a meal. I had started with a baked potato, heaping all the nearby toppings onto it until it had a good coating of butter, sour cream, cheese, bacon, and chives, but then I realized that all the good toppings were at the salad bar, so I went there and added ham, boiled eggs, shredded carrot, sunflower seeds, and Thousand Island dressing. When I was done, the potato was so indistinguishable underneath the toppings that the woman who rang me up charged me for the salad bar instead.

I went to a table by a window and mechanically shoveled at the food, trying to empty my mind, thinking only of the surprising flavors and textures converging in my mouth. Ten minutes later I put my fork down and sat back, vaguely sickened. I kept picturing the photos, thinking of that innocent birthday gathering and feeling like I had somehow violated it, chastising myself for letting the gypsy languish in filth while he waited for the police, wondering what had happened when they arrived to extract him from his plastic prison. I pictured him stumbling out in his soggy work clothes and my throat clenched. I looked away from my plate of slops and into the cafeteria, trying to fix my gaze on something that might distract me. My eyes slid over the soothing waxy green of a boxed plant and then fell on a person at a nearby table. It was Mitch.

He had just glanced up from a bowl of soup, the spoon still hovering in the air near his face. "Natalie?" he said, obviously surprised. "What are you doing here?" He put his spoon down with a look of unhappy confusion.

He was wearing his usual collared shirt, royal blue, and his hair was gelled into little black spikes. On the surface he seemed tidy, but his face had that chiseled-down gray-white look of exhaustion that he used to come home with after a twelve-hour day of studying in the library. I didn't feel that inclined to answer him.

"Did something happen?"

Yes, something had happened. A lot had happened.

"My dad," I said, trying to keep my voice even.

He furrowed his brow at me in an expression that was serious, but not exactly concerned, and I recalled how little he had liked my father. "What? Is he all right?"

I could have said that he was recovering from a car accident, or that he had a concussion, but I didn't. Instead, all I could think of was: "He had emergency brain surgery."

He looked shocked, then dismayed, and then he tried pulling his face together into a look of haggard sympathy.

I dropped my head, staring down at my potato. He would be looking uncomfortable by now, not sure whether he should come over to my table and not inclined to either. *He's an asshole,* I told myself. *He's an asshole.* I chanted it several times over until I could lift my head and meet his eyes.

"That's... awful," he said.

I nodded.

"Is he going to be okay?"

I shrugged. I thought of the good news, that he was awake now and speaking, but I didn't bother to say it.

"Well," he said awkwardly. "I hope he is."

Now I was supposed to thank him for his concern. I cleared my throat. A moment of expectant silence passed. I said, "Working a long shift?"

He nodded, looking as if he didn't know how to talk about himself under these circumstances.

"Hmm. Dr. Psychology," I said, calling him the name my mother had called him. That name was like a sharp jab to the chest, and I followed it with my equivalent of an uppercut: a hard little smile. "Must be tough."

For a moment he looked at me, reading my attitude, reading my thoughts. Then he dropped his head and wagged it a little, making a show of how quietly disappointed and sorry for me he was. "Okay," he said, standing and picking up his half-full bowl of soup. I noticed there was a fortune cookie beside it, rocking on the plate. Apparently, I had missed the Chinese buffet offering. I remembered how much Mitch had always liked egg drop soup. *You will meet an old friend,* I thought.

"Well I have to get back," he told me, making the lie that obvious, and I could see him struggling with himself, wanting to put me right back in the place he had left me over a month ago, but feeling guilty for doing it under the circumstances. "I hope your father is okay." His eyes flashed once again with some poignant expression I couldn't name, something genuine and heartbreaking.

"Yes," I agreed.

"Bye Natalie." Trying not to make it sound final. Just like the last time.

When he was gone I tried to finish eating, but found I had no appetite. After a few minutes I left and went home. When I got there I hung up my coat and stripped off the rest of my clothes and got in the shower, hoping I could lose the memory of the day in a haze of hot steam. I wanted to forget about the gypsy and about Mitch too. But Mitch clung on like a bad funk. I would never understand the way he had left me. I had been trying to understand that since it had happened. What had the fortune cookie said? *The hunger for knowledge is never satisfied.*

The next day was Saturday, and stepped into my father's room a little before noon, I found him bathed in a glow of bright sunlight. He was alert and watching the doorway, as if expecting somebody. When he saw me his face soured.

"Hello," I said, pretending I didn't notice. "How are you feeling?"

"Hrm," he said bitterly.

"I hear they're moving you to a rehab facility next week. That's good, don't you think?"

With a scowl he pointed to the other chair in the room, where everything he had been wearing on the day of the accident was neatly folded.

"The chair?" I said. "Your clothes?"

He flicked impatient fingers. "Give me those."

"Oh I think you have to wear the gown. I can ask them if you want." I stood up to push the call button on the handset, and his hand fumbled over it as he tried to intercept me.

"What? You don't want me to ask? Fine." I lifted my hands in the air, feeling my exasperation boil up. I dumped my purse in the chair, ready for a confrontation. "Dad, I need you to tell me what's going on. Why were we in Mom's old neighborhood?"

His eyes cut away from mine, toward the door. Jenna stood looking at us with a hesitant expression. I told her it was nothing—I had mistakenly pressed the button. She paused, deciding whether or not to say something. Finally she did: "Your father had a visitor this morning."

"A visitor?" I turned to Boris, surprised.

He didn't look at me. His face was turned to Jenna and on it I could see the same glowering look he had given me moments ago.

"Sure did," Jenna said, her cheery voice sounding artificial. "Your brother came."

"My brother?" I croaked. *My brother?*

I looked from Jenna back to Boris. He had raised his arm suddenly aloft, and with a jerk he flung it forward and something launched through the air and hit Jenna in the hip.

I looked at it in a daze of disbelief. It was the book, the one I had been reading.

"Excuse me, Mr. Krupin," Jenna said as Boris let out a hoarse groan. "I really don't appreciate having things thrown at me." She turned to me. "Why don't we talk in the hall for a quick sec."

Boris sat up in bed as if he were going to get out and follow her.

"No," he barked.

"Mr. Krupin," Jenna said with surprising firmness. "You need to calm down. I don't want to have to call somebody in here. I'm just going to talk to your daughter."

I watched him sink back down in the bed, fuming. I couldn't think of any words to say to him. This was a mistake, I told myself. I put one foot in front of the other and eventually got to the door. On my way out my foot kicked something, and blankly I reached down and picked it up. The horror fan's book. It would follow me until the end. As soon as I was in the hall Jenna started talking.

"I came in at ten o'clock and your brother was here," she said. "Your father was asleep. When I asked about it later he became really agitated. He didn't seem to know your brother had been here."

I put my hand on my chest where my heart was beating, thwacking my ribs like a dull ax. "I don't get it," I said. My voice sounded like somebody else's voice. "This doesn't make sense." I could see Jenna's perplexed face as if it were a picture on a wall somewhere far away. Then her arm came through the vast distance between us and I felt its warmth on me, firm and steady.

"Oh my gosh," she said. "You need to sit down." I was clamped bodily under her arm and walked toward a chair against the wall. She let go and I drifted downward.

"Why would he come here?" I heard myself say.

"I don't know, hon. Why? What's wrong?"

"I thought he was—" I didn't finish the rest of the sentence out loud. *Dead,* I thought. *I thought he was dead.* Had I really believed that? In a croaking voice, I said, "He's been missing for a long time. He ran away."

I watched Jenna's eyes widen in alarm. "Oh my. Well, no wonder your father was upset. Oh gosh. And he just showed up and didn't tell you?"

I nodded. My whole face felt stiff as ice, unable to shift itself out of the tight stricken look I could feel there.

"Oh, I mean how strange," Jenna said, looking as disturbed as I was. "I just don't know what to say. Why would he show up like that and disappear again?"

I shook my head. All I could think of was how long it had been since I'd seen him. More than ten years. The person I pictured when I thought of him was still that wasted-thin seventeen-year-old who had left with no hope. Was he better now? Or was he still the same?

In a feeble voice I said, "What did he look like?"

"Well, he looked a lot like you. He was tall. And thin. Dark skin. Darker than you I'd say. He didn't say very much."

I nodded. That sounded like my brother, but I still couldn't believe it. He was unreal to me now, no more than a memory, more distant than I had realized. How could this be? How could he have been here? Why had he wanted to see my father?

I stood up sharply. Jenna took a step back and looked surprised. "What's wrong, hon? What do you need?"

"I think I should talk to my father," I said in a wavering voice.

"Oh, of course. That's a good idea. You see what he says. I'm so sorry," she said. "You let me know if you need anything, okay?"

I thanked her and walked away down the hall. Would my father have any idea why he had come? I walked in through the door and found him on his feet, swaying unsteadily at the side of the bed, holding his pants out in front of him.

"Dad—what are you doing?"

He turned a desperate eye on me and kept going, wobbling as he tried to aim his leg into his pants.

"Stop," I said. "You're going to fall." I stepped back and called into the hall for Jenna.

My father grunted and a set of keys fell from his hand. Then it struck me what was happening. He was not just trying to get dressed. He was trying to get dressed and *go*.

12

IN THOSE LAST MONTHS BEFORE MY BROTHER LEFT, BORIS HAD MADE the mistake more than once of going into Eliot's room, blustering and insistent, all his good intentions undone by his own methods.

I could still hear the coarse rumble of his voice, demanding to know what my brother was doing to his body and who was giving him those cuts on his arms and who his friends were and how he was spending his time with them. Through the crack in the door I would hear my brother's brutal replies.

"What these?" he'd say. "Well these ones here were a knife my friend did for me and this one was a razor blade I got from your bathroom cabinet—"

"Stop that! Is it those boys at school again? You tell me what they're doing to you."

"Well the boys at school like to drag me into the bathroom and pull out their dicks and piss on me," my brother would say, his jeering voice rising up, flighty and wild.

"Do not talk like that. Why do you have to make this into a joke?"

"I'm not joking. I'm telling the truth."

"Stop with that voice! I'm being serious."

"*Gee, Dad,*" my brother would say, as if the word itself were a joke. "I can't help it. I'm a fag. I have a fag's voice."

At this point my father would burst out into the hall and I'd hear him in the kitchen ranting to my mother. "Your son is a liar! He just sits in there and tells lies to me!"

My mother never said anything. I could feel her standing back and refusing to take my father's side on those nights, and I seemed to be the only one who felt sorry for him as he went fuming into the living room by himself. It seemed like my brother's words and my mother's silence were teaming up on him, like they were combining efforts in a silent bond of resentment, and I couldn't understand why. It was somehow linked to the other mysteries of that summer, the feeling that my mother and brother were working together, conducting some secret life that neither my father nor I could share. Boris either didn't notice or didn't want to notice. He had always been good at not paying attention, and my mother had a talent for deception. She knew that if you ever want to hide a thing from someone, the best way to do it is out in the open, with complete transparency.

For months I had been using that exact technique to deceive her, after she had driven me to new levels of desperation with her stance against my reading habits, forcing my eating experiments to expand in secrecy beyond paper and books to the wide-ranging world of rubbers and plastics and woods and leathers. Every day I went walking through my house with all sorts of raunchy, unexpected things in my mouth, and the fact that I wasn't trying to hide myself was what made it all invisible. My mother never suspected a thing.

At that time she had been busy practicing stealth operations on my book hoards and I had been losing ground. For months we had been in a secret unspoken battle over territory as I moved my books to new hidden locations all around the house, and she followed behind me and eventually uncovered each one, studying my traffic patterns and waiting for me to lead her to them. In a brash act of protest one spring I began eating up my schoolbooks. This turned out to be a mistake when, at the end of the school year, my mother had to pay three fifty-dollar replacement fees for my science, history, and math texts after they went back with more than a few pages missing. For that I had been massively punished with a series of humiliations involving the disappearance of my entire wardrobe and the appearance of thrift store replacements consisting of all the things I hated most—stale ruffled dresses and long heavy skirts and crocheted lace and shoulder pads. My mother informed me that I would be wearing these clothes all summer, and I would earn back my old wardrobe when the school year started again, and she withheld my allowance money so she could pay for the school books and also prevent me from buying any new clothes.

This was the summer that would live forever in my memory, the summer that began with my dressing like a dusty Victorian doll and ended with my brother running away. I had responded to my mother's punishment-by-clothing by cutting and ripping and sewing the overly stuffy articles into deranged punkish creations that my mother promptly confiscated and replaced with more floral prints and puffed sleeves. I had been so busy with sartorial alterations—and the strange intense short-lived friendships with other strange intense girls who would enter my life briefly and then disappear just as quickly, leaving their mix CDs and manga doodles gathering dust under my bed—that I hardly had time for my brother, who was spending his summer being carted away every other day by my mother to some unspoken destination. When they left, I would steal back my reading time, creeping to one of my few remaining secret nooks the moment my mother was out of sight, and spending those stolen hours in fevered bliss. Despite her frank warnings to my father not to let me read—that I would eat the pages and poison myself—these accusations only drew snorts and derision from him as if she must be crazy. My father's tendency to ignore the obvious worked in my favor on these occasions, and I gloated at her with my eyes as she slammed the screen door and departed down the sunny walk, the long limp body of my brother trailing after her.

I realized then that the only reason my mother allowed me this time to myself was because she was trying to get away with something too, hoping that Boris would continue for one more day to conveniently ignore her mysterious excursions with my brother. I was jealous and watchful as they left me at home on those days, dressed in some preposterous dress or another, noting that their casual behavior was always a little too careful, seeing in it their efforts not to rouse my father's attention. My mother knew that I knew, and I understood that she was paying me off, giving me my disgraceful hour of stolen time in return for silence.

One day while she was gone I asked Boris to return my wardrobe from the shed in the backyard, where it was locked up.

"No," he said, his face turned down into his newspaper. "Your mother told me not to."

"Don't you care that she's torturing me?"

He looked up, vaguely offended. That day I was wearing a stiff yellow gown of the kind Cinderella had worn to the ball that was two sizes too big. "Look at me," I said. "Look what she's doing to me."

"What? I don't see anything."

I flapped the dress at him in anger.

"You like dresses," he said.

"No I don't. I hate dresses."

"I've seen you wear a dress before. What's so wrong with it?"

"Can you see this dress? It doesn't even fit me. Look at it!" I demanded, lifting my arms. I thought he would surely acknowledge the utter absurdity of my situation, but instead he gave me an indifferent frown.

"Leave your mother alone. She has her reasons."

Denial had become my father's method of avoiding all the discord that surrounded him in our house. He preferred not to notice anything about his family that might disturb him, an effort that made us feel all but invisible. It was even this way with my mother, or perhaps especially with my mother, whose every act of cruelty and negligence upon us and every act of unhappy self-destruction over the years he had faithfully ignored in simple preservation of his love for her. He didn't want to get angry at her. He didn't want to mistrust her. He didn't want to look at her and see beyond the contented wife he had constructed in his mind.

Over the years I had learned from my mother's example to accept the inventions of personality and dress that my father had given me in his effort to see me as an ordinary girl. I finally understood that blindness for him was an act of love, a tireless effort of devotion in the face of daily strife. My mother knew it too, and I could see it drove her crazy. She carried on the activities my father would rather ignore right under his nose, with a defiant resignation, as if she were still hoping that she could rouse his anger, or disappoint him at least, and lift the fog of blindness from his eyes momentarily. But it never happened. In fact, the only one of us who was ever able to reach Boris with the awful truth was my brother. I had seen him use it on my father too many times, as if it were a weapon he had for sending Boris flying away over and over in confusion and outrage.

And my mother put up with it. In her silence, she condoned it. She was allowing my brother the voice she didn't have, and taking some vicarious satisfaction in witnessing the powerful damage it did to my father. But when my brother left, that voice disappeared, and it seemed at the time that a peaceful quiet descended on the house. My mother went around in a silence that was deeper than ever, as if the very breath had been snatched from her.

She waited eight months and then pronounced my brother gone from our lives, as though she needed to finalize what he had started—and she did it the same way she did everything—brashly, unsentimentally, with a finality that was terrifying. One day she appeared in the school parking lot wearing a dark burgundy dress I had never seen before, her hair looped around her face in curls that flopped about in the stiff breeze. I wondered for an instant if this woman in front of our powder-blue Oldsmobile was really my mother. Had I ever seen my mother's hair curled? I got closer, not convinced, and she held something up at me—a black piece of cloth that flapped like a banner of death in the air.

"Put this on," she said. I heard in her voice the same burnt resolve that had always told me when I didn't have a choice.

"Where? Here?" I said, hoping she couldn't be serious. The parking lot was crowded with teenagers yelling to each other over the loud engines of the buses. There were older kids filing through the lot around us, going to their cars, cavorting and laughing, but my mother and I were held instead by some delicate magnetism to this dark skin that she had given to me and I had taken, already far away from this carefree light-filled afternoon.

"Get in," she said. "You'll have a chance while I drive."

I kept the dress in my lap while we drove through the city. By the time we got out to the long strip of desolate highway I knew where we were going, and with a single sideways look from my mother I knew I was expected to put on the dress. I started at the bottom, unzipping the back of the dress and squeezing off my jeans and then pulling it up over my hips, and finally taking off my shirt and pulling the padded shoulders up and perching them dutifully over mine. Then I lifted my hair and turned in my seat to the window, where the vast glittering ocean spread out beside us, and my mother reached over and yanked my zipper up. I felt cold in the dress, nearly unclothed as the beach wind sucked it hard against my body and then sent it billowing away from me. I was fifteen and my brother, though we didn't say it to each other, would be eighteen today.

The towels we unrolled on the sand almost blew away from us before we could sit down. My mother twisted down out of the wind to light a cigarette, and then threw the box at me. I pulled one out and held it in my hand, as if I wanted to warm it first. It was a complicated moment, in which I felt myself stepping over a threshold of childhood into a world my mother had finally permitted me to enter, by clothing me in this dress and tossing me her cigarettes. She had now dragged me up from the heavy waves to stand apart from my brother, now just a vacancy in our lives, to grant me a passage into adulthood and deny my brother his, wherever he was, as if my life necessitated his death. We sat for a long time staring at the waves.

They were big that day, rolling up in tall heavy stacks of blue and dropping away in a fierce turbulent roar, spitting white foam that hissed all the way up to us in a thin reflecting sheet that paused, then retreated. *He's dead,* I thought, *and I'm alive*. It was a terrible idea, and it was my mother who was holding me down hard inside of it, who had already succeeded in pressing it around me with the force of the ocean air and waves, with a weight that was so endless and continuous I couldn't move a muscle against it. It felt as if her final word was sounding in the ocean roar and riding through me in the mournful battering wind. I put the cigarette up to my nose and sucked up the dusty scent of decayed leaves, and my mother looked over at me. Her neck stood out in thick cords, and I thought of those afternoons long ago on the beach, my brother and I chattering in her company, feeling nothing but the pleasure of being alive, and my mother looking on, disbelief on her face. What was my mother thinking now? Whatever it was, I didn't like it. With an enormous effort I stood up. I put the cigarette in my mouth and snapped the end off and sucked on it as I walked away down the beach toward the tide pools my brother and I liked to visit when those days we spent here long ago had been almost over. This had been the part when we left my mother, so that we could come back to her later and see her packing up our things, finally ready to take us home.

When we did go back home that afternoon, my mother disappeared into the kitchen, and an hour later she served my father's favorite dinner.

After we had eaten it, all of us quietly chewing, she brought out a cake.

I recall the look on my father's face, intense and choked, as he looked from the cake back to her.

"I thought we could say goodbye," she said.

On the cake, instead of *Happy Birthday, Eliot* she had written *Bon Voyage, Eliot*. For my mother it was almost a romantic gesture. For my father, it was almost criminal. As my mother cut it into slices and handed them out, he stared at her with his eyes gogged like a madman. He seemed to be asking her what this meant. She shrugged at him. After a minute he picked up his fork and held it over his cake, staring at the spot where my brother should have been sitting. Then finally he sensed me watching and looked over. For a full minute he fixed me with a fierce unwavering stare. It was a look of total concentration, as if he was focusing everything inside him just to hold me there. *You're still here,* he was telling me. *You're still here.*

In the end it seemed like my father had suffered the most from my brother's disappearance, because he had tried not to see it coming. He was a man who suffered not only the event but his own denial of it. It was in this way that he endured all the difficult events of his life, meeting one miserable reckoning after another until he ended up with a runaway son and a dead wife and a burned-up house and a squalid little apartment down the street from a daughter who couldn't get herself a college degree or a decent man, and each thing he had suffered through with the same uneasy denial, the same absent heartache that had come to prop him up through the years like a lonely king on a throne, peering into his diminished kingdom, his lost family somewhere out there in the darkness, just beyond his sight.

And now, when his son had come back to him, here he was putting on his clothes—to what? To go after him this time? To make up for the accident of avoiding him, of failing to embrace him all those years ago? What had gone through his mind this morning? Only he knew. And he wasn't talking.

13

I WOKE UP IN UNEXPECTED DARKNESS, STARTLED. WONDERING ABOUT my brother. Had he come because he'd heard about our mother? But then why hadn't he come before, directly to me? My brother hated my father. And for a long time the feeling had been mutual. In fact, when I thought about it, I couldn't recall a single memory of my father and brother getting along. Those memories surely existed, but they were buried in the distant past, lost beneath all the things I *could* remember. Those terrible last nights just before my brother left.

For a moment I had no idea where I was. And then I remembered that I had driven home from the hospital expectantly, hoping to find my brother waiting for me. I had fallen asleep waiting for him instead, spread out on my bed, over the covers, leaning back against the headboard, reading.

The horror fan's book lay next to me. I had put the book in my pocket at the hospital, while two nurses were coercing Boris back into bed. An accident more or less.

The clock by my bed said 7:47 P.M. How could I fall asleep at the end of a horror novel? Had I even finished it? I tried to remember the last thing I had read, but something was bothering me. Something didn't feel right.

I got out of bed and crossed the room on tiptoe. Cautiously I looked out my door into the short empty hallway going to the living room. All was still. I stepped out, the silence growing like a balloon around my head. I told myself to pull it together. It was only 8 P.M.—the evening was just beginning for most people. They wouldn't be doing illicit things for hours yet. When I was done with this pep talk I was at the end of the hallway and I peeked around the corner into the living room.

It was well lit with moonlight and everything was still. Seeing all my new furniture perched in the dark, the seating aggressively out of scale with the coffee table and television, I felt like I was looking at a child's nightmare, a dollhouse come to life. The kitchen chair I had gotten at the school junk sale had inspired me toward a children's theme, and most of what I had now was small battered furniture in bright candy colors that had been outgrown by some child and dropped at the thrift stores in the neighborhood. A squat little armchair and pill-sized ottoman lounged beside the plastic shopping cart I was using to store my extra movies, and the entertainment center had been replaced with a fairy-tale castle flanked by two turrets with open shelves, the television tucked behind a frothy pink curtain in the center archway. The couch was a caterpillar.

What, exactly, was I going for here?

Whatever it was, my diminutive furnishings had become creepy in the darkness, pricking my unease up to an irrational fear. But of what? Briskly I crossed the room to the light switch and turned on the overhead light, and then did the same in the kitchen and moved to the switch in my shallow entry space. While I was there I felt the urge to open the apartment door to the safe and reassuring emptiness of the public hallway. I flung it open, but the hallway wasn't empty. It was occupied by a tall figure in a light pink shirt, and a fist was approaching my face through the air.

"Oh," I gasped.

The fist stopped short and fell. "Oh hi—I was just... Natalie," Mitch said, looking me over nervously. "What are you doing?"

In the mystery and horror novels I read in my adolescence, it was often the romantic interest who turned out to be the villain, driven always by passion and jealousy to do loathsome things. As I got older these plots got more subtle—maybe the romantic interest didn't even like the girl, but was only using her to get to somebody else, or something else: a secret, a room, a weapon. Sometimes the romantic interest was the one who died right before the truth was revealed, as if a final sacrifice had to be made in order for the revelation to become truly profound. Or else he was the guardian of the central secret that would reveal a web of hidden loyalties—a liar, yes, but only because he was forced to, or tricked to, or trying to protect someone, and so the lover could be dismissed as a mental or emotional weakling before leading the protagonist to the truth. And then sometimes the lover had nothing to do with the rest of the story, and was only there to make the reader wonder and to distract the protagonist from the truth, showing up at unexpected moments and then explaining himself, missing dates and then producing an excuse, creating ripples and smoothing them over, all of it adding up to nothing: a red herring. Now I looked at Mitch with the same avid distrust with which I had watched all those other lovers whose blood had been spattered on so many grim and turbulent afternoons of my life.

He raised his eyebrows at me and looked down with an awkward, halting expression, and for reasons I didn't know I reached out and shoved him, as I'd imagined doing in the cafeteria.

"Hey," he said, touching his chest. "What's wrong with you?"

I tried to ignore that and gave him a hard suspicious look. "What are you doing? How did you get into the building?"

He put his hands up in a defensive posture. "I have a key."

"You gave me your key," I said. "And I gave it to Boris."

He looked embarrassed. "I know."

His appearance was unusually rumpled. His pink dress shirt looked as if it had spent some time crushed into a ball and his hair was twisting out of its precisely gelled spikes into little roughed-up clumps. I had always preferred him disheveled like this, but he used to insist it was unattractive and sloppy. So what was he doing out on a Saturday night, and at my building—like *this*?

"I don't understand."

He looked uncomfortable. "I have other keys. I came up here to tell you—in case you ever saw me in the building."

"Keys to this building?" I said, bewildered.

He let out an uneasy breath. "I'd been planning to come up and talk to you, and then when I saw you the other night..." He paused, looking like he couldn't decide what to say next.

"What are you talking about?"

"Okay, Natalie. I was here, visiting somebody."

"Who?"

"I'm dating someone in the building."

My heart sparked out like a popped bulb.

Mitch said, "Do you know Amber down on the second floor? She lives in the apartment under you."

So that was her name. I had noticed her when she moved in last summer, and every time I saw her I was overcome by an ambiguous fear and dislike. She was one of those pretty dark blondes, with large gray eyes that always seemed vaguely wounded or confused, as if she had forgotten what her own apartment building looked like and hoped she was in the right place after all. And though I never explicitly saw it, I suspected too that she was drawing Mitch's sideways gaze every time we passed her in the parking lot or the building.

"I met her when I came back to move my stuff out," Mitch said. "It was just an accident. We sort of ran into each other."

I could feel a slow, poisonous rage boiling up inside me now. Here it was. The real reason for the breakup.

"You must think I'm stupid," I said.

"Natalie." He was using his tired impatient voice. "I wanted you to know so that you wouldn't have any unpleasant surprises."

"Uh-huh. Like the unpleasant surprise that my boyfriend cheated on me," I said, to my unpleasant surprise.

"I did not cheat on you."

I decided to go with it. "Well you obviously wanted to. I saw the way you looked at her."

He dropped his head and rubbed his hand over his face, almost too tired to defend himself. "I didn't come here to argue with you, Natalie. I was hoping we could be friends."

For some reason the idea of being friends hurt my feelings. I stared him down for a few moments in the dim entry and then I remembered what I had been doing before he so egregiously interrupted me. I stepped back and flipped on the overhead light on the wall beside me, brightening the space around us. He mistook this as a cue to come in, and after a few steps into the entryway his eyes settled on the apartment behind me.

"What the hell?"

"What?" I turned around to share his view. The tiny-tot redecorating scheme had all been done since he moved out. Seeing it through his eyes, I could guess that he wanted to make something out of it, some tragic regression to better times—or, better yet, since he knew my childhood: idealized times I never had. He wouldn't be all wrong, but he wouldn't be all right either.

"Let's not bother," I said. I looked up at his ghostly white neck, every follicle newly bursting with fresh black stubble, and noted that he hadn't shaved yet today. I crossed my arms, trying to ignore the soreness in my heart. He was not worth it, I told myself. He was an asshole.

He was giving me a curious look. "Are you okay?" he said.

"I'm fine."

"How's your dad?"

This caught me off guard. For a moment I struggled, thinking about today's catastrophe, and then I decided I didn't want to go into it. "He's better," I said. "He's going to a rehab facility."

"That's good." He watched me and I watched him watching me. We were standing three feet apart and I remembered when I used to simply close that space at a time like this and rest my head on his chest. Then he would put his arms around me and quietly sigh, as if he vaguely disapproved of this display of neediness but couldn't help giving in to it anyway. I tried not to feel like I missed that.

Now he bent his head and rubbed his hand over his face again like this conversation had drained the little bit of energy he had come here with. He blinked his red eyes at me.

"So are you okay?" he asked again.

"I'm fine. Why do you keep asking?"

"I don't know. You don't look good."

"Oh, well thanks. I stopped exercising."

"You know what I mean. Have you been eating? Normally?"

"What are you, my doctor?"

Mitch gave me a look that said he pretty much thought he was my doctor. "Seriously. I don't want you poisoning yourself, Natalie. Your habits—you worry me."

"Oh I do?" I said, suddenly angry. I knew from experience that I only worried him when he was in the mood to worry over me, which was when he wanted to feel good about himself. Most of the time I just bothered him. "Well, you didn't seem too worried about what I was going to eat when you left me to go frolic with Amber."

He tilted his head back at the ceiling, but the gesture seemed almost satisfied, like I had confirmed something he had already guessed.

"Jesus," he said, quietly. There was nothing I hated more than that tone of superior disbelief, that look of condescending regret over something I had said or done, as if it was up to him to feel for me what I wouldn't feel for myself.

"Well," I said. "I'm tired. And I can see you're still worn out from all that lovemaking you did last night. So why don't you go home and take a shower."

He looked offended, but there was a charge between us now, that nervous electric spark that had once stood for passion in our relationship and now stood for something else, something much less pleasant. After a moment he shook his head at me and smiled quietly down at the floor.

"Okay Natalie." He glanced at his watch. "I give up then." He stepped away and put his hand on the knob of the door. He turned back, opened his mouth, then closed it and shook his head.

A sharp sadness pierced my chest. "I know you still love me," I said, before I could help myself.

He flinched, and then he frowned deeply, looking aggrieved and saddened by my outburst. But the moment I said it I felt a dizzy pleasure rise up through me, as if it were actually true. Mitch lowered his gaze, walked into the hall, paused like he would say goodbye, looked momentarily stricken in the attempt, and then changed his mind and closed the door behind him.

I listened to his footsteps fading out in the stair well and then I went to the window and looked6 out. He left the parking lot on foot, which made me wonder if he had been parking down the street so I wouldn't recognize his car in the parking lot. I remembered the man I had seen walking that way in the early morning. I had been right the first time. Or was it the second time? Whichever time it was it still applied and would always apply: he was an asshole. And still I watched him go. Still I stayed at the window.

14

When I thought about it later I realized I was being unfair. The truth was that I couldn't entirely blame Mitch for our problems. Our relationship had always been about timing. When we first met in college, we were each coming to the end of a long, difficult journey. For him, the journey was the four and a half years of study and hard work to get his double major in psychology and biology, an effort which was about to carry him into the more exclusive world of medical school. My journey through college had been somewhat different. For me, college had been a long four-year experiment that I had continued to pursue every semester out of fear of my parents and fear of getting a job. As long as I was in college, my parents continued to pay for my tuition, rent and food, trusting that one day I would emerge with a degree and take care of myself. In their generosity they had let me take their money as far as the downtown campus, where I had started out in a shabby dormitory with a tiny redheaded roommate whose petite features shifted too often into a vague, sickened expression whenever she looked at me.

One day she caught me tilting the pencil sharpener up to my mouth as I was studying for a math test. Before I noticed her enter the room she was there, studying me cautiously as I munched away on loose grit and shavings. Another time she watched me from the open doorway while I fished through her sweater on the back of her chair, took a bite out of her strawberry lip balm, and rubbed it smooth again with a tissue. After that I had to spend my time carefully avoiding the roommate and four or five people on my hall who had also seen me in the midst of devouring the usual assortment of inedibles: papers and notebooks at my desk, food wrappers with lingering crumbs and powders still clinging to them in the trash cans of study rooms, flyers from the bulletin boards along the dimly lit corridors, all those places of high exposure where we were expected to fraternize with each other constantly, leaving doors open and straying in and out of rooms like college was one big aimless party. It didn't take me long to realize that I hated college, and that college hated me. But it was here that I learned, finally, that I could no longer hide myself from the world. And since I couldn't hide, I was going to have to change my habits and survive.

In order to accomplish this I had to first find the rule by which I would learn to live, the first and final rule of my existence: *Spit, don't swallow.* I started by creating a heavy poultice of the most unswallowable materials I could imagine—five pieces of gum embedded with nutshells and thumbtacks and bobby pins and staples. Every time I had an unnatural urge, I put this in my mouth, my mind rigid with the fear of swallowing. It was like slow torture—the muscles in my throat flexing, demanding, twitching against the incompletion of the act—and my mind repeating its mantra: *Spit, don't swallow, spit, don't swallow.* After twenty minutes of chewing and working my way around the sharp pricks of pain, I took it out, relieved, and saved it for my next urge.

There was only one thing the ball hadn't worked for, and that was reading, because my mind wasn't always there to remind me it was needed. So I did what I had to do. I started by giving up the textbooks for my classes, leaving behind their thin satin pages and the passing grades that reading them would have granted me. What was hard—nearly impossible—were the pulpy horrors and mysteries, those cheap grainy meals I had loved since I was a girl. I was still reading those, and even more of them, as if they were a soothing balm at the end of days fraught with academic failure and rigorous self-discipline. As it turned out, I couldn't have taken the final step and rid my life of books had I not gotten a certain boyfriend at the time. His name was Scott, and he was one of those earthy bohemians—lean and tall with kinky blond hair and a long wiry goatee that I nibbled like a rat.

Scott's accommodating tolerance of this particular behavior had initially coaxed me into new and more troubling urges, eventually driving me to a voracious sensual chewing that left him chafed and pink, so that I couldn't look at him without feeling panic and guilt. Even worse, my book eating had become a lurid source of arousal for him and he had concocted a sort of foreplay for it, feeding me sexually explicit pages from sordid books and magazines that he brought into bed with us, ripping each one out and stuffing it into my mouth as we went, and then climbing all over me with animal desire. When my pica wasn't being used for sex it was being used rather badly for intellectual exercise, theories produced at the breakfast table, like the idea that my impulsive consumption was an intuitive response to the earth's agony, to the wasteful spending we humans did with the earth's precious resources, an urge to *recycle*. Slowly I began to recognize that I was becoming enslaved by his dehumanizing lust and belittled by his idiotic philosophies, and I started refusing the books in bed, shunning his sex games and going back to my staple crop of horrors and mysteries instead. I spent two weeks pushing away his attempts to turn me back onto our old routines. Eventually I had to leave him. This was harder than I expected. He called me for weeks, and it wasn't until I began relentlessly hanging up the phone on every begging plea that he finally disappeared.

In those weeks I tried to forget the humiliations of our intimacy, but I found that my books were all tainted by his memory now, and in a drastic effort one day to purge my life of the filthy memories I emptied my apartment and sold everything to a used bookstore. Then I celebrated by going to a café and eating a meal of real food with the cash. And it was at that café that I met Mitch.

He had been there drinking coffee for hours and studying, and he had torn his hair out into that rumpled look that I liked. We met at the sugar-sprinkled counter, where I picked up a fork and he picked up a handful of white packets with long, ink-stained fingers.

"Wow. That's a meal," he said, looking impressed.

"I'm getting over a sickness," I told him.

That night I learned that he was graduating in December with a BS in psychology and biology, and I told him, even though I was nearly failing all my classes and hadn't made much progress in the way of gathering credits, that I was a fourth-year junior in media studies. We had a nice conversation and he asked for my phone number. I went home that night, and without the white noise of books to put me to sleep I found myself sitting up thinking about him and about our conversation. First I was impressed by how smart he was. Then I thought about how I had let him assume that I was also a hardworking college student on her way to graduation. It occurred to me suddenly that I would never graduate college. I wondered why I was spending all my time posing as a college student, just to accomplish nothing. Then I thought to ask myself a question. What did I want from all this?

It was as if the books had clouded my brain, and it wasn't until I finally shut the door on that gaudy landscape of terror that I actually found myself in my own life, and had no idea what I wanted from it. The next day I didn't go to any of my classes. I didn't go to any the following day either, and pretty quickly it occurred to me that maybe I had gotten what I needed out of college—not book knowledge, not a degree that would put me in a better salary category, but a painful socialization that had forced me into a prolonged trial-and-error effort of self-discipline. This had been the intangible preparation that I had needed for being in the real world, and now I was done.

The day after that I dropped all my classes. Then I went to the news station where I had been working as an intern and begged the station manager for a real job. He looked me over, asked me how I liked working with Salt Pfeiffer, ignored my answer, and then offered me the job of becoming his personal assistant and wrote up a job description for me. I took it, and the next day Mitch called. I told him, perhaps to warn him, that I had dropped out of school and become a coffee and memo girl. He seemed happy for me. And the next night we went out to dinner.

As the weeks went by and he kept calling, I began to wonder about myself. I realized I was a college dropout with no legitimate interests, not many talents, not much ambition. As I got ready for our dates I looked in the mirror and found something even more perplexing—myself. Here was a face I hadn't spent much time noticing—skin the light honey bronze of a good tan, brown eyes rimmed in a fine, glittering green, a nose a little too long and narrow but balanced by a bare sculpted mouth—and I understood what all those inexplicable attentions had been telling me all along, that this was an attractive face, an undeniably pretty face. *Was that possible?* I wondered. *Who was I?* That was around the time when Mitch started asking the same question. Who was I?

I was a person poised on a threshold, about to enter a dark room where she would learn something, and Mitch was there to turn the lights on. He turned lights on all spring long, left me blazing in my own illumination until I was stunned and seeing. He *helped* me. He explained my regressive tendencies. He told me I had brought childhood fears with me into adulthood. I had a masochistic love of punishment. At some point in my life I had been traumatized by my relationships. Plus, there was the oral fixation. He was the one who diagnosed me, gave me a name for what I had.

"If it were serious you'd be dead by now," he told me, looking down his eyes at me. "You wouldn't be able to live alone without constant supervision. You wouldn't be able to make any choices at all about what you put in your mouth."

"Well, thank you for giving me hope," I said.

He looked at me, his face ironic and half amused. "So how did you get so screwed up?" he said, putting his arm around me. This was where his affection had always come from, what he had seen in me from the beginning—a complex problem, an unfortunate misfit, in need of his help. Eventually he got around to asking me about my parents.

Who were these people? he asked jokingly. What did they do to you?

After three months of dating I took him to the house for dinner, not without warning him first. My mother spent thirty minutes being polite, then, having come to some conclusion and having finished her second Scotch and water of the evening, she stopped calling him Mitch and began calling him Dr. Psychology. Mitch laughed nervously and often, looking at everybody as if he were a dog that wanted to play along but didn't quite understand what we wanted. I didn't understand either. Here was the career-oriented college graduate on his way to medical school who could whisk me into the upper classes and revive all my parents' wilting dreams for me, and my mother hated him. That night on the porch she had given me an acid look.

"What?" I said.

"He's not good," she said.

"Well thank you for the warning."

"Listen. Don't let him tell you what you should think about yourself. Don't let him choose your problems for you."

"Of course not," I said, thinking *you already did that,* thinking, naively, that because I finally recognized my mother's power over me I was no longer her victim—I was free.

But she had been right, because once he had discovered all he needed to know about me, he got quickly tired of dealing with the very personality challenges that he had found so stimulating, and he broke up with me. That summer I lived alone and dedicated myself to the increasingly unprecedented duties of my assistantship to the local weatherman. I rarely went out and barely spoke to my mother—and when I did I lied about Mitch. I was just getting up the nerve to confess that we had broken up when school started up again, and he came back.

He had missed me. He had spent the whole summer working with delinquent bums at the psych hospital and he was depressed and badly rested and underfed. He looked sallow and weak, and I felt a loving pity for him that I hadn't felt since I had seen my brother waste away. Mitch rarely gave me the chance to pity him, and I liked it. It occurred to me months after I had taken him back that what he seemed to most need me for was money, though he would never admit it to himself or to me, and I spent the next three years experimenting on and off with various punishments to see which would make me feel better about this discovery—withholding sex, leaving piles of food and dishes around the house for him to pick up, forgetting to give him phone messages, and so on. During this time I was treated on a daily basis to Mitch's therapeutic attacks and every few weeks to my mother's slow and weary scorn whenever we got together for dinner.

After a while Mitch refused to go to the house, so I always went alone, and then came back ready to be subjected to his scrutiny and criticized for my weakness—the weakness he was sure I must have shown there—pulling at the edges of our recounted conversations, asking about the looks I'd received from my mother, what her tone had sounded like, every minute detail, until I was exhausted by both of them. Then one day, as if my mother too were exhausted and had decided finally to claim some sort of resentful defeat, she sent me a card, a get well card, with a short message inside it, cryptic and mean: *Call me when you get over this infatuation. Mom.* I read it, and then I read it again. What was this? Had my mother just devised a new punishment for me? Did she mean to suggest that I was not to speak to her again until Mitch was out of my life? I thought about it for a week, making up my mind about how I was going to get her back for this. Then, before I could call her up, before I could tell her these would most certainly not be the last words between us, that I wouldn't let her make this choice for me—she died.

For three weeks after the funeral there was something strange between Mitch and me, but I thought it was only natural after what had happened. I spent those days feeling my mother's fire still going inside me, burning a dry white heat that would destroy me from the inside out. Mitch watched me as if he couldn't trust me not to do something crazy at any moment.

"What?" I said.

"Nothing."

I opened my mouth. Every time I wanted to say out loud the thoughts that had been plaguing me I tried to resist it, but I couldn't. "I don't understand."

Mitch gave me an uneasy look. "You don't understand what?"

"She sent me a card. Right before she died. A goodbye forever card."

"Stop, Natalie."

"And then she set herself on fire."

"She did not set herself on fire. It was an accident."

"She wanted to punish me."

"Do you realize what you're saying? You're saying that your mother killed herself to punish you for being with me. You're saying that it's my fault your mother is dead."

We stared at each other. I could see that my accusation had hurt his feelings. But I knew what my mother was capable of. I knew the kinds of punishments that she had used on us over the years. Was it possible she would do this?

No—he was right. It was going too far, way too far.

Mitch sighed. "We need to talk about something. Something else," he said, and paused to look meaningfully at me.

"Okay, you're right," I said. "I'll stop."

He shook his head. "I was going to talk to you before. But then your mother..." As if he found it exhausting to keep looking at me, he rubbed his hands down his face and kept them there. "I'm sorry," he said. "I wanted to be here for you."

"You are here."

"I know this is bad timing." He looked warily up at me.

"What?" I said. I didn't get it.

His eyes searched my face. "You don't know what I'm trying to tell you?"

And then I did get it. My heart stabbed up into my throat and I stared at him, unable to speak.

"Look Natalie," he said, his voice low and unsteady. "We can't do this anymore. This is not working."

I let out a breath and a weak sound followed.

Then he told me he was moving out.

It had taken almost four years for us to finally get done with each other. When it was over I wondered how long I had simply been biding my time with him, holding on until the inevitable end, ready to accept it whenever it came, and unwilling, for some reason, to hurry that moment along. By the end my problems with Mitch were reduced to a confounding simplicity: I knew he was making me unhappy, and I knew exactly how he would go on making me unhappy, but it was because of how well I knew him that I couldn't leave him. When you know somebody you don't just get up and walk away. You don't just remove yourself from that person's life. It took both of us a long time to realize that sometimes that's the most merciful thing you can do. One of us had to do it, and it may as well have been him.

PART FIVE

IN LOCAL NEWS

15

WHAT IS THE NEWS IF NOT THE ORIGINAL HORROR STORY, THE ONE that leaves us stuck in that murky landscape of fear and uncertainty—our lives at risk, our jobs at risk, our money at risk, our health and sanity at risk. Every night we return for the latest installment, eager for new twists, different angles, fresh hints and allegations—the facts dubious, the rumors tempting, the silences damning, the righteous intent plastered all over the faces gazing back at us from our televisions, those clean and attractive mannequins sitting complicit and exempt at once, a placid skyline behind them. And of those figures that tuck us in at night, the one who is least complicit and most exempt is the weatherman, with only natural phenomena to report—just a simple sky gazer who wants nothing more than to prepare us for the mercurial whims of Mother Nature. We either depend on him or we ignore him, and a clever station manager understands that the right weatherman can be propped up before us year after year in loyal humility to speak of sun and snow and heat and cold and the coming and going of every season until he becomes the apple of our city's eye, the salt of our earth.

This morning I had sent our Salt out fresh faced and ready to perform his humble duty, and just as I was getting ready to leave, Raina's new boyfriend appeared to take her out to breakfast. I'd seen him once before, and today his appearance corroborated the data I had gathered on him the first time. He seemed to be one of those sporty guys who always wore sleeveless shirts and workout shorts, as if he were perpetually on his way to the gym. As he approached us, Raina looked at me, then he looked at me, then they looked at each other like they were talking about me with their eyes.

Raina said, "Greg, this is *Natalie*." She might as well have added, *The girl I was telling you about*. "Greg went to your high school."

"Oh." I tried not to appear disturbed by this. "When did you graduate?"

"Four years ago."

"Oh, that's way after I was there," I said, relieved.

"Huh," said Greg, still smirking. Had he heard something? Had my reputation lingered there, haunting the halls, skulking like a miserable ghost?

"Well we're going to breakfast," Raina announced, and looked at my station in displeasure.

She gave Greg a look that seemed to say, *See? See how messy she is?* And then they turned around together. I noticed that something seemed to be very funny as they walked away. "She even eats my Q-tips," I heard her say, giggling, and she cast a little naughty look over her shoulder as if half afraid and half hoping I was still paying attention.

"What a psycho," said her boyfriend, apparently unaware that I was still listening.

So, I thought, Raina had gotten her panties in a wad over me. She was like the girls in high school, just like I had suspected. Well, at least I hadn't tried to be her friend.

But this thought did little to soothe away that squirming sense of shame that came so easily to me after so many years of exposure and embarrassment, and I spent the rest of the day feeling like a reject. When I got off work I was still thinking about what she had said about the Q-tips. I loved Q-tips—they were paper put into a dense, snappable stick. Sometimes I put one in my mouth for a moment when I was working on Salt's eyes, so that I could blend with my finger, and then I didn't want to take it back out. I would have to stop doing that.

As I drove, I noticed the trees overhead all had budding new leaves. A breeze was turning the delicate green shapes over and back again like swift, tiny heartbeats. As I had done many times in the past several days, I thought of my brother. Where was he right now? He had never come back, and I had no way of finding him. I was realizing how hopeful I was at even the possibility of having him back, and that made his lack of contact all the more hurtful.

I pulled into the lot of the rehab facility where Boris was now, prepared to press him for answers. This morning I had packed a suitcase of clothes for him, and I took it out of the backseat and headed into the building. When I got to his room I found him facing away from the door, sitting on the edge of his bed, his shoulders rounded, his head down. He looked like he was praying.

I walked quietly up behind him. No, he wasn't praying. He was looking down into his open wallet at a photograph.

"Dad?" I said, cautiously.

His head jerked back in alarm and he dropped the picture. With a grunt he bent down and snatched it up, then gazed up at me, panting hard.

I sat down on the bed beside him, ready to start my round of questions, but the photo distracted me. Looking at it over his shoulder, I could see what he held was an image of himself and my mother, one that must have been taken at the county courthouse where they got married. My mother was wearing a yellow dress and Boris was in a navy suit and brown tie, and behind them was a wall of dark wood paneling. It occurred to me that Boris had kept this photo in his wallet for decades. It was now the only picture he had of my mother, the only picture of her at all. The fire had burned up all those years of her life and now here she was, purified in the brightness of youth. She hardly resembled the mother I knew. Boris was more familiar, almost lean in his suit, his smile nervous and expectant, but my mother was like a true foreigner beside him, deep bronze and supple with youth, only seventeen—her smile closed and barely curved, her dark eyes radiant and intense and at the same time guarded, like she was holding a fragile hope for happiness that she was afraid she might any moment spill and lose.

In that face I looked for the traces of who she would become in my childhood, for the Americanness she would gain that would take away that cautious, foreign look and replace it with a harsh readiness, for the attitude that would make her see her life as a thankless chore. But I saw none of that here.

Without a word, Boris put his thumb on the photo and slid it to the side, uncovering another one underneath.

Now I could see that he had been carrying a whole stack of them, and they were of all of us, photos that he had kept in his wallet for decades and never bothered to throw away or update. He paused on a second grade school photo of me right after a bad haircut, then moved on to a school photo of my brother, another early one from third or fourth grade. There he was, baring those large, scraped-white teeth, his gaze flinching and unsure. I felt a familiar ache when I saw that picture. I wanted to reach my arms out and console the child there, who already felt timid and exposed, who didn't like to talk in school because of his speech problem, who got bad grades and had no friends, who would never, ever fit in. At such a young age, it was all there, all over that face. What broke my heart most was the smile. Still, he had smiled.

Boris was holding this photo out like he wanted me to get a good look at it. I could feel that he wanted to say something. He let it drop to the ground. "Not even mine," he said.

Then he stood up.

"Wait." I bent down and picked it up. *Not even mine?*

But he was leaving the room in a hurry, stumbling away from me as if he had said too much. I watched him go out the doorway, and then I stood up and walked out behind him. Under a sign with an arrow pointing to restrooms, he turned, and around the corner I heard the men's room door swing open.

I stood in the hall for ten minutes, my mind blasted clean by confusion, discreetly chewing up a disintegrating corner of the cork bulletin board at my shoulder—putting pieces of it in my mouth as if they were nuts. Why had he said that? *Not even mine.* What could he have meant? That he wasn't Eliot's real father? That was crazy. Of course he was. I had heard the story. Uneasy now, thoughts going off in my head like bright, dangerous sparks, I waited for what seemed like a long time. Finally, I went down the hallway and knocked quietly on the men's room door.

"Dad, are you okay?" I said in a hushed voice, loud enough for him to hear me through the door. No answer. Cautiously, I pushed it open. I was looking at two urinals and an open stall. Inside the stall my father was sitting, holding his head in his hands.

Without lifting it, he said, "Leave me be." His voice stretched like taffy, full of pain.

I stood frozen, unable to leave him like this and unable to think of anything to comfort him. "Should I get the nurse?" I asked, knowing it was the wrong thing to say.

My father shook his head, slowly, as if he weren't even hearing me.

I didn't know what to do. For a minute longer I stood holding the door open, watching my father cry, then I let it close and took a step back. Right beside me was another door with a metal push bar. I pushed it open. Bright afternoon light flooded my eyes and I sank down onto a set of concrete steps leading down to an empty residential street.

I was still holding the picture of my brother in my hand, and I looked down into his sad, brave little smile. His skin was as dark as my mother's. I had gotten that dose of whiteness from Boris, but Eliot hadn't. He had always been the dark one, the one who my mother said could pass for a true gypsy.

Could it be true? Could Eliot not belong to Boris?

But then, who did my brother belong to? If not my father, then who? I couldn't help it. It was the first name that came to my mind. Emilian.

I stood up.

I thought about all those times that Eliot had called him *Dad*, as if it were a joke, or an insult. Unfortunately for my father, it cut both ways. The first time I called him Boris instead of Dad, my father had stuck his finger up and shook it at me.

"No. Not you," he said. I remembered how my brother had laughed about that, like my father had said something that was more appropriate than he knew.

My brother must have known. Either he had found out himself, or somebody had told him. No, not somebody. I knew who had told him. My mother had told him.

And now my father knew. It was going to be hard for him, I thought. The rest of his life was going to be hard. I stood up and walked to my car. There was nowhere I wanted to go, nowhere I could be right now. I felt cast out by my father's grief, unable to cross over that void of incomprehension to comfort him. And I felt too as if I were suddenly bound to a betrayal I could hardly understand. Why had she lied?

I got in my car and started driving. How and when had my father found out? By the way he had been looking at that photo, the way he had been acting these last few days, it seemed like he had only recently found out. Was it at the hospital, when my brother visited him? Or before that? Did this have something to do with his trip to the church? I drove past the empty streets of downtown, my thoughts flitting rapidly like the shadows on the pavement. I thought all the way back to the night my father had pounded on my door and sat in my kitchen, trying and failing to tell me something. How long had he been chasing this mystery? There was the note in the cigarette case, and the other line in the road atlas. Feeling very strange, I passed under the bridge and kept going. The turn for my street came and I didn't take it. I was driving east. I had a feeling I was going to go somewhere I didn't want to end up.

Perhaps I was here out of some sense that I would find something—a clue, a whisper, a guiding sensation that I needed to feel before I could consider what was before me now. Nobody was out in their yards and the hard spring light was fading quickly.

I could see all the way to the bottom of the backyard, which sloped down, where our one big evergreen tree was charred black on the side that had been exposed to the heat of the fire. I was standing on a mound of dirt they had used to fill in the basement. They had removed everything—ducts, pipes, walls, glass, insulation had all gone into the dumpsters. Since the outline of the house was still here I could imagine where I might be standing, which was in the hallway that passed from the living room down to the bedrooms, the hallway where we'd had all the family pictures hanging.

The whole world was silent. No birds, no breeze to move the leaves, nothing but the air endlessly expanding around me and the shadows quickly melting into dusk. It was like a graveyard. No—it was a graveyard. My mother had died a violent death here right in front of the gas stove.

I could still see the image on the TV afterward. It seemed like the fire trucks and camera crews had arrived at the scene at almost the same moment. The news hook repeated itself in my mind. "A local woman is *dead* tonight from a raging house fire."

A local woman. Tina Krupin, they had called her on the news. That was her official name after she married my father, after Tina Thomas had married Boris Krupin. But Boris had always called her Alepa—her *nav romano*, her true name.

I stared into the vacant yard, unable to comprehend it, unable to put any of the pieces I had recently gathered into a complete picture. After a while I realized my eyes were fixed on the crabapple tree, my brother's tree, standing forlorn and tilted in the grass, blooms already gone—like an accident that had happened here when nobody was looking.

I buried my hands in my coat. I felt the hole in the pocket lining that had swallowed up my keys more than once. That was my life, I thought. The startled confusion of finding a hole where I thought there was something. Things disappearing, slipping through my grasp.

I stepped away from the kitchen and the ashes and dust. I stepped out of the house altogether. I walked down the withered yard to the curb. All was quiet. All was empty. All was waiting.

16

I WALKED INTO MY APARTMENT, STILL WRAPPED IN THAT STORY OF betrayal and loss that had become my father's life, still wondering what would come of it. I closed my door behind me. Then I felt something. In the silence around me there was a prickle of expectation, a slight bristling that made me guess I was not alone. I stood immobilized, unable even to lift my hand to the light switch.

Then to my horror, a molten blackness moved in the kitchen at my left. A light came on and out of the darkness appeared the lean, whittled face and kinky hair and crimson shirt. The sight of the shirt registered as pain, and I winced.

The gypsy opened his mouth and words came out. "So," he said, "where is it?"

He twitched his head back, as if he'd been jolted by a little spark of electricity. I noticed a sparse layer of black bristle growing on his upper lip, not quite a mustache. "I've looked the place over and I don't see it. So if you don't mind getting it for me."

We both stood there waiting for something. I was aware that he wanted me to get him something. I opened my mouth, and the noise that came out of it was little more than a wheeze.

He raised his eyebrows. "What?"

I put the words together and said in a choked voice, "I don't know what you're talking about."

"Really?" He pointed at my purse. "Hand that over."

I stood against the wall, my arms dangling like lead weights at my sides. He seemed to recognize that I was unable to follow his directions, so he reached out and lifted the strap gingerly off my shoulder.

"That privy had vents at the top. I could see you the whole time. It took me a while to figure out where I had seen you before."

I stared. Had he just said *privy*? The gypsy pulled out the blackened cigarette case and looked at me with a grin. His jaw flexed and the smile fell from his face. With his dark, somber eyes on me he dropped the case back in the purse and leaned against the doorframe. He put his hand in his pocket, pulled out his own box of cigarettes, and packed it against his palm.

"Want one?"

He held one out to me like I was a horse he wanted to feed a carrot to. When I didn't move, he shrugged and put it in his mouth. "I just want to talk," he said, looking me over. His eyes were huge and full of soft pulsing blackness. "Why don't we go sit down?"

He took a step closer to me, holding his hand out toward the living room to gesture me ahead of him. I felt a surge of nervous adrenaline and my legs stumbled forward down the hall and took me into the living room.

"Sit down," he said cordially, as if this was his room and I was his guest.

Behind me were two stuffed cubes I had placed on one side of my coffee table. I sat down on one and the cheap foam crushed down audibly under me. He stood over one of the two little armchairs at either end of the table—the one covered in the cheap lavender fur that was put on stuffed animals. Before sitting, he reached into his pants pocket and pulled a lighter out and lit his cigarette.

"Go ahead," he said, leaning across the table and tossing the pack of cigarettes and the lighter into my lap. He sat down in the chair. It was so low for him that his knees rose up into sharp jagged peaks. He looked at them a second, putting his free hand on one. With the other, he brought his cigarette to his mouth and drew in a breath until a little red bud of fire appeared on its tip. He exhaled, watching me.

His eyes looked into my lap. I thought maybe he was waiting for me to take a cigarette, so I reached down for one and brought it up to my mouth. I didn't want to smoke it. Smoking made me sick. So I did what I knew I would. I clamped down on the filter with my teeth and began to chew.

I hadn't had a cigarette this way since college parties with my first boyfriend, who had enjoyed it so much for the novelty that he would feed me cigarettes all night from his pack. Now the feel of the delicate paper and smell of earthy decay took me back to all those nights and I felt instant revulsion. I wondered what the gypsy was thinking. So far he was only looking at me.

"Who are you?" I blurted.

The cigarette lurched in the air on its way up to his mouth.

"A name," I said, dizzied by my own bluster. "Your name. I mean, you're in my apartment."

He glanced around, as if to acknowledge my apartment. "It's Bobby," he said.

I flattened the filter down and bit it off. *Oh, yeah, right,* I thought, pushing it to the side of my cheek where it would be out of the way. *Bobby.* I took a bite off the stick and began crunching up the brittle flakes.

Bobby said, "So why did you look through my camera? I'm curious." For a while he looked at me, waiting, and I tried to think of an answer for him. It was a good question.

"I'm talking to you. I'm asking you a question."

"I don't know," I admitted.

"Hmm." He seemed to be thinking something. "What did you think of the photos on it?"

Why was he asking me about the photos? The photos were totally meaningless. Or had I failed to notice something important? Nervously I snatched another cigarette out of the pack and put it into my mouth.

"Are you some kind of freak or something?" he asked me. He was looking at me with disgust, and this made me feel a sudden rush of aggression.

I took the cigarette out of my mouth and said, "Fuck you, Bobby."

He jerked his head back and laughed a little. But he looked taken aback.

The next words came out just as unexpectedly. "I could tell somebody."

He paused with the cigarette on his way to his mouth and said, "Tell somebody what?"

About your scam, I thought, thinking of the paid receipts, and wondering if I was stupid enough to say that out loud. Was I really going to try and threaten him now, while he was here threatening me?

"Well?" he said. "Do you have something to tell me?"

"Why are you here?" I blurted out. "Why are you threatening me? Why don't you leave me alone?"

He attempted a smug grin. "For your information, I don't want anything to do with you. You're the one who's bothering me. Why did you follow me?"

The question I had been desperate to ask finally spilled out. "What was my father doing at the church that day?"

He looked at me thoughtfully. "Why don't you ask your father?"

I shook my head.

As if he had read the truth in my expression, he said, "Maybe he doesn't want you to know." In the darkness I watched him shrug his sharp shoulders. "Look. I can't tell you anything. I don't know what they were talking about."

"They who?"

Bobby shook his head. "It has nothing to do with me." He leaned forward in his chair, put the cigarette out directly on my plastic table, and stared at me with huge, pondering eyes. "I came here to tell you that I'm not involved. So don't bother me, and I won't bother you. But if you do bother me..." Without finishing the sentence he stood up. "I know where you live. So just stay away from now on."

For a moment he looked down on me from his towering height, then he turned. He was leaving. Without telling me anything. I tried one more thing. "Who's Emilian?"

His head moved abruptly in the darkness, and the brief silence that followed seemed like the silence of somebody who was surprised.

"Tell me why Emilian might have wanted to see my mother," I said in a rush.

For a rigid moment, he stared at me. Then he said, "You lie."

"I have a note," I told him, my voice breaking on a snag of nerves. "Maybe you could tell me who wrote it. Maybe you would recognize the writing."

"Show it to me."

I was about to get up for my purse when I realized that he wanted to see it—he was eager to see it—and if I used it right I might get him to tell me something. "First tell me why my father was at the church that day. Who was he talking to?"

In the darkness he looked down at me, his body stiff, his face still. Then he said, "I might have something you want. Show me the note and I'll give it to you."

I was surprised. "What?"

He reached into his pocket and pulled out a small object that glinted in the moonlight and tossed it into my lap. It was a key.

"What is this?"

"It's how I got in tonight, *Natalie*."

I turned it over and saw the small, round yellow sticker that had been on it ever since the landlord had given it to me, with *Natalie Krupin: 3B* written in pen. It was my spare key. The one I had given to Boris. The one I thought was still on his key chain.

"How did you get this?" I had had my father's key chain in my possession since I took it from him at the hospital on Saturday.

"I paid a visit to my father," said Bobby.

"To your father?" With a shock it hit me. He had been the one at the hospital that day. He had visited Boris. He had taken the key. The description the nurse had given me matched him perfectly. "You said you were my brother," I said, my heart sinking in dismay.

"Show me the note," he said.

I blinked several times fast in the darkness. "How did you find my apartment?" I asked hoarsely.

He paused, as if considering whether or not to tell me. "I followed you from the hospital."

From the hospital. Was it that same day? When I raced home thinking Eliot might come to see me after sitting with my father? But it hadn't been Eliot. It had been a stranger, watching my father sleep, going through his things. "How did you even know my father was there?"

He stared at me. "Show me the note," he repeated.

His voice had a sharp edge in it now. My purse was still in the hallway, on the floor, and I pointed to it, afraid to walk past him. "My purse," I said, and watched him go to the hallway and come back with it. He dumped its contents out on the coffee table and looked at me expectantly.

"In the cigarette case."

He picked up the cigarette case, opened it, and unfolded the note. When he was done reading, he looked up in the darkness. "What can I say?" His voice was unsteady now, wavering with anger. "Your mother's a slut." He took a jerking step back, dropped the note, and took three strides into the entry hallway and put his hand on the door.

"My mother was not a slut," I said, my voice boiling out of me. "She got *married.*" But not to the man who got her pregnant, I thought, and my heart welled up.

He opened the door and walked out into the yellow light of the hallway, where his shirt lit up again to a blistering red. "You don't even know," he said. The eyes that looked at me this time were hard and dangerous. "Leave my family alone." His lip twitched. "And if you're keeping something from me..." He held out his open palm, as if to give me one last chance. When I did nothing, he slammed the door shut behind him.

17

When he was gone I picked up the phone. After three rings there was a hoarse noise on the other end that sounded something like hello.

"Is this a bad time?"

There was a brief silence. "I just worked a double shift. I haven't slept in twenty hours."

"I need you to come over," I told Mitch.

"Now? No."

"Somebody broke into the apartment. He was here tonight when I got home."

"What?" I could hear the haze of sleep lift from his voice. "Have you called the police?"

"I don't want to do that."

"What do you mean?"

I let out a trembling sigh. And then I seemed unable to respond.

After a while, Mitch said, "Okay, so you don't want to tell me." He expelled a tired breath. "I probably don't even want to know."

There was a deep, short silence. Then he seemed to be rubbing his hand over his face, smearing his breath as he exhaled. "If I come over there, you're going to tell me what this is about," he told me. "Right?"

"Right," I said, not sure at all.

After I hung up the phone, and after standing anxiously still for several minutes, listening to every noise and twitch of the building, I looked down at the coffee table and saw the loose contents of my purse and began putting them back inside. When I came to the photo of my brother, I stood looking at it for a minute before deciding what to do with it. It had been a long time since I'd seen his face in a photograph. Sometime after he left home, my mother had taken them all down and stored them somewhere out of sight. There was only one she didn't take, and that one I had put in the back of my closet shortly after Eliot ran away, perhaps anticipating her inevitable purging. It was a photograph that had been taken of us that summer, sitting in the yard with our heads close together over a game of cards, a blur of tree bark behind us. My mother had snapped the photo before we noticed her there, in some unprecedented impulse to capture an image of her two children, an impulse that seemed at the time to be strangely foreboding. Later that summer, the day my brother disappeared, I came into my room and found the photo on my pillow. He had left it for me as a goodbye gift, something to remember him by. Once it was tucked away, I never looked at it. Even when I moved to my apartment, I gathered it up inside a heap of sweaters and threw it in a box. But I was glad for that picture because it was the only thing I had of him. I had put it in a cheap plastic frame so I wouldn't be tempted to eat it, and I buried it in the back of my closet again, where I wouldn't have to look at it and be reminded of him.

Now I fished it out and slid the school photo into the corner of the frame on top of it. I allowed myself only the briefest glimpse of our faces, two shades of bronze, before retreating to the kitchen to find solace in my midnight snack bowl. I was still trying to get over my disappointment. It wasn't my brother at the hospital. After a while I heard footsteps come down the hall and stop outside my door. A knuckle gave three peevish taps, and I took a deep, calming breath and went to the entry and opened the door.

Mitch stood clean-shaven and gray-white under a navy-blue Red Sox hat. "Okay. I'm here," he said, eyes barely parted. He walked past me and sat on the first piece of furniture available, which was the same tiny purple armchair Bobby had sat in. Mitch was heavier than Bobby, and the chair was meant to take one-third of the weight that was in it right now. He watched it crease and fold around him. His knees came almost to his face, propped up in front of him. He gave me an incredulous look, then rested his head on the back of the chair. "So what happened?"

I hesitated. Mitch picked his head up and looked at me over the coffee table. "You said you would tell me, Natalie."

"I will." I went into the kitchen and put away my snack bowl and came back out.

Mitch was gazing at the table where I had left several items out of my purse. "Hey," he said. "What's this?" He leaned forward and picked up the cigarette case. After he had turned it over once to examine it, he gave me a stricken look. "Is this from the fire? It looks like"—he opened it—"a case for cigarettes."

I had put the note back inside and now I didn't stop him from unfolding it. He read it silently. There was a long, troubled silence as he looked at me.

"Does this have anything to do with your mother?"

I paused, one second too long. "No," I said. "Why would it?"

"Yes it does. This has something to do with your mother." He shook his head wearily. "What are you doing, Natalie? What is all this?"

"It's a long story," I said.

He sighed. He put his arm over his eyes. "So you weren't lying to me about this guy? He really did break into your apartment?"

"Yes," I said.

"Are you in danger?" he asked.

"No," I assured him, though when I said it I wondered if it were true.

Mitch yawned. "Whatever it is you're doing, stop. Please. Don't do this to yourself." There was a deep heavy sadness in his voice, or else exhaustion.

"You don't even know what I'm doing," I said. "I'm not doing *anything*." It was other people doing things around me, or to me. It was hard to tell.

"Well you haven't told me anything yet," he murmured. "I'm still waiting."

"You don't seem like a very eager audience right now," I said.

Mitch didn't answer.

"I'm going to make some tea first. Do you want some?"

Nothing.

I went into the kitchen and made myself some tea. When I came back I stood over him, listening to his calm, even breaths. I poked his shoulder gently. As I suspected, he was asleep.

I sat down in the other chair and sipped my tea, sucking the floating bag into my mouth and chewing it for a while, letting my nerves settle. I felt better now that I wasn't alone. Several light taps at the window told me it had started to rain. I waited to hear it become a steady patter, but it continued intermittently, broken by long gulps of silence. When the bag shredded and I had a loose poultice of bitter leaves in my mouth, I got up and rinsed my cup and went into the bathroom and swished my mouth out, then brushed my teeth. I went around the apartment turning off lights and got into my pajamas. I came back, and after looking at Mitch for a minute longer I decided what to do. I picked up his hand and gently tugged it, coaxing him into a standing position, and walked him to the bedroom, where he dropped instantly down on his side of the bed. I pulled off his shoes. This I'd done many times for him when he came home too tired to do anything but collapse in a chair. Back then it was a much bigger and more comfortable chair, but still, I never liked to leave him like that, all cramped down and breathing into his neck while I was spread out in a comfortable bed. Tonight he seemed to be going through the familiar motions of our ritual as if nothing had happened between us, nothing had changed.

I slid into the cool sheets beside him. Rain was now hitting the window steadily. Lying in bed next to the ex-boyfriend who had recently left me for the girl living downstairs, I should have felt shame, I should have felt anger, I should have felt guilt, I should have felt something other than what I was feeling. All I felt with his body beside mine was a deep undisturbed contentment, as if my life had been put into its proper alignment once again.

I watched his back rise and fall, his breathing deep and even, and a calm settled through me such as I hadn't felt in weeks. We weren't doing anything wrong, I told myself. We were just lying in the same bed. That was all. I closed my eyes and relaxed. I lay there for a long time, my mind vague and soft. I didn't even feel myself sinking into the long black stillness of sleep.

In the middle of the night, something woke me up. It took me a while to understand. Mitch was kissing me. His warm mouth was pushed over mine and gulping all the air out of me. And I was kissing him back, energetically. Then I could feel the firm tender clutch of his hands finding me everywhere, and the smooth warmth of his body as my hands went around his back. My whole body blazed up at once. Was this really happening?

"I love you," Mitch murmured, in a desperate, unhappy voice that was possibly still half asleep. "I can't help it."

I got up on my knees and straddled him. He reached up and pulled off my shirt.

"Natalie," he said. "We have to stop."

But we didn't stop, and soon we were moving together in the languid rhythms already familiar to us, half asleep, half awake, our bodies unhurried and receptive. The soft drizzle outside the windows seemed to expand and still the air, holding us gently inside a delicate conscious dream, and we woke slowly, distant from ourselves and close to each other, until we were both there, inside a single body that seemed like it had been ours forever. The moments that welled up in the dark seemed vast and expanding, and in that darkness was a pinkish haze of light, pushed into our room by the clouds and the streetlight. In that light we were meeting each other in a place we had never been, not in four years, not ever. And then we fell asleep.

The next morning, it was after 5 A.M. when I lifted my head from the pillow and glanced at the clock. Startled, I looked out the window. Had I forgotten to set the alarm? The rain had stopped falling and now all the moisture of the night was lying quietly in the air in waves of mist. I rose out of bed into the drenched morning hush and put on clothes. I made sure not to wonder what last night had meant. Somehow it felt like it already belonged to another world, and should stay there, untouched by talk and untainted by my thoughts. When I was dressed, I went to the other side of the bed and woke Mitch. Then I left him in the bedroom and went to splash some water on my face. I came tiptoeing back and he was sitting up on the side of the bed, looking at something. With a jolt I realized it was the photograph. I had left it there last night. I sucked in a breath and said nothing. He hadn't sensed me in the doorway yet, and as I retreated I saw him turn the frame over and look at the other side. I had never spoken much about my brother to Mitch. Now it occurred to me that he was reading the note my brother had left me, his final goodbye. I went to the hall closet for my coat and shoes. I tried to remember the words he had written.

I was putting on my coat when Mitch came out and gave me a faint, beleaguered grin. I couldn't tell if there was regret in it or not.

As we stepped into the hall, I could feel the silence shifting between us, the tight sharp wingbeats of his mind going once again in swift retreat to some private deliberation without me. I wondered what he was thinking. Maybe he was thinking about Amber. Or maybe he remembered what he had said in his half-sleep to me. I remembered the confession, the voice that was urgent and so unhappy. I felt it with an ache that seemed like one I had carried with me for a long time already. It was almost consoling. Now that I had heard the truth, I understood that the truth wasn't enough to help us.

Mitch stopped me outside the door. "Natalie," he said, with such a look of suffering on his face that I felt like I could forgive him for everything.

"It's okay. Don't worry. I won't tell anybody."

He cupped his hand over his eyes. "Right. That's good." Then he lifted his face and said, "This is… I don't know."

I wasn't sure what to make of that. "I hear it happens," I said.

He sighed. "Maybe I should go first."

Mitch waited for an awkward pause while I struggled to understand what he meant. "Down the stairs," he said. "It's probably better if I'm not with you."

"Oh." I got it. Because of Amber.

"I didn't mean…" He gave me a hesitant look. "I don't know what to say. I'm sorry."

I gave him a little smile. I didn't know what to say either. I didn't even really know what we were talking about. Were we sorry for what we did last night? Or were we sorry for something else, something more?

For a moment more we looked at each other, as if there was something left unsaid but neither of us knew what it was, or how to approach it. Then Mitch said, "Well, I better go. I don't want you to be late."

I watched him go down the stairs, and I wondered how long I should wait. I dug my keys out of my pocket and went back into my apartment and to the window, looking for him to come out and walk away like he had the other day. When his tense hurried strides had carried him out of the parking lot, I turned from the window. I went back to the dresser in the bedroom and picked up the photo in its cheap plastic frame. I wanted to see what Mitch had seen. I turned the photo over and read the note on the back:

Little Sis,
I dare you not to eat this. Be good to yourself.
Friends forever,
Eliot

I couldn't help it. When I looked at the faded scribble of my brother's writing, I felt a hot blast of grief, as if I had unlocked some dark box in my heart, and out he had stepped.

I had put my brother away for so long, afraid to think of him, afraid to ask myself what had become of him, afraid to admit to myself how injured I had been by his disappearance. He had left me and never come back. For years I thought either he was dead or he didn't love me. But now I could feel that missing love in the photograph I had buried away, in his last words to me, written in that cramped scrawl that I hadn't seen in so many years.

I heard a car go by in the street, slick and wet. *Friends forever.* I felt again the charge of those words, reminding me how much more they said about us than a compulsory *Love, Eliot* would have said. Eliot had been my only friend growing up. It was so familiar, this note, like looking at something I'd never put away. I was placing it back on the dresser, gratified that I hadn't destroyed it, or lost it, seeing my brother all over again in the slant of the script—the jammed-up left-handed posture he wrote with, the sweetness and decency he always tried for, just a little long-lost bit of him—when a thought struck lightly in the stillness of my mind. I reached into my purse and pulled out the cigarette case. One more time I opened it and unfolded the paper inside.

Emilian is dying. The writing was identical.

I was late getting to work, too late to assist Salt in his morning preparations for the newscast, too late to makeup and dress him, and too late to shepherd him out in front of the cameras. With a sense of peril, my mind spinning out of focus, I tiptoed into the studio just before the news was starting. Birnoff was speaking, calm as a cookie, and Salt was standing by his blue screen, dressed in a gray suit with a steel-cut gleam, like a kitchen knife under pot lights in a cooking show, his lipless pallor ghoulish above an Easter-yellow collar. Gunmetal gray and yellow? My mind clanged with discordant discoveries, and I stared hard across the room as if the sight of my weatherman would clear my head and slow my heart back down to a normal pace.

He looked puckered and cadaverous under the lights. Clash of color. Grim reaper. I don't know how long I continued to stand in place, staring with dry burning eyes and feeling the hot breath pass over my lips like wind from a fire. Then I felt my attention rush out into the room around me, where the noises in the studio crackled like kindling flames. I knew I was in trouble. I knew before I saw the station manager, folded arms, chin burrowed into his thin navy windbreaker, silver hair shellacked down, his wet-combed look, still clutching his car keys, jags of tension gusting off of him and buffeting the air, sending stiff waves of warning over to me. He was waiting for the weather forecast. Somebody must have alerted him. Not somebody. Birnoff was already a minute into his pitch: mild morning greetings, gentle teasers about if you live downtown you might have heard a pesky bleeping that was not your alarm this morning, and speaking of noisemakers, there's a new kind of protest down on Dross Avenue, and we'll tell you what's got people in an uproar right after we take a look at your morning weather forecast—slabbed head in rotation, cuing Salt—*Sure seems like a morning you might wish you'd stayed in bed?*—the prompt smoothly offered but a little withholding, tilting up and back, pinched courtesy—but why should Salt stumble? It's the same as every morning, some question that will fit the formula of his two-word turn, brisk and genial—*Right, well*—moving into his report, always some folksy self-contained chitchat, nonreferential of Birnoff's turnover (*not a day to take your mom out fishing*), and then the numbers and dew points and barometric pressures, all in earnest and oblivious of Mr. Swenson, bearing down in the shadows like some apprehensive football coach, staring not at the studio set but at the monitor, getting the viewers' take.

I could feel him ignoring me intentionally, but he knew I was here, had seen me come in—I was sure of it from the angle of his body, turned partway to the door I had just entered through, his shoulders signaling everything to me—his disapproval, his guarded warning: *You better hope this comes off.* And when it was almost over, no snags, perfect execution, a turn of his head, flagging me with flat brutal eyes, chin flicking—*come over here*—not at all forgiving—why? As I approached, wondering what reason he had to reprimand me, other than the unflattering wardrobe—yes bad, but not *so* bad; he was wearing a suit at least—I saw the half shot and exactly what was wrong just as his finger tapped on the monitor accusingly: the corner of Salt's mouth, where a trembling black crumb, like a spider, caught the stream of his breath, and I knew it was the cinnamon cake that I wiped off his face every other morning when he tilted his head back to receive his morning makeover.

Damn.

"My office, please." He ducked his head and puddle-walked over cables and duct tape to the studio doors, pausing for the cut to commercial. He waited, not looking at me, and I felt myself walking on rubbery legs in his direction. Then he was out the door and I was moving behind him through the offices, floating it seemed, unaware of my feet on the carpet, passing cubicles and the clicking of keys and the ringing of phones. I had one job, one simple job. I got paid as much as the cubicle dwellers to do image management, basic human upkeep, no specialty training or education here. People around here resented me. I could see the quick, keen glances as I followed behind the boss, and I felt like I was walking farther and farther away from this morning's discovery, into a diorama stillness that held a gravity that meant nothing at all. The early-morning light was casting a cold unfeeling radiance on everything, a strange, bleared light that seemed to hammer everything thin and made the open door to my boss's office look severe and flimsy at once, his black leather chair distorted and prop-like. I sat down in the chrome-and-cloth chair opposite him. It was all a set, a lie, a game.

"Thirty-nine minutes late," he said, and held up a hand, as if convinced that the world he was in mattered and existed. "I get it," he said, "emergency. Your dog ate a pincushion. Things happen. Here's what we're going to do. You're going to schedule a crew to go out and film a promotion segment to go in the three p.m. slot." He looked at me, thinking, head thrust forward, reaching up and pinching his nose. "You know," he said, deflating like a bag of air, "probably one of those with his arms around downtown pedestrians in front of shop windows, 'He's my weatherman—rah, rah.'"

"You got it," I said. "Rah, rah." My voice wobbled like tin.

"Maybe get the new museum building. And actually take Ray—he's all you need. Just—this is serious. Natalie." He blinked at me, his eyes little blue jewels sparkling on a backdrop of watery pink. "We're teetering on the edge here. Your job is about to become obsolete. Just so you know."

PART SIX

THE LONG FIRE

18

IN MY CHILDHOOD IMAGINATION, MY PARENTS' STORY HAD ALWAYS been one of forbidden romance, one I had gathered up over the years after listening to it in many versions—all those reveries and confessions, drunken midnight ramblings and conversations speckled with suggestion and innuendo—and after sifting through all the accounts and hints and clues that had slipped past my attentive ears, and embellishing everything to my satisfaction, I had what seemed a fairy-tale account of how they had met and married.

From the way my father spoke, his whole life had been arranged so that he would find my mother and fall in love with her. It was as if my mother was the key to a future that had been locked away from him in a dark room, and all the life that had come before her had been leading him to that door.

But my mother, on those nights my father fell asleep in his chair, had told a different story. She had met my father in a moment of restless discontent, soon after she had been officially promised to a man in another family. She was disillusioned with the future that stretched ahead of her, and out of bitterness she had allowed herself to be seduced by a gajo. It wasn't clear if Boris had been a momentary impulse for her, or if she had only found him in bitterness and then fallen in love with him. I, of course, had supplied the love that was left in question. But later it wasn't so easy.

Later I couldn't imagine that my father had seemed very special to her. He was a gajo, for one thing—but not exactly all-American, with his stoic Russian upbringing. He had come back from Vietnam and had spent three years taking one drab government job after another without any clear idea of what to do with himself. His mother, by now, was dead. She had died while he was away.

I had sometimes thought of my father during that time, back from war, full of the terrors he had seen and committed there, all alone, no future he could envision, and I had understood how he decided to do what he did next. As he told it, he decided to contact his father, to tell him that his mother was dead, and to pick a fight with him that he had been waiting to have for fourteen years.

His father, Nikolas Krupin, had immigrated under the assumption that in America he could do anything he pleased, and before he had quite found his feet to act on this fervor, he met Boris's mother, then a twenty-year-old young woman who had grown up in America from the age of eleven. They got married a little sooner than they got to know each other, and almost immediately he began to live a life outside of that marriage. He drank, he fought, he stole, he gambled, he visited prostitutes, and he came and went as he pleased, going to jail over and over—and each time he got out even more stubbornly determined to reward himself with a lawless life. Finally Boris's mother divorced her scoundrel husband and raised Boris alone in an apartment near the home where she had grown up. Providing for them with the money she made as a seamstress, with little help from her family, their life was whittled down to a stark subsistence. Growing up, Boris watched his mother position herself deeper and deeper inside the attitudes of hardship—in which she came to see expressions of love and joy as extravagances, wasteful expenses of the vital energy it took to live. And it was his mother's attitude that made him want to excuse his father for his transgressions and later his abandonment, because he saw her as the probable cause of it, not the victim.

But while Boris in his middle age had outgrown this notion, and had frequently denounced his father's treatment of his mother, whenever he spoke of the actual man he had known briefly at the age of twenty-four, he did so with affection. When Boris had tracked him down, his father had stood on the porch and wept. He embraced him, he took him inside, he begged for forgiveness, he received the news of Boris's mother with respect and regret, he told his son how much he thought about him and how much he loved him, and said he had wanted many times to contact him but had been too afraid. Despite what happened later, my father never doubted his father's sincerity on that day. For the rest of his life he believed in it, and that was how he kept his original forgiveness intact.

In the year that followed, his father invited him wholeheartedly into his life, and Boris saw firsthand what it was like to move under the radar of the law, to pursue a network of loyalties and confidences made through surreptitious meetings and furtive exchanges, conducted through a language of suggestion and nuance. All of this spoke directly to the cynicism and malaise Boris had felt since his return from the war, and soon enough he was deep inside it, taken in again as he had been for those two years at war by the danger and exhilaration of submitting to the worst inclinations buried in himself. He was beginning to think that person was who he was. But then—and this is why I think he could never resent his father—all these underground operations had a center of contact to which his father was taking him, giving him slow hints and minor details, testing out his interest and loyalty with bits of information, place names and people names, and it was when they arrived finally into the last ring of contact, while all of those preparations were being consummated in a neighborhood of gypsies, that he met, like a moving arrow, straight and true, with my mother.

I never learned the scam that brought them together. All I knew was that she was the daughter of a gypsy broker, and he was the son of a Russian broker, and their fathers were making deals in secret meetings that left Boris just outside the door, not to be trusted completely yet with the details, and my mother, passing him in the dark halls of the house, signaled him with her burning night eyes, and he sat spellbound, looking back once, twice.

Soon she slipped him a note, and so arranged their first meeting. All of this she had told me in her own words too, her eyes glazed and bright with bourbon one night and gazing past me to a romance I couldn't fathom. I had looked at her then and seen only her unraveling age, a woman withered by slow physical resignation, sinking toward some undesirable end.

But all through her willing deterioration, Boris had been held captive to my mother as in a trance, her beauty never forgotten, his early worship of her still reflected in his rapt gaze. My mother was for him an exotic discovery, a mysterious being of power and grace, but there was also something instinctively familiar in her. I imagined it was her furious survivalism that had given her a familiar imperious beauty, that had whittled her down to an ardent will, a pure fighting passion that was too bright and hot for warm expressions of love and affection, but that seared him all the way to his core and drew from him a love that was like worship. In the end, he had fallen drastically in love with a woman who was much like his mother in her grimness and her gravity, but she had revealed herself to him in the hidden world of his father, had burned there like a fire for him and then come out into the light a dying flame.

When it was exposed, Boris's father's connections with her family were severely threatened, and to save himself he cast Boris out of his world just as my mother was cast out of her father's world. Boris took her to his mother's family, and nobody liked her there either. She was strange, dark, secretive. She seemed to disdain them, to resist their questions, to look on them with scorn. They warned my father about her, but he didn't listen. He took his bride to the county courthouse and married her, with no family present. And then they left town, together in exile.

All this I had believed. All this had been true for me. Until now. Now I didn't know what to believe. Now, inside this forbidden romance that I had thought belonged only to my parents, somebody else had insinuated himself—a third party had stepped in, and he stood like a shadow at the edge of what I knew. There was only one person who could answer my questions now. And I hadn't seen him in thirteen years.

How was I supposed to find him?

I was back in my apartment, with the picture in my hand. There we were, fourteen and seventeen. We were outside, the summer he ran away. The same summer my mother began taking my brother to mysterious places, having quiet conversations on the phone. Had she been in contact with her family all along? Had she brought him to them? Introduced him to his real father? And since then had my brother been living, all this time, under the radar, among gypsies? If that was true, then he was a gypsy. And maybe he wouldn't even want to talk to me.

There was only one thing I could think to do.

Brackish puddles flashed in the road and churned up under the car tires. A cold sun had parted the clouds and the light was smeared like a glaze over my windshield. I shielded my eyes, driving blindly down the same pitted streets where now a wet dazzle made everything strange again. I parked on the busy street and stepped onto the weedy curb alongside the church. Standing water in the gutter brought a pond smell to my nose as I picked my way through soggy vegetation. I was on the chapel side, with its small gloomy windows made of amber pebbled glass, set into the brick wall. When I got to the corner and turned I saw with relief that the fortune teller's porch was empty. The rest of the street was heavy and still, all the buildings leaning down on themselves as if suffering some deep, morbid depression, with the white afternoon sun lying flat and silent on everything. For a second it felt like I was walking into an abandoned movie set, a place where nothing was real.

I walked past the freshly gouged trunk of the cypress tree and up the steps into the deep shade of the porch. I reached out and touched the cold knob of the door. It was locked. What now? Could a person knock on a church door? I lifted my fist and tried. No answer. I walked down the steps back into the sun and looked across the street at the fortune teller's house. There was no way I could go in there and ask her about my brother. Who knew what she might do to me. The sun wasn't warming anything, and I burrowed my hands into my coat. The cars on the busy street whooshed by, splattering up geysers of water. I stood there trying to imagine my brother living on this street, conducting meetings in this church. Had it been him in there that day? I took a few steps and looked down the side of the building. No doors. I found myself walking through the dead sodden grass anyway, making a slow circle toward the back of the church.

When I rounded the corner I could see there was only a few feet of dirt between the church and a chain-link fence that separated it from the side wall of a business that faced the busy street. I startled when I saw a man on the other side of the fence, standing beside an open door. He looked vaguely in my direction.

I tried a polite smile. I hoped he didn't think I was trespassing, which I realized was exactly what I was doing.

"Cold day out," he said in a rough, briny voice. I noticed he was only wearing a t-shirt, and it hung almost to the knees of a pair of black-and-white-checkered pants that were hunched up over large rubber boots. He had rumpled gray hair, and he stood with his head hanging low in front of his neck, like a barnyard animal. On inspection he didn't look very lucid.

"You should try wearing a coat," I said, trying to be cheery.

He nodded, looking at me out of the corner of his eye. "Yeah I had a coat. My cat didn't like it though. It was a wool coat."

I stepped closer to the fence. "I was wondering, do you know the people who run this church?"

He nodded slowly, as if he were drawing up another thought from a long way off.

"Yeah, that coat, my cat just keep tearing holes into. He figured it was a creature or something." He shot a little burst of laughter out his nose. "And then my other cat pulled the drapes down on himself one day." He waited to see what I thought of that.

"Cats are funny," I said.

"Yeah my cats want to go outside in the winter but I won't let 'em. At night they see those bats and they want to go out and hunt, but it's too cold."

"Bats?" I said.

"Feels just about as cold as night out here today," the old man said.

I nodded, trying to think of a way to bring the conversation back around to my question.

"That's a nice coat," he said.

"Oh. Thank you." I decided to be blunt. "I'm looking for somebody."

The old man got a faraway look on his face as if he was trying to block that out.

"His name's Eliot? Or maybe he doesn't go by that now. He's around thirty, tall, dark, thin." I realized I was probably describing a lot of the men in the neighborhood.

He chewed on his lower lip. "Yeah, I don't know."

I reached in my purse and pulled the picture out. "This picture is like ten years old, but have you seen anybody who looks like that?"

The old man glanced at it, or maybe he didn't. Now he seemed to be looking me over.

"It's nice to have a hood. Then you don't need a hat."

Why the obsession with the coat? "I don't really use it," I told him.

The old man nodded. "I can't afford a coat right now. When I get money I'll get myself another coat. Not a wool one though."

It occurred to me that he might be trying to barter for the coat, trade it for what he knew. "You should go to a thrift store," I said, trying to gauge his reaction. "That's where I got this one."

"Yeah. I have to pay rent on my apartment." He put his thumb over his shoulder. "I live over the shop."

I looked up at a steel staircase that ended in a banged-up door. I nodded, and then noticed he seemed to be waiting for me to say something. "Nice."

"Yeah. My apartment has a window where it looks out on the street. My cats, they see the cars out there and they think it's bugs on the window."

"Really?" I said.

"They like cars. They watch 'em off the back of the couch."

"Huh." I shook the photo idly, trying to get his attention back to it.

He glanced down at it then back at me. He blew air into his hands. "Hard to stay warm on a day like this," he said.

I stood there indecisively, watching him look past me. Should I offer him my coat? It would never fit him. And it was my favorite coat.

"Somebody's pulling up," he said.

I turned and leaned forward to see around the back of the church. A black car was pulling up to the curb. Shiny, chrome trim, spoiler—it looked brand new, except for the mass of silver duct tape over the front bumper.

"I seen him before," said the old man, as the driver got out and came around the hood. There was something about the car that looked familiar. Had I seen it before? "He works in that Chinese grocery around the corner. I go in there sometimes."

I could see now that it was the Chinese guy, the one I had seen on my visit to the store, and who I assumed Bobby had been to visit with the briefcase.

"You ever been there?" he asked, turning to me with a little smile.

I nodded and glanced back over my shoulder, afraid he might see me. He was going up the church lawn toward the steps. Did that mean somebody was in there? Or was he meeting someone?

"You should ask him," said the old man.

I looked back at him. "Ask him?"

"About your friend." There was an odd look on his face now—something wily about his smile. Or was that just the way he smiled? I pointed back at the photo.

"Ask him about him?"

He nodded. "I seen him go in that grocery. When he come they don't let me stay. They kick me out."

"They kick you out of the grocery?"

His smile wavered a little. "The back part. Behind the curtain."

I tried to picture a curtain. I didn't remember seeing one.

The Chinese guy was coming back down the stairs again. I felt a momentary rush of panic as I watched him stride toward his car. He was leaving. Should I try to go out there and talk to him?

"That's a nice coat he has," said the old man.

He was already going around the hood, pressing down some duct tape over the caved-in front corner.

"Looks like he needs some body work."

I wondered if I should follow him. If he went to the grocery, I could go in and talk to him. The engine revved roughly to life.

"You know I seen him do that."

I glanced at the old man. There was something new in his tone. "Do what?" I said.

He nodded out toward the car as gas sucked through the wheezing engine. "Ran right into a car on this road not two weeks ago."

My heart gonged in my chest.

"Saw it out my window. Got me this scratch," he said, putting out a knobby hand with a crusty red scab on it. "Cat didn't like it none bit." The old man huffed out an amused breath. "Cat thought it was comin' for him."

I watched the car pull away from the curb. He had fled the accident. But why? It wasn't his fault. Suddenly I had the urge to trot to my car. "I have to go," I said, turning to the old man.

He nodded, like he knew that already.

"Get yourself a coat," I suggested as I stepped away.

He snorted. "Maybe. Not today anyway."

I threw a wave over my shoulder and hurried to my car, then sat waiting for the lanes to empty so I could do a U-turn back in the direction the black car had gone. I tried to remember the name of the street from the road atlas. When I got going I passed two streets I didn't recognize and then came to Harbor Street. That was it. I turned left, and there were all the landmarks I remembered—Rhonda's Burgers and the paint store and the auto body shop. When I found the grocery there were no cars in the lot, but I hadn't seen his car the last time I was here either, the day Bobby had been to visit him. He probably parked in the spaces behind the building. I took a deep breath and steadied my nerves, trying to think of a plan.

I was parked right in front of the heavy glass window where I remembered the register to be, staring at its fishtank murk. Nothing but dim shapes inside. I hoped nobody was at the counter. I got out and walked toward the door and opened it gently so the bell wouldn't jingle, and then braced the door as it pulled closed. I was alone at the front of the store. I looked down the long counter to the back wall and saw a curtain. Black, or maybe dark blue. On either side of it were two metal posts like those in a movie theater, with a red velvet cord draped between each pair. On the wall above the curtain was a sign drawn in black marker, *ADULT XXX*. Oh. Was that why the old man had given me that smile? The hours posted said *3 P.M. TO 12 A.M.* I checked my watch. Lucky me. It looked as if the storage closet for porn had opened for business ten minutes ago.

As I headed for it I instinctively ducked my head. I heard loud shifting sounds down one of the grocery aisles, like somebody was stocking shelves. I wondered what the shopkeeper, Lin, had to do with this little enterprise inside her store. Maybe this smutty entrepreneur was family, a son or a nephew. Whoever he was, it didn't bode well that he had fled the scene of an accident that wasn't even his fault. Maybe he was driving without a license or insurance. I was hoping I could use that as some kind of leverage if I needed it. I was at the curtain now. I pinched it open and stepped into a dim little alcove, with brown walls and maroon carpet adhered to the concrete floor, the color of a movie theater. I was alone in the room.

Directly across from me was about eight feet of wall covered in plywood shelves. Under a sign that said *Films*, DVDs were placed like books in a bookcase, only their titles showing. Under a sign that said *Baseball* were shelves of binders full of what I assumed were baseball cards. There was another sign that said *Hockey*. It was like the disgorged contents of a teenage boy's room. The air was stale and warm, the product of some heat vent working overtime, and a grimy fan mounted in the corner of the ceiling blew a tepid breeze on me. A desk sat on the wall to my left, with a miniature TV on it. Next to it was a door standing barely ajar. After several moments of silent listening I heard a distant rummaging coming from the crack in the door—probably a basement. I wondered if I should go back out and try again in a few minutes. Then I heard footsteps coming up stairs.

He came into view holding a box that looked heavy. When he saw me his expression went from an effortful frown to a startled flinch, and then a hard slick flatness seeped over all this features.

"Oops, I'm sorry," I said reflexively, then regretted it. In the car on the way over, I had told myself to be tough from the start.

He dumped the box on the floor and swiped his hands down his chest to brush off the dust. He was wearing a white collared shirt turned up jauntily at the cuffs and a maroon sweater vest and faded black jeans, a preppy stylish look that was somehow sinister on him. Maybe it was the fact that he stood rigidly with all his muscles flexed, emanating hostility. He didn't even muster up a hello.

"I'm looking for somebody," I said. "I heard that you know him."

He seemed displeased by this and walked toward the desk, then drove a hand through the glossy black tuft of hair that was leaning softly back off his forehead. The hand made a sharp plunge down and was by his side again.

I took the picture out and walked it over to him. "Maybe you could tell me where I can find him? It's an old picture," I said. "I think he lives over—"

"I've never seen him," he said flatly, looking down at the photo.

I tried not to be deterred. "Are you sure? I was told that he comes here."

He furrowed his brow as if perplexed. "Whoever told you that is wrong."

I considered this. The old man could have been wrong.

"Maybe you don't recognize him from the photo," I said. "He's older—"

"Who are you?" he said.

"Who am I?"

"Yeah—who are you? Why are you asking me about this person? Who sent you here?"

"Who sent me here?"

He crossed his arms over his chest and looked menacingly at me, apparently waiting for me to stop repeating his questions. I tried to call up the explanation I had rehearsed in the car ride over.

"He's my brother," I said. "I just found out he was living around here. I want to find him."

"He's your brother?" He had a look of cautious curiosity on his face now. He glanced back at the photo. "Does he know you're looking for him?"

"I don't think so." Now that I thought about it, he might.

He paused. "Do you think he would want you to find him?"

"I don't see why he wouldn't," I lied. I had no idea if Eliot wanted me to find him or not.

He looked at me for a moment as if he was considering something, and then in a sharp gesture he cracked all the knuckles in his right hand at once against the palm of his left hand. It was like a firecracker going off, and I jumped. This seemed to amuse him and he smirked. "I don't know him," he said with a shrug. "Why don't you ask at that body shop."

"Why would they know?" I asked.

He seemed to be caught off guard by this question. "You said he was one of those gypsies."

"Actually, I don't think I said that."

Now he looked uncomfortable. "He looks like one," he said, glancing at the picture.

"Does he work at the auto body shop?" I asked.

"I said I don't know him," he snapped.

"Then why were you asking me about whether he'd want to see me?"

He gave me a piercing look. "I don't have time for this. I have to work."

I looked around the room as if to ask him what work he could possibly have to do in here.

There was a look of nervous agitation on his face now, and he came around the desk and walked over to the box he had brought up. I watched him pull the tucked flaps open. Inside was what looked like a sliding mass of magazines. He was trying to ignore me.

"I know you know him," I said.

"Either buy something or go," he said without looking up.

I took a deep breath, dreading what I was about to do next. "That car you're driving," I said. "I took the license number down."

He glanced up at me, eyes narrowed. "What?"

I told myself to exhale. "It ran into my father's car a couple weeks ago." My nerves were buzzing so hard they rattled my teeth. "Out on that street by the church you visited today."

He dropped his arms. "What the fuck," he said. "You're following me?"

"I was in the car when you hit us." My voice was scudding through a clenched throat, trying to get out and be done with it. "I have another witness who saw it too. I could press charges."

"I don't know what the fuck you're talking about."

I felt myself cock my head at him, like a curious dog. *Really?* His expression seemed jittery, little twitches under the stone surface. My growing incredulity was like a bite of something too big, riding up inside me. "You don't remember how your brand-new car got wrecked?"

"Fuck," he said, pulling both hands through his hair. Then he looked at me with a grimace. "Some fucking white supremacist assholes stole it. They brought it back like that the next day."

Oh. I found myself coughing down the imaginary obstruction. I wondered if I should believe what he said. Then I wondered if it mattered. "I guess..." I said, talking into my balled fist, "if you didn't report it stolen..." From the look on his face I could see that he hadn't.

"Well, okay." This really was agonizing. "Since you didn't report it, nobody's going to believe it wasn't you driving." A guilty grimace spread my mouth wide.

"Are you serious?"

I kept having to swallow that big clot of flexed muscle back down my throat. "I don't think you want to be charged with a hit and run." I sounded like I was sympathizing with him. "And my father has some pretty steep hospital bills."

He shook his head and glared at me for a long tense moment. "Bitch," he said. "You bitch."

I let that pass, my breath edging in and out of my pinched throat. It was not the first time I'd had to take that word in the face. I couldn't help thinking of my college boyfriend, how he used to use that word with affection. What a mess, I thought.

I held my smile, trying to steel myself against all that inner susceptibility, all that benign acceptance that always made power so remote to me. I tried to think of my mother. She knew how to wield power, even when it wasn't hers. Power was just a state of mind. "I think you should tell me where to find him," I said.

Still, it had sounded so polite.

He looked away, staring at the fan on the ceiling. "Fuck," he said. "Ahhh fuck."

This seemed like progress. I put my hands in my pockets, letting the silence whittle at him for a bit. I noticed how warm I was getting in my coat.

"I don't know where he is right now."

I felt a surge of triumph. So he did know him.

He was reaching into his pocket, and before I knew what was happening he had his phone in his hand and was tapping the screen. "He won't answer my calls." He put the phone up to his ear.

"Wait. What are you doing?" No, I thought. Don't do this on the phone.

He gave me a peevish glance and didn't answer. He seemed to be listening to it ring. I found myself holding my breath, hoping Eliot wouldn't answer. I didn't want to do it like this. I didn't want some quick introduction and then a phone in my hand and my brother on the other end.

He shook his head at me and ended the call. "I can give you his number." His offer had the sound of something sour, like the words tasted bad. He seemed to know this wasn't very good. I wondered if my brother ever picked up his phone.

Was there something better I could ask for? I took out my phone and opened a new contact. Maybe he knew more than he was saying. I didn't even know if he had really called him. "How do you know my brother?" I asked.

He didn't look up. Maybe he was pretending not to hear me. He started reading off numbers and I hurriedly tapped them in.

"Give me yours too," I said.

He gave me a sharp glance. "Why? How does it help you to have my fucking number?"

I shrugged. "I won't call it unless I have to. Like maybe you lied to me and this isn't his number. Maybe I need to tell you that I'm reporting you to the police for a hit and run. Who knows?"

He narrowed his eyes at me and shook his head. He seemed to be waiting for me to change my mind. I raised my eyebrows in a *go ahead* expression.

"This is fucked up." He gave me the number and I put it in under a new contact.

"What's your name?" I said.

He blew out a scornful jet of air. "Ian."

I typed in IAN XXX. Fine. Good. "I'm going to test it right now," I said, and made him show me the incoming call on his phone.

"Are we fucking done here?"

I looked at the two numbers in my phone. I tried to figure out if this was all I wanted from him. Somehow it gave me a sinking feeling to see those digits, sharp and remote at once. What was I going to say? *Hey, how you been doing bro? Glad to know you're alive and totally avoiding me.* The phone went into my pocket.

"For now," I said.

19

IT WAS SIX O'CLOCK AND ALMOST DARK. I HADN'T TURNED ON A LIGHT in my apartment. I liked the way night slid in at this time, how it made me feel like I was going underwater, slowly, without fear. The deepening sky was like one big slow wave washing through me, easing me out of my separateness. It was the kind of good feeling that I had to be still for, that didn't last long once I started noticing it. The streetlights flushed slowly on outside my window, and after a few moments my apartment was much darker. All the black shapes bobbed around me.

I had the phone in my hand, ready to call, but still somchow far away from doing it. I felt like I did when I was young, heavy and adrift, looking up from a book in my hand, the aqueous blue world welling around me. All those times when the darkness seeped over the page and the words got lost, and I'd find myself struggling in the midst of that delicate delay, those long slow minutes of blind reading before I finally fumbled for the lamp, shining that cone of light that would make a black wall of the night that I could turn from, rejecting this world in favor of that.

Intermittently I could hear the muted sounds of people coming up from the street below—a car door snatching open, a skittering of seed pods underfoot, the faded clink of coins, even an almost imperceptible softness, like a jacket shrugging on, a dog breathing. As apart as I felt, here was evidence of other people, all around me. It was a strange thought, when the light seemed to brew up some thick broth of seclusion. It was the same with those distant evenings too, those lapses in the dark of my room, when I would rouse to sounds that told me I wasn't alone. The flat, incessant pop of a basketball several houses down, the low sinuous thrum of clarinet practicc, thc distant clatter from the boys on the corner, circling the curb with their skateboards—my brother probably among them, probably getting flicked with ash from my mother's filched cigarettes, ready to come home with evidence of some fresh assault. I remembered how he used to shamble down the hallway, hover in my doorway as if maybe he was going to say something, and through the fog of reading I would register that bleak and needy pause, tugging at me gently, waiting, and then before I had quite dragged myself up to shallow waters he'd be gone, his door shutting down the hall. A lot of those times, I'd be coming around in the aftermath of this, waking on that very shoreline of afternoon and evening, when another sound would finish what my brother had started. I could almost hear it still, the scuffing that was right there in my ear, raspy and close—such a secret, insinuating sound that I sensed its private communication before I heard it, like a static hiss in the dream I was waking from. Then I became aware of myself, sitting sideways at the foot of my bed, back against the wall, head propped on the jutting sill, a crag of pain streaking out as I lifted it away. I would listen, perking my ears, and if I turned in time I could usually just make out her black, skewered shadow whisking away, a moving thicket of darkness—the old woman.

Some nights—and this was the part that made my heart catch—another shadow would meet her on the sidewalk, one that was hard enough to pry out of the darkness that it often felt imagined, but if I could catch it gliding down our walk I could follow it all the way to her side, like a dummy rolling out on greased wheels, a black bending form that seemed to extend out a limb and brush the woman's sleeve, and then an exchange, a handoff.

I knew it was a handoff because I'd seen her do it from the kitchen too. If she happened to look out the window at the right moment, she'd clutch a towel in her hands to blot away the residue of whatever task she'd been doing and grab something—a banana, a bag of roasted nuts that Boris had been eating—and go swiftly out the side door. I would watch, and my mother would hand over the food and the woman would take it, her shaggy head turning vaguely and her hand lifting obediently, her feet still shambling along. I always wondered, Did she eat the banana? Did she even know she had it?

For those long moments after the two shadows had melted apart I stayed wondering, How did a woman like that keep living?

I hadn't thought of that woman in a long time.

She lived across the back alley and two houses down, the one with the yellow fiberglass overhang on the back porch and an old, self-standing ladder that rose like a staircase to nothing, perhaps the remnant of some long-abandoned gutter project, evidence of a time when home maintenance was still on her mind. I could look down into her backyard from our dining room window and inventory the precarious mound of teetering objects that seemed to spill little by little out the sliding glass door—metal chairs and small appliances, various hoses and canisters, an overturned exercise bike, a portable dishwasher, planters covered in heavy mustard macramé, a wooden stool made to look like a chicken, white dowels and brass poles from some previously dismantled furniture. We had to pull the curtains all summer long to block out the blinding flare of sun on metal—and sometimes I suspected that those polite-sized aluminum foil casserole pans I'd seen neighbors walking around the block were what was catching the light, sliding down the pile and lodging partway into crevices, glinting their goodwill up the long slope of our backyard.

On Sundays sometimes I'd catch Susan and Paul from up the street—a childless couple who worked at the university—go by with one of those pans, after church probably, and I couldn't help thinking of my mother, her darting shadow and cloaked generosity, compared to this cooked meal and deliberate journey, these citizens conducting their charity by the light of day the way normal people did. The only reason I was outside to see it was because my mother would strand me out here, descending unexpectedly on my musky reading corner, her hand a stiff talon on my neck, snatching me up and thrusting me through the living room and letting me loose on the porch with a command to move my limbs, get some exercise. I'd sit in the grass, jittery and anxious, pulling up tough blades and trying to make that reedy whistle Eliot was so good at, then furtively nibbling them down, the fleshy tubes at the bottom of the stalk leaking bittersweet juice into my mouth. Soon I'd cast an eye at all the dandelions growing up in the tough grass on the other side of our driveway, fiendish with temptation, and decide to do some weeding.

I'd settle down under the tree and start sampling the fuzzy choking head of a dandelion, looking on cagily as Paul and Susan strolled in my direction. One or both of them gave me a smile that I had seen already enough times to know that they were trying for my sake to pretend I didn't make them uncomfortable.

"How's that lollipop tasting?" Paul asked once, and I nodded, making my face big and innocent as if I were six, and not thirteen, but then I pulled it out as if I didn't know how it got there. Spores stuck to the roof of my mouth like hair. I made a spitting sound.

"I'm playing a game," I told them, in a voice that sounded oddly belligerent to my ears when it was spoken out here to their open, expectant faces. But it was my normal voice.

Paul nodded. I tried not to flinch away from the guttering sheen in their eyes as they wondered what exactly was wrong with me, if my condition was nutritive or mental, if I was a candidate for charity casseroles or something else.

"Natalie, right?" said Susan, her pace slowing, but indecisively, not sure she wanted to prolong this moment. I didn't answer. Their friendliness made them seem afraid of me. I gave them a face-splitting grin to show how offended I was.

When they passed I followed them, skulking behind parked cars and trees, making a game of it, hearing snatches of conversation that were as peculiar to me as this organized undertaking—Susan's voice saying something in a low, melodious lilt, Paul responding with a smile in his voice, ducking his head to laugh. Their intimacy made me uncomfortable. It was like they were amused by each other's company, like they had never outgrown some high school infatuation.

Around the corner and looking on at the speckled siding of the old lady's house, I watched them pick their way up the walk between a thicket of old sunflower stalks and weeds, a mix of tough green and nodding yellow and brown flaking chaff, baked dry from multiple seasons of neglect. After ringing the bell, they stood for a long time on the porch.

The woman was not coming to the door. I was sure of it. What did she know about doorbells?

But then, a greenish dishwater murk parted the white facade, and Susan's voice carried across the street. The woman's head bobbed in the middle of it, a sizzled cloud of white, dissolving in a toxic gloom.

I'd seen her in daylight before, pacing back and forth in front of the neighborhood grocery store, one white leather shoe in her hand. She was bony and tensile, skin like a cooked hot dog, race and age indeterminate, arms twitching and batting at invisible airborne irritants, fingers scratching away at scaly brown scabs all over her bare arms and neck. I remember how my mother swept past as if she hadn't seen her.

I tried to point her out. "Isn't that the—"

My mother turned and gave me a look that said to shut up.

What? I thought, looking back at her. *Wasn't that the woman?*

Now I knew it was her, coming out of her dark house like a spider, stepping tremulously between the do-gooders and continuing down her own stairs, her arms flicking at the open air, pausing, turning back at Susan's voice, coming back up. Paul had a smile on his face that I could see from across the street. A brown cat came out on the porch and curled around his leg like an eel, and he turned and looked down at it a second before twitching it away. I watched Susan hold the offering out. The woman lifted a fidgety arm and fumbled with the pan as if she only vaguely understood the rules of the exchange, and then Susan thought better of it and stepped to the threshold, saying something to the woman, trying to get her to follow. As they waded in I imagined her taking the dish through the living room to the kitchen, winding around piles of unopened mail and soggy newspapers, picking her way across a shag carpet dotted with cat feces, strewn leather shoes and handbags, dust and grit granulating the air, hairballs, tufts of fur, her breath held at the deep sweet reek of cat musk, rotten food, last week's casserole, and every banana my mother had ever given her. I felt my jaws working, the muscle clotting up deep in the back of my throat. Suddenly, and senselessly, I wanted to go in that house. I wanted to delve through the evidence, inventory the refuse, pluck up clues, sniff and scratch at the tragic bouquet that I was sure was this woman's life.

I never had grandparents. I never got to wander the cool musty grottoes of knickknacks and memorabilia, solemnified by the loud ticking of ageless clocks. All I had were the stories my mother told about her mother—fierce hair rituals and cleaning superstitions that made her both whiskery and bald, a love of sardines, a blinking terror of white dogs. The spatula that she used to slap her children's faces with, whipping it right off the hot pan, its melted plastic cooking a cheek and a bit of ear, frying strands of hair down to brittle sprigs—my mother describing it with more reverence than revulsion. There was the way my mother had gazed, with a delicate stillness in her face, that afternoon in the aisle of the grocery store when she found a near replica, its plastic springy as she flexed it against her palm, turning it on her own arm with a stiff whack that made my shoulders jump, and told me who she was thinking of. I remember how she looked at me, her eyes going dull.

"What?" I said.

She dropped the spatula back into the bin with a tired flick of her hand. What a shame, she seemed to be saying, not even acknowledging my actual presence so much as looking through me to her own private thoughts. And then I wondered, Did she miss her mother? Was she looking at me and wishing for a daughter who could make up for that absence?

There was another habit she had, of noticing old women wherever we went. She seemed to be trying to make up for something, letting them ahead of her in lines at the credit union, giving them the fruit she had just picked when they came up beside her at the produce bin, opening doors and pulling carts free for them, usually confusing them with her terse, unsmiling solicitude, her odd mixture of deference and standoffishness that didn't want to make anything social or friendly out of it. It was as if she was doing this thing for somebody else, making due with flimsy stand-ins and warning them not to intrude. She never said anything about it, but I felt oddly like I knew a lot more about her in those moments than I could have explained. Her intense and superstitious regard was something to count on, something I had come to count on without knowing it.

But that day so many years ago, when she ignored the old woman, my thirteen-year-old self was left at a loss. I had fully expected her to lean into our cart and whack open a plastic bag to find some food item she could walk over and put in the lady's free hand. But instead she passed by.

When she ignored my questions I said, "Don't you recognize her? She's the one who lives around the corner—"

A silencing gaze stopped me again. I looked back. It wasn't even the point that she lived around the corner. The point was that she was here. The woman my mother fed in the dark outside our house, now plainly in range of her old-lady compulsions and badly in need of something. She could not overlook her. She could not change the rules.

"Look at that," said my brother, his voice glassy and private. He was high or low on something, and had spent the whole time at the store shivering and tossing his head, pushing more pills into his mouth when my mother wasn't looking. He had that wet-clay look and that pungent art-room smell, and he kept putting his arm around me and taking it back off until my lower back ached and I wanted to shove him down. By the time we left the store I was so sick of him that I was gnawing my fingertips raw. My mother would not look at me. Was she mad because of Eliot?

"Lots of people give her food. Susan and Paul take her casseroles every week," I said. I wasn't sure why, but I wanted to irritate her.

My mother made a noise, unimpressed, vaguely disapproving, and opened the trunk.

"What?" I said, staying back while the smell belched out—warm and moldy from years of soggy upholstery that never dried. Our trunk had a leak, and the rusty water pooled in the depressions around the wheel wells. "It's better than you."

I expected a distracted lashing for this, maybe a smack on the temple with the butt of her hand. But my mother leaned into the trunk with a grocery bag, shaking her head. She stepped away and pointed into the cart. "Do the rest."

I glanced at my brother, staring over the roof of our car, taking shallow breaths through a slit in his mouth.

"Why do you even care about that woman?" I asked.

She pulled out a cigarette, gave me one of those crushing stares, like a wall of hard water coming down on me. "Natalie. Don't talk to me."

I watched her flick the lighter on in the same hand that still held the box of Newports. I stared at the box. *Where's my case?* I wanted to ask.

"What did I just tell you."

My brother made a low, huffing noise and slumped down to rest his cheek on the corroded top of the car. I looked from him to my mother, and my heart curled like some hammered-down scrap of metal. "I hate you," I said. The words came out and my mouth felt empty and puckered, like a hole of dry sand.

My mother, without seeming too disturbed, grabbed a handful of my hair and yanked it. She jerked my head into the foul-smelling trunk and for a second I thought she'd slam the lid right down on my neck. I felt my mouth fill with liquid, so much that it all came flowing out onto the plastic grocery bag under my face, a loose stream of drool, then she let go and my head snapped backward. I stood back, woozy, a bolt of pain in my neck and my scalp searing.

She got in the car and turned it on. I watched dumbly as my brother stirred at the vibrations and lifted his head and looked at me. His eyes were black and shimmering with a blind, reptilian heat.

"So," he said, in a strange upward lilt, his eyes tracking back and forth aimlessly across my face, as if it were part of some distant setting, "I'm probably going," and then he ducked his head and got in the car. The trunk was still open. I sank down on the curb.

We all sat for a long time in silence, breathing the gas fumes puttering out of our rusted exhaust pipe. I chewed on my hair and my mother smoked with the window open. My brother's head sunk out of sight.

"The ice cream's melted," she finally said.

I got up and fished it out of a bag in the cart. I turned and threw it over the row of cars parked behind us and heard it thump on the grass on the other side. I dumped the remaining bags in the trunk, slammed the lid down hard and got into the backseat, far away from my brother's wilted figure at the window, wanting to get this ride over with, wishing now I hadn't prolonged it. I should have admitted sooner that the only way my mother would have left me here was if I had wanted her to stay. I sat gnashing my teeth in fury the whole ride home, wishing for a car accident that would kill us all. When we were back on our street, my mother rolled up her window and ground her cigarette in the ashtray. "I'm dropping you off," she said.

I didn't say anything. All the words felt blown out of me and I wanted to die.

She pulled up at the curb and rolled to a stop. I opened the door.

"Natalie."

I didn't turn and neither did she.

"Is your brother breathing."

I looked at him, face squashed into the crevice behind the window, mouth yanked open by upholstery. He could be dead, I thought. I gave her eyes in the rearview a hard angry look and closed the door.

As I walked up the lawn my heart spun and clattered in my chest, like a disorienting, directionless game of pinball.

"If your father asks," my mother called out the window, her steady voice like the pit that sucks the ball down with a clunk, "tell him I went to get Chinese."

It occurred to me now that my mother might have been being merciful, letting me out in front of the house, not making me wait those forty minutes in the purple aquarium lights of the Chinese restaurant as punishment for my insolence, not confiscating my allowance to pay for it as she would normally have done. I knew it was my fault she was getting takeout—I had kept her too late at the store. But she clearly had more on her mind than that. Now I wondered, What had happened after I had slammed the front door behind me and marched into the blank, humming silence of the kitchen, feeling suddenly hot all over? Did she turn and lean into the backseat to check his breathing before driving off? Did she decide whether it would be the hospital or Chinese? How did she get him to wake up? Did she yank him out of his delirium and drag him into the restaurant? Did she turn to him under those red lacquer fans, slippery in the shrill light, and say in her voice, *I'm going to tell you something. You can't repeat this to your father.*

Because I still remember that meal, the crumbled texture of the rice going to my mouth, like the desiccated larvae of some prolific insect, my whole meal inedible as I watched Eliot, strangely revived and ravenous, slurping his flavorless broth with a jovial bob of his head, Boris popping dumplings in his mouth and eyeing us all sharply as if there was some secret he could cut out of us.

I remember his mouth opening just a second before the phone blistered over the silence. We never answered calls at home because none of us had social reasons to receive them—they were all either telemarketers or political advertisements—and I put another bite in my mouth, hearing my father say something cranky and suspicious about my brother's sweaty face, which he kept swiping with the sleeve of his sweatshirt, and that was when my mother got up and answered the phone.

20

"HELLO?"

A jolt went through me. Somebody had finally answered the number I'd coerced from Ian.

"Oh, shit. Never mind. Not my phone."

"Wait—" I blurted, but she had already hung up. After years of not speaking to my brother, I'd been afraid I wouldn't recognize his voice. But the person on the other end made it easy for me. It was a woman. I called back. The phone rang and rang and rang.

For almost a week now I'd been calling the number. Every time I dialed I was afraid that he was going to pick up, the sound of his voice whirling me into a moment of no return, and every time I ended up listening to the ringing go on forever. A dull, mechanical trilling, both near and far—like an echo extending into some long gray tunnel, taking me in and leaving me there.

"No not her—!" Salt yelled too loudly at my side, and I jumped. We were at a downtown intersection, recruiting fans for our beloved weatherman spot. I glared at his profile as he criticized the prospects walking by—the little purses under his eyes, the steep length of his nose, just a narrow nub of flesh over a bare hatchet of bone. "She's too ratty—not our demographic—looks like a street person. Hello there! How are you, miss?"

The subject gave us a pinched look as she hurried by, her fluted patchwork skirt flapping at her ankles. I smiled awkwardly. Ray was mouth breathing down at the camera as he made adjustments.

Finally, I thought, there had been a glimpse of light—strange, aslant, the disappointing slope of a voice I didn't expect. But still, someone was there.

Salt shooed at the next pedestrian even as she tried to ignore us. "No—another one—this is all wrong. Why are we here by the college?"

"We're not by the college." Ray's husky voice, barely polite. "We want to get the new museum building in the back. Could you just—"

Salt cut him off, "Oh, there, let me grab those two."

"Nat, what's going on? Who's on the phone?"

Just checking something, I mouthed to Ray.

I hit redial. The broken staccato blips of sound were still falling, falling, falling. *Pick up,* I thought as Ray rolled his eyes and started after Salt. I was on phase two of my calling plan: having established that my brother was not answering during the afternoon and evening times that I had been incessantly calling, I was trying other times of day. Now there was superstition at work too—maybe if I called at a time that was inconvenient to me, fate would have him pick up.

"Mr. Pfeiffer. Nat, he's walking away."

I hung up. Salt, hair ruffled by a breeze, was striding up to two women who were looking off down the street, poised to part ways, one with her finger pointed as if she were giving directions.

"We won't be able to use it. He's still in his coat."

"He's done segments in his coat before."

"Have you seen that fucking thing? Coffee dribble all over it. Some crusty snot smear that picks up the light. You have to get him to take it off or we're wasting our time."

I bit my rubbery phone casing, trying to strategize as I watched Salt perform his Bob Barker tilt over the two women, fingers barely grazing the elbow of the one in the teal beret. He said something and with mannequin grace began rotating them in our direction, even as the one was warmly effusing and rearing back with a joyful blurt of his name. Nothing was coming to me. Salt was clucking some response, solicitously sweeping them along as the women, looking at each other, shrugging and smiles faltering, seemed a bit befuddled. It was cold out. Everybody was wearing coats—it would not look right if Salt was without one. His was light camel hair, and Ray was right, the last trip to the dry cleaner had not worked its usual wonders. Chili and onion soup, coffee, dandruff, and some kind of gluey lacquer that very well could have been snot, but might have just been doughnut icing, plus there was a sludge of gray where a cigar had plopped its ash—it looked like a coat only a destitute would privilege for its warmth. Like the old man I had met behind the church. But he had those cats. No natural hair coats for him.

"Hello ladies," I said, dropping my phone in my pocket.

"Hellooo." One of the women, approaching, pulling the word long as she closed in on us. Her enthusiasm had mellowed to a slightly withholding geniality.

Ray said, "Mr. Pfeiffer—"

"These women knew me right away. They said, 'Salt Pfeifer, my favorite weatherman,' and I said, 'That's exactly what you can tell the camera if you just step over here.'"

"Well, that's not exactly what we said—" The shorter woman shook her head, as if to press reset on her words, and smiled stiffly. She was wearing a bulky black scarf, so thick her chin was resting in it.

"Ma'am," I said, and as I spoke I thought I felt a buzz against my thigh. "If you could remove your scarf for the shot..."

"Oh. I guess."

The buzz came again. My phone, swaddled in layers of heavy cloth, was ringing. I stuffed my hand into my pocket—where was it? My fingers caught on the hole in the seam. It had slipped through into the lining. With the ladies staring at me, I lifted the bottom of the coat up toward the pocket to get my fingers on the phone. *Hurry.* There was a crunch of something else in my hand, loose and sliding, more than one thing in the lining—some change? I pinched the phone by its corner and fished it out.

"Should I just—" The woman had unlooped the scarf and was holding it uncertainly now.

"I'll hold it, out of the way for you," I offered, looking down at the incoming number.

At the sight of the digits I felt myself go stiff, like a sudden onset of tetanus. My jaw cranked tight. I felt the scarf pile its warmth into my cold hand. My brother was calling me back.

I looked up, as if I wanted someone to see my need and answer me, and the woman's eyebrows spiked up uncertainly. Salt had stepped up and was impatiently hovering, an irritable vampire. "Let's not delay."

"Do you—" The woman pointed at the phone. "Is that a call?"

Propelled by her question, I pressed the answer button as Salt held his arm out for her in an impatient yet gracious arc, the hand itching for her shoulder, white and raw knuckled, a flutter of long fishy fingers. "If you'll just turn this way, miss."

There was a pause during which I should have said hello.

"So, both of you will say exactly what Mr. Pfeiffer just said—" Ray barked frost into the air.

"Hello?" It was the woman's voice again.

"No, I said I wanted only the one to speak," Salt moaned.

"Hellu-oh. Can you hear me?" The voice was high and seemed to melt around the words—everything liquid. "Eliot? Is this you? Who are you with?"

"What are you doing, Ray?"

Eliot? Why would she think that? I let out a percussive breath, almost an answer, staring hard as Ray's hand fluttered and snapped at the air in my direction.

"I wasn't looking through your phone, I swear," the voice kept going. "I just kept seeing this fucking number come up *all the time* and then suddenly I thought, *Is it him?* Don't be mad."

With the phone to my ear, I followed the urgent directive of Ray's hand, plunging forward and lifting the hand he was gesturing at, confused momentarily to see the scarf in it, and then stalling as he pointed at Salt and then made some tugging motion around his own neck.

"What are you doing—" Salt was asking. "No, don't bring her—"

"Fuck you, are you even going to say something?"

"Let Nat help with the shot, Mr. Pfeiffer. Nat, get off the damn phone."

"Wait—" I cleared my throat. "I'm Eliot's sister. I'm trying to get—"

"You're going to say 'My favorite weatherman!'—a little enthusiasm, you know," Ray's voice was loud and brisk, cutting mine off. The silence on the phone was so deep I thought she might have hung up. "And please everyone I need your attention this way."

"Hello?" I said. "Don't hang up again."

"I'll count down from three," Ray said, holding up three fingers, everyone stiff and waiting for me to do something, I realized, with the scarf I was holding.

"You start speaking right after the third finger goes down," he told them. "Nat hurry up with that."

"I'm trying to get in touch with him," I said as I lunged forward hastily into the shot. "Do you know where I can find him?" Then I ducked behind the trio and draped half of the scarf over Salt's far shoulder, still getting those perplexing nods from Ray, wrapped it behind his neck and brought it down flat on the other side. The woman whose scarf it was, smiling into the camera, twitched her head slightly but didn't turn to verify what I had just done.

"You said sister?" said the voice. It was cautious.

I stepped out of the shot, to the side and back, turning away so as not to distract the women, the phone still pressed against my ear. "Yes."

"Shit I—never mind. I'm not even supposed to be on this phone. He's—I mean for all I know he's dead."

"What?" I said. *Dead?*

"Exactly!" Salt's voice jumped in. "Only this one should speak. That's what I was saying. You get the two of them saying it together they'll sound like giddy schoolgirls. We want a mature—"

"Excuse me." I looked up from my phone. I registered the face of the woman whose scarf I had taken—her chin drawn back into her now bare neck. "Do you just want me out of the way? I don't need to be in this at all. Trust me."

"No," said Salt, "you stay. For balance. You're very attractive—just don't talk."

The teal beret snapped open her mouth and then, startlingly, caught my eye and laughed. "Oh my word." Southern accent, lilting and clear. I stared. What was happening here?

"Mr. Pfeiffer, please—it's fine. Natalie—!"

I stuck the phone back in my pocket and stepped abruptly forward as the two women leaned forward to eye each other with astonished smiles. "Did he just say what I think he said?"

"Okay stop talking please. Are we all ready for another try?" Salt asked them.

I cringed and tried to figure out what my role was here. Ray looked at me with hard eyes.

"Who are these people?" the scarfless woman said to her friend. "I think I'm going to call the station. This is insulting."

Now I sensed the full crisis. Salt's reputation. My job. "Ladies—"

They were both giddy with indignation. "That's his first name?"

"Be quiet please now. Ray needs to cue us."

"Oh of course. So sorry—oh my lord he's wearing my scarf, Layne."

"Your scarf?"

Blast of air from Salt. I pressed my mouth tight. Don't make it worse.

"Oh—this is hysterical—here, he's cuing us."

Ray's fingers were in the air.

"Remember not to talk."

"You know what Layne, I'm out of here."

And before I could do anything else, the women were detaching, walking briskly away from us, threatening to call the station and report our behavior, wishing they had it on video. Flummoxed, Salt deflated, nothing but a hurt old man. "That was rude," he murmured, and swiveled his head to peer over his shoulder. He was already looking for two more victims.

21

INSTEAD OF RETURNING IMMEDIATELY TO THE STATION, I VENTURED on foot to buy a coffee. I had recouped some standing with Ray by finding two more victims for Salt and ushering them through before they could be offended, but I knew there would be consequences regardless. I wasn't in any hurry to return to the station.

I jammed my hands in my pockets and remembered the phone call. I still heard her words in my ear. *For all I know he's dead.* My fist popped a thread in the lining and actually poked through the pocket, and I let it go all the way to the bottom and fished for the loose change I'd felt there. Instead my hand closed around a cluster of metal—long notched shafts. My keys. They were always getting lost down there. I took them out. There was a red rubber tab with the name of the auto body shop printed on it, and a small gold ring. I stopped walking. These were not my keys.

These were his. Bobby's. I stood very still, letting this sift down through me. I had taken them from him. At the abandoned lot, when I went through his car. I must have put them in my pocket. Suddenly, I had a different, more urgent matter to address than buying coffee.

I parked along the street in front of the auto body shop, and before I could second-guess myself I stepped out and headed toward the business office. I could hear the loud hurried pounding of a mallet beating dents out of somebody's car in the garage as I walked over the broken asphalt, past the cars for sale and to the door. I opened it and stepped inside.

Bobby was sitting behind a counter. When he looked up his eyes widened and his head jerked back as if a string had yanked it from behind.

"Hello," I said, and was suddenly aghast at the high quiver of fear in my voice.

The air inside the little shabby room was cold and the smell of gasoline was like a thick, choking haze. I cleared my throat. I placed the ring from his key chain on the counter in front of me. I had wanted to toss it, I had imagined myself tossing it, but instead I placed it. Then I said the line I had been planning out in the car ride over—the only one that had come to me. "How about an exchange?"

He looked at the ring, then back at me, his eyes glinting with a black, fevered intensity over a pair of faded navy coveralls, the canvas scuffed and steeped in pools of brownish-green.

"Your keys, for a conversation with my brother," I continued in a quaking voice. "You know him? Eliot Krupin."

He crossed his arms over his chest and shook his head no.

"I know he wrote that note," I said. I was thinking that he might be dead. That he wasn't answering his calls.

"I can't do it."

"Yes you can." My voice shook now with more anger than nerves.

Bobby glowered at me. "No."

I breathed out a sigh, and all the rising pressure with it. "Why not?"

The phone behind the counter rang, and he put his finger up and went to answer it. I watched him roll his chair over to the computer monitor, huge and prehistorically beige, and look something up. Every few seconds his eyes darted over to me. A door opened behind him and a man in navy coveralls came into the office, letting in a volley of noises from the garage, and got some water from the cooler in the corner. I felt a jolt of alarm as I looked at the frizzy tangle of silver hair on his head. Could that be him? My mother's father, my grandfather? He was frowning deeply as he filled his cup, breathing as if he had just done some heavy exercise. He stepped back, leaving greasy fingerprints on the casing, and walked back out without even looking at me.

Bobby was typing something rapidly on the keyboard. A name tag pinched at his pocket corroborated his alias. He hung up the phone and we looked at each other.

"Give me that," he said. I had put the ring on my finger in a fit of nerves. Despite the size of the jewel, I realized now that it must be a woman's ring. It fit me perfectly. From the tense way he tilted forward in his chair I suddenly feared that he might vault over the counter and attack me for it.

"Whose is it?"

He watched me and said nothing. A loud drilling started up in the garage and I jumped. Bobby said, "It was my father's."

"He had small fingers," I said stupidly.

The drilling stopped and Bobby cracked his jaw and looked over his shoulder again. "He was a jeweler. It was the first ring he ever made. He left it to me. I want it back."

"A jeweler?" I said. "Then why aren't you a jeweler? Isn't that how it works?"

"Works how?" He held me for a moment in his large, lightless gaze, thinking something, then looked away. "The shop burned down."

I couldn't believe it. Another fire.

Something feral now had crept into his stillness, a poised intent. "Just a second," he said, and got up abruptly and went into the garage.

A few minutes later he opened the garage door, yelling out something in another language over his shoulder. There was a shouted response from inside. He swung the door shut and put his hand to the top of the file cabinet. "After you talk to him you give me the keys," he said briskly, and pulled down a flat metal tablet. He started to come around the counter at me, and it was so sudden and decisive, so all-business, that I jerked back and pushed opened the door. He stopped.

"What's going on?" I said.

"I'm taking you to see him."

Ten minutes later I stood on the steps of the church. Bobby had directed me to drive here, go into the front vestibule, and wait. This was exactly what I wanted, and yet somehow I felt like I was walking into a trap. I took one deep steadying breath and pulled the door open and stepped inside. I was plunged into the sudden darkness of a windowless space, and before I had time to adjust I had walked right onto the heels of a tiny woman. She turned and looked up at me.

"Oh. Excuse me," I said.

She gave me a little smile and looked me over. She was Asian, with small features and a silver fluff of hair. Behind her was a cluster of people crowded just inside the door, in a shabby little lightless entrance, a pair of double doors just being opened into the chapel beyond. There was sudden light, and I saw the peeling wallpaper, yellow like dried glue, with little flowers going down in vertical columns. The group began moving through the doors, and Bobby, still in his solvent-smelling coveralls, was standing just outside the threshold, impatiently directing them up to the altar. As they drifted down the creaking aisle toward the front, somebody was speaking loudly in another language. It was a woman, wearing a wedding gown, her heavy yellow hair propped on her bare shoulders like a hood. I was surprised. Was this a wedding? A man walked just behind her, dressed in a beige suit, his hair black. Something clicked. I had seen these people before. In the photos I had looked at on the gypsy's camera. The bride's name was Michelle. The groom was the guy from the Chinese grocery—Ian.

Two other women, tall and blond, had paused at the side of the entrance to let the Asian woman through, and they were speaking some Slavic language, cold and sludgy. The door opened behind me. I moved to the side, and was disturbed to see the old man I had met behind the church, bundled up like a parcel in a puffy beige coat. He gave me a vague nod, devoid of recognition, and muttered, "Cold as hell out there."

He slid his coat off and hung it on a peg beside several other outerwear items.

"Good thing it's an indoor wedding," I quipped.

He wore a dark blue suit jacket with a shirt underneath that had the browning look of paper left out in the sun. He nodded. "Not to mention—" He pinched his thumb and forefinger together and rubbed them, then went through the chapel door.

When they had all cleared the entrance and I was the only one left, Bobby looked at me and wordlessly closed the double doors in my face. Now I was standing alone in the tiny entry. To my left was a bench. To my right was a narrow table with six champagne flutes on it and a two-liter bottle of ginger ale. Beyond that, on the far wall, was a closed door.

I sat down on the bench. Twelve o'clock on a Wednesday seemed like a strange time to have a wedding. And the ginger ale and champagne flutes were an odd choice too. I looked back at the closed door. I wondered for the hundredth time what my father had done in here. Maybe he had been a wedding crasher too. Then I heard a creak from behind the door. Almost like another door was opening somewhere on the other side. A murmur, a squeak of old wood, and a huff like somebody sitting heavily, and then another voice, someone quietly responding.

I held my breath, straining to hear the other voice. Several seconds went by, my eyes burning as I stared at the door, and then there was another sharp murmur and the sound of weight on squeaky boards, as if someone were standing. The disembodied voice, so thin and high, said something into the room and I heard Bobby responding. He was in there. My brother. Talking to Bobby.

I stood up. The sounds of shifting weight turned suddenly to footsteps, echoing into the low-level murmur in the chapel. They were moving in there.

I was finished waiting—I needed to see him. On tiptoes I crossed the scuffed, creaking floor and turned the knob on the chapel door. Silently, I cracked it enough to peek through, and stood back from it, listening. I could still hear Bobby speaking between pauses, and somebody's feet were moving. It sounded as if nobody had noticed the door open. I moved my face to the crack and peered in.

I knew him instantly—the tall forehead, the long nose and chin, the nervous, quick expression on his face. He was up at the altar, behind the bride and groom, dressed in white and black robes. He was standing still and clasping a book. Bobby was busy arranging the couple, moving the bride and groom to face each other, telling them to smile, then directing my brother to open the book and speak. My brother opened his mouth, looked very grave, and in his sallow, mournful voice, he said, "Hello. Here we are. This is what it is."

My brother was speaking nonsense.

Bobby snapped pictures. He made a waving motion, and two men I hadn't noticed, hovering by a door on the far wall in sweats and t-shirts, shuffled out of the shot. After that, he came forward and gave the bride and groom each a ring, and told them to take turns putting them on. Then he told them to kiss, and while they kissed he took another picture. The people watching in the seats sat there politely, and he turned to take their picture.

"Look happy," he told them, and then he saw me. His head snapped back and he forgot to take the picture. Everybody turned to look. I took a step back from the crack, just as my brother shifted his gaze to the door. Maybe he saw me, maybe he didn't, but he was walking toward me.

"Leave it. Leave it," he said in a tight rising pitch. "You got the pictures. That's enough."

His fast footsteps clattered down the aisle and then the door opened and he was right in front of me in the entrance, all his heat, all his overpowering life, sweeping down on me. A look of surprise broke over his face as he stepped forward, and I winced, shrank back, suddenly afraid of everything I had been seeking. Then he hugged me.

22

I STOOD VERY STILL IN HIS ARMS, CHOKED BY THE FORGOTTEN NEED for his affection, waiting for this man I didn't know to become my brother again. Then I felt him kiss me on top of my head and stand back.

"My little sister," he murmured, his voice like the breaking of my own heart. "I missed her."

The moment I looked at his face I felt a sob pull up through me, and before I could stop myself I was crying. He pulled me against his chest again and clutched me there hard. "I'm sorry," he said. "I'm sorry."

After I had drained a good deal of my misery onto his chest, when there was nothing left in me but a slow, hollow ache, I stepped back. He shifted me in his embrace, walked me through the entry to the closed door, unlocked it, and led us into a small, sunlit room.

"Sit down," he said. I felt him disappear into the entry behind me, and when I turned, he was coming back in with a beige coat in his hand, puffy like the old man's. He gestured for me to sit and hung the coat on the back of the door and went to a chair behind the desk.

The chair I sat in was low and soft. I wanted to tell him it wasn't my coat.

My brother pulled his chair around and sat facing me.

I waited, squinting in the sunlight, my eyes sore. Behind him the sun was coming in the window in a bright shaft, falling across the floor and spreading halfway up a door on the far side of the room, touching the knob with a sharp pinpoint of light. I looked at it. That must have been the door that had let him into the chapel.

"Well." My brother watched me with weary eyes and a crooked grin.

I managed a smile. All the questions I had had, all the doubts and suspicions, were spinning away from me in a blur of relief. Here was my brother. Alive and well. And he was happy to see me. For the moment, that was all I cared about.

"You look good," he said, his reedy voice quaking slightly. "You look grown up."

I nodded, taking in all the familiar features: the white teeth, the quick, expressive eyes—the quiver of pain still there, yet gentler somehow, as though sometime in the last thirteen years he had left the torments of youth behind him and stepped into a better age, a better life. "So do you," I admitted.

He lifted his hands. "Better than last time you saw me." He attempted a smile that died quickly. "I've cleaned up."

"And you're a minister, or something like that."

He looked down at his robes as if he were surprised to find himself wearing them. "Oh. That's right."

"I interrupted you in there," I said apologetically.

My brother widened his eyes and looked at the door. "Oh no. We were finished. I was just doing a favor for a friend."

I didn't like the look in his eyes, the subtle shift across his face, all the human features quietly turning to wood.

"A favor?" I said.

As if I'd touched a button, my brother rapidly went into an explanation. "The bride asked us to get a few photos so she could send them overseas to her family. They got married in here last week," he said, "but they forgot their camera. They're Eastern Orthodox, so it was a big deal to have proof of a church wedding."

You're lying, I thought. As if he had read my mind, my brother leaned suddenly forward in his chair, his eyes earnest and repentant. "Anyway, not important," he said.

I wanted to hold this against him, I felt like I should hold it against him, but somehow I couldn't. I looked down at the arm of the chair, the busted seam at the edge where my fingers were already busily plucking at the yellowish froth of exposed stuffing. "So you're a gypsy now," I said, and it didn't even sound like an accusation.

My brother shrugged.

"And you've been living here since you ran away." When I said this my heart went cold as a distant star, and in this deep chill I found myself tugging some of the stuffing loose. It came out with a gentle, fibrous tear. My brother looked away from me into his lap.

"Well I didn't exactly run away."

I felt a flicker of surprise. When he didn't say anything more I asked, "What do you mean?"

"You didn't know?" Now we were both looking perplexed and expectant. My brother raised his eyebrows.

"What?" I said.

"I thought at least she might have—" He wagged his head. "Why would I ever think that? You didn't guess?"

"Guess what?"

He let out a thin breath and looked at the floor between his feet. "Okay, well Mom brought me—was bringing me. That summer, you remember?" he said, looking up.

I nodded, feeling suddenly as oblivious as Boris. Had he assumed I knew all along? Had he given hints, told me in ways I hadn't noticed? "Right," I said.

My brother went back to staring fixedly at the floor, his eyes moving rapidly across the grain, as if reading his history on the wood. "So, we both know I was in a bad place. I couldn't get straight. I was killing myself. Right? When she brought me here I didn't want to come. I was—I had no idea what to expect of these people, or what it meant coming here. I wanted to tell you about it—I did. I just—" He glanced up, pained. "Anyway, all summer she kept bringing me, and I knew something was up. I knew there was a plan they weren't telling me. I didn't even have it in me to resist. I just let it happen." He sighed. "She only did it to help me. I understand that now. She didn't know what else to do."

He was bending over his knees, his hands dangling out in front of his legs. I sat transfixed, staring at my brother's taut face, rolling my fingers around the stuffing. "So one day she left me. Locked me up, actually." The stuffing in my fingers was soft and densely packed like a cotton ball. "She had it all set up," he said. I knew what was coming. I got it over with before my brother looked up. It tasted like wadded cobwebs, like spun dust and decay.

"They tied me to a bed in a basement for three weeks. This basement, actually." He hooked his thumb over his shoulder at a door behind the desk, almost too casual. I noticed, uneasily, that there was a camera mounted over the door. My brother peered at me, his expression off, but not in a way I could read. He circled his wrist with his fingers. "That was how I got clean," he said. He waited for me to say something.

I felt too stunned to conjure a proper response. "That was how you got clean," I heard myself echo.

My brother spread his palms and breathed a sigh, as if to say, *It just is what it is.* "So I was like a prisoner for a while. The minister of this church, the man who did this to me, he was well respected. And when I came out of it he started taking me around, showing me to people." He leaned back. "I met all her relatives, all my relatives. They didn't trust me of course. I'd been living with gaje for years, and it was like I was toxic. They were careful, but they weren't mean. They seemed to want to help me. I don't know," he said, avoiding my eyes. "I've thought about this a lot and I don't know why I didn't leave as soon as he untied me. He couldn't have made me stay. At first I didn't know what to do with myself. It was like I had come out the other side of something and ended up in this other world, and there was no going back to where I had been. And I was still angry, you have to understand. I hated her for doing it. I could have left and gone somewhere else, but I had no ideas. And the people here, they took me in. Gave me a place to stay. Gave me jobs." He shrugged. "After a while I traveled, so I was in and out a lot, but I always came back."

"You came back," I said. "You traveled a lot but always come back." *Here. To them.* It dawned on me now that what I had always assumed, without realizing it, was that if he had gotten clean, if he were lucid and well, he would have come back to me, at least to explain, at least to ease my mind, maybe to ask my forgiveness. But here he was, and I had been the one to come to him.

My brother smiled. "I see you've still got your little habit."

I'd packed another tuft inside my mouth and I was tonguing it like a bit of pesky lint. I shrugged. I didn't want to be doing it right now, right here, but I was.

"I've been thinking about you lately." His smile faded as he brushed his hand through his hair, dropped it, turned his wrist in a slow circle, working out some stiffness there. "Been doing a lot of reading. Every time I read a book I think of you." He looked up, expectant.

I couldn't look at him. All the hurt I had felt when I first saw him was hardening into anger. I unzipped my purse, reached inside, found a tissue, and wiped my tongue clean. Then I pulled out the cigarette case and watched my brother's eyes dart down to it. I opened it up and unfolded the note and handed it to him.

"Who's Emilian, Eliot?"

For several seconds he fixed his gaze on the note, as if he were thinking about what it meant that I had it. Then he nodded. "She kept it."

"What does that mean, 'she kept it'?" I asked in frustration. "Why did you write her this note?"

I watched him place the note on the desk and stare down at his hands, rubbing them together slowly, deliberatively, trying to decide what to say. "First of all, I didn't want to write her that note. If I hadn't written that note none of this would have happened. Boris wouldn't have found it and come here. And you wouldn't be here right now."

I felt his words raise hackles in my heart. "Well, sorry I had to put you through this," I said, standing. "Sorry you had to see me again."

My brother gave me a look of flinching chagrin. "I wanted to see you," he said, "but I never wanted to have to tell you any of this."

He bucked forward and raked his hands through his black hair, then gestured me back into the seat. "I'll tell you," he said. "You deserve to know." His eyes floundered over my face, swift and uneasy, begging me for some understanding. I felt the hardness inside me sink away, just like it always had, just like all those times he had come home with my mother and those eyes had begged a kind of silence from me, implored me not to ask him where he'd been, not to make it real. Maybe he was right, I thought. Maybe I shouldn't have come. But it was too late now. I had to finish this.

I said, "What about Mom? Did she meet you after this note? Did she go back to see him?"

My brother looked away, his eyes bleak. "No," he said, his voice hollow and thin. "She didn't go."

That was not the answer I had expected.

He lifted his head but didn't look at me. "When she didn't show up I went to get her. It was the least she could do. And when I got to the house I found her." His eyes were fixed somewhere on the wall above me, and for a moment they touched me—bitter, glinting—and then moved away again. "She had taken all the pills in the medicine cabinet. She was in bed, a cigarette still burning beside her. That was how I found her."

For a slow moment I stared at him, at the swags of light hanging still and heavy in the air behind his head, as if some curtain had been pulled back behind his blot of darkness. So she had done it to herself. I realized that I was not surprised by this. Somehow, I had expected this. I had been waiting for it all along.

"I tried to make it look like an accident. I didn't want you to know what she had done." My brother stood up and moved through the lighted air, stirred it with his presence. "I didn't want you to ask these questions. I was trying to protect you. It seemed like the least I could do."

"You set the fire?" I said.

He didn't answer. He was behind the desk now, the note I had given him pinched in his hand. He pulled a set of keys out of his pocket and with a glance over his shoulder—at the camera, I realized—he bent down to unlock his bottom desk drawer. His head disappeared momentarily behind a picture frame propped on the desk. He locked the drawer and stood up again. "You might as well read it now." He held out a piece of paper.

I took it. It was another note—short, written in my mother's untamed, loopy script. All it said was:

I haven't lived right. It's too late to ask for forgiveness. I don't even want it. I just want to die. Then everyone can live in peace.

I looked up at my brother. My brother looked down at me.

"So now you know," he said.

I stared back at the note, wanting to think that "everyone" included me. But I realized I didn't know. I didn't know anything. Not yet.

"Who was Emilian?" I said. "Was he your father?"

With a careful expression, my brother bent down and took the note out of my hand. He took it back to the desk and locked it up again. He didn't seem surprised by the question. "Did Boris tell you?"

I nodded. So it was true, I thought. "Is that what you told him when he came to the church that day?"

His expression made the answer obvious—hot eyes, glowing coals. "What was I supposed to do?" He folded his arms across his chest. "He came to the shop first, and when he saw me there he called me a murderer, called me a liar, looked at me like I was a monster. He thought I had killed her. Written the note and lured her to some deviant plot, because that's what I am. A deviant." He stopped, looked out the window. "I didn't want to tell him the truth. But I had no choice. I said

I would tell him what had happened if he met me here. I knew he wouldn't believe me, so I had to show him her note."

I watched him looking out, moving his wrist in slow unconscious circles, wincing with unresolved anger, all the old hostilities back again: my father, his prejudice galloping out ahead of him, Eliot, wielding the weapon that would wound him forever. It seemed to me that from the moment he had known, my brother had wanted to wound my father, had wanted to tell him he wasn't his son. In fact, he had been telling him all along. Every time he called Boris by his name, he had announced that he was not his son. Now I felt disloyal for using his name like that too.

"You tortured each other," I said.

My brother only shook his head. A thought came to me that it could not have ended any other way between them. My father had been the first one to teach my brother shame, the first one to step away in apprehension. And years later my brother had been equipped with the knowledge to punish him for it. How else could it have turned out?

"When he came here, all I did was tell him the truth."

The truth was what I had come here to find. The truth was what I was still waiting for. "I want to know why she lied to him back then. I want to know what happened to her."

My brother sighed, and looked at me with those bright, wary eyes, as if I were asking him to trespass on a place he didn't like to go. The wooden face was gone, and I was looking directly at that core of quivering pain that would always be my brother. Here was the brother I had lost. Here was the brother I had loved. But he was not here to stay. That much I understood.

23

THE STORY WENT LIKE THIS: ONCE UPON A TIME, THERE WAS A GIRL. A girl who lived in a world where promises were given, prices were set, and marriages were made.

When she left that world and grew older, she spoke to her two children about it, telling them she had left because she had been sold by her own family to a man's family. That was the truth. When she said it was against her will, that was a lie. When a gypsy father sells his daughter to a man's family, he does so with her consent. She had wanted to marry this man. She was in love with him.

The man's family name was Emilian le Stevanosko, son of Stevan, a jeweler by trade, and the woman was Alepa o Mirceosko, daughter of Mircea, owner of the neighborhood car dealership, both of them children of fathers who were big figures in the kumpania. They had grown up together, they had played together as children, and when they reached that age when the body loses its innocence and becomes a liability, they were pulled away from each other as all of the others were, kept separate by the boundaries of their sex. They could not be alone together, they could not talk without others listening, they could not even pass close to each other for fear of polluting the air between them. And while she was kept guarded, protecting herself and her purity so that it could be kept for the man she would marry, he was sent to get his experience with gaji girls, the unspoken rite of passage, the *marime* act that earned him his manhood. But he didn't want experience with gaji girls. And she didn't want to protect herself from the man she knew she was going to marry. So they kept playing. They played just out of sight, behind the dealership and the jeweler's shop, around the corner of the old Chinese grocery next door, down the dirt alley, at the end of the street behind the concrete drainage pipe, crouched low, whispering in the twilight, their voices bare, their hearts trembling, their bodies ready.

At seventeen, Emilian was already making jewelry for the family business. When he wasn't with my mother he was at the shop with his father, practicing the family trade, learning the business of acquiring and selling gemstones. The jewelry in his family's shop was procured the gypsy way, some of it hocked and traded with other gypsies and gaje, but much of it plundered, bartered, bought and sold on the black market, pieces plucked apart and refashioned so that they were no longer recognizable. In his spare time, Emilian was fashioning a ring for my mother with a topaz that had come in, her birthstone, which he had bought himself from his father, and he was going to give it to her on her birthday. In three months she would be seventeen. He was helplessly in love with her, with her willowy grace, her fierce heart, and that quick and ready tenderness in her hands, which was only for him, only when they were together and no one else was watching. The families had seen a good match a long time ago, and when Emilian's father was ready to pay for her, the bride-to-be was priced highly. The deal was made for a wedding in the spring.

While the couple waited, they continued to meet. And one night Emilian told her about a job he was going to do, one of the many scams that brought money in, and said he was promised a good cut of it to set them up after they were married. He was going out that night to set a fire.

The property had been purchased and insured, and the other two individuals involved, gypsies with experience, knew how to start a fire that showed no sign of human agency, so that the insurance company would have to pay out on the damages. But that night there was an accident. A spark in the basement too soon, and the stairs blew out from under him, and he was trapped in the burning building until the rescue crews, gaje in their fire suits, could come and haul him out through a narrow window, his body seared and shriveled, melted down to a wick, his throat too charred to scream out in agony.

The emergency crews saved him and took him away for a month to the pollution and isolation of a gaje hospital, subjecting him to torturous procedures and operations to treat and replace his melted flesh, piecing him together with gaje skin and forcing his pain and terror into submission with injections that left him slack and listless, unable to resist, unable even to uphold his dignity with scorn. The kumpania despaired. What a terrible loss, what a terrible punishment, to be shamed and transfigured in the gaje institutions of sickness and death. To be permanently corrupted by their flesh. They mourned for him, they gathered money and prayed, they did what they could, waiting for his return, but they wouldn't go near him in that place.

His bride-to-be was wrecked. Her father called off the wedding, reclaimed his daughter, and kept the money that Emilian's father had paid as compensation for his trouble, for the near taint to his daughter's purity by their son's stupidity and bad luck. With all regret, the boy was now polluted, disfigured, unfit to be her husband. The girl spent that month in her father's house, wretched with grief. When Emilian returned, she stayed inside, afraid to see him, afraid of what she would find changed, afraid of what she would find the same. She heard much of it anyway, and all about his physical mutilation—his face and arms smeared with scars and foreign flesh, flesh that wasn't even his, and his remaining flesh tightened over his bones and curling him down like a weakened claw. The breath came out of him ragged and scorched, his speech was a raspy husk of sound, unrecognizable, and his eyes, once so dusky and full, were blanched and colorless, two bare melted slits in the bald lump of his head. While she languished inside her house, tortured by these images, losing sleep, losing weight, her father was making plans to match her up quickly with someone else, looking for a marriage that would cure her of this despair, that would let her find peace in her womanly role to serve, and he decided on a nice young man from their vitsa, a second cousin. He proposed the idea to her, hoping for his daughter's consent, coaxing and cajoling, while she said nothing, passed in and out of rooms, her haunted eyes flickering on the men who came to the front of the house for business.

She was learning to hate herself. Her own love was turning toxic inside her, burrowing into her like a poisoned thorn. It was her love that kept her inside the house, that made her wish never to see him again, that made her afraid of the ambivalence in her own heart. Whenever she thought of him, the anguish over what he had suffered and what she had lost was always gilded with a terrible relief, and the thought she could not fight off was that it was better to lose him entirely, better to feel that he had died, than to accept a tormented life so near to the wreckage of the man she had loved. The only way to survive was to stay where she was, in this half-light, until everything inside her was erased, until she could be nothing more than this body, a room with no windows. She could see no way out.

She practiced turning off her thoughts and feelings, reducing herself to a body that moved through the house among other bodies—and some of those bodies were her family and her friends, and some were strangers, and some were there to do business—and she tried to pass by all of them as if they were the same meaningless body repeated over and over. But her eyes kept catching on the Russian broker and his son, a gajo who was so sullen and lonely looking, white as a ghost, his eyes haunted like a ghost too, as if he had seen some portion of the horror she felt. She watched him, and she let him watch her, and it seemed that the punishment of his eyes on her was a punishment earned. Whenever any thoughts came into her mind, bitter and unbearable thoughts, she thought about the desolate gajo to shut them off. And when she thought about him she hated herself. And because she hated herself, she felt that he was what she deserved.

Almost six weeks had passed since the accident. Inside her, in the darkness, something was growing. She was pretty sure now that it was there. She couldn't get rid of it. She didn't want to. And she didn't want to live with it here, tormenting herself, tormenting him. And so she did the only thing left to do. She wrote the gajo a note.

There were secret meetings, new ones, these as strange and dreadful to her as the others had been thrilling and sweet. But despite everything, she liked this man's bewildered infatuation, as if she was raising him from the very dead just as he was lowering her down. There was something sacred about the way they had met at a time of need. And when that need became expressed, when she first felt his arms around her, it was like a fire burning everything away, all her connection to her family and her past, until she was empty at last of her thoughts and numb with the searing disgrace of what she had done. She needed this disgrace, she told herself. It was this man, and only this man, who could give it to her. And her need for this man became a kind of love for him that was dark and urgent and damning. When the time was right she told him she was carrying his baby. And when she had done it, all she had left to do was wait for this life to end and another to begin.

The burned lover, who knew he had lost his bride the moment he woke in the hospital, had spent these same weeks recovering in his house, curled frozen over his work in the jewelry shop, trying to forget the girl who had withdrawn into her father's house to escape the anguish of meeting him. But he couldn't forget her. Even after she ran away with the gajo, disgraced and polluted, he felt nothing but heartache and pity, because he understood that she had chosen this ruin because of him. Even years later, when he had taken over the jewelry shop, married a wife, and had three children, there were days when he would look down at his little finger where he wore the ring he had once made for her, the ring that held all the hope of first love, and feel heartsick.

When he died the ring went to his youngest son, who was seventeen, whose birthday was three days after hers, but he never told his son the story. The only person he did tell was his first son, the tainted one, the one who had lived with the gaje for the first part of his life, the one she had brought back to him, stepping back into his life like a mangy dog, the beauty yanked out of her face, the heat lost from her eyes. But still he felt something when he looked at her. When she told him they had a son together, that she had left here with a piece of him because she couldn't stand to lose it, that she had told the gajo the boy was his and let him raise him, he felt again what he had felt when she left, that she had chosen her own ruin because of her need to suffer, and he forgave her. He should have been angry, should have thrown her from his house in fury, but he didn't. Instead, he agreed to meet the son. And then he did everything he could to fix the boy.

But the boy was sick, more sick than he realized. Not only had his gaje life corrupted him in all the usual ways—made him weak, dull, afraid—but it had made him speak like a girl, and had made his heart like a girl. The best cure for that was marriage, but the boy was too fragile for marriage, too tainted to ask for any of these girls. So he took him in and tried to cure him. And it took years. And little by little he took the boy into his heart. And little by little he learned that what was in the boy's heart was there to stay, and he let it be. He began to think of the boy as a son. And the boy began to think of himself as a son. And when the father was dying he asked his son to do him a favor.

He asked him to bring his mother back one more time to see him. He wanted to give her the ring that had been meant for her so many years ago. He wanted her to know that he had never blamed her for what she had done. He wanted to tell her that there was still a place in his heart where he loved her. The son dutifully wrote his mother a note, and though he didn't want to, he prepared to see her again after thirteen years.

But his mother didn't come. As was her way, she gave no mercy, and then took none on herself.

I left my brother in the church that day, his eyes dark and drowning, his story finished. I left thinking that between the two of us, I had been the lucky one. I was not injured by the truth as my brother was. The truth had forced him to look into a past of misgiving and violence, to enter that suffering that had been done around him, all the pain that had forged him in the fire of his creation. I, on the other hand, had come after all of that, and though that made my brother the child of love and me the child of lies, at least I was far enough from those fires not to be withered in them—at least I was standing well beyond them, lapped up on the merciful shores of another life, where one story had ended and another had already begun.

24

OUTSIDE, A LITTLE BOY WAS POKING A TOY AT THE GASH BORIS HAD left in the cypress tree. It was a fake silver revolver with a red handle. He heard me on the steps and turned.

"Want to play?"

I was surprised. Was he allowed to talk to me? I gestured at my car, half afraid that somebody would see me with him. "I can't. I have to go."

He followed my finger with his gaze, then pointed his gun at the fortune teller's shop. "My *bibio* wants to read your fortune. She said for me to ask you. She wants you to go in."

I looked up at the window, sparks raining in my chest. It occurred to me that this was the boy I had seen looking out the fortune teller's window on the day of the accident. He had looked out at the whole thing with the same untroubled expression he was giving me now. "Sorry. I have to go," I said, and started walking. Aside from the little boy everything was conspicuously desolate. Where were the people who had gotten married? Where was Bobby? I put my hand in my pocket and felt the ring there, suddenly wondering when I was going to return it to him. For now I had to get back to work. I crossed the street and opened the car door and got inside, eager to be away from here. The boy watched me as I closed and locked the door, and then he turned and walked across the lawn of the church, swinging his gun as if it were something heavy and important.

I started the car and pulled around the same way Boris had, but this time more slowly, while I watched the boy crouch down in front of a basement window. He put his gun up in front of the glass and pointed it, as though he were taking aim at his own reflection. Just as he cocked the hammer and got ready to take the shot I passed him. I turned my face to the road and drove away from there like I had no time left to escape. I felt as if I were breaking up inside, all the new pieces sliding and poking and cutting. I kept coming back to the same thoughts—that my mother had killed herself, that she had loved somebody other than my father, and that my father now knew.

There was no denying my mother had written that note. The swift swooping curves of the letters were all hers, aggressive and large, angling drastically forward, the ink dark and heavy. I wondered what it had been like for my brother to walk in on her. Did he blame himself? It was he who had written her the note to come back, after all.

"When do I see you again," I had asked him before I left. But there had not been an answer. There'd been no exchange of information, not even a phone number. At a certain point, I decided not to ask about the woman who had answered his phone. The one who had speculated that he might be dead. She had guessed wrong, and maybe that was all I needed to know.

I drove, hardly seeing the road, my thoughts a dark tunnel. Already I seemed far away from my brother, and as I contemplated that distance into it dropped two bright words. *Friends forever.* That sign-off, from the note he had written me so long ago, was like a sign blinking on in darkness. It was strange to recall the moment that those words had become important for me, and now I couldn't help wondering if he only wrote them to make me feel better. Had he been lying to me all along, ever since that day in the grocery store, that day he popped more pills than I'd ever seen him do, that day his life seemed to be really veering out of control—when I still naively imagined myself his closest confidant and when he had inadvertently struck a limit on what I could be for him?

It was always the same with my brother back then—hilarity drifting into headache—Eliot half there as he shambled down the cereal aisle tapping boxes and saying, "He's hot." First it was the basketball player on the Wheaties box. "He's hot." Then the boxer with taped hands, a gristle of nose. "He's hot." Then the fake tan with a dumbbell propped on his shoulder like a parrot. "He's hot."

I tried one. Olympic swimmer, water streaming down his goggles. "He's hot."

He sniggered. "Hey do you think I could get Adam Coors to like me if I lifted weights?"

I scoffed, until I realized he was serious. Adam Coors was the one who had stuck a toothpick in his ear and punctured his eardrum. "Why do you want Adam Coors to like you?"

He shrugged. His smile was still, vibrating. "Because he's hot."

I knew this was a confession, one of the many quivering horrors he held inside and then gave to me in moments of weakness, to bear away. "Eliot," I said. "Adam Coors is a prick and an idiot. Remember when we saw him hitting baseballs at that concrete slab on the practice tennis courts and they kept coming back and hitting him?"

"He's color-blind," he said, almost tenderly. "He wears orange pants to school and he doesn't even know what that means. Orange."

His voice had gone cloudy and soft. He turned, staring at a display of knit bags dangling off a hook in front of the sugary cereals, and I stole a glance at our mother, a little ahead of us, plunking a massive can of coffee into the cart. "Here," he said, snatching one down. "Chew toy." There was a rubber duck inside, which he put in his mouth and bit down on, then held out to me.

My mother looked back at us. I had my hoodie drawstring in my mouth and I shook my head at her. Eliot was looking at his hand now as if he didn't quite know why he was holding it between us. He let the duck drop to the floor and put his arm around me.

"I wish you could be my friend and not my sister."

My mother turned and kept shopping. His other hand came darting up to his mouth. I tried to slap it away before the pill went in.

"Hey, do you know how Kurt Cobain killed himself?"

I reached swiftly into his open sweatshirt pocket and closed my hand around a pill bottle. I pulled it out and put it into my sweatshirt. "Why can't I be your friend *and* your sister?" I said.

"Why did he do it like that? Why didn't he just OD?"

I felt my heart twanging, like a chord struck slightly wrong—a mix of relief and worry at once. I shoved his arm away playfully. "Answer me," I said.

He stumbled and then snapped his fingers—a buttery, fumbling gesture—half keeled over against a rack of oatmeal tubs. I looked back again but my mother had turned out of the aisle. I felt righteously aggrieved, thinking that I had been the one to do something about this. It was me, not her, who took care of him.

"Why can't I be your friend?" I said.

His mouth opened to say something.

"Eliot," I said.

But he shook his head. He pretended like he hadn't heard me. He was singing the words to some song I didn't know.

I was almost at the freeway when I pulled the car to the side of the road and stopped. I felt as overlooked now as I had that day at the store. I remembered coming home and standing in the kitchen after they had driven away, taking his pill bottle from my hoodie pocket. I might have saved his life. There were several little solid white tablets still in the bottom and who's to say he wouldn't have polished them all off? The label on the prescription bottle said Vicodin. The name of the patient was Caroline Dell. My brother was popping pills that somebody else needed. Either he had stolen them or one of his friends had given them to him. I went to the bedside table in my parents' bedroom and started to put it there for my mother to find. Then I changed my mind. I went back to my room and hid it in a shoe in my closet.

I waited two weeks, and then tried to catch him off guard one night as he passed by my bedroom doorway. "Hey Eliot. Who is Caroline Dell?"

"Who?" he said, turning in momentary confusion. "Oh." His thumb went over his shoulder. "That old woman around the block, isn't it?" And then a twitch, a secret blankness spreading across his face, as if he realized he might have given himself away. "Why?"

I shrugged, my face prickling with heat. My brother was stealing from the old woman. He waited for me to say something. "Just wondering." My voice sounded pinched. "We got a piece of mail."

"Oh," said Eliot, rubbing his nose vigorously, hesitating in the doorway. I realized he didn't believe me.

I raised my eyebrows, signaling that he could leave me alone, and lifted my book again. If he could keep secrets so could I.

I couldn't wait until the next day. I closed my bedroom door and got the pill bottle back out of the closet and shrugged on my coat. I slunk past my mother's cooking sounds in the kitchen and out the front door. Skittering around the block in the dusk, heart pounding with an odd mixture of trepidation and glee, I tried to figure out how I would return her pills to her. I could put the bottle in her mail slot—it went right into the house like ours. But who knew if she'd open the little door in the wall to check it? I could try to find a window, maybe the kitchen window, slide it open and put it on the sill inside where it would catch her eye. But there were screens over the windows. Or I could just knock like Susan and Paul, hand it over to her. It was dark out and there was no light on her porch. I climbed the steps and stood at the screen door. The button for the bell was aglow like an orange ember, a little bloodshot skewer of electricity inside. I pressed it. I didn't hear anything. As I stood there I tried to remember if Susan and Paul usually knocked. After a minute of waiting, and a glance over my shoulder, I turned the grinding metal knob and pulled the screen open a few inches. I tapped on the wood. Impatiently I waited, then put my hand on the door handle and felt it turn smooth as grease.

With a little push I had the door cracked. Sudden yowling at my feet kept me from opening it more. I could see an animal snout pushing hard against the crack in the door. I tried gingerly to push the cat's nose back with my foot but it was persistent, wiggling its head through to the neck as the door opened a little further with my efforts. I felt suddenly trapped in this position, not wanting to let the cat out, holding the incriminating bottle in my hand. Could I just toss it inside? Where would it land? Now a warm putrid smell was seeping out the door. Urine? Tobacco? I couldn't close the door. Could I let the cat out? This wasn't one I had seen wandering the block. I tried lowering to my knees, keeping my hand on the knob, and pushing the cat's face with my hand, lifting it off its two front feet now with a shove and banging the door closed in the suddenly too-quiet night.

I turned, startled by my own noise, and my heart vaulted to my throat. There was a dark figure in the walkway.

"What are you doing?"

I gasped, panting. It was Eliot. "You scared me."

I stayed there for a minute in a crouch, breathing heavily. I had let the bottle of pills roll out of my hand as I pulled the door closed. Now it was somewhere on the floor inside. "Mail," I said. "I told you we had mail."

My brother made some move in the darkness. I could hear his coat shifting. I thought I saw a flick of bright cinders. "I know what you were doing."

I was suddenly furious at him. How he just stood there, smoking, looking down at me as if I was the one who had been caught. "You stole her pills," I said. I wanted off her porch, and I stood and lunged down the steps and past him, reaching out on my way to shove his shoulder. "Asshole." He let me push him aside and then followed me out to the sidewalk. "Unlike you she *needs* them," I said.

Eliot trotted forward to catch up to me. "She doesn't need them. She's addicted. Mom says."

I turned and stared at him in the dark, shocked.

"Mom takes them from her. Not me."

It was too dark to see his face, but his voice was flat, matter-of-fact. My surprise tipped all the way into disbelief. "She takes them? No she does not."

Eliot did one of his shrug-nods, his apathetic gesture for *it's true*.

I started walking again. "And what, am I supposed to think she just gives them to you?"

He leaned over into my face and let his mouth fall open slack in a look of stupidity. "No," he said. "She used to keep a whole stash in her bedside table."

I kept walking, head down, starting to believe him despite myself. Why did I never know the truth about anything?

"I took some before she knew I knew. Now she does something else with them. Probably throws them away. Total waste."

"You're going to kill yourself, Eliot."

"I don't take all of them," he said with a little smile in his voice. He seemed to be enjoying this. "I sell some of them."

"Who do you sell them to?"

"Friends."

"You don't have any friends," I said. "You're a loser. Everybody hates you." It wasn't true anymore and I knew it.

Eliot was silent in a way that told me exactly what he was thinking. That he knew it wasn't true either. That I was the one who didn't have friends. That I was a loser. "Leave me alone," I said.

"Natalie. Just chill out." His arm went around me again, amiably. "I'm not mad at you."

Tears sprung to my eyes in the dark. I wanted to believe him, to trust his camaraderie the way I used to. It used to be us against the world. But it didn't feel like that anymore.

He nudged a cigarette out of his pack and offered it to me. "Just don't say anything to Mom."

I used to think that drugs had made my brother stop caring about me. At the end, if he wasn't high he was always half paying attention to something else. It was that same distracted quality that I had felt in his office. Something else was happening, dividing his attention, something he wouldn't—or couldn't—say. Bobbing up in my mind were other doubts, other misgivings. The camera over the door—a strange place for such a security measure. The way my brother had glanced repeatedly at it. The way he had rubbed his wrist and winced.

I reached for my purse and took out my phone. I called the number again. The same unanswered ringing. *For all I know he might be dead.* I reminded myself that Eliot hadn't asked for my help—Eliot had *never* asked for my help. But that was almost beside the point. There had never been any such thing as help for us. There was just that fatalism of self and circumstance, that impossible wall we never saw the other side of. And there were choices, all the choices we made from the side we were on. I had thought there was companionship in mutual suffering. But I could have been wrong.

Now I had to ask myself: Did I want to find out? Either I did or I didn't.

I did a U-turn and drove back toward the neighborhood.

25

When I got back, the old man was up at the top of the stairs over the shop, looking down at the church, smoking a cigarette. He was still as a gargoyle, watching me cross the lawn. The church door was locked. Once again I lifted my fist and knocked. Nothing happened. I came back down the steps in view of the old man. How long had he been up there? Had he seen anyone leave? I tried a tentative wave. No response. He didn't have his coat, I noticed.

My phone produced a whispery vibration inside my purse and I took it out, half afraid now of any incoming call. It was only Meredith from work. I dropped it back down and let it buzz.

The man took the cigarette from his mouth and leaned forward onto the railing, turning his head away from me to look into the street. I thought he was ignoring me. It took me a second to realize that he was crooking his finger. *Come here.*

Steadily, head down, I walked over the lawn and passed the chain-link fence between the church and the shop. I saw the sign over the door—EDDIE'S VACUUMS—and started up the metal staircase bolted into the brick facade. It popped and shuddered as I went, like a rickety version of my old high school bleachers.

The old man had made some room for me on the top of the ledge, and he was still leaning forward, his blue suit jacket rounded up like a turtle shell, watching me out of the tops of his eyes. "Wouldn't stay down there if I was you."

"What do you mean? Is someone still there?"

He shrugged a little.

"Where's your coat?" I asked.

He smirked. "Special delivery." He turned to look at me. "Took your advice."

"What?" I said. What advice?

"Got it for twelve dollars at the thrift."

I stared, still wondering what I was to make of this. Special delivery. What did that mean?

The man took another drag on his cigarette. He didn't seem inclined to make any more conversation.

"I'm going to go back down there. Look in the window," I proposed.

He gave me a vague, sidelong look I couldn't read.

I turned and began descending the stairs, feeling his rheumy gaze sloshing down on me. I crossed back into the churchyard and went along the side of the building to the window where my brother had stood looking out. The glass panes were reflecting sun and crusted over at the edges with brown paint. I heard the door over the shop open and close. I was alone now. I put my face to the glass and looked in. Curtains. Mustard yellow.

I backed away from the window and went through the heavy quiet light back to the front of the church. All I could hear were my footsteps in the grass, and they sounded far away from me, thin and unreal. I stopped at the basement window where the little boy had been.

There was a piece of cardboard behind the murky glass, water stained and old, as if it had been there forever, blocking drafts and light, and I imagined it was there even when my brother had been tied down inside that room for three weeks, held hostage by a man he barely knew, and not just a man, but his own father, a gruesome figure whose tortured appearance was terrible to behold. I wondered what it would be like to writhe in that room without light or air for three weeks, to be buried alive until I was sure I didn't exist anymore, to be stuck inside one unending moment that had begun before I was aware of myself and would end only after I could no longer recognize myself.

Had I just heard a sound beyond the glass, down in that room? I bent down and put my head close to the window. It was not even a noise but the phantom of a noise—a muffled clatter and scuff, like feet on concrete. Or the leg of a chair tilting up and then scraping the floor. For a long moment I squatted there, straining to hear. Was my brother down there now? All around me, the silence throbbed like a slow, heavy heart. Then out of it came a striking double crack that went off almost inside my own head. I felt my knees buckle and my shoulder jerk backward as if somebody had yanked me from behind. There was a bursting pain somewhere high in the center of my body.

It seemed to radiate through me and move everywhere at once. I felt the thick, heavy luster of the sun on my head and shoulders, and the wet, sliding pain all up and down inside me.

I was on the cold grass, and the chill was seeping up through my knees and into my legs like black water. Something like water seemed to be rapidly rising, swimming into my vision to block out light, and as I concentrated all my effort on keeping my eyes on the window, on not passing out, I saw in the small portion of murky glass that was left in front of me, a tiny hole, the size of a nickel. I stared at it, the distinct black circle that had not been there a moment before in the middle of the pane of glass, my mind groping slowly toward it, as if wading into its dark infinite center. My breath felt ragged and unsteady. I couldn't understand why this tiny well of blackness had appeared to me. But I couldn't lift my thoughts from the spreading darkness.

As somebody who has learned to sleep after reading a horror novel, I know about the place on the way in or out of a nightmare, that long, delirious moment when I can feel myself stuck in this paralysis of near sleep, not awake enough to wipe away the distortions of my mind, and yet still awake enough to feel their sharp edges grazing me, tormenting me with the certainty that I am not safe, that any moment I will be in sudden peril, and I cannot move to stop it. Now here I was in this place, still strung somewhere between waking and dreaming, locked in that halfway world that takes minutes or hours to pass through, waiting for sleep to either come or go, to shift me deeper into my mind or lift me finally from its sucking weight and deliver me into the world of the living.

Panic lifted my head. I felt a spray of cold silver light on my face, and then a jagged pain split across my chest like a bolt of heavy lightning. I was on a cold, hard surface in the dark, but a tiny spool of sunlight from somewhere seemed to be falling right on my face, flaring in my eye. I turned my head and followed it to its source. It was a window, small and high in the wall above me. The light was coming through a tiny hole in a piece of cardboard covering the glass.

My heart gave a sudden thump of panic and sent a shard of pain through my chest and shoulder. I was in the basement I had just been looking down on. I had somehow become tiny, passed through the little hole and landed on the floor. I sat up, and the air blurred and thickened, and I thought I was going to pass out again. I stayed very still, taking in deep, choking breaths of sooty basement air, my eyes searing in the new darkness, listening to a noise that seemed to be in my ears, like a dull, muted static. After a minute the shadows thinned and the light seemed to glow and fade as if it were moving and changing. I could see indistinct forms piled high against the wall to my left, and to my right I could see the crisp edge of a wall thrown into dark relief by the flickering light just beyond it, as if this basement turned a corner. My eyes smarted against the harsh, bilious air, and every breath I drew stung my lungs.

Terror got me on my feet. There was smoke. I stepped to the wall, my legs strange and flimsy underneath me, my left arm dangling at my side like a shivering cord of pain. I brought my hand up and felt wetness on the shoulder of my coat. *It's blood,* I thought. *My blood.* I rounded the corner. There it was, in a small square space—a ragged cluster of flame, burning white-orange petals against my eyes, concentrated at the foot of a dark flight of steps going up to the basement door. With a jerky, panicked momentum I found myself moving closer to it, trying to see a way around the fire and up the stairs, and now I could make out the solid outline of something that was burning—a soft, slumped shape, like a bag of trash on the bottommost step. I flinched back, a bone-deep shudder telling me the horror-truth, that it wasn't a bag of trash, and at the same time I saw a dark form, somehow tangled up in the banister, the length of an arm extending up to it, and the undeniable contour of a hand—one digit sinking outward, like a petal adrift—a thumb.

I staggered back around the corner. I had to get out of here. I looked up at the window with its point of white light. That was where I had to go. It was the only way out. My mind filled with the looming importance of this one task, and I looked around for some way to get up there.

I saw the shapes stacked up against the wall and hurried over and put my hand on them. A dry husking stiffness—cardboard. They were boxes. I began dragging them to the wall under the window with my one good arm, because the other one refused to work and there wasn't time to check on why. Quickly I started to stack them up like a staircase. They weren't empty, and some were heavier than others. As I was doing this hurried labor my face kept hitting something in the darkness, like a string flicking me lightly. I reached out instinctively to swat it and realized it was the pull cord to a light. I snapped it on, and saw what I already knew, that the basement was cloudy with smoke. Through it, I could see the boxes, and an old cot folded up against the wall. Nothing else.

I could hear the fire crackling and bursting behind me now, the gathering smoke smothering out the light a few feet away. I had already dragged the first box against the wall, a tall, heavy one that came up to my knees, and slid a second box up the side of the first until I could push it on top. I used my right arm, my damaged left arm dangling at my side. It was the kind of spring-cleaning task that seemed appallingly mismatched to the sparks of panic going off in my head, the smoked flesh right around the corner, the almost careless way my mind seemed to empty every time it approached the thought of who that body was. I got my fingers hooked under the edge of a third box, nails scraping concrete, and lifted it up all the way over my shoulder one-handed, trembling, though it was light. My lungs were now alternating between big toxic gulps of air and pinched little sips, my head whirling.

The top of the boxes was now within two feet of the window, good enough to open it and crawl out. I sat down on the bottom box and let the cardboard crush in under me, then I brought my legs up and stood, bracing myself with my good arm, and climbed to the second box. I reached up and tore away the piece of cardboard covering the window and a flood of natural light hit my face. Cranking the window open, I felt a gush of cool air before a hot breeze sucked past me out the opening. I felt scorched and limp, and I put my face up to the open window to gasp at the fresh air. Across the opening was a brittle screen that had curled back at two corners and I used my good hand to tear it out, little by little, scraping and gouging my hand against the rusted metal for a furious several minutes, listening to the fire roaring and popping and devouring the room behind me. Then I put a knee on the top box and hoisted myself up onto it.

All I had to do now was rotate to face the open window, but my body seemed to be moving with a nearly sluggish disinterest, the box tottering beneath me. Finally when I was turned, I took my bad arm by the sleeve and lifted it out onto the dry grass, the pain twisting inside like a sudden knife. Gasping and breathless, I pushed my head and shoulders out of the window. I caught sight of the vast tilted blue sky, and for a moment my mind went blank with relief.

My legs were still jutting into the room behind me, and I squirmed across the ground inch by inch to get them out, like a soldier in a trench, my wounded shoulder dragging beneath me, my body conveyed now by some will that was beyond mine. I could still hear the sound of the fire in my ears, with me even now, but there was something else layered over it, a thin, uneven noise that seemed to toss around on the air and get closer and louder every moment, like the predatory language of some wild animal. I lifted my head and looked up just as I felt something close around my hand, something dry and warm and firm, and I saw a wild face plunge down at me, the eyes black and wide, the mouth open and making that thin harrowing sound, a brittle tangle of black hair falling toward me from her bent head.

In the moment before I understood, I thought I was looking at my own mother. Then I realized it was the woman from across the street. It was the fortune teller. She had taken my hand and was pulling me away from the building.

26

I BUMPED AND SCUFFED FACEDOWN FOR SEVERAL FEET, AND THEN suddenly my arm dropped and hit the ground and a hand pressed roughly on my shoulder and rolled me onto my back. I blinked up at the hovering face, blacked out by the brightness behind it, and felt the fresh air touching my damp cheeks and forehead, passing in through my charred throat as I pulled in deep breaths, streaks of twisting heat unraveling in my shoulder and arm—and I closed my eyes, trying to calm the chaos. I heard her shrill voice fleck the air again, the words called out above my head. Then the voice was gone and the air around me disappeared—a curtain lifting away into the folds of the sky—and I felt myself rise into the weightless expanse, both near and far from myself. A clutter of distinct sounds rushed past my ears, footsteps and two other voices crossing over each other, one of them loud and close and breathless, as if somebody were running by in the grass. Feet scratched the air by my ear and there was a hurried, bated pause, a moment of pure silence, and the woman's voice above me fell through it again like a scythe. She was speaking in another language, urging somebody in the near distance. My eyes were still closed, and they seemed impossible to pry open, lacquered down by a heavy glaze of sunlight. I could feel myself going hot and cold at once, my body burning and baking at its center, while my left arm seemed dipped into a cold black well, frozen there like a distant, forgotten part of me.

Hours or minutes could have passed. The next thing I knew, something hard was nudging my cheekbone. My eyes fluttered open to squint into sharp light and then shut themselves. Another firm prod against my cheekbone, and this time I looked up at a rough rounded bulge, hovering inches above my face. I startled upward and my cheek grazed its raspy surface. It lifted from my face. It was the heel of a foot. The woman squatted down over me.

"Get up." Her hand went under my shoulder and tried to tilt me forward. She pointed somewhere I couldn't see, then looked away from me and called out something in that other language and stood up. I managed to turn my head. A bulky dark figure was moving toward me against the light.

"Wait," I said, realizing what this meant. The man leaned down over my head with a puff of air and roughly gripped me under the arms.

"Stop," I wheezed. "Let me go." The woman had taken hold of my ankles and I tried to shake them loose.

They hurried me into the street, my shoulder bumping with pain at every labored step, and I saw the boy for an instant, hovering shyly at the edge of a lawn. He turned sharply and ran out of view. We tumbled from sunlight into shade and thumped up some steps. I saw a can brimming with cigarette butts, then a screen door, pawed open by the man's hand. Inside a sharp chemical odor, and dark shapes looming in ambiguous gloom—a round glass table catching sunlight that reached vaguely through the window. The floor we shuffled over had some kind of cloth on it, thick canvas bunched and strewn and twisted by feet, randomly streaked with green. Again the man took a hand out from under me and opened a door. I had a last glimpse of the satin gleam of the totally bare walls, a moldering pea-green color that seemed vividly lit in the gloomy light, and realized they were painting the room.

Now there was a cold outdoor feel. A piece of darkened concrete floor and the front fender of a car. We squeezed in beside it—a sky-blue sedan with speckles of rust across the hood—and hurried down the side. At the back they dropped me on the greasy concrete. A stabbing pain shot up through the inert clay of my shoulder, reminding me that it was still a part of me. The man stood back and let the woman go through a set of keys, and she stepped over me and opened the trunk, leaned in, and pulled out a stiff yellowish square and began to unfold it. It was a blanket. She flapped it a few times and a spray of stale dust filled the air over my head. Then she leaned back in the trunk with it, stepped away, and she and the man bent at the same time and lifted me.

I got a confused glimpse of the blanket spread out flat, and then they were bumping me up over the rim of the trunk and dropping me down inside.

"Oh," I gasped. My head hit something hard and a rough hand reached in and bent my knees and crushed them down.

The woman lifted her arms to the trunk lid, with its blue-and-brown lace of corroded metal, and pushed it down at my face. A stunned blackness closed over me, and one bewildered second later I heard the trunk click shut.

"Wait!" I yelled, realizing too late that I was trapped. I banged on the inside of the lid and flakes of rust fell onto my face. I heard a door open, but it was not the car door. It was the door to the garage. It opened, and then it shut. I could smell the tang of rust above my face, like blood.

I began to count—somehow, somewhere, I had learned this. If you are stuffed inside a car trunk, start keeping time. It was hard, because I was incapacitated by fear. They were going to leave me here to die, I was certain—a long, suffocating death. Finally, just before reaching one thousand, I heard a noise—the muted sucking whoosh of the door opening. I held my breath and listened to footsteps coming down the side of the car. There was a pause, and a loud rattling noise that must have been the garage door pulling open. The footsteps passed the trunk again and the driver's-side door opened, and I felt the car sink down slightly. The door closed, and the engine started with a halting, uncertain rumble. With a lurch of movement, the car backed out.

I didn't lie for long in that moving darkness, but the motion seemed almost instantly to slide me out of myself, and I felt the way I did in all my dreams, vividly alert but bodiless. I was suspended in a dark puttering eternity, leaning into the periodic tuck of a turn, pitching forward to a complete stop and rocking reluctantly back again. I felt the last rolling pull of a gentle stop, heard the engine cut off, and sank back into the dull, pounding reality of all my limbs again.

I heard another hollow rattling sound, very much like the one made by the garage door pulling open minutes before. A key was inserted into the lock of the trunk and the lid parted with a slice of blinding light. The physical world returned with a sharp, startling clarity—the square metal lid of the trunk above me, and two people standing over me—the tumbling black mane of the woman who looked like my mother, and the broad, sturdy man from the auto shop with the sizzled gray hair. My eyes stuck on the man's face. This was the man I had seen just this morning in the office. The man who could be my grandfather.

He peered down his nose at me. It was an ugly nose—a swollen bulge of red, pitted flesh that looked like ground meat, flecked with bits of white, and under it was a small mouth between a pair of loose, square jowls. His eyes darted from my face to my shoulder and back to my eyes, as if he were staring into me to find some secret fact. With a slow, deliberate movement, full of a restrained power and dragged down by the sinking weight of his flesh, he stuck out a big meaty hand.

"Come on, come on," he said, shaking it with an impatience that didn't seem to match its bulging mass. "I help you out."

Dazed, I watched the hulking figure lean toward me and plunge the heavy hand into the trunk, clasp my forearm, and lift my torso until I was propped up like a dummy, still sitting inside the trunk.

"Stop, wait," I muttered, anger welling up.

He shook his head and turned to the woman, who blinked furiously. Tears poured silently down her face and soaked into the scooped purple neck of her top. I watched her move away into the garage as the man held me swaying in his one hand. He pointed with the other hand at my bloody shoulder.

"It not so bad. We take you to hospital. But first we go into the office. We talk."

I looked at my shoulder and wondered how he knew that from looking at my coat. For the first time I wondered: What exactly *was* wrong with my shoulder? The garage echoed with a loud, squeaking rattle, and the woman appeared on the other side of the trunk wheeling a rolling stool. The man gestured to it, my purse clutched in his free hand.

"You get on that?"

Without waiting for a consensus on his proposal, he reached forward and yanked my legs out of the trunk and hung them loose over the side and pulled me up onto them. I dangled there off his raised arm for a moment, twisted and unstable, before he spun me around and rolled the stool underneath me. I slumped down like an invalid and he pushed me back with his heavy paw until my spine hit a metal bar, and his hand braced me against it as he wheeled me slowly across the concrete floor.

"Now we go for ride. To office. I not hurt you. I ask questions."

As he wheeled me away I saw the woman get back in the car and shut the door and put her face in her hands. Something had deeply upset her since the last time I had seen her.

The man rolled me sideways with a grim unreadable expression, pushing me toward a doorway off the garage where a small room was lit with deep oily light, one glass window in the wall facing into the garage. Another office. He rolled me straight inside and positioned me to the side of a metal desk. There was a chair and two tall metal filing cabinets and a big square safe in the room, every surface smeared with greasy black fingerprints. I watched the brass doorknob disappear in his hand as he shut the door, and then he turned and plunked my purse on the desk.

I tried to remember the last time I had had my purse. I hadn't had anything when I crawled out the basement window. Somebody must have found it and given it to him. He stuck his hand inside and pulled out my wallet. He opened it, looked at my license, my health insurance card, my bank card.

"You are Natalie," he said, as if introducing me to myself.

He counted the cash in the billfold—only three ones—and looked up again. "I am Dennis."

I wanted to ask if he was my grandfather. I wanted to ask if his real name was Mircea.

He seemed to regard me as if he knew my thoughts and didn't like them. He found the pocket behind the license window and dug his huge finger into it and extracted a thin strip of paper. He pinched it between his forefinger and thumb. I realized what it was. The fortune I had put in there. *You will find luck when you least expect it.*

Dennis tossed it aside, then turned the whole purse upside down and shook out the rest of its contents. All that was left was the scorched cigarette case, my keys, and my cell phone. He spent some time going through my cell phone, and then picked up the cigarette case. He looked at it, opened it, gazed at the inside, and looked back at me. He pulled a cigarette out and ran it under his nose. Hand rolled. I started. Where had that come from? He dropped it on the desk with the rest of my things and clasped the case shut.

"This was nice case once. Now is all black from fire." He peered at me with an expression that looked almost upset by this. "This very special to you."

I shook my head, and felt my shoulder convulse like a speared fish. I looked at my shoulder. My shoulder was special to me too. "I need a doctor," I enunciated slowly.

"I see initials. A.K."

Alepa Krupin—I'd had it engraved with half my mother's true name and half a nav gajikano. Stupid. But I was only twelve. I had no idea who she really was.

For a long moment he scrutinized me, a roughness in his eyes that was also somehow intimate. It reminded me of the look my mother gave me. Then he put the case aside and swept his arm across the desk, scooping everything back into the purse and plopping it down on the floor as he lowered himself into the chair. I watched the shoulder strap flop over and something fall out—the cigarette, rolling past his foot and coming to rest against the leg of the desk.

"Now you tell me. How you get that?" He pointed to my shoulder and bent forward over his belly and looked at me with needle-sharp eyes. A wave of spicy sweetness momentarily soaked the air, either his aftershave or cologne, and a rush of nerves dizzied me. I told myself that being scared of him wouldn't help.

"I'm sure you know."

He stood up and with a lunging step forward gave me a tough poke in the shoulder. A jagged spasm of pain erupted there and I jerked backward into the crossbar of the stool, gasping for breath. He kept looking at me with harassed agitation, like I was merely a misbehaving animal or child. Again, I thought of my mother. It seemed to me now, looking at this man, that all her expressions had come straight from him.

"Tell me why," he said. "Why you've been shot. You're lucky. It went in the front and out the back without breaking much."

My eyes widened. "Shot," I repeated.

"That's right."

I could feel something happening to me under that gaze, like a stone was rolling aside in my heart, heavy and slow, returning me to an old, precise misery of which I knew every contour and every sensation.

"Where it happen?" he said.

Where? I tried to think. "The window," I realized aloud. "It must have come out through the basement window."

He raised his eyebrows, not exactly surprised, and sat back. "A bullet come out through the basement window?" Then he shook his head as if this were wrong. "But *you* come from inside basement. We see you come out."

"Somebody put me in there—"

"Who?"

I took a moment on this, my mind churning at the reality that this man was probably right: I'd been shot. "The person who shot the gun?" I guessed.

His harassed expression had taken on a set look, as if he were concentrating on maintaining it for my benefit. "And you not see this person? This person put you and you not see?"

"No," I said, and I wondered if he didn't already know the answers to his questions. "I was passed out. I blacked out on the lawn."

"And you wake up in basement and climb out?"

I nodded.

"And you see nothing? Not in yard or basement?"

I shook my head. He continued to watch me with a sharp feral expression, like a cat that wants to trust you but can't, then abruptly he whipped his hand down through the air.

"You say you see nothing. You know nothing. You go to church. What you doing there?"

I hesitated. If I mentioned Eliot, would that give something away, put him in danger? He put his hand up before I could speak.

"I know why you're there," he said. "You look for your brother. You speak to him in there. Why?" He gogged his eyes as if to startle the answer out of me.

Here now, it seemed, we had gotten to the real source of his curiosity, and now anything I said had the potential to unleash some furious assault from him. But I was still more afraid to be silent. I said, "I wanted to talk to him—I hadn't seen him for years. I just wanted to know if he was okay."

The man shook his head before I had finished my sentence. "No. He not okay. I tell you about your brother," he said, leaning forward again. "He sick."

He seemed to freeze after he said this, and then he shot back in his seat as if on a tightly coiled spring. "No," he said. "No. First you tell me this." He reached into the breast pocket of his blue coveralls and pulled out a piece of paper. He unfolded it and held it out in front of my face, his eyes bugged. It was the note. *Emilian is dying. He wants to see you.* Somehow, between the time I took it out at the church and now, the note had gotten into his hands.

"You ever see this?"

Confused, unable to keep up with what was happening, I only stared.

"And don't lie," he warned me, pointing his finger at me in a way that reminded me of Boris. "I know if you lie."

I looked at that finger and felt a sharp twist of pain in my shoulder, as if in anticipation of its probing forward and stabbing me again. I looked at the note and nodded.

His eyes blazed. "Yes you see it. Where? Who this note for?"

"I found it," I said, backtracking to why I had the note in the first place, trying to show that it was accidental. "In my mother's things. After she died. I wanted to know if she went to see that man. I wanted to know who he was."

Slowly, thoughtfully, his eyes bore into me. After a minute he nodded. "What he tell you? He tell you she go to see him?"

"No," I said. "He said that she—" I stopped, the words lodged in my throat.

"She what?"

"Killed herself." I took a gulping breath.

"He lie!" He pulled the paper out of my face and stood up, as if the outrage was too much to take sitting. For a full minute he stood there drawing coarse, heavy breaths and staring down at me. I couldn't tell if he was upset by the idea of my mother killing herself or upset at the idea that my brother had lied. Either way I felt assaulted by his gaze, limp and immobilized under the predatory distraction of his eyes. Suddenly a brutal spasm contracted across his face, as if he were physically pushing his fury down, and he looked down at the note, thinking.

"You know a woman. Rita George?"

I shook my head. The name meant nothing to me.

The gypsy stood there for a few seconds looking down at me, his eyes barbed and ready, then he sat down again in the chair. He leaned forward, his finger out in the air again. "I tell you something. You brother. He do something very bad. This you need to know." He bucked back in his chair and then came forward and started talking fast. "He come years ago. He *marime* when he come. Bring all filth of gaje with him—right?—of you people—" He gestured a thick hand at me, his face vaguely contorted with disgust. "But he full gypsy. You mother gypsy and he has gypsy father. His real father say that he true Rom. So we take in. But he bring *prikàza*—bad luck. His father get gaje disease from living with him so long. So he go travel. On boat—to outrun prikàza. He come home three week later and he look better. One week in house and he too sick to get out of bed. One month later, he dead. Now this," he said, holding up the note my brother had written. "We know your brother write it. It say Emilian want to see your mother. So I think *Mamioro* come—bad spirit. Emilian want to forgive your mother, but this make your brother crazy. He can't forgive. He meet mother and do something to her. Maybe he get her back for what she did to him long ago. He do this to you too." He motioned to my shoulder. "Gun go off in basement. He come out. He see you, put you down there. Set fire." He was nodding his head at me vigorously as a sudden terror chilled me. "We can't prove this but is true, all of it." His hands gestured aggressively in the air. "He disappear now. We find him, do a trial—Rom way. We don't murder," he said. "Not like he murder."

The gypsy stood up and went over to the desk and gazed at me from behind it.

No, I thought. *No.* "My brother is not a murderer—he would not have done those things," I said firmly, surprising myself.

The gypsy seemed to disregard my response as he picked something up off the desk. He came back to me in the chair and held it in front of me. It was one of the birthday photographs I had seen on the camera that I had looked through, the one with the man and woman on the couch. "You know this man?"

I looked at it, wondering what he had to do with any of this. The gypsy shook it impatiently in front of my face.

"He—" My voice faltered, sinking back into me with the weight of mud. "He works in that Chinese grocery down the street."

He nodded, his eyes lingering suspiciously on me. Then he walked back to the desk with the photograph and picked up Eliot's note and the cigarette case. I watched him walk with them over to the opposite wall, where he bent over in front of the safe. As he turned the knob, he said, "If there something you not tell me, you come back. You come back here and tell me, okay?" He opened the door a crack and then put the case inside the safe. "This you care about, I know. I keep this here and give to you when you come to talk more." He closed the door and turned the knob again. "I keep it safe." He stood up and crossed the room again and looked down at me. "Police," he said, and tapped the air in front of my shoulder. "When they come talk to you, you tell them this was accident. Car drive by on road. Not us," he said. "We do not do this." He stood over me, ominous, waiting, and I had the idea that this was a required condition of my release. I nodded. Then he leaned down and took my arm. "Good. Now we take you to hospital."

I sat in the backseat. The fortune teller drove, and a small nervous man in coveralls sat in the passenger seat beside her, stealing sharp little glances at her as she brought us down serene sunlit streets, while I sat stunned and woozy, basking in the innocuous light of day as if it were cleansing me of the cold, cavernous dusk of the garage we had just left. When the hospital came into view she turned down the street that led to the emergency entrance and abruptly pulled the car to the side of the road and stopped. She turned and looked at me with glazed red eyes. She looked so much like my mother. "Are you sisters?" I didn't notice the question until I had spoken it out loud.

"What?"

"You look like my mother."

"The hospital," she said, pointing. "Go."

I got out, and she stepped on the gas and veered into the right lane again and puttered off. I walked across the parking lot in the direction of the glass entrance doors. Every breath I took felt raw, as if the air itself were sharp and granulated. Still I felt myself walking on. I arrived into the shade of the concrete overhang and drifted toward the entrance doors. They glided open and two people looked at me with startled eyes. I passed by them and stepped into the familiar waiting room. I remembered there was a desk somewhere, and I found myself already walking toward it, looking straight into a pair of large, moody eyes that stared back at me from the other side.

"I've been shot," I said, but there was already a phone in her hand and her mouth was moving. My own voice had made a hollow noise in my ears like a toneless echo that reverberated in a soundless room. I felt a convulsive heave start deep in my stomach and ripple up my throat, and I promptly bent over and wretched. The last thing I remembered was the pattern on the linoleum—a speckled beige embedded with bits of mica, like the sand on a fair and sunny beach that was far, far below me, the distance so great that it was dizzying.

27

I WATCHED A NURSE GLIDE IN THROUGH THE PALE SQUARE OF LIGHT. The woman's eyes glanced up at my face and back down, but she didn't say anything. There was a pain, but it was hard to place, slushy and floating. It was so quiet here, such a relief not to talk. I listened to some muffled noises she was making at my shoulder, and then with a sedate smile she turned and went to the wall and flicked a switch that made my room go from dim to dark, and she slipped out again. I turned my head and gazed into the shadows where my IV bag was hanging. Behind it was a window covered in blinds. It seemed like it was late at night. My eyes closed again, and I could feel my body sucking gratefully away from me, into the dark current of a heavy sleep.

The next thing I noticed was that a doctor was speaking to me. He had a round waxy face and rimless glasses. I blinked my eyes rapidly, trying hard to concentrate.

"I can see you're still a little out of it. That's okay." I realized he was patting my forearm. The room was much brighter, and the blinds at my window glowed a radiant peach. "Let me tell you what's happened here," said the doctor.

He explained that I had been in the hospital overnight, and then he gave me a technical description of the bullet wound I had arrived with, describing the point and angle of its entry into my shoulder, its trajectory and exit, followed by an explanation of the procedure that had knitted me back up, and then he finished by assuring me how insignificant the wound was as far as bullet wounds went. He told me I would be held until tomorrow and then I would be sent home with two prescriptions, one for antibiotics and one for pain medication.

"Alrighty?" he said, cupping his warm hand on my forearm again. "Anything else I can do for you?"

I shook my head, still too dazed to speak.

"Okay, Natalie," he said, "feel better," and he was gone.

Later, when I was more lucid, I began to process things. Two nurses were now tending to me. They brought me to the bathroom and handed me little cups of pills. Each took a turn asking me who

I wanted to contact, who did I have to call, but in such a relaxed way that I didn't feel any urgency about it. I let it go for a while. I slept again. Night came. I woke up. When I turned my head, a new nurse was flipping a switch on the monitor beside my bed.

"We don't need this anymore," she said.

The light in the room told me it was morning. Now I remembered that the doctor had said I would be leaving today. When the nurse left I picked up the phone beside my bed and called work to explain my situation to the station manager, and then I called the rehab facility where Boris was staying and spoke to his doctor there, who very gravely expressed her sympathy and reassured me that my father was doing fine.

In the afternoon a police officer appeared to take my statement, and I told him what the old gypsy, or Dennis, had instructed me to say, fearful the whole time that he could sense me lying. But all he did was nod and ask questions about the car and the driver in a blunt, disinterested voice. I told him I couldn't remember if the car was blue or green, and I hadn't seen the driver or passengers at all. "Not a great neighborhood," he said glibly. "Not the worst, but—" He shrugged. "Street violence. Vandalism. Shootings aren't as common." I felt myself sour on him. Was he bragging? His black uniform was harsh on the eyes and his cop accoutrements jangled whenever he shifted his weight. When he was gone, I lay with my head buzzing, wondering if I had done the right thing. Though my grandfather had said they weren't murderers, I wasn't convinced, and anyway I didn't think I had the wherewithal to tell the story as I knew it.

When it was time to get discharged, I finally called Mitch. He said he could come after the end of his shift in two hours. His staggered concern exhausted me almost immediately. I would need to buck myself up for his coming inquisition. As I waited, I tried to find distraction in getting out of bed and going to the window. My legs were clumsy and weak beneath me, my arm stiff and unwieldy in a bulky padded sling. I looked out at long shadows already cutting across the parking lot, blue as ink. *What's going to happen to me now?* I thought. I felt like I had taken a big, long step out of my own life, and I didn't know quite how to get back inside it again. I turned and delicately picked up my bloody coat, which the nurse had politely folded on top of my pants in case I wanted to have it cleaned. The coat did not look salvageable, and I didn't want to wear it ever again anyway. I wobbled over to push it down into the trash can, reaching in the pockets to be sure that they were empty. I felt the torn lining inside the pocket and remembered Bobby's keys, which I had put back in the lining for safekeeping. Once again I extracted them. I wanted them out of my possession, and everything else that tied me to that family to be erased, my mind swept clean. But that thought only triggered a chain of unwanted images—the shackled hand in the dark, the black bloated thumb, how Eliot had sat rubbing his wrist, glancing at the camera over the door, the old man's coat on the door, special delivery. The gunshot. The body. The fire.

Who was it? Who had been in the basement with me?

I slumped down in the chair by the bed. The remote was on the arm and I aimed it at the TV. I stared at two women arguing. I got a flash of the gypsy woman crying as she drove me to the hospital. I pushed a button to change the channel, and I tried to do the same to my thoughts.

"It was an accident," I told Mitch when he came to pick me up. I had decided to give a little embellishment to the story I had told the police. "I just stepped outside, a car sped by—you know, tires squealing, in a rush to get away—and a gun went off through the window. I'm sure it was an accident."

He was looking at me with a wary mixture of disbelief and concern, standing just inside the doorway, once again wearing the baseball cap that made him look paradoxically gaunt and unsporty. I eyed the plastic bag in his hand. I was still in the room's only chair, and I had been watching daytime TV for two hours. I had already put my gray slacks on under my hospital gown.

"Does this have anything to do with that guy breaking into your apartment? Or that note?"

I stood up. "No. But can we talk about this in the car? I'd really like to take this gown off now."

A look of apprehension crossed his face, as if he thought I was going to take the gown off right then and there, and then he came forward with the bag and dropped it on the foot of the bed and stepped back into the doorway again. I felt my heart go rigid. So that was where we stood, I thought. And only a few nights ago we had been in my bed together.

"I brought a t-shirt and a button-down," he said, hovering uncertainly. "I didn't know which would be easier."

I put my hand in the bag and pulled out a puffy wad of fabric. It was a jacket. "Button-down," I said. "And I'm going to need you to help me." That was just to see what he would do.

"Oh," Mitch said. His face tried to look unassuming. "I could get the nurse."

I pulled out the button-down in one hand and gave him a look of disbelief, a look that asked him if he was serious. "Never mind," I said.

Mitch took a step back, more than ready to retreat into the hall. "Are you sure?"

"Fuck you," I told him. Now I was not thinking about the shirt anymore. I sat down on the edge of the bed and looked up at the TV through a glaze of unexpected tears. How could this be happening? I did not want this to happen.

A moment later I felt his weight sink the bed down deeper. He let out a deep, aggravated sigh. "Natalie," he said. "What can I say? You shouldn't have put me in the bed."

"Oh so this is my fault?"

I expected another blast of air, something disappointed and condescending, but the silence trickled by, complete and unadorned. "I'm sorry," he said at last. "That's all I can say. I'm sorry." His voice cracked.

The tears in my eyes had not spilled, and I blinked them back. I didn't want him, I reminded myself. I didn't want him.

I sniffed and stood up. "Okay well let's go," I said, and to make it easy for him I added, "Get out so I can put this on."

He stood up, his face battered and uncertain.

"Don't be an ass," I said.

He winced, and then he turned and walked silently out into the hall. I took my time with the buttons and eased my arm gently out of the sling and into the sleeve before returning it to its perch. Then I slipped into the huge fiberfill jacket, blue and red, obscurely sports fan looking, and I paused in a moment of incredulity—had I ever seen him wear this? Was it new? I joined him a few minutes later in the hall and he fell into step beside me, his usually hurried strides slow and carefully paced. He stood in respectful silence as I signed the checkout forms, then led me down another hall and through a lobby and out the sliding doors into a frigid evening, clear and starless. We walked with heads ducked to the car, where he opened the door for me with all the care of a father helping a small child.

"If you don't mind," I said, feeling positively sick of all this politeness, "I need to go pick up a prescription before you drop me off."

Mitch nodded. I could feel him trying to think of something more to say, something that would prove he wasn't the double-cheating ex I was making him into. We pulled out of the parking lot and turned onto Harbor Street, the street I had become so familiar with over the last week. For a while I looked at the dark buildings passing in the blue evening light, and without wanting to I found myself waiting to see the auto body shop, my nerves strung tight.

Mitch opened his mouth to try to say something, then closed it. A few seconds of silence went by, into which my stomach released a sudden hungry grumble. Mitch glanced at me.

"Are you hungry? We could stop somewhere."

"No thanks."

More silence. We were nearing the block of buildings I had driven up and down almost three weeks ago, when I was following that line in the road atlas—when I still knew nothing.

"So," Mitch said, tentatively, "where were you when it happened?"

"What?" I was distracted by my thoughts, hardly listening to him.

"The shooting."

"Oh." I stared out my window, wondering how to answer. There was the convenience store where I had parked on my stakeout a week ago, ablaze with light, and past it, aglow in its illumination, was the sign for the Chinese grocery. "At a Chinese grocery," I said, almost without thinking.

Mitch looked over at me. "What were you doing there?"

My stomach gurgled again. "I was hungry." There was a silence, during which I waited in dread for his next question.

"What were you doing out of town anyway?"

"Look—we're about to pass it," I said to avoid the answer.

"What?" He jerked his head in surprise.

"If you look to your left"—I adopted a mock official voice—"you will see the scene of the crime." I pointed. "Pull over into that parking lot."

"Why?" said Mitch, startled.

"I'm hungry. I want to get something to eat."

Mitch looked at me in the darkness, and I knew there was astonishment in his face. "From the place where you got shot?"

"It wasn't their fault. It happened outside. Please," I said, knowing he would have to do it if I asked.

He sighed and slowed the car and made the turn. "I don't understand you," he said, pulling into a parking space and stopping. We were now in the same spot Bobby had parked in the day I followed him. I shrugged. Neither did I. But now that I was here it seemed there was a reason for it.

"They have good food," I said.

The grocery smelled like warm grease and stir-fry this time, an almost good smell. One velvet rope was strung between two poles across the entrance to the back curtain, signaling it was closed. As I walked ahead of Mitch toward the dry foods aisle, I listened to the clatter of metal and water running in a sink at the back. Each aisle I came to I looked down, but I didn't see anybody. It occurred to me that I was looking for him—Ian. The last time I had seen him was at that bizarre wedding photo shoot. When I stepped into the last aisle, I saw the fluffy head of the clerk, Lin, leaning over something in the area behind the back counter. I bent for the cookies.

"That's what you want?" Mitch said. "Don't you want something more substantial?"

I gave him a guilty look.

He smoothed his face out into a careful, neutral expression that I knew well. "It looks like they have prepared food at the back." He pointed at several large trays sitting under a heat lamp. "Are you sure you don't want to look at it? I'll pay for it."

I knew what he was doing. He didn't like the prepackaged, paper-inclusive meal I had picked out for myself, and he was trying, with all the pretend patience of a father tending to his finicky child, to redirect my attention. I decided to compromise. "Okay, but I'm still getting these."

He held his hands up to show how cooperative he could be. "Okay. Fine."

We strolled down toward the thickening aromas at the back of the store. Lin was at one of those deep utility sinks, washing dishes, and when we came down the aisle she turned off the water and dried her hands on an apron and came forward. I was inexplicably tense, my heart pounding in dread as I studied her for any signs that something was wrong. What was I afraid of? Lin put on a pair of thin plastic gloves and looked at me.

I studied the selection—lo mein sitting like greasy worms in brown sauce, broccoli and beef scattered like dark glistening turds, and two kinds of rice mounded up in separate trays. Lin picked up a pair of tongs in the lo mein as if to encourage me. I looked up at Mitch. He didn't seem bothered at all. I wondered how I could be picky about real food when I was willing to put almost anything into my mouth.

"I guess I'll have the lo mein," I conceded, and pointed at the smallest of the three boxes on display above the heat lamp. Mitch ordered beef and broccoli and white rice, and Lin scooped the food into boxes and put everything in a white paper bag and told us to meet her at the register.

While we waited, I looked at a new sign taped to the counter, showing the grocery's spring and summer hours and written in the same quivery script I had seen on the "Have You Seen Me?" card when I was up at the register last.

Front Grocery: All Days 9 A.M.–9 P.M.
Back Video: All Days 12 P.M.–2 A.M.

"So, are these hours wrong?" I pointed at her sign.

She lifted her eyebrows, punching buttons. "No, they right."

I gave her a look of confusion. "But the back is closed."

"Oh. Video. My son run that, but he gone." She put my cookies in a plastic bag and pushed both bags across the counter. "Maybe he be back after weekend. He don't tell me. I don't know where he go." She shook her head, clearly irritated with him. The dread came galloping back. Maybe he was on his honeymoon.

"Didn't he recently get married?"

She puckered her face at me. "Married? No. Why?"

"Oh, I thought maybe I knew him. I guess I don't."

She continued to look skeptically at me. "You think of Ian? My son?"

"No," I said, waving my hand and shaking my head. "Somebody else. Never mind." I picked up our bags and thanked her.

"Okay," she said, still frowning. "Bye-bye."

Mitch was staring at me as we walked outside.

I ignored him. I was trying to put something together about this woman's son, Ian. Had he gotten married or was that a lie? And where was he now?

I reached into the bag and opened the fortune cookies.

Mitch stopped at his door and looked over the car at me. "Why did you think you knew that woman's son?"

I could tell from his tone that he thought this was a significant clue to what I had been doing here the day I got shot, and I made a show of concentrating on the difficult task of holding a bag of groceries and getting my door open with my good arm at the same time. Then when we were sitting in the car, I read my fortune out loud to distract him.

"The truth hides in small places. You must search to find it."

"Why did you think you knew her son?" Mitch tried again.

I stared at the message. "What?" I said in a distracted voice.

"Are you going to tell me what you were doing here yesterday?" Mitch said. "Who is that woman's son? Do you know something about him?"

I shrugged, trying not to look as if I were holding something back. "No. I don't know anything." It was mostly the truth. All I knew were a few disconnected facts that didn't match up. I knew Ian had been at the church yesterday, and his marriage to the blond woman was pretty obviously a sham of some kind. There was the old gypsy, Dennis, asking me if I knew him. And now he had disappeared. And my brother had disappeared too. *Supposedly,* I thought. There were things I couldn't accept yet without a deep, chaffing sense of untruth, a scouring skepticism that left me raw inside.

I looked down at the scrap in my hand. Words on paper. Notes. Clues. *The truth hides.* I didn't want to do this. I didn't want to search anymore.

I put my head back on the headrest and let out a tired breath. I felt Mitch glance over in the darkness.

"Go ahead and eat," he said.

My hands stayed limp in my lap. Mitch had a rule: no eating in the car.

"What?" he asked.

I shook my head and reached down and grabbed my purse. I was not going to let him ease his guilt by giving me special permission to break his rule. I found my wallet and started to tuck the fortune in the window behind my license, where I had put the other one that was now floating loose in my purse somewhere. I could suddenly feel the old gypsy's eyes on me.

"You're hungry," said Mitch.

It was like a nightmare moment, gasping awake. The piercing stare. The yellow room. Jab of pain. Harsh smell of engine oil.

"Natalie?" Mitch was peering at me.

I breathed to steady my nerves, trying not to inhale what was only in my imagination. Cavernous cold. Crackling flame. "We're in the car," I said.

Lights popped out the window like flashbulbs. My mouth opened to speak. Had I said something?

"It's not important," Mitch said.

I glanced at him. Behind his head, light sliding over dark. Cringing strokes. Hand in shadow. Had I even really seen it? Had I imagined it?

I turned away.

"What?" said Mitch.

Was there something I wanted to say? The sign was upon me now, its soiled glow. BIG M's. The gypsy, his animal heat bearing down on me. A dash of white, thin and long, out of the corner of my eye.

Oh. Swift, sudden drop, the world yanked out from under me.

"Natalie. What do you need right now?" Mitch was speaking to me from a long way off. "Tell me."

I turned. All around me black lapping waters. Luster and sheen. "I need something," I said. *No. No.*

"What?"

"I have to go get it."

"Where? What are you talking about?"

The cigarette. The hand-rolled cigarette. How could I discount it? The thing that didn't belong. The extra bit. Small thing. *The truth hides.*

28

THE SHOP WAS SUNK IN DARKNESS NEAR THE BACK OF ITS LOT, THE closest streetlight far out past the other end of the building where the garage was. I stood at the door to the business office. Three SUVs for sale along the curb shielded me pretty well from the street, where I had asked Mitch to park.

The keys were hard to maneuver because my hands were shaking. My heart was squeezing my lungs flat and I could hardly breathe. After trying two keys I found the one that fit and opened the door. In a rush I stepped inside and closed it behind me. The moment I did this I panicked, realizing I could have just set off an alarm, or been caught on a camera. I looked up into the corners of the room, where cameras usually are, and saw nothing. Neither was there an alarm sounding, nor any security device that I could see. I let out my breath and quietly inhaled the heavy gas fumes that lay on the cold stale air. It occurred to me that a family-owned business that was kept in a shambles like this one perhaps didn't bother with alarms or cameras. Even if they put them in their churches.

I kept the light off and made my way past the black outline of the counter along my left. At the end of it I turned toward the back wall where the door led into the garage. I fumbled in the dark until I got it open, and the blackness of the office was suddenly thinned out by a shaft of light coming into the cavernous garage through one square window cut high into the back wall, where a floodlight across the back alley was shining.

I closed the door behind me and crept toward the interior office. This door's handle also had a lock. I had to go through each key again, sticking them in and pulling them out with rising doubt until—last one—it juttered into the groove and turned and opened the door. There were no windows in this room, and I decided I could safely turn on the overhead light. I paused in the fluorescent yellow flicker, listening to a clock ticking in the silence. It was almost six thirty.

I walked to the desk and crouched down. Still there. A little white stick, like a discarded lollypop. The gratification of seeing it made me want to put it right into my mouth, but I didn't dare. I plucked it up—thin white paper, brittle crunching flakes—like any other cigarette. I untwisted the end and tapped it in my palm. Had Eliot put it in the cigarette case for me to find? It was packed tight. I needed to peel it open without tearing it. Or slice it. I was trying to remember if the cigarette case had ever changed hands in his office. I was pretty sure I had never given it to him—only the note inside. Then when? When I was in the basement? I studied the top of the desk for something sharp, a scissor I could use like a blade, a utility knife. A car door opened and closed somewhere outside. I wondered if Mitch was getting out to look for me.

I stopped searching and pinched the paper and started tearing, little by little, right along the glue strip. Quickly I unrolled it and at the sight of the loose leaves, acting on instinct, I tipped it up and shook it into my mouth. Smoked earth, bitter and eye watering, delicate crumble. Looking at the paper, brushing leftover dust away with my damp fingertips, I found it. Inside, lightly penned in black ink, were numbers. A phone number. And a four-digit code of some kind. In the silence of my contemplation, a voice suddenly called out my name.

It was Mitch, shouting for me from somewhere outside, his voice thin and twanging in the quiet night air. Then my phone vibrated. I picked it up.

"I'm fine," I said.

"Where are you?"

"I'm fine. I'll meet you at the car in five minutes." I hung up.

My fingers trembling, I tapped in the number on my phone. After one ring an automated voice picked up and asked me to enter my security code. I entered the four-digit number on the paper. There was a pause, and then the voice told me I had one saved message, left on February 16.

I heard static, a confused burst of sound, and then a voice picked up at midsentence. "—at the Ruckett Marina," it said in a quick, gritty whisper. "A7. If you don't come soon I'll be dead." The last word was nearly cut off by the faraway clatter of the phone dropping onto some hard surface, then there was a click and the line went dead. My heart bucked in my chest. I had heard this message before—or something like it—on my father's answering machine. It was the same message—the same husky, irritable voice—except this time it was louder, and clearer, and beneath the ragged tones was a person I had known my whole life. My father was right. It was my mother.

I stood still, trying to understand. On the day of my mother's death she had called somebody and left a message. Two months later, Boris had gotten the same message on his machine. This must have been just after he had gone into that neighborhood, irate with accusations against my brother. How had the message gotten from this person's voice mail to his? The transfer had been weak and unclear. All the important information was indecipherable. But Boris had known it was her. And the next day, he had brought me to the church, where my brother had told him my mother had killed herself.

At the Ruckett Marina. Soon I'll be dead. So my brother had lied.

PART SEVEN
SURVIVED BY

29

HALF INSPIRED AND HALF SICKENED, I LEFT THE AUTO BODY SHOP. When I emerged into the night air and stood on the other side of the locked door, I saw Mitch only twenty yards away, standing sharp and stiff in the yellow-tinged light that gilded the darkness under the streetlamp. For a moment I stood there, poised, tuning in to the more elusive motions of my mind, and then I was moving from the car lot to the dirt alley, going in the opposite direction, my steps quick and light. After a moment I realized what I was doing. I was running away.

At the first cross street the alley brought me to I turned left and kept running, taking shallow breaths of glassy night air, and soon I could feel the slow undulations of pain in my shoulder far below my pain medication. A cold, unhealthy sweat beaded at my temples. I turned right, then ran four more blocks—until I was standing out of breath at my own car, on the side of the church, on the edge of that unlucky neighborhood where my life had almost ended less than two days ago. Amazingly, the car appeared to stand unbothered and intact, waiting for me.

I unlocked the door and sat down in the driver's seat, catching my breath, my whole body suddenly shaky and limp. I reached inside the pocket of Mitch's coat and pulled out my phone and dialed his number.

"Natalie, what the hell?"

"I'm sorry," I said, my words coming out in short breathless spurts. "But I don't need you to take me home anymore."

"What? What is going on?"

"I'm at my car."

"Your car?" His voice was pinched high in agitation, and in my mind I could see the expression on his face—eyes squinted, teeth bared, chin jutting.

"Something just... came up. Anyway I'm going to drive myself."

"Natalie, what—"

"I can't talk about it. I'm okay. Everything's fine. Thanks for everything you've done," I remembered to say.

"Wait a second. Don't—"

"Bye. I'm sorry." I hung up, turned off the phone, and threw it with my purse into the seat beside me. With an unsteady hand I found the ignition and stuck the key in.

As I pulled away from that neighborhood I cracked my window to cool my face. The air had that bright cut-metal scent of melted and refrozen snow. Little dirty deposits of it were still piled up at the curbs, almost totally gone in the late spring melt. When I got on the freeway and the air began to snap loudly at the cracked window, I opened it further until there was a dizzying gush of wind all around me. I was alert, but it was an unnatural alertness, probably a medicated confusion that only seemed like alertness, one that made me feel jittery and slow at once. I seemed able to take only shallow breaths and my heart felt like it was jumping in and out of place. I drove with my right hand jerking the wheel, and my left arm resting in my sling.

I knew that Ruckett was south of Boston—I had seen signs for it along the freeway before. But I didn't know anything about the marina in Ruckett, or how to get there, or what to do once I was there. *A7,* I thought, making sure I remembered the number—the one my mother's voice had spoken, haggard and strained, barely recognizable. I flinched to think what had happened to her there. *A7.* Was that the dock slot for a boat? *A7,* I told myself again, trying to empty my mind. I chanted it again. Soon there was nothing in my thoughts but the number, repeating itself over and over like a numbing incantation, taking me to that unthinkable yet inevitable destination.

Eventually, in the middle of that trance, I saw the exit sign for Ruckett—white letters aglow against a green background. I pulled off in a slow, curved descent that delivered me to a stop sign, where I could go either left or right. Which way to the marina? There was a gas station standing alone on the corner, and I decided to turn in and ask for directions.

A girl was working the register, with a round face and a long trickle of brown hair pulled forward over her shoulder. With her fingers she combed through it as she stood politely waiting for me to approach.

"Hi," I said, trying my best to look steady and courteous. "I'm trying to find the Ruckett Marina."

Without a word she reached for a pad of thin white paper and a pen and slid it across the counter at me. I realized she wanted me to take notes on her directions. I took the pen in my hand and she ticked them off, as if she were a machine that had done this task so many times it was wearing down its circuits.

I left the shop, the blackened fringe of trees hissing in the breeze, and above their dark bristles I saw the soft, dented lobe of a half-moon—these two shapes put together as if to say there was no malice without first a terrible, imperfect softness. I could feel that softness in me, warm and melting, pulsing painfully as I drove away from the convenience store. Ten minutes later I was driving down the street leading to the marina. I could see that it was not so much a marina as a dilapidated little docking place for local boats, with a cluster of buildings on a bumpy strip of asphalt leading down to the water. The water was black as oil, slicked down under a pink sheen from the nearest streetlamps. I passed a darkened rental shop and a run-down motel and a restaurant/bar with a huge carved-wood anchor out front. On the corner was a burger shack called Ron's, and inside the bright windows a man in a checkered shirt was leaning over and swiping a table with vigorous circular motions. The street swerved left at a metal railing, and a little farther on the road dead-ended in a gravel parking lot. I parked and got out, listening to the lethargic suck and swallow of the water against the dock and the boats. I felt the crumpled ball of directions in my hand, squeeze and release, squeeze and release, soft and a little damp. The brackish smell of ocean water and gasoline hung in the air, and under it the souring odor of beach and seaweed. There were maybe twenty dismal boats docked and knocking around in the darkness. As I looked at them I felt a terror I had not known yet in all of this, for that walk out over the water to get to those boats seemed like the last destination I had left in the world.

I had the feeling I would find on that boat the answer to every mystery that had driven the world through its secret and certain evolution since the beginning of time. And neither could I resist or refuse this calling now that I had heard the directive, now that my mother's own voice had commanded my presence here.

I listened to that voice in my head as I walked through the parking lot down a sandy gravel slope and out onto the dock. My mouth was full now and my teeth had taken over what my hand had started, clamping and releasing. I could feel the creak and bend of old wood under my weight, announcing my uncertain suspension above the water below. I came to a cross length of dock that divided into three extensions where the boats were tied up. I imagined I was looking at extension A, extension B, and extension C. Wooden posts stood waist high in front of each boat, painted white with stenciled numbers. The first and second extensions had only a few boats docked close to the pier, nothing farther out where the numbers got higher. I went to the far extension. I took six hollow steps and stood even with the first pair of boats. Even from here in the dark I could see that the space I was looking for was empty.

I walked all the way up to it and stood looking at the slot of black water, moving in lazy little swells, slopping at the sides of the dock. I stood there for a long time trying to think of something. The boat was gone. I stared down at the water and could feel it drifting inside of me. This was it, I thought. This notch of black water moving and heaving inside of me, this fathomless mystery was all I would have for the rest of my life.

I sat down on the cold wood. There was a little air rolling over my face, wet and heavy, and on it a long low whistle came floating through the darkness, as if somebody were calling his dog back out of the night, back toward home.

Inside the bulky warmth of the jacket I felt the grazing tremor of fresh pain, as though that other me that had been forgotten under the medication, the one that had been pushed down into some remote place, moaning and wounded, was coming back out to the near edges of my body.

If I concentrated, I could still hear the voice from the phone message far in the back of my mind. When I had heard that voice, it was as if she was still on this earth talking to me, and all the power she had held in my life had come instantly back. I had felt what I had been missing these last months, the force of something holding me to my life, the existence of my own self pushing back on someone real. She was real,

I thought—my mother was real—but still I hadn't known her. Maybe for that reason it was not my place to know what she had been doing out here, or what she had died for. As I looked out on the black waters I realized that this had all been done without me, a long time ago, and assuming that I had any part in it, or any obligation to find out about it, was to assume that I mattered somewhere in my mother's story. But all I had found out in this process was that I didn't matter, that I had been flicked lightly away from the center of things years ago without even knowing it. And now here I was.

I leaned forward and touched my hand to the rough plank of wood, my mind a slow blur of pain, sliding into unease as I realized the throbbing in my shoulder was returning and I had no painkillers, no medicine. I braced myself and stood up. I lifted my feet one by one and began to walk back toward land, feeling as if I were still floating somewhere above my own body, severed from myself by the water moving underneath me. I stepped off the dock and onto the sandy gravel that led up to the parking lot, listening to my footsteps crunch. There was another whistle, sweet and melancholy, followed by a little sprinkling of music from a dog collar. At the edge of the parking lot I looked up, and saw that I wasn't alone. A dark figure was walking slowly along the far side. As if it had seen me at the same time I had looked up, it listed in my direction, a thin haze of hair standing out darkly against the streetlight.

"Hey," said a voice, rusty and loose. "Hey can you help me out? Is that your car?"

I watched the figure come on in the dark, my heart pumping, and I looked at this person as if it had just become the last unnamed creature in this landscape, the bloated thing of terror that was not to be discovered or approached.

"I'm trying to get out of town," said the voice. I could tell it was a woman now, coming forward on lean ropey legs, dressed in cutoff shorts and a bulky hooded sweatshirt. She was holding something in her arms, and after a few more steps in my direction I could see it was a little dog—a profusion of light fur with a tiny pointed face in the center, its black eyes shining at me in the darkness.

"I'm sorry to bother you." She came all the way to the edge of the parking lot where I was still standing. "I saw you out here and I wondered if you could give me a ride to the next town. I'd take a taxi but I don't have money."

I thought I should speak, and tried to muster something, but the woman spoke over the effort without noticing it.

"I need to get to the hospital to get my stitches removed." She took one arm off the dog and gestured up the street behind her. "My husband's up there in the bar right now and I'm trying to get away before he sees me. He stabbed me in the leg. See look." She pointed at her leg, where I could see a big white square of medical gauze above her knee. "I had to go to the hospital and get stitches. They put me on pain medication and while I was in bed he took all my money and spent it. That's why I can't take a taxi. I'm trying to get away from him." She stopped talking and looked at me, her eyes widened in an expression that was both pleading and reproachful. The dog in her arms was somehow like the excess of that look, the little surviving fiend that had been stolen out of her over the years and lay vanquished in the night air, peering with suspicious resignation, a spirit too listless and feeble to stir.

She didn't seem very old, but she looked somehow mummified in her age—preserved in a state of early decay—dry, sizzled hair, skin sucked deep into the hollows of her cheeks, a blackness in her mouth like a tooth was missing. She seemed to understand what I was thinking and said quickly, "I know I look like shit, but I'm not lying. I just need a ride to the next town. If you could spare some money I could call a taxi. It's fifteen dollars to get there and I only have five."

Now she wanted money. That was something I could say no to. I had spent all my money on fortune cookies. "I don't have any cash," I said, my voice coming out thin and high.

"You have a debit card?" said the girl. "You can get cash at the bar up there. Just buy a drink. The drinks there are cheap. Like two dollars. And then you can get cash back. Look I wouldn't ask you if I wasn't so fucking scared to be here right now. I'm so fucking scared," she repeated, as if she had found something in this phrase she liked. "I'm just trying to get away from my husband."

I stared at her, the only thing that had come to me out of this empty journey, coming out of the night to tell me these lies, or to drop these bitter truths in the bucket of the night, like stars put one by one back into the sky so that I could remember the world I had come from and the world I was going back to. I could just barely hear the dog in her arms, its breath wheezing in and out at her chest.

"I still have some of my pain medication from the hospital."

"Some of your pain medication," I echoed. I looked around in disbelief. Had this woman been sent to me?

She reached into her sweatshirt and pulled out a little plastic bag. "It's not in the bottle anymore because I had to take it out to hide it from my husband. That asshole was trying to take my pain medicine too, after he stabbed me. It's not street stuff," she said. "It's prescription. I still have the bottle at the motel. I'm staying at the motel right there by the bar." She pointed up the street. "Maybe you're interested, I don't know. I saw you out here and I thought you might be up for something. I just want to get money for a taxi."

I looked at the pills, little capsules lined up end to end along the bottom of the bag, and their two-tone uniformity, *white-red white-red*, sent a cringing pain through my shoulder and down my arm, like nails screeching on a chalkboard. I shuddered, and she seemed to interpret this in some way. "I also have a joint," she said doubtfully, reaching behind her ear. "I know it's not worth ten dollars but I sort of need to keep my pain meds. I mean, I'll give you whatever," she trailed off.

"I don't have money," I repeated.

"You can get some at the bar," she said, and it was suddenly as though our conversation were on a loop. For a moment it seemed like we might go on and on talking to each other forever, our words moving us deeper and deeper into some deranged other night, unless I did something to stop it. I was too tired to push against her need, whatever it was. All I could do now was get her the money.

I started walking through the parking lot.

She turned and fell into step beside me. "I don't know what I'll do if I have to stay with him one more night. I'm afraid he's going to kill me or something," she said, still tense with uncertainty about where I was going. The pain in my shoulder had sharpened to bright sudden shards, as if a hot poker were jabbing it over and over.

"Let me get my wallet," I said.

"Okay." She stood back politely—now that she knew what I was doing—and waited while I opened the passenger door of my car and took my wallet out of my purse and put it in the pocket of Mitch's coat. I left my hand in the pocket with the wallet and started walking.

"Thank you," she said in a voice suddenly lustrous, and stepped up beside me. "Here. I really appreciate this. So you go in and get the money and I'll be waiting on the steps of the motel." I took the joint she was offering me and put my hand back in the pocket, feeling loose change at the bottom. Several quarters and a few dimes, the cold assorted shapes sliding around against each other in a friendly fashion.

"Just don't tell my husband," said the girl. Her voice in the dark beside me was gleeful and sly. "He's in there right now. Who knows what he'd do if he knew I was leaving his ass tonight."

30

THE BAR WAS ONE OF THOSE SHABBY SEASIDE PLACES, WITH HEAVY ropes tacked to the walls outside and an anchor looming above the front door, a place that had dingy out-of-the-way glamour despite itself—a place more actually weathered than fashionably weathered, the kind of place college kids from Boston sought out to feel authentic, hoping for cheap, bad drinks and amusing conversation with the local drunk at the counter. It was just that group of gelled and shaven figures that came out of the heavy wood door as we approached, all looking rather subdued and stopping in a cluster to discuss their next destination. Three guys, all in crisp button-up shirts of various pastel colors, clapping their flip-flops on the pavement and lighting cigarettes and looking at each other, ignoring the only girl, who was small and bare shouldered and stood with her arms crossed in the chill. Then they saw us, all at the same time, and together as one beast they slid their eyes over us without turning their heads. I could feel my face sewn up in grimacing pain and imagined how my expression must have looked to them, maniacal and ragged and predatory. I couldn't help it. Striations of bristled white heat streaked up and down my arm, and under them a heavy rolling ache thundered against all my nerves.

I turned to the woman. "Give me a pill."

She looked distractedly at the group of observers, who were still talking idly but obviously watching us. "What?" she said. In the light I could see she was as young as I had originally thought, maybe thirty.

I reached into my pocket and pulled out change. "Here, I'll buy it."

She turned to me suspiciously. "You said you didn't have any cash."

"All I have is quarters."

She frowned, then stuck her hand into her sweatshirt pocket. "Okay but you're coming back out right?" She held the dog in one arm and worked her hand down into the plastic bag in her pocket and put a pill in my hand. I stepped up to the door and her gaze flicked over to the group of people again. The door hadn't closed behind me before I heard her voice talking to them. Maybe she would get a ride from them, I thought. Maybe I would come out and she would be gone.

It was dark inside the bar, and the oiled counter slid from one end of the room to the other like a heavy black ooze. At the far end were two men, one of them overlarge for his bar stool, his green sweatshirt hitched up on his flabby white waist. The other one was skinny and leaning forward with his head at a tilt, mouth smiling in a red-brown beard. The fat one heaved back in abrupt laughter and then turned, conscious of his noise, with an expression both sheepish and belligerent, and fixed his eyes on me. The other one glanced back and saw me too. The bartender was in the corner plucking glasses from a table with his thumb and finger, and he walked back to the bar with several hanging off each hand. I followed him up to the bar and waited for him to throw the glasses in a plastic bin and turn around. He cocked his wide, melting jaw at me and raised his eyebrows.

"Can I get a beer?"

The bartender looked at me with a studied disinterest and named off all the beers he had, then I ordered a bottle and he put it on the bar in front of me and asked for three dollars. I told him I had to pay with a card. He went to the register and rang up the beer and had his hand out waiting for the card before I got to him. I was right beside the two men now, and the skinny one tilted his head sideways to look at me.

"Do I know you?"

His eyes were floating cores of clear blue rimmed in red, and he had a little knowing smile cut out of his beard.

"No," I said, barely.

He was nodding, his eyes wandering down from my face and back up, and suddenly I was grateful that I looked like hell. Behind him his friend was looking pointedly straight ahead and tipping his beer into his mouth.

"You're not friends with those others that were in here, are you?" he said, pointing his thumb over his shoulder and turning to his friend with a smile. The other man snorted over his beer.

"College brats." He spoke past me to the bartender. "Why you let them in here, Derek?"

The bartender shrugged. "I don't mind taking their money." He handed me the ten dollars cash back I had requested. I put the money in my pocket while the skinny one gazed at me, still smiling.

"You staying here in town somewhere?"

I felt a nervous jolt in my chest and then a streak of pain skewered my shoulder, and I gave a vague shake of my head and walked away.

"Cause Henry here owns the motel next door," he said to my back. "If you need a room he can get you one for cheap."

"She doesn't want a room, man. Leave her alone."

"Okay. I was just asking. She don't want to talk to me she don't have to."

I sat down at the table nearest the door and their voices started up again, lower. I reached into my pocket and pulled out the pill. If it was what the woman had said it was, then it was exactly what I needed. Still I hesitated, remembering my brother. I had never been the least bit susceptible to the compulsive drug consumption that had been Eliot's undoing. I wanted the full-bodied feel of an object bumping around amiably in my mouth, not laboratory concoctions sliding down unnoticed, zinging me to a place out of my control or understanding. But tonight was different—tonight, I told myself, I was nursing a bullet wound, so I threw the pill into my mouth and washed it down with the beer. As the pill slid down I heard the voices of the group outside, sharp and inquisitive. I wondered if the woman was telling them about her no-good husband. The one who was sitting right here in the bar with me. Which one was it? I looked back at them. Not the motel owner, I answered myself right away. Then it rolled over me, big and swift with breaking clarity.

"Motel next door," I asked out loud, and both men turned to look at me. "There's a motel next door?"

"You walked right by it."

I heard it loud and clear, my mother's voice once again telling me where she was. "A7," I muttered.

"What about it?" Henry asked, narrowing his eyes.

"That's the honeymoon suite, isn't it Henry?" the skinny one cackled, as Henry shook his head.

"You want a room?" Henry asked. "You look like you could use one."

Without another word, my pulse rushing in my ears, I stood up and walked out of the bar.

There was nobody on the sidewalk. The girl and the group were gone. I walked a short distance, back in the direction I had come. Past the bar I found a porch with a single stair. RUCKETT MARINA MOTEL, the sign over the door said. An empty wicker bench was plunked on the porch like a thrift store donation waiting for pickup. I stepped up on the stair. I smelled wet wood and something else—an earthy musk of decay. I noticed that my hand was on the knob of the door—that I was doing this—and then I was bathed in a yellow light looking down a short narrow hall. My heart was in a lot of places at once, filling my tongue and eyes and limbs, squeezing my breath away. There were doors all the way down this hallway on both sides, painted brown. Doors with letters and numbers. The musty smell was stronger in here, like wet animal fur. I heard a click in one of the knobs and a dry creak of weight shifting behind it and suddenly I realized there were people here. Not just the ghostly reminder of my mother's last days. Hopefully not my mother's ghost.

The hallway oozed and pounded around me, and behind all the doors I could hear little skitterings and tickings, as if everything small and secretive had come out to warn me away. I turned to another door, and found myself staring at it. *A7*. A thought swept through me, slow and rich, like a heavy curtain rising with beautiful ease. Here I was. This was the place. *Too late,* came the next thought. Then something happened. With my hand on the knob, it turned, without me, and the door opened.

A figure stood peering at me from out of a long matted waste of salt-and-pepper hair. I felt my heart swiftly plummet, like a stone tossed down in water. A white tendril rose before the face, like a strand from the crinkled mane leaking upward in sinuous defiance of gravity, and then I saw the bony arm holding the hand with the cigarette aloft. It was smoke. A wide sleeve of faded aqua green was sinking back from the wrist, corded with big purple veins like fish pushing under the surface of the skin. I saw all this in a glimpse as the hand with the cigarette in it seemed to reach out for my eye, and I flinched back. It arced past my face and sank into my shoulder, a tight, unrelenting claw. I felt it tug me forward. My heart staggered in my chest, and I felt for a second like two separate people—one coming and one going.

Before I understood what was happening I was stumbling through the doorway, pulled forward by a force too inevitable to resist. And then I was in the room.

31

THE BODY CAME CLOSE, SMELLING DANK, AND I STOOD TERRIFIED AS it reached an arm around me and the door closed behind me. Then it stepped back and thrashed out a rattly, convulsive cough that sounded painful—the sound of a throat torn ragged. I stood pinned to the door as this robed stranger hacked and sputtered, its head bent over the faded terrycloth hanging slack and twisted over its gaunt upright carcass, then it lifted a clawlike hand and spit into a crumpled white wad. The head raised and there was a twitch of features, a cringing malleability before they settled into place, and in the dim light I saw a dark milky-yellow face with eyes pushed deep into collars of bone, black as the earth's mantle, burning me to a wisp of smoke with a fevered stare.

"Don't look at me like that," said the stranger's voice, scaly, clacking with mucus.

I felt my knees quake under me and I tried not to sink toward the filthy brown carpet, where grit was scattered like beach sand and where twisted shimmering objects swarmed and glittered like waves in an ocean. For a moment I swayed above the shifting floor until the waves stopped moving in my sight and I could see what they were. They were packages, trampled and twisted but still bearing the telltale contours, the deeply familiar blue-green shade, the shape and color that had filled my life, quietly lapping against my consciousness, set down in all the rooms of my childhood like an incidental part of my very soul. They were my mother's brand. They were Newports.

In the silence that trickled over me I heard a dry curdled noise, low and primitive, a dying moan that was almost worthy of a horror novel.

"Don't do that," said the ghastly mummy before me, as if I had made the sound myself. "Sit down." She stepped back and motioned me deeper into the room, toward the mangled bed centered under a dirty yellow light. I was having some sort of dream. I had a vague memory of taking something I wasn't supposed to, and now I was trapped in the living horror of my own subconscious mind. The room spun around me in its phantasmagorical waste and detritus—strewn sheets and litter and blinds—gnawed-up and half-digested wreckage that looked as if it had been coughed out by some humongous beast and left to settle under a sifting layer of baked ash. I felt a hand nudging me through the chewed-up abyss and delivering me safely to the foot of the bed, where I sank onto its creaking springs.

"So you found me." The body leaned its face forward to peer at me, eyes squinted. "What is this?" she said, reaching forward and plucking something from between my fingers.

I looked back at her, this conjured nightmare, draped in her filthy seafoam skin like some hideous mermaid of death, drowned and resurfaced. A squall of noisy silence filled my ears and I dropped my eyes to the floor. I saw one white slipper and one bloated purple boot that I realized was a bare foot. Then a heavy wave of darkness rolled up over me and I shut my eyes against it. I could hear a voice speaking to me from inside the ocean roar. Was that her? I tried to move my mouth but it was already doing something.

Sometime later I could hear the voice again, beetle-small and speaking right into my ear, chewing its way in until I could almost hear what it was saying.

"Natalie," it was saying. It was mean and snappish, as if I had done something wrong. It got louder. "Natalie. I know you can hear me." It was a tool sharpening itself on me, over and over. "Open your eyes! Right now."

I opened my eyes. And looked at my mother. Her haggard face was hovering over me and I was closer to the floor now, tilted back against something firm and solid.

"Listen to me," said my mother, speaking in a sandy voice that broke into a long cough. "You need," she said, "to tell me"—she straightened and pressed the stiff, balled-up tissue to her mouth and hacked out the last words—"how you got here." I stared up at her. She was looking more and more exactly like my actual mother every moment. What was she doing here? What was she doing alive?

"Did your brother send you? Did he tell you about Danielle?"

I could hear myself breathing rapidly through my open mouth, gasping in and out of the tight croaking passage to my lungs. She was waiting for an answer, her black eyes slow and steady, pools of oil burning low in the dim room. *What was the question? Danielle? Who was Danielle?*

"I don't know," I said in a choked voice.

I watched my mother's shoulders rise and sink down with a sigh I had seen so many times before, an exhausted disapproval that was worked into me like an incantation of shame. She held something up in her hand, a long white stick. "Now listen," she said, and paused, her eyes boring into me, making sure I was listening. "I know where you got this."

I looked at the thing she was holding up in her hand. I recognized it. It was the joint. The joint that girl had given to me.

"That girl. She gave that to me."

"I know," said my mother. How did she know that? Did she know that girl?

"Who is she?" I asked.

My mother shook her head at me, vexed by this question. "She's a friend of your brother's," she said, pulling another crusty white ball from her robe and unfolding it. "He was keeping her here."

I stared at her, unable to comprehend the meaning of this. "Why?"

I watched her move through the pounding air, and then she was putting the tissue to her mouth and hacking into it. She finished and shook her head at me. "You're completely useless right now. You can't even think."

She tossed the tissue into the corner of the room and opened another door and turned on a loud, humming light. I heard a tap going and I realized she was in a bathroom. She came back out and held a cup of water down to me. I took it, realizing that my mouth was very dry.

While I drank she was talking to me from someplace where I could no longer see her, saying things I didn't understand. "Vermont where it's legal..." She appeared again to take the glass away. "—why you have it now." She came back with the glass, full again, then looked down at me and shook her bedraggled head. "Are you hungry?" she said. "I have some chips from the vending machine."

Two unopened bags fell into my lap. I lifted one and popped open the package, famished, while my mother walked behind me out of sight. The smell of the salty powdered cheese floated up to me and I reached inside and pulled out an orange triangle and put it in my mouth and crunched it up. I did this mechanically for some time in a heavy cocoon of utter silence. I was content not to turn around. Soon both bags were empty. I turned them inside out and licked all the bright crumbs away. Then I crinkled up the shiny foil and put it in my mouth, feeling it compress and expand, compress and expand. It was too big to swallow, and it wasn't getting any smaller, so I took it out and put it on the floor. I sat in front of a brown dresser with a split bottom drawer, a sideways crack in it jagging through the wood. There was a clock on it with red digital numbers that said 8:50.

I realized my mother had disappeared. I looked around at the blinds hitched up crooked and yellowed and the corner of the room with the tissues piled up like stale eggs and the chair with the crushed cigarette boxes strewn all around it. She had been in this room with me just a minute ago. But she wasn't here now. My heart swelled up like a hot welt. Where was she? I stood up, my bulky sling unbalancing me, and braced my legs against the mattress behind me. I turned around. She wasn't on the tangled-looking bed. The door I had seen her go through was open and the humming light was still on. Could she be in there? I walked over to it and peeked inside.

She was sitting on the edge of a bathtub full of sitting water, her aqua robe hitched up around her thighs, her legs poking out like skewered sticks of meat. Her head was down and her eyes were closed. I stepped back before she noticed me, disturbed and wonderstruck to see my actual mother, her body wasted away but still there, still breathing life, and I carried myself to the edge of the bed and sat down on it. The springs squeaked beneath me. On the floor where I had been sitting was an orange pill bottle with long white sticks in it identical to the one I'd seen my mother hold up minutes ago. I picked it up. I stared at the black letters on the prescription sticker. RITA GEORGE. A second later I heard a long strip of toilet paper yank off the roll, and then my mother's throat drew up some heavy mucus and she spat. She stepped out and looked at me.

"Coming to your senses yet?"

Her voice was hoarse and strange, hardly recognizable, yet here she stood, so perfectly like herself that I couldn't recall a moment of her being dead, and I wanted to weep with both bitterness and relief. She reached for her cigarettes on the dresser and shook one out, this gesture so automatic, so natural, that I only noticed it because of the tremors that shook her hand, and the way it steadied when she pulled the cigarette out and ran through the familiar motions with the lighter and then looked at me through the first plume of smoke.

"I wish you hadn't come here," she said.

This hit me like a fist in the throat.

"I can only hope your father doesn't know." She peered at me, waiting, it seemed, to see an answer appear on my face. "If he did it would kill him."

I thought suddenly of what my father did know, and how it had already killed him, and how my mother stood here not aware of it yet, searching me with her look, but not asking to be told. She took another drag on her cigarette. Her eyes, full of a grim lusterless intensity, pierced me through the smoke.

"Well, what should we talk about?"

My throat was so tight I could barely breathe. There was so much I wanted to talk about, like how she could be alive right now when she was supposed to be dead, and what she was doing all the way down here, and why my brother had lied. I wanted to accuse her of lying too, of carrying on a secret life, of leaving our lives in ruin, of leaving my father in ruin—but looking at her so savagely wrecked, so forsaken in this dismal waste of a room, I couldn't summon the blame.

"Well for starters," she said. "You can see I'm dying." She squinted at me. "You probably already knew that. Did that boyfriend of yours tell you he saw me?"

I stared at her. What?

My mother's face seemed to loosen with surprise. "Maybe he didn't see me. He got on the elevator at the hospital." Her hand waved absently. "Months ago." What was she doing at the hospital? She looked at me bleakly. "I suppose you're still with him."

I felt a twinge of shame—her tone of knowing disappointment twisting in me like a sharp little screw. I cracked my throat and pushed out a response. "No," I said, my voice unsteady, not convincing at all.

She cocked an eyebrow. Suddenly her face contorted and she turned her head and coughed. When she was done, she said, "So how did you know I was here? Did Eliot tell you?"

"Eliot told me you were dead." The moment the words were out I felt the anger from that lie swelling up hard and huge inside me.

My mother didn't seem surprised. "I guess he showed you that note he had me write." She turned and bent over coughing again, not stopping this time until her face went purple with strain and the breath she drew was feeble and choked.

I watched, stricken by the sight of her, and by the unfathomable thought that this was how she had been living for the last two months, keeping barely alive in this foul little room where she had nothing to do but linger in agony. Why? Why was she here? What had happened to her on that day that she was supposed to have died?

And this thought struck another one, bright in the darkness of my mind. *Somebody* had died in that house. There was a body. And if it wasn't my mother's, then whose was it? The question burned like a sudden revelation and I blurted it out. "A body was in the house."

My mother glanced up at me, drawing the wadded tissue out of her robe again. I could tell by her face that she knew about the body.

I felt as if all the wind had been knocked out of me. Had Eliot killed somebody? Somebody *else*? I thought, remembering the body on the basement stairs. A sudden wave of fear and dismay rolled over me. *Who was my brother?* I thought. *What had he become?*

My mother spit into the tissue and folded it away. "Your brother did what he had to do. And I don't blame him for it."

"You don't blame him for what?" I said, breathless with rising panic. "What did he do?"

She gave me a short hard look. "It has nothing to do with you."

She started across the room, hobbling on her blown-up foot to the chair in the corner and lowering herself down, sucking in the pain—not paying any attention to me. There it was, the familiar barb of my mother's dismissal and rejection. I felt it like I had always felt it, that little prick in my heart, fast and unexpected, sharpened this time by the terrible truth of what my brother had done, of who he had become.

"He killed somebody," I said.

My mother gave me a sharp disapproving look. "What do you think this is? One of your murder mystery books?" She sounded almost amused. "Your brother has his problems, but he doesn't kill people."

But she didn't know about the body, the one I had seen in the basement. And she didn't know what he had tried to do to me. "He tried to kill me," I said. The words were out before the thought was even complete.

My mother looked disconcerted. "What?"

"Somebody did." My voice throbbed in my throat, and though I could hardly believe what I was saying I went on. "That gypsy told me it was Eliot."

"What gypsy?" My mother's mouth was parted in a hard incredulous gash. "What are you talking about?"

I took a gulping breath. "The one in the auto body shop with the gray hair."

My mother stared at me for a few moments, saying nothing, then leaned forward with a heavy sigh and crushed her cigarette out in the ashtray on the little round table. "You met my father."

So it was him. I pulled at a handful of bedsheet and twisted it between my fingers.

"What did he tell you?"

I hesitated. I couldn't start with what the gypsy had said. I had to begin before that, with what had actually happened.

"I got shot," I said. At these words I felt my throat clench shut.

My mother looked dumbfounded. "Shot? Like with a gun? Where?"

I cleared my throat, trying to open a passage, and pushed the words out. "I was outside the church. Somebody shot me in the shoulder."

"The church?" my mother said.

"The one in your neighborhood." I felt strangely guilty, as if I had just confessed to something I had done, not something that had been done to me. "I passed out. Somebody locked me in the basement." Again I could see that blinding spray of flames and behind it, darkly illuminated, the silhouette of head and shoulders. When I spoke again it was in a hoarse whisper. "They set it on fire." I didn't mention the body. I couldn't. "That man—your father—he told me it was Eliot."

My mother stared at me, her eyes bright and hot, then she put her face in her hands and sat bent over, her elbows braced on her knees, one crusted tie of her bathrobe hanging limp between her legs. I found the bedsheet still in my hand, twisted to a tight knob, and I put it in my mouth and chewed. It smelled sour and felt slick and cool against my tongue, thinly coated in grease, and it repulsed me at the same time it comforted me.

"No," my mother said, shaking her head to throw off the suggestion. "It was not Eliot. Your brother would not try to kill you." She looked up, and her eyes were suddenly filled with a molten sadness so deep that it startled me. I felt a sharp ache of yearning, a hurting hope that my mother would say something I needed to hear, that she would tell me she was sorry for everything that had happened to me, that she would heal me as only she could.

"Don't do that Natalie."

I realized she was talking about the bedsheet.

"That's two months of my rancid sickness on that sheet. Two months of all my nasty secretions and dead skin and whatever else is coming off me. Do you want to suck on that?"

I shrugged. Maybe I did. And it was not a fair question anyway. My mother watched a moment longer in disapproval, and then sighed in exasperation and looked away like she couldn't stand the sight of me. We sat there, the moments trickling by, my chest tight and my heart swollen huge inside of it, each beat momentous and grave, heavy with longing and disappointment. I realized how much I wanted her to say she was sorry. But she hadn't. I took the sheet out of my mouth. My voice came out in a trembling accusation.

"He told me," I said, "your father told me—that Eliot was crazy."

My mother shook her head and reached for her cigarettes. "Of course he did. He believes Eliot is crazy." She plucked one out and lit it, then sat gazing into the room and shaking her head, as if she couldn't abide by any of it, as if some deep offense lay at the center of it all and left her resigned and hopeless. "Let me explain something," she said in a voice that was low and strained. "What your brother is—my people, they don't allow it. They think it's a craziness. If you're like him, you pollute yourself and the whole family."

I didn't understand. "Like him?"

"You know what I mean Natalie," she said, her voice suddenly hard and impatient. "He's a queer."

The word went off like a spark in my chest. I had known it—we had all known it of course—but it was the first time I'd heard my mother say it. I watched her suck on her cigarette, the cords of her shriveled neck standing out like bones. "I shouldn't have sent him there," she said. "I knew what he was. I knew it would cause problems, sooner or later. But I thought he would leave before that. I never expected him to try to live with them. I never expected him to stay there and pretend he was something he wasn't." She turned her face down and gazed at the point of her cigarette. She seemed unwilling to look at me. "There are things about my family you wouldn't understand. Things I've never tried to explain. You have to try to see things the way they look at them."

She stopped talking, sinking down into her thoughts, and for a moment I thought she wasn't going to say any more. Then she started speaking again, in a voice that was quiet and tense, strung with careful thought—a voice I had not heard her use before. "My people—they believe sickness is something that possesses you. Your thoughts, your feelings—nothing you feel or do is your own when you're sick." She gazed in my direction but her eyes were looking through me. "And who says it ever is? Who says that part of us isn't always the property of something else, something terrible that gets inside of us and has us at its mercy." She put her cigarette to her mouth and drew on it and took it away. Her face was like yellow wax, still and ponderous, her eyes feverish and staring. I didn't know who this person was. She did not seem like my mother.

"That's the life we live. We live under the command of something other and above us. And the rules that we make are there to keep us clean in the eyes of that other. All those stupid rules," she said, waving her cigarette in the air. "Don't wash skirts with blouses. Blow on your hands to prevent illness. If you're sick, get married. If you're crippled, get married. If you're queer, get married." She stopped talking abruptly and peered at me, pinning me down with her stare, as if trying to decide how much more to say. "That was the trouble with Eliot. When he didn't get married, they thought he was sick. He was making Emilian unwell. He was possessed to do wicked things, things they could never condone. He was bringing bad luck. So that's why my father told you he was crazy." She shrugged. "He's not crazy. He's the same as he's always been."

The same as he's always been. But he'd always been possessed to do crazy things—he'd always been compelled along by a kind of sickness. And he had done this to my mother, hadn't he? Or had he? My mother puffed out smoke and looked into the room. "Look at what a place this is," she said, as if she were waking from a trance to see it for the first time. "Look at what a dump."

"What are you doing here?" I said, overwhelmed suddenly by everything I didn't know, by my mother sitting here before me, looking at me through a bitter cloud of smoke and ash, languishing here in a room she couldn't or wouldn't leave, either trapped or hiding here, by whom or from whom I couldn't guess. "Who did this to you?" Now I could feel all the desperate, unfathomable confusion rising in me like an iceberg and sticking high in my chest. "What happened?" It felt like no question was good enough for all I wanted to know.

"It's a long story," she said with an exhausted sigh. The breath snagged in her throat and she coughed. "It doesn't matter anyway. As soon as you leave here, none of this matters."

How can she say that? I thought. *It matters to me.* I heard my voice come out as if it didn't belong to me—a dry, trembling husk of sound. All I could say was "Why?"

My mother shrugged, her eyes dull and tired. "Because." She leaned forward and stamped her cigarette several times into the ashtray. I watched her drop it beside the other one, two bodies tossed down in twisted ruin. Then she looked up.

"Tonight I'm going to die," she said.

32

SHE ALMOST SEEMED TO SMILE AT THIS, AS IF IT GAVE HER RELIEF JUST to say it. "You got here just in time."

My lungs felt pounded thin in my chest, like bright, hard disks with nothing inside.

"Since you're here, I have one favor to ask of you."

Favor? My thoughts were completely shaken loose, drifting in deep confusion.

"On the day after Memorial Day, Tuesday," she said, "I want you to go to the beach at noon, the one I used to take you to, by the bathrooms where we used to go. If you see a woman there—somebody who looks like me—" I could hardly understand what she was saying. I felt dumb with shock and refusal. "Natalie," she said. "Listen. If you see her—she's my sister—I want you to give her this." I watched her pick up a stiff card, write something on it, and then hand it to me. "She needs to see that."

Numbly, I stared down at it. It was a missing persons card, and in the top corner, trembling and unsure, a familiar phrase was written: *I pity dafoo.* I felt a jolt of recognition. It was the card from the Chinese grocery, the one that woman, Lin, had written on. But there was more writing now in my mother's script, beside the age-progressed picture of the missing boy: *This is why he did it. Luca's safe—with E. Don't blame yourself. Don't come for me.* My mother's initials were below it. What was this? I looked at the picture of the boy, the big eyes, the schoolboy smile, eager and a little tentative. He looked familiar—a little like the picture of Eliot from my father's wallet, but it was not Eliot. Where had I seen him? Suddenly I knew where I had seen him, or a boy who looked almost like him, outside of the church. With the toy gun. And inside the front window of Madame Zadie's shop before that, on that first day I had been to the neighborhood. I stared at the card. The boy's name was Matthew McGowan, and his age had been progressed five years. He had gone missing when he was only a baby.

"What is this?" I said, my chest tight with apprehension.

My mother looked ruefully at me. "You didn't know," she said, just now realizing it. "Your brother has a son."

For a moment, I sat in stunned silence. "What?"

"It's not his by birth. It's hers," she said, pointing with her thumb to the door. "The one across the hall."

I stared at her, hardly breathing, trying to wrap my mind around this, and then looked back at the card. There she was in the other picture, her blond hair like a static around her face, the woman who had asked me for money in the parking lot. I looked at the information below the picture. Danielle McGowan. The card said she was missing too.

"Who are they?" I said, unable to make sense of this. "Are they both here? In the motel?"

"No," said my mother, reaching again for her cigarettes and shaking one out. "The kid hasn't seen his mother for years. He doesn't even know her. Eliot keeps her here, out of the way."

"Out of the way?"

My mother waved her hand as she lit her cigarette. "She's up here strung out all the time. You saw her. She has some trashy husband now who sticks around for the drugs. Eliot gives them what they want. He pays for the room here and keeps them satisfied." She stopped and peered at me. "You didn't recognize her? She's from his high school. She used to come over to the house. Your father always hoped she was his girlfriend." She snorted. "She was one of the people I had to ban that summer. You remember how much she was hanging around that summer, right before he ran away."

That summer. The weight of those words swung through me, deep, resonant, painful. All I remembered of that summer was my own suffering, how I had languished those months in a shroud of crinoline and taffeta, witnessing the covert crimes of my mother and brother—the mysterious outings, the hushed voices, the evasive answers—like some secret club pursuing an objective I couldn't guess. And then at the end of it he was gone. But he hadn't run away.

"You *took* him away," I said, and I thought, *Away from me.*

My mother's head twitched back, as if what I had said had momentarily surprised her, but then she nodded, gazing absentmindedly into the smoke from her cigarette. "That's right. I did. I took him away because I knew Emilian could help him." Her voice was hard and unapologetic. "I knew he would do what I couldn't, what your father couldn't." She must have seen something in my face, something that showed her the power of my hurt over her sense of rightness. She looked almost startled. Then she shook her head and sighed.

"Okay, look, Natalie. I knew if he took Eliot in, if they knew Eliot was his, Eliot would be accepted, for a time." She lifted her hand, as if to stop some force in the air. "I told Emilian to hold him there for six months. After the six months he was free to do what he wanted. He might go back to drugs. He might come back in the night to kill me, or run away and start some other life and never look back—whatever he did, whatever he chose, that would be his choice to make. But I wanted him to be able to make a choice, to decide that he didn't have to keep killing himself senselessly. That's all I wanted. I was trying to save his life," she said, her voice thrumming in her throat. "I did save his life."

I felt the knot of pain and anger loosen inside me. I knew she was right. But what had happened to him since then? She had saved my brother so that he could become despised by the same people who had taken him in, so that he could live a false life among them, pretending to be what he wasn't, stealing some kid away from his mother and hiding her up here. I didn't understand it. I held the card up in the air.

"Why did he do this?"

She gave me a tired look, and I was afraid she wouldn't tell me, but she started talking. "After I sent him there, for a long time I was talking to my sister." She pointed her cigarette at me. "Nobody knew about that then and nobody but Eliot knows it now. That's not something you can tell anybody," she warned.

"Okay," I said. I wondered what it meant to keep that a secret.

"She told me that he was cleaned up and staying on, and then he got involved with some of the kumpanias down the coast, some of the car scams, and he was driving back and forth, months there and months gone, and I expected to hear one day that he had left and not gone back. He was making people uneasy. He must have known it. It was hard to hide what he was. But he always went back." She shook her head. "Emilian was the only one keeping your brother there. The respect they had for him, the influence he had, kept Eliot in good standing. And Eliot was good at what he did for them—he always made them money, he never got caught.

"And then once he came back after being away down the coast a full year, and he brought with him this wife and a one-month-old baby. The real father had been Puerto Rican or something. He'd left the girl when she was still pregnant. Eliot had run into her somewhere, or maybe he had sought her out—I don't know. She was strung out and all alone with this baby, didn't think her parents would help her. He promised her all the free drugs she wanted if she pretended to be his wife and lived in the neighborhood, lived according to our rules, and he would raise her kid and take care of it. So he came back with her and said the baby was his."

I didn't get it. "But she's white," I said.

"So?"

"Didn't they kick him out?"

"For marrying a white woman?" said my mother. "No, that's not a crime."

"But," I spluttered. "Dad was white. You were kicked out."

My mother smiled grimly. "That was different. I was a woman. I wasn't married to him either. But a gypsy man can marry a white woman if he wants. She's tolerated as long as she lives like a gypsy. But that little woman," said my mother, pointing, "of course wasn't doing any such thing. The house was a mess, she did what she wanted, dressed as she wanted, spoke as she wanted. So Eliot got rid of her. He brought her up here, told the vitsa that she ran away, and he kept her son. By that time he was more Eliot's son than hers anyway. He had raised him. I heard he was a good father." She raised her eyebrows and inhaled on her cigarette, as if she couldn't exactly believe it but couldn't deny it either. "Of course it didn't look good that now he had a son and no wife. But she wasn't really the problem. The parents were the problem."

"The parents? Whose parents?"

"Hers. They came looking for her. A few months after my sister called and told me Eliot had come back with a wife and child, the girl's parents showed up at the house."

I was disconcerted. "Our house?"

My mother nodded. "Apparently their daughter had mentioned Eliot's name to them in some phone conversation sometime before she disappeared. She had said they didn't need to worry anymore, that her friend Eliot was going to take care of her. Of course that had worried them," my mother said drily. "They remembered him from years ago, and they remembered his disappearance, all the attention it got at the school. When they came to the house they wanted to know if I knew where he was. I had to say no, of course." She seemed too nonchalant to be telling me all this. It was old news to her, but I couldn't help feeling sorry for those worried parents, still without a daughter or grandson, still living with the question in their minds of what had happened to them—and probably with the heartache too, of what they imagined in answer to that question. "They said they had filed a missing persons report, and they asked me to tell them if anything came up, and promised they would do the same, and went on their way." She pointed at the card in my hand. "For four years I said nothing. But then this card showed up somewhere—who knows how often they circulate those things, if it was from that original report they had filed, or if they filed another one—but somebody recognized the picture."

"Who?" I said.

My mother shrugged.

I looked down at the card. I had first seen it in the Chinese grocery. Could it have been Lin, since she was keeping the card? Or Ian? Maybe he had noticed it. Maybe he had recognized the picture. He must have seen the boy in the neighborhood. Or even Danielle.

"I saw this," I said. "At that Chinese grocery."

My mother looked at me in confusion.

"This exact card," I said, flapping it. "With the writing. How did you get it?"

She flicked her hand dismissively. "Eliot had it. It was in his things," she said, not saying whether he left it or she took it. "Whoever he took it from had been gouging your brother for money so he wouldn't tell." She let out a sputtering cough. "Then, to make it worse Emilian got sick. Eliot was taking care of him. The whole kumpania was staying away from them. He was worried about his son. His time was up." She pitched forward and began hacking again, her hair nearly in the ash on the end of her cigarette. When she was done, she sat back, listless and weak, noticed the smoking stub still in her hand, and put it out.

"Water," she said. "Get me some water."

I got up and went to the bathroom with the glass and turned on the faucet in the dark.

As I filled it I stood looking at my dark reflection in the mirror, unable to piece this part of the story together with the fact of my mother sitting out there in that room, her body broken, her life lost, strewn like wreckage in my brother's wake. How had his problems led him back to her, to his old house on that February day, where my mother was likely walking the house in her bathrobe, refusing to go and meet him, and thinking who knows what? What had happened that day between them? How had it ended with her coming here?

I walked back out and handed my mother the glass of water. She took several small sips, as if each one were a torment and not a relief. I watched her. She was dying, I thought. For almost three months my mother had been here, dying. Of what? Emphysema? Cancer?

"What is it?" I said. "What do you have?"

She glanced up, dully, not understanding the question.

"Cancer?" I said.

The look on her face—*So?*—was affirming and dismissive at once.

Did she think I knew? How was I supposed to know? "You didn't tell us," I said, the words pouring out in confusion. "You had cancer. When did you find out?"

My mother looked at me. She didn't say anything.

"Why?" I said. "Why didn't you tell us?"

She shook her head. "It was easier that way."

"What was easier?" The moment I asked it I was afraid of what her answer would be.

My mother opened her mouth, but paused. "Forget it, Natalie."

But I didn't want to forget it. "Why did you have to keep it from us? And whose name is this?" I pulled the canister out of my pocket. "Rita George?" Once I said it the name seemed to linger in my mouth, like rust.

My mother gave me a penetrating look, a look full of attention, as if it bothered her to hear the name too. Then she sighed. "Rita George was an old name," she said. "It was just convenient."

"Convenient for what?"

"I didn't want it on my records, Natalie. I didn't want anyone knowing that I had cancer," she said, as if it irritated her just to say the word. "I didn't want any phone calls, or bills, or letters coming to the house. I didn't want your father finding out and trying to make me take the treatment. I didn't want the argument, the exams, the doctors, the money wasted—" She cut herself off, disgusted. "I didn't want any of it. I just wanted to know if I had the damn disease."

A lump had risen in my throat. Of course she would do it that way. She couldn't share her life with us, so how could we expect her to share her death? "But we would have found out about it anyway," I said. "When you got sick."

"I wasn't planning on getting sick, Natalie."

For a moment I didn't understand. And then I did understand. Now I felt the truth fold back on itself, bringing me one more time to what my brother had told me. It was no longer the lie I thought it was, at least not completely. My mother hadn't killed herself, but she had been planning to.

But something had gone wrong, because here she was, right in front of me, dying of cancer. For some reason she hadn't done it—something had changed her mind, or something had stopped her.

"I need a cigarette," my mother said, and took one out and stuck it between her lips. "Look what you're doing to me." She bent to light it, and then leaned back again and looked at me, her eyes sparking, alive again with some portion of that hot luster she always carried in her gaze, as if just having that long stick of fire in her mouth had partly revived her. "Just so you know," she said, pulling a drag and tilting her gaze up at the ceiling. "I was going to make it look like an accident. I knew there would be an investigation, and I didn't want anything on my records that would seem to give me a reason to do it. I wanted to spare your father of that at least." She raised her hands, dismissing that concern and acknowledging her defeat at once. "But anyway here I am. You can thank your brother for that."

I was hit now with the full realization of what my brother had done for my mother when he had come to the house that day. He had really saved her life. But he had also prolonged her suffering. I wondered, Did he know that was what he had done? Did he know, when he was bringing my mother here, that she was already dying? I looked at the medicine bottle. At some point it must have been clear to him, because he had made an effort to keep her alive.

"Why though," I said, my voice loud with agitation. "Why did he do it?"

"Because," my mother said. "He needed me."

33

"EMILIAN WAS DYING. YOUR BROTHER NEEDED HIS MONEY."

I was surprised. I had thought this was about Eliot's son, and about his falling out of favor with the gypsies. "Why?"

"Because he had nothing." My mother widened her eyes like it was obvious. "No high school degree, no skills, no trade, no people he could count on outside the gypsy community—all his connections were through them. He knew he couldn't stay after Emilian died. He couldn't keep paying the cost of keeping his son a secret there, with somebody blackmailing him—he was afraid," my mother said. "He didn't know who else would recognize the boy. And if it came out what he had done with the girl, he could go to prison for drugs, human trafficking, child abduction. Even if he had a good story—even if he could say he was raising the boy after his mother ran away—he knew the way it would spin, he knew the courts wouldn't be lenient. He was a gypsy. He needed to get as far away as possible and he needed money to do it."

At this I imagined plane tickets to some South American country, my brother living on a load of cash. It was like some book I had read. "But Emilian couldn't have had that much money," I said. I had seen that gypsy neighborhood. There was no money there. They were poor.

"He owned a jewelry shop," my mother said. "He had money from losses when it burned down." She stopped there, but I knew what it meant. I had heard Eliot's story—fires, insurance claims.

"So it was a scam," I said.

My mother eyed me fiercely. "Gypsies have a lot of enemies," she said, then immediately shook her head to move us past that thought. "That money was supposed to go to the vitsa. The family," she said. "But when Emilian got sick your brother had him write out a will."

I sat thinking this over for a moment in silence. Did she mean that Eliot had taken the money meant for the family? "So what does that have to do with you? Why did Eliot want you to go see Emilian?"

She seemed a little disappointed by my inability to put it together. "Because Emilian left all his money to me."

"To you?" I said, stunned. "Why?"

She put the cigarette to her mouth and raised her hand in a dismissive gesture. "In the last weeks of Emilian's illness, he wasn't thinking right. Eliot made him suspicious, confused. He told him the vitsa was out to get him. He told Emilian lies about what the rest of the family had done to Eliot while Emilian was sick." She sat back, looking uneasy. "Emilian had a brain tumor. He was half out of his mind by the time I got there. He was convinced," she said, and turned her head and coughed. "Eliot had convinced him—" She stopped talking, and her face contorted and she got lost in another heavy fit of coughing. The cigarette was still in her hand and she put it out, grinding it down beside the other ones—four in all now—while she struggled to draw breath. She pulled out a tissue and spit a gob of brown mucus and stringy blood into it. "Never mind," she said. "All you need to know is that I went, and a few weeks later, he died. I didn't know about the money until after that." She stopped talking.

I sat quietly, letting my mother rest, listening to her raspy breaths go in and out, trying to finish the story in my mind. After a pause I said, "And now you have Emilian's money and they want to get it back? And that's why they're looking for you?"

My mother made a noncommittal noise and looked at my hands, where I was ticcishly scraping the sticker from the pill bottle with my fingernail. The *R* in Rita George was gone, balled up into a little sticky pellet I had rolled between thumb and forefinger. I put it in my mouth.

So, was this a fake name? Another nav gajikano? *Convenient,* my mother had said. An old name. I remembered the old gypsy asking me if I knew a Rita George. Why was he asking? Didn't he know it was her?

And then it clicked. "Is that how the money was left to you, as Rita George?"

A sigh, as in *yes.* "You know how that goes. Paperwork needs to be signed, money needs to move. Once it was there Eliot didn't need me anymore."

For a while we sat in silence, and then slowly I realized that my mother was done. There was nothing left to say, no questions left to be answered. The story was over.

I thought about what it took for my mother to tell me this, to empty out the past, to put it out where she could hear it and where she knew I could hear it. And it seemed there was almost nothing left of the mother I knew in the figure before me, her eyes listless and grave, her mouth a furrowed slit, pulled down into some final, unknowable regret. I had no idea what she was thinking, or what she regretted. I had no idea how much of this had been forced on her, or how much she had willingly participated in. As if she could sense my remaining unease, my mother picked her head up and leveled a stare at me.

"But let me just say this for your brother. We have to pick our loyalties in this world. Everything he did to me he did for his son. And I can understand that."

At these words I felt a prick of misgiving. *Why?* I thought. Why had she let him do this? Why had she forgiven him? And why did it pain me to know it? But the answer came to me: because my mother had picked her loyalties too. Just like Eliot, everything that she had done to me, and to my father, she had done for her son. But I couldn't understand it. And I never would.

Her eyes were still on me, their lightless sheen like a mirror that threw me back onto myself, that would leave me stuck in this place of misgiving and doubt forever. "It's time for you to go," she said.

My heart snapped like a twig. "Wait." The realization of what this meant, of what she was going to do when I was gone, broke through me like a hard sudden wind, and my voice buckled. "No," I said.

My mother stood up. "Tell my sister there was nothing she could do. And don't tell your father anything," she said, sharpening her eyes on me.

I wanted to speak but my voice was sucked away by this heavy gust of anguish. After all that she had done to me, all that she had failed to do for me, here I was, swept down by grief, like I had never grown apart from her, like I had never grown up and never decided I didn't need her. My mother walked past me toward the door. I opened my mouth, but when nothing came out I sprang up from the bed, my legs as wobbly and confused as a newborn calf, as if I was going to stop her. But once I was standing I didn't move.

"Well." She opened the door and heaved a sigh that made her cough again. "This is goodbye, Natalie."

I couldn't believe what was happening. I stared into the gloomy narrow hallway outside the door, and it seemed not like the place where I was going but the place where my mother was going—an ugly, irrevocable corridor, a place where doors never opened, where despair swallowed the light and soiled the air. "You don't have to do it," I said, my voice skidding in my throat. "Why do you have to do it?"

She answered with a sallow breath. "Don't make this hard."

What was there to say to this? I had walked forward and was now standing on the edge of the hallway right in front of my mother, wanting to grab her and pull her back, waiting for one of us to do something, waiting for something to happen.

"You'll be fine," she said in a parched voice. "And your father," she said. "The two of you."

"The two of us?" I couldn't even think. *The two of us?* I had the terrible feeling that my mother was missing her last chance to do something, to make something right for us in the end, since she was making this the end.

I wanted her to say it was her fault. I wanted her to say she was sorry. I wanted her to say she loved me, despite everything. I wanted her to tell me that whatever it may look like, everything she had done had been in part for me, not in rejection of me. But my mother only looked at me wearily, as if she had no idea of all that was still waiting to be said.

"I'm tired," she muttered.

I felt a surge of adrenaline, so much that it dizzied me. I realized I wasn't going to do what she wanted, and out of that rushed a whole slew of possibilities that tried to impel me to disorienting action: grab her, push her, throw something, slam the door, yell, sit down, punch the TV, grab the phone, call—who? Call Boris, Eliot, Mitch, the police. I was breathing hard, taking bull breaths that seemed to be stirring me up to some unlikely physical feat, enraging me so deeply I wanted to scream in her face.

"Okay. When you're ready." My mother's voice, sliding into that tone of dismissal as she walked away from the open door and toward the bathroom.

I saw the dark glint of standing water in the tub and pounced. Got to the door before she did, stood in her way. "No no no," I said—furious, inarticulate. "No. You don't." I had no idea what I meant, only that she was wrong, so wrong, and I wanted to shove her back into how wrong she was.

Without a word my mother let out a sigh, eyes receding bleakly toward some inner thought, then turned and started toward the open motel door. I moved in front of her. I swung it closed. She turned back to the bed and sat down. "Okay, you want to stay and make me suffer? Go ahead."

"I'm not leaving," I said.

"Why don't you hand me my cigarettes."

"I'm not handing you your cigarettes. I'm not letting you smoke any more cigarettes."

My mother looked at me in silence. "Well I'm going to get in bed." She stood up, walked around the side of the bed, sat down, coughed for a few moments, and then feebly kicked her legs up over the side and pulled the sheet to her chin.

I listened to her breathe. "So, that's it," I said.

No answer.

"Nothing? You're not going to say one thing to me. One fucking thing."

I felt stars in my head. I didn't expect my mother to respond.

"I've been here, all this time. *All this time,*" I said, not really understanding my own meaning. "You can't—" I felt my throat clenching down. "Can't you—I mean—" I was on the verge of crying now, and it filled me so full of outrage and despair to listen to myself, to hear my raw voice, trying to ask for something from my mother, practically begging, that I breathed out a low, furious scream before I could let myself do it.

My mother, eyes closed, raised her eyebrows, cleared her throat.

"Why do you hate me?" I said. "I didn't do anything. All I ever wanted. I mean—couldn't you ever—you were so fucking mean to me."

She coughed, weakly, as in *really?* A drab silence followed and I hung my head.

"I wasn't that mean to you." This murmured up at the ceiling.

I scoffed. "You weren't ever *nice* to me." Shamefully, I noticed the relief I felt that she was speaking to me again, that her signs and signals were back on. "What nice thing did you ever do for me?"

She sighed. She seemed on the fence about whether or not to keep bothering with this conversation. "I don't know, Natalie." I thought she was done, but then she said, "I threw your books away."

"That wasn't *nice.*" I was raising my voice now, nearly yelling. "Do you know why I read in the first place? Because nobody would be my friend. Nobody would come close to me. I was an outcast at school—I couldn't look anybody in the eye. Do you remember how you used to take us to the beach? How you would yank my hair to get me to put on my swimsuit and then drag me out to the car, how I cried all the way there, how I begged you not to make me go in the water? Did you think I would just be a normal person who could make friends after that? I was afraid of everybody. All I had were my books. And you took them from me."

After a long bleak pause, she drew in a wheezy breath. "It wasn't my job to be nice."

"Wasn't your job?"

My mother didn't seem compelled to respond to this.

"You never played with me. You never cared about what I did in school. You never tried to help me *like* anything else. You threw my books away. You gave me money and made me buy my own Christmas presents at the mall. You left me at the Laundromat. You hoped I would die, or disappear—"

"I didn't exactly hope that."

"Didn't exactly—? What did you hope? You wished I had never existed then." I paused only for an instant, realizing I was afraid she would answer this with a telling silence. "Maybe you didn't want me, but I was a human being—your *daughter.* Wasn't there ever a moment when you felt glad I was alive?" Again, a question I didn't want to leave hanging. "I mean, remember that old woman across the alley? The one you used to feed? You were nicer to her than you ever were to me. And she was senile. She was deranged. She couldn't even appreciate it. You treated her more like a human being than you treated me."

I stopped, out of breath, feeling like I had begun to talk to myself, unraveled and spun out, a hamster in a squeaky wheel, my whole existence lived inside a different set of concerns than the other body in this room. Bleakly I kept looking at my mother, breath rattling in her chest, nose up, resting there coffin-style, waiting to die, and wondered how this was going to go, what I had signed myself up for when I refused to leave. I went to the little round table and sat down. I should have left when she told me to. Now I had to stay.

My mother cleared her throat. In a murmur, she said, "I read to her."

"What?"

"Your books." She parted her eyes and tipped her head up slightly, then dropped it. "You want to know where they went? I took them to her house. Piles of them in the living room. So many books," she said hazily.

My mouth, I realized, had opened. "My books? Read to who?"

"Many nights," my mother said, her voice drifting. "I couldn't sleep. She was always awake. It steadied her, to hear a voice."

I could not utter a word.

"Her daughter—put in that home. Retarded. House falling apart. The elderly—" she fluttered her fingers, tone sour. "The way this world treats them. It's just not right." For a while she said nothing and I found myself staring at the tabletop—ashtray, amber glass, fake wood grain. None of it made sense. "You're not like me," my mother said. "Someday you'll have a daughter and be her best friend. My mother—" she shook her head and roughly cleared her throat. "We all take. We all lie. We don't pretend this life is precious. That's where I come from. We live. We serve. We're lucky or we're not. That's it. End of story."

My mother broke into a ragged cough and when it was over she lifted up on her elbows to breathe.

I stood, drawn up to my feet, about to do something. I could imagine my books in that house. In the gloom behind the crack in that door. And my mother herself had stacked them there.

"Don't stay, Natalie. I don't want you to."

Then I did it. I took four plunging steps over to her and scooped my good arm underneath her, lifting her up, light as a wishbone, grizzled hair against my cheek, musky and sour, the claws of her nails scrabbling against me, my arm churning with rivulets of pain again. Now that I had her rib cage firmly clamped I started dragging her from the bed. The only place to go was the bathroom, and I was already moving in that direction as if I knew exactly what I was doing. My thoughts lagged behind my body, spinning circles in place and then suddenly racing forward, and I started talking as I dragged us through the doorway. "Full tub of water?" *Was that the plan?* "Probably not warm anymore." I staggered in the dark with her as she sucked in big wheezing gulps of air and fumbled to get her legs under her. "Let's just get it over with," I said, huffing the words out as our heads knocked together. "Always your choice. I'm here to help." But I couldn't drop her in the tub. I couldn't do it. I plunked her on the toilet, roughly so that her head snapped back and hit the tank, still talking fast as if to outrun my panic. "Push your head under? Will that make up for it?" I saw her arm jab out in the dark and cover up the glint of something on the side of the tub and a sound—little metallic chink—made my heart skitter with sudden inexplicable horror. I recognized what I had seen as I grabbed for her hand and she fumbled the razor between her fingers and raised her other arm like she was trying to slice it wide open right under me. Our hands clawed and scrabbled and she expelled a rattling gust of air and I felt the raw sting too as my forefinger pressed on the blade and then slipped down it, blood flowing between our hands as the razor fell and I got my shoe on it.

"No!" I yelled, still holding one wrist, all bone and sinew. My mother let it go limp. "No," I said again, this time quietly. I stood over her, catching my breath, realizing I was going to keep her alive until she died, that whatever pain she suffered from here until the end would be all because of me.

I stood frozen in tension over her, a coiled spring, air pounding in and out of my lungs, thoughts firing. "I'll take you to the hospital," I said, trying one last thing. "Use your fake name. It doesn't matter anymore. They won't find you in time."

My mother gave me a black withering stare.

"I'll leave—you can be alone. You won't even know you're dying," I said, even though I knew every word I said was a lie. The way her eyes lost focus on mine and retreated, as if from some cruel, glaring light—she must have seen something, my desperation looming over her, like the menace she'd been outrunning all along, the nameless punishment she'd always felt coming to her. For a desperate moment I thought I should force it on her—she would never agree to let me take her but maybe some part of her was relying on me to do it. The thought passed and so did the volition to go with it. I sat down on the edge of the tub, scraping my foot against the floor to bring the razor over. My mother slumped down, taking broken sucks of air she probably wished she could stop working so hard for. The light coming in on us from the other room was murky, apocalyptic, mustard gas and smoke. In the mirror I could see my own silhouette and a few frayed strands of my mother's wayward hair. Towel over the shower rod above my head, racks all empty, counter barren, nothing but a dark square mass on the toilet tank behind her. I kept looking at it—not a tissue box. More the size of a book.

I noticed the hammering in my shoulder, a cardboard stiffness there, a mismatched queasy slurring in my stomach. My mother's breathing was even, but prickled, full of sand. I reached behind me and flipped the drain open and the tub started to glug. I turned the water on, hot as it could go. I would get her breathing again, at least for now. I flipped on the light switch. Two bulbs lit up behind a cracked, tawny piece of plastic over the mirror. I closed the door, reached over my mother's prone neck, the top of her spine poking out like an elbow, and picked up the book.

As I sat back down, swaths and shoals of steam began gusting all around us, like a spell being cast in a faraway land, a whirl of pure and perfect magic.

"Mmm." My mother's voice, telling me she knew exactly what I was doing, echoed off the walls with a roundness and luster it never had in real life.

Then the grim ministrations. The disjointed hours going by in a fever trance—death labor, dozing off, panic and exhaustion and the nasal vibrations of my voice reading words and a tight, infectious tingling over my entire body. Somewhere in this swirling vortex I turned another page in the book, gingerly, but the sheet came out, breaking clean of the binding with the brittle heft of something stiffened by water damage, something that had been sponging up the humidity of that bathroom for who knew how long. I held it in my hand a moment before letting it drop, an ungainly paper aircraft falling down like the ones I had made in my youth. Mine never flew. Eliot's always did.

I reached up and turned off the lamp. I wouldn't let myself eat these pages, and so far, one hundred pages in, the plunging vertigo and brimming nausea had convinced my pica to obey me. It helped that it wasn't a very good book. The kind my mother used to read on the beach—windswept Tarzans in tattered trousers courting schoolmarm Janes on an island paradise. Missionary aid workers, succumbing to their insatiable eroticism. No irony whatsoever. It was a romance novel. My mother would have loved it.

And who's to say she wasn't loving it? Right now, she was in one of her blackouts, those sudden hiccups of deep sleep that were cut short by ghastly spasms and waking inhalations. The air going into her lungs was now a red mist, a fine spray that would slowly suffocate her. She no longer had the strength to cough. I, myself, was running out of strength for steam baths. But I would keep giving them. I realized that. I would carry her to the bathroom, lower her to the toilet, get into my kneeling crouch to keep her from sliding off, and balance there panting for twenty minutes like a bodybuilder revving himself up right before an outlandish lift. I was learning my own strength, here in this room.

Cold morning light slipped watery through the blinds. Which morning were we on? It seemed impossible that it could be the third. *May 7th*, I said in my head. A Monday. Already the start of workday doldrums for some people—fishermen, lonely weathermen, delivery boys and dog walkers. Me too, if I was where I should be.

A few minutes ago I had heard the sprinkle of a dog collar in the hallway. Now I was wondering about Danielle. Was that her? Had she really gone to the hospital? I was nervous about how much she knew about this room. She had given me that joint from my mother's supply. Did she know my mother was here? At some point would she come bursting in, demanding to know where Eliot was, waving his forsaken phone in the air?

"Huhn-kuh." My mother's eyes parted, barely. She began to make the zombie noise into the pillow. Sometimes, though it made things worse, she broke into words upon waking, the sleepy fretting of a sick child. Her mouth moved, and I could see this was one of those times. After some inarticulate whispering, she mumbled a phrase.

"Mine now," it sounded like.

"Mmh," I said, a tonal exhalation, trying to ease her as gently as possible into her awareness of me, the room, the event that was taking place.

Her face twitched slightly away from a red scribbling on the pillow. That blood had started as just a speck, a dry little incidental mark. But with all the trips from the bed to the bathroom and back again, it was forming a ghastly little artwork under her head. Violence, pure and unraveling.

Her eyes settled on me and focused.

"Hi," I said.

A pause. A whisper. "You."

"Me." That's right. Me. Every time a discovery. I parted the paperback again and held it up. *Want more?*

My mother, blinking, scrabbled her finger at the sheet. She seemed to want to point. She was pointing something out to me. I looked down, the medical apparatus upon me already a dirty, soggy thing. The wound inside was hard as bone.

"You hurt," she muttered.

Yes, I nodded. *I hurt.* And admitting the obvious, I felt for a clear vaulting moment an exhilarating relief. There was a moment of calm in the room, a top-of-the-mountain awe. My mother and I sipping together on thin glorious air. Stillness, peace between us.

Then she scraped for breath and we went sliding down the mountain. I stood up to get the hot shower going again in the bathroom. I came forward and dabbed her crusty mouth, untwisted the mangy blue pelt from her legs. She was so weak. All her bones sliding in her skin. Would we even make it to the steam this time? Standing over her, I had a feeling, a deep, deep feeling, that we wouldn't. I retrieved the book and sat on the edge of the bed. My mother, scoured, drowning in blood, flicked her fingers for me to go on with the story.

I read, and she closed her eyes. I read and eventually she died.

When I finally left that room, hours later, the night air sweeping me down to the end of the road, I saw an old world. Big moon, bright and steady overhead. Black water, sheen and starlight. And down the beach, a fire.

34

I PEEKED INTO THE PEEPHOLE OF MY APARTMENT DOOR AT A MAN IN a pink shirt, hefting an exuberant throng of flowers. *Oh no,* I thought. *More to eat.*

I opened the door, and he kept his prim smile planted as he foisted the splattered mess of petals and wax leaves onto me. "Thanks," I said, my tone doubting my words.

A card roosted on a plastic stick right in the middle of all that, the envelope so thick it could have come with an eject button. That was going to be a guilty pleasure later on. Inside were signatures from everyone at the station—the news team, the staff writers, the interns, Swenson himself. Salt had written out his entire name, as if he were autographing the flowers for me. Oh, someday I was going to miss him. That day was already here.

I carried the flowers spewing their scent like a can of tear gas out to the living room and hesitated, unsure where to place them. They were bigger than most of my furniture. I picked the only spot I could imagine them fitting, on the notched pink battlement atop my fairy-tale castle, and I stood back to view my arrangement. Whatever warrior princess was up there ready to sink her arrow into the caterpillar across the room would now have proper coverage. I looked around me. I felt a tad bit squeamish. It was probably time to get new furniture.

I went to the bedroom to finish dressing. All men's button-downs for ease of ingress these days—a totally new look for me. Mitch had loaned me some. The shirts I would replace with ones from the thrift store soon, and return to him. Then I would see. Not all friends are forever.

I was heeding the pill bottle's advice not to operate heavy machinery, so I would be walking instead of driving today. No coat necessary in this weather. After a twenty-minute stroll through sunlight that was as mild and tepid as a good sedative buzz, I walked into the rehab center.

Boris had his chair pulled up to the little table in the corner and was arranging a game of solitaire. My first thought was that it looked like the table where I had sat in my mother's room. He took one look at me and puffed air into his cheeks.

I lifted my hand in hello.

He shook his head at me.

"Don't tell me." My father held his hand up. He looked me over, his eyes blunt and searching. "You're fine?" he said, and I actually cracked a smile. "You're fine."

In a way, it was true. If there was one thing I could always count on, it was my father's insistence on the fact that I was fine.

I watched the corners of his mouth pluck down, and before he turned away I saw a look come into his eyes, that look that stirred up every now and then in those brown foggy waters—that clear wellspring of love that was there, that had been there and would always be there, in the cool untouched depths of his heart—whether he acknowledged it or not. He fixed his eyes on the table and continued to lay his cards down. There was nothing more to say, so I sat down and we played solitaire together.

On the day of his release from the rehab facility there was a message on his machine from our old neighbors, Susan and Paul, inviting us to a barbecue on the Sunday afternoon of Memorial Day weekend. Her voice, its deep melodious thrum, moved through the stale city gloom of Boris's apartment. I wondered if Boris would want to go to the barbecue. I finished tidying and drove to the facility. When I stepped into his room, I found him watching my news station.

A single suitcase lay packed on the unmade bed beside him. He turned and caught my eye and gestured at the TV. "That's somebody else doing the weather," he said in husky disapproval. "Where's Pfeiffer?"

"Oh. He's retiring," I said. "This is a new guy they're trying out."

Turns out, Salt had not survived my weeklong absence. While I was gone, Raina had been installed as my temporary fill-in and had quit almost instantly, at which time the station manager had experimented with letting Salt prepare himself for the forecast, a risky gamble that had been lost when Salt had appeared chipper and disheveled before the camera one morning, white stubble glistening and hair uncombed, tie stripped roughly loose, looking like a drunk who had just been caught off guard by the bright lights of a squad car come to make him sleep it off.

"What, he's going to take over?" said my father, looking in surprise at me, his expression fading into disappointment. He looked back at the TV. "He shouldn't take over. He looks like Howdy Doody."

I smiled. "I won't tell him you said that."

We watched TV for a while longer, and my eyes glazed, and the silence between us loomed. As had been happening, I thought of all that I hadn't told him, and what little I had. I told him I'd twisted my arm tripping down some stairs. I told him my brother had left town for good, and that I didn't know where. I thought about my brother, and the body in the basement, and with dread I thought about the possibilities.

"Are you sure Dad?" I asked now. "You don't have any... questions?"

He glanced up at me.

"I could tell you a little more, just so you don't think—"

"No, I don't think so," he said gently, almost politely.

I tried to be okay with this. For some reason, I didn't want him to think Eliot had done this to me, even though I didn't know myself.

My father stood up. "We should go."

He looked depressed about this prospect. I knew he didn't want to go back to his apartment. I had been dreading this moment too and now I didn't know how to help him, how to take his mind off the dismal homecoming that awaited him.

"What do you think of going to a barbecue this Sunday?" I said, throwing out the question a little too brightly.

He glanced over at me, then walked forward and turned off the TV.

"At Susan and Paul's? They invited us. It's their yearly neighborhood get-together, remember?"

"No," he said.

"No you don't remember or no you don't want to go?"

He gave me a scorching stare that told me all I needed to know.

"Okay," I said, and patted the air reassuringly. "We don't have to. I didn't say we would go."

He lifted his suitcase off the bed and let it drop clumsily at his side. Without a word he walked to the door, and I followed. I knew how he felt. I felt the same way about going back there. It didn't seem possible, after the way we had left.

I remembered those last two weeks right after the fire, when my father was staying in Susan and Paul's guest room, before I had found him an apartment, and I was driving over every afternoon to see him. I remembered how barely tolerated he had been by the other neighbors, turning up in their streets and alleys and yards with his garbage bag like a bum they could neither evict nor ignore. Often I would see him as I came driving down the road, the air still sharp and singed, the shell of the house still there in the background, not yet torn down, his body stooped down by some neighbor's bush or staggering away from a lawn ornament he had mistaken for his own debris, his face clotted with misery. And sometimes I would see neighbors too, finding each other over hedges and speaking in urgent voices, looking concerned and resentful, staring away toward our house, which was now the eyesore of the neighborhood, the grim evidence of their diminished property values. Something needed to be done, I could almost hear them saying. Then seeing me, the men's expressions would turn into nervous looks of apology—tentative smiles of sympathy—and the women would come forward while I got out of the car, unsure, giving me tearful hugs of consolation, sometimes producing cards they had bought and muffins they had baked in other more generous moments.

It seemed they had realized too slowly what a terrible thing it was that happened to us—that strange family down at the end of the block—and if not for Susan and Paul they may never have found the resolve to accomplish that belated feat of neighborly charity that they threw themselves into, at the end donating items from their closets and basements, filling up the guest room with a formless tower of coats and shoes and lamps and bowls and cooking supplies and towels, heaping up their garage-sale discards on us with mounting guilt and urgency, until they had ushered us, indebted and encumbered, out of the neighborhood and out of their lives.

My father was right, I thought. The barbecue was a bad idea.

"Well, what do you think about going to church on Sunday?" I asked as an alternative—back to our old routine.

He grunted at this, as if his insistence on church had been a bad idea he'd given up in the time he'd been here.

Finally, I said, "There are other apartments, you know. Maybe we should skip church and start looking for something a little more..."

He glanced over, his eyes stoked with interest, and he nodded with a vigor I hadn't seen since before the fire.

"Okay," I said, mildly cheered. I followed him out of the room, and hopefully out of the last place where our wounds were made plain to us by our need to be there.

35

I SAT LOOKING OUT THE WINDOW AT A LOOSE BUNDLING OF GRAY clouds. It was the day after Memorial Day, the day I was meant to serve as final messenger for my mother. I had spent the morning watching the weather collect itself as if it were going to rain, only to see the sheet of clouds whitening and breaking apart again in some new part of the sky. I could still see that woman in my mind, the original villain of this whole ordeal—gaudy and false and malicious that first day in the neighborhood, trying to snatch out my father's eyes like some fairy-tale witch. I wondered what she would do today if she saw me walking down the beach in her direction. I wondered if she would even be there. Part of me was certain that she would be, because my mother expected that this ritual would be played out even in her absence, and my mother herself was a creature of ritual. But there were things that my mother didn't know, things that had happened while she was in that motel room, things I hadn't mentioned when we talked.

At eleven o'clock, exactly at the time I needed to leave to be at the beach by noon, and when my courage was waning, and when I had looked to the window for a last signal from the weather, the clouds quietly lifted and flattened in the sky, and a trellising of rays broke through and burned the air into white vapor, like the cold and conscious breath of some great deity. I took this as the sign I needed and got in the car and drove to the beach.

I remembered Eliot as I drove, sitting with me in the back of the car as we made the trip to the beach. There was a game we used to play on those trips—one of our many made-up games that had been our distraction as our mother sat at the wheel ahead of us, smoking a cigarette in grim silence, marshaling us swiftly toward our own demise. The Hypnotist. That was what we called the game.

"I dare you to hypnotize me," my brother would say, and all the unhappy apprehension I felt would trickle up my spine, like something light and easy.

Then I would say, "You're getting sleepy. Very sleepy."

My brother would let his head drop. His eyes would almost close.

"Your eyelids are very heavy. You can't open your eyes. You're putty in my hands. You'll do whatever I say."

Now he moaned in drowsy acquiescence and hung there like a puppet on a string. "You're a wave," I said, my brother now at my mercy, and he sucked his body up and lifted his arms in a round arc that crashed down into his lap. In a bubbling voice he said, "Tidal wave," and started sucking himself up bigger and bigger, looking like he was going to crash over me, and I said quickly, "Now you're a tree." He went stiff, his arms out beside him. After a moment a swishing and howling came like a distant gale through his mouth. "Whoo. It's windy," he said, and the branches bent and flung and whipped out at me. "You're a flower"—or you're a dog, or a kite, or a raindrop, I would say, stopping him every time he changed the game. I always ended by saying, "You're a dead body," and he would lie back and fold his arms across his chest and hold perfectly still.

"Okay, you're Eliot," I'd say, giggling, but he often held the rigor mortis pose well beyond my patience, waiting until I had proclaimed my disgust with the game and then—when I had turned to the window to show him that I was done, that his performance had finally tired me out—he would come back a mummy or a ghost or a zombie and prod me with tickling fingers until I begged him to stop.

And that was how the game went every time—my brother and I entering happily into that contract of servant and master that was so familiar to us, that we were so often made to play without our consent, and coming out at the end giddy and pleased, satisfied to be at each other's mercy. He was the only one, I thought. The only one who had never put me at his mercy without first putting himself at mine. But somewhere along the way that had changed.

I thought about what my mother had said, that my brother had picked his loyalties, and though it meant that he was no longer playing fair with me, at least it meant that he was playing fair with somebody—or trying to—even though the child was not his.

I turned into the parking lot, its patchwork asphalt and sandblown spaces exactly as they had been all those years ago, their familiarity made unreal by the passing time and by the strangeness of my purpose here. I got out of the car and looked across the beach, marveling at the expanse of sand and water, the dizzy loss of perspective, scanning for the single figure, picturing in my mind the black hair and bright fabrics from that day on the porch. Almost immediately I spotted her, down the shore fifty yards—a tall willow branch of a body in a billowing orange skirt. As I stood above her in the parking lot, my thoughts full of nameless misgiving, I watched her gaze out at the gray curling waves, looking as alone as my mother had looked all those years ago when she had forced us out here to imagine ourselves lost in that momentous scheme that owned and maneuvered us moment by moment.

Then it happened, almost as I knew it would. Another figure came darting up at her from the sliding glass of the tide, where he had been crouched like a rock, his black hair blowing up like feathers in the breeze, looking from this distance like the image of my brother himself.

At the sight of him I felt my heart snag, catching on all the worst premonitions I had carried with me to this meeting. And at that exact moment, as if she could feel some furrowing in the fabric of the universe, some movement of the inevitable forces that were folding us together, the woman turned and looked at me.

At her glance I felt all her familiarity and strangeness pierce through me. Hers was a face more broad and round with health, a body taller, softer and more deeply bronzed, not the same as my mother but somehow exactly alike in stance and gesture, as if they held an identical gravity on this earth. I came toward her, afraid and hoping for the protection of some willing God, some extension of mercy that was beyond the capacity of the flawed and human figure on which I was depending in this moment.

A chilly wind was tossing and the sand shifted under my feet with a coldness that felt wet. A thin plume of cloud still covered the sun, but it would be out soon. Nobody was in the water, but there were several figures dotting the beach, a few clumps of people together and some solitary walkers. As I got near, the little boy scampered up again from the tide, looked at me, and shied back. He turned his face to the woman, his expression bright and uncertain, waiting for her cue, and she glanced distractedly at him and said something that was blown away in the wind, then gestured him back to the water. Doubtfully, sensing the adult exchange about to take place, he turned and skipped back—as if by his own lightness he was trying to convince himself that the morning was still all in good fun.

Out of a nervous impulse to receive some sign of recognition from her, I lifted my hand. She looked at it, then brought her arm up and inhaled a cigarette I hadn't noticed when her arms were crossed. I stopped a few feet away from her, and saw the look in her eyes, not friendly and not hostile, but pooled and still, besieged and waiting.

"My mother sent me," I said. My voice was hardly audible over the roaring tide. I didn't know which way I should sound for this woman—angry or hurt or compassionate or indifferent. I didn't know which way I should feel either.

She continued to look at me with that poised apprehension in her eyes, as if she were waiting for some great sorrow. She must have understood by my presence here that my mother was dead.

"She wanted me to tell you something," I said.

She spoke something in a language I didn't understand.

"What?" The question came automatically, and I bent closer to hear.

Suddenly her face was like clay melting before me, her eyes streaming. Those eyes that were so like my mother's eyes—eyes that seemed as if they'd been fired like glass in some perfect creation of cold, inscrutable passion—were now soft and weak and wet.

"I let her die," she said.

Part of me wanted to let her take this on, bear the final burden, but my head was already answering her with its shake of assurance and denial, finding some authority beyond me to reject that sense of blame that my mother had not wanted her to have.

"She had cancer," I said. "There was nothing you could do." Once the words were out I realized she may have already known this, and anyway that was not what was important. This woman had wanted to be there. She had wanted to go to my mother. She was the one, I understood now, that my mother would have really wanted at her bedside.

She sniffed, watching me shake my head, her eyes moving over my face with some grim need to see something there, perhaps some resemblance in me that could make her glimpse my mother. "I shouldn't be talking to you."

I nodded. But I didn't move to leave and neither did she.

After a minute I remembered what I had in my hand. With the boy here it hardly seemed necessary to hand her the card, but I did.

She took it and looked at it, then looked at the boy, crouched in the sand, digging now with great concentration in a child's effort to ignore us, and she tapped the card with her thumb, thinking. I could see her reading over my mother's handwritten message. *This is why he did it. Luca's safe—with E. Don't blame yourself.*

But he was not with Eliot, as my mother had thought. He was here. And now I could feel the question that I didn't want to have answered pushing its way up through me, my voice coming out in a high keen, a gull cry almost lost in the wind and sea, whisked vanishing from my mouth to her ear.

"Why is he here?" I said. "Why didn't my brother take him?"

The woman looked at me, her mouth twisting down, and I knew the answer. I pictured again the spray of flames in that dark underground place in which I had woken. My brother had made the choice he had to make. He had fled the scene of his crime. He had left his son behind.

Even so, my heart broke anyway, to think of my brother swept away like this, wrecked by circumstances he designed, jettisoned out of his own life all over again. He had not carried the plan off. He had not escaped. It felt like he would always be suffering the misfortune that had begun long before him, without his consent, as if he were one of the unlucky few who had been fashioned too near the fire, too near his own destructive heat to rise above the damage of his own life. He would never escape, I realized. It was not in his makeup to escape.

Dropping her cigarette, the woman folded her arms across her chest. "His brother," she said, and looked at me with hesitation, as if maybe I didn't know Eliot had a brother, "you know? He came to your... ?"

"Apartment," I said.

"Marko," she said. So that was his name. Marko. "He found out that his father left money to your mother. Family's money. Your brother was going to leave the kumpania—the... neighborhood—with it." Her expression was doubtful, as if she didn't think I could follow this, but I nodded her along. "So they tied him in basement—not to hurt him. Trying to get him to say where the money was. To give it back." With a pang I thought about how I had shown that note to Bobby in my apartment—the note Eliot had written to my mother, asking her to go and see Emilian before his death. I remembered the look on his face, how he must have known in that instant that Eliot and my mother were working against the family, how it was me—I had been the one to give Eliot away.

"Your brother—in the church that day, after you came, he had a gun. It was the one from the Beletsky wedding, the Chinese, who started it, waiting around to see him, he wouldn't leave. After you left they let him go in. He's asking about money, your brother shushing him—*not the time, not the time*—looking at the camera, they think Chinese must be in on it, they go in, *what is this?*" She raised her eyebrows at me, demonstrating their agitation. "The two watching Elya, your brother, they try to intimidate the Chinese, he won't say what it's about, starts pushing, they go out the office with him, try to cool things down, get him away from Elya, get him talking. Marko is there and he stays, he tries to take Elya to basement, talk to him without the camera, has no idea Elya has a gun." She was looking down now, burning through the details, talking fast. "So Elya threatens, probably doesn't think Marko will go after him like he does, gun goes off, Marko—" She swallowed, as if a lump was rising, making the word difficult—"shot"—a vague gesture, somewhere near her rib cage. "Upstairs Chinese runs off, they go down to Elya and he has the gun out, Marko in the ties, he makes Stevan give him the key, goes off, everything is disaster. Marko needs help. They go out and see you there. Bring you down to figure out what next to do." She glanced at me. "So Stevan came across the street and told Yenoro what had happened—my husband. They go. Then in my back door, Elya comes. Wanting to know, is Marko okay, where's Luca, *I have to take him, I have to take him now.* But Luca was at the shop—with my father. The look he gave me. He told me somebody was after Luca, and they would take him away. I didn't know what to think," she said, her voice agitated and sharp, as if she was still thinking about it, still trying to decide what to do with this warning from him. She looked down at the card.

"This?" she said to me, flicking it angrily. "This is it?"

I was on edge, my throat too constricted at first to answer. "Uh—his grandparents. They're looking for him."

I thought of what else she needed to know. "I think Ian—the Chinese guy—knew about it."

"Wanted money," she said, nodding. She looked back at the boy with an almost defiant toss of her head. I wondered what she was thinking. After a few seconds of watching him, throwing clods of wet dirt into spitting waves, she dropped her gaze and turned partly back to me.

"Your brother," she said. "I should also tell you."

These words sent a chill through me. There was more?

"He asked me to do one other thing. He asked me to go to you and tell you about your mother." She looked at me, her eyes abraded and fierce, as if apologizing for something she couldn't speak out loud. "I told him I couldn't—" For a moment she was quiet, then she said, "I tried once before, with Luca, you wouldn't come, not after that first time—" She broke off and looked away. "So I put the cigarette, hoping you would find it. That was all I did."

I took this in. The cigarette. That was enough, I thought. It had been everything. I realized I was not very surprised to find out it was her either—I hadn't been able to convince myself that the cigarette had been my brother's doing, hoping but not fully believing, not knowing how to reconcile this with the tidy script inside or with the accusations the old gypsy had made in the garage. If not for the old gypsy leaving the cigarette out of the case, or for Bobby's keys, lost in my coat lining all that time, I wouldn't have come back for it, I wouldn't have sought out my mother, I wouldn't have been here on this beach.

It hit me now that I still had the keys—I had brought them, just in case I decided I could trust her to return them. I opened my purse and fished for them and for the ring. I hadn't decided if I was going to keep the ring, but now it seemed wrong to hold on to something that had so little to do with me. "These are—" I stopped myself, realizing what this really was. My chest felt suddenly tight. It was Bobby, I thought. In the basement with me. I was returning the possessions of the dead.

The way she looked at those keys, the ring—such an astonishment in her eyes, a wild, cutting look, like she didn't know if she should be furious or grateful. She scooped them from my hand and pressed the closed fist to her lips.

"When I came out of the basement and you were—" I didn't know how to continue. "What happened?" I said. "The fire... ?"

She closed her eyes, shook her head, and spoke to me from behind her fist. "Accident. He asked Besni for a cigarette. Besni lights it and then goes upstairs for not three minutes to get water, something to wrap the wound for now while he waits. Marko—his jumpsuit covered in gasoline. He pass out, cigarette falls. That's what we think." She stopped talking, shook her head again.

I stood letting it sink in. Starting with the moment I saw my brother through the crack in that door, his religious robes fluttering down the aisle at me, then getting ushered into that office, the coat on the door, the camera, my brother's readiness to talk, his openness hiding a delicate restraint, that handled so deftly that I left unaware of it at first, walking out of the church compliant and accepting, then going back drained of that feeling, bending at the basement window, the violent plunge back into grass, waking in the basement. The darkness, the heat, the shudder of flame.

An accident. As I let those words work their way down, past my cringing recollections, a second thought came to me, sharply—that my brother had not left me in there. He had not intended me to die.

Neither, I realized, had this family, to whom I now felt inextricably linked, strung by some invisible cord to the same destiny, in a way. All of us, I realized, had been seeking my mother. For different reasons we had searched without knowing that it was she who we were looking for, and it was in this blind heat of our searching that we had all found ourselves together, in the same trouble.

As I stood there, stifled and smothered in the blaze of my thoughts, the sun came out, cool and startling, and the water exploded into a million glittering white prisms, the light trembling loose on the surface. I looked out at the cool shimmering expanse of it, taken briefly away from my own heat and up into the broad, trackless indifference of all that water, all that sky. Like a part of some unending dream linking me back to my past, the little boy sprang up with a small, muted cry and trotted up the sand toward us with his hand outstretched.

"Bibio," he said, "look what I found." In his hand he held two pebbles, milky and pink. "I washed them in the water. Look they're like jewelry."

He pinched one up and put it in her hand.

"Oh yes, this is very nice," she told him.

He gave me a hesitant look, and then he reached out and offered me the other one. Surprised, I opened my hand for it and he put the wet stone there. "I'll find another one," he said, and ran back, a random scattering of limbs.

I looked down at my pebble, creased and bulging like a pale clotted muscle, and imagined it tucked into my mouth, beating there like the buried heart of some clean, bloodless amphibian that had been here since the beginning of time.

The woman had watched the boy go back to the water's edge and now she let her eyes flick uncertainly over my face, as if she wanted to cross the distance that was still there between us but didn't know how. There we stood together, my anguish lashed to her anguish, neither of us equipped to offer out comfort and neither of us desiring the imperfect expression of the other's comfort. She opened her mouth to say something, perhaps make a conciliatory comment, but just then she saw me do something that made her close her mouth.

I couldn't help myself. I had put the stone in my mouth and now I was sucking the warm primordial salt from its slippery contours like a busy infant at a nipple. This pica—it was my destiny and my doom. It would always be calling me back to my weakest places, into my deepest vacancies.

"You put that in your mouth?" she said.

I shrugged.

"That's dirty. That comes from the dirt."

"It helps me," I said around the pebble.

She gave me a long, doubtful look. "Your mother said something like this," she began, trailing off, to finish in thought what she hadn't said aloud.

"What?" I asked. "What did she say?"

"She said you like to do this. You put things in your mouth. Like a baby. Putting the whole world in there like you don't know the difference between inside"—here she put her two hands together and held her fingers in a tight cluster in front of her chest—"and outside"—and here she released her fingers and scattered them before her. "Inside is clean," she said. "Outside is dirty. You let too much of the outside in and it eats down your spirit."

I nodded at this. *Eats down.* I liked her phrasing.

"You should stop this," she told me, like she was offering me a new choice I had never considered.

I shrugged, unable to make any promises. The woman gazed at me a moment longer, unsatisfied, and then turned her face back to the shore where the child crouched. I stepped backward in the sand and spit out the stone. It was time for me to go, to leave them here, to put away these two figures from another life. I fixed the boy in my sight one more time and then my eyes left him there, motherless, fatherless, digging in the sand for some great find. "I should go," I said.

The woman nodded. "Goodbye," she said to me.

I thought about wishing her luck. Too quickly the moment passed, and I turned and walked back up the beach to the parking lot, the sand grinding between my toes. As I went I couldn't help thinking of all those other afternoons I had walked up this beach, with the sound of the ocean behind me and my mother leading the way ahead of me, my brother and I giddy and laughing with relief, straggling behind, exhausted but finally free of her imprisonment. We walked up from the water as if we had accomplished some worthy feat out there that day, some important performance of faith and courage, and though we didn't know what we had done to earn the punishment that had forced us onto this beach, we also knew that we must surely have deserved it, because our mother had said so, and it was she who had made us and she who was our first and final judge.

ACKNOWLEDGEMENTS

I am honored and gratified to be able to thank the people who have offered their support and encouragement in the making of this book. I am indebted to my agent, Andrea Somberg, for her persistence and her guidance throughout this process, and her many affirmations that graced the way. I want to thank the editors at Unnamed Press, C.P. Heiser and Olivia Taylor Smith, for their exhilarating enthusiasm, their commitment and integrity, and their great ideas in the final stages of this book. I could not have written this book or discovered the world within it without the work of Isabel Fonseca, Anne Sutherland, Marlene Sway, and Jonathan Lethem.

I thank my friends and family for their cheerful support and loving esteem, right now and over the years. To my colleagues at UCCS, thanks for your integrity and your community and your friendship. Special thanks to my grad school friend Jillian Cantor, for your steady supply of advice and encouragement, and for setting an example that kept me on the path. I also thank my old friend Samantha Ruby, because your big heart and brassy humor are here in this book and with me always.

I am grateful for the love and support of my mother and father, Anita and Bill Tifft. Thank you to my mom for caring and believing, and for telling me all your stories—a glorious stockpile that has entertained, inspired, and enlightened me. Thank you to my dad, my first reader, for all your generous devotion over the years—reading, critiquing, discussing, listening—always with a keen eye, an open heart, a real respect. I am indebted to you for these remarkable gifts that once showed me what I could do, and continue to lead me back to the courage and discipline to do it better.

My supreme and eternal gratitude goes to my husband, Tony. This debt bends space and time. Thank you for your extraordinary brilliance. For lighting this world with your humor and play. For sharing your law-breaking talents, your intelligence, your passion and your insights. Thank you for listening and talking and caring deeply, for the copious reading and writing and the wicked all-nighters. Thank you for your feats of fortitude, your constant sacrifice, your tremendous love, your true partnership. Thank you so much for making this book with me.

And thank you finally to our daughter, Blake, for doing your part, for sleeping well, for your magic and the luck you brought with you.

MEGHAN TIFFT

About the Author

Meghan Tifft grew up in Los Angeles and Tucson, Arizona. She has an MFA from the University of Arizona and teaches writing at the University of Colorado, Colorado Springs. She lives in Colorado with her husband and daughter. This is her first novel.

OTHER BOOKS FROM THE UNNAMED PRESS:

Nigerians in Space by Deji Olukotun

Good Night Mr. Kissinger by K. Anis Ahmed

Walker on Water by Kristiina Ehin

Escape From Baghdad! by Saad Z. Hossain

The Fine Art of Fucking Up by Cate Dicharry

The Paper Man by Gallagher Lawson

Remember the Scorpion by Isaac Goldemberg

FORTHCOMING IN 2015:

The Revelator by Robert Kloss (September 2015)

Eyes Full of Empty by Jérémie Guez,
translated by Edward Gauvin (November 2015)

Rus Like Everyone Else by Bette Adriaanse (December 2015)

Year of the Goose by Carly J. Hallman (December 2015)

@unnamedpress

facebook.com/theunnamedpress

unnamedpress.tumblr.com

www.unnamedpress.com